# Special Delivery

Zoë Barnes was born and brought up on Merseyside, where legend has it her skirt once fell off during a school performance of 'Dido and Aeneas'. According to her family, she has been making an exhibition of herself ever since.

Her varied career has included stints as a hearing-aid technician, switchboard operator, shorthand teacher, French translator, and the worst accounts clerk in the entire world. When not writing her own novels, she translates other people's and also works as a semi-professional singer.

Although not in the least bit posh, Zoë now lives in Cheltenham where most of her novels are set. She shares a home with her husband Simon, and would rather like to be a writer when she grows up.

Zoë Barnes is the author of seven best-selling novels including *Wedding Belles*, *Bumps* and *Hitched*. The others are *Hot Property*, *Bouncing Back, Ex-Appeal, Love Bug, Just Married, Split Ends* and *Be My Baby,* also published by Piatkus. Zoë loves to hear from her readers. Write to her c/o Piatkus Books, 5 Windmill Street, London, W1T 2JA or via email at zoebarnes@bookfactory.fsnet.co.uk

# Special Delivery

## Zoë Barnes

PIATKUS

Copyright © Zoë Barnes 2007

First published in Great Britain in 2007 by
Piatkus Books Ltd.,
5 Windmill Street, London W1T 2JA
email: info@piatkus.co.uk

**The moral right of the author has been asserted**

*A catalogue record for this book is available from the British Library*

Hardback ISBN 978 0 7499 0842 3
Trade Paperback ISBN 978 0 7499 3808 6

Data manipulation by
Action Publishing Technology Ltd, Gloucester

Printed and bound in Great Britain by
Mackays Ltd, Chatham, Kent

For Grizzle, Tino, Pizza, Jupiter and Jim, without whose feline 'help', writing this book would have been a whole lot easier . . .

Prologue

# Prologue

**One very ordinary Monday morning at the unfashionable end of Cheltenham ...**

'Mum, I can't find my pants,' wailed a young male voice over the din of the cartoon channel on the kitchen TV.

Ally Bennett half-turned her head towards her son as her hands automatically went on filling the two plastic lunch boxes on the counter, while keeping one eye on the ancient toaster that could go from anaemic to carbonised in a nanosecond. There was a smear of margarine in her hair, but that was nothing new.

'Which pants? I left some for you on your bed.'

'Not those, my Little Britain ones!' replied seven-year-old Kyle, in an exasperated tone that implied no other pants in the world were worth wearing. 'My *best* ones.' He was standing in the kitchen doorway wearing his school shirt and jumper, twinned with a pair of half-mast pyjama bottoms.

'Well they're not in the wash,' replied his mother, 'so I haven't a clue what you've done with them. You'll just have to wear the ones I put out for you.'

'But I want *those*—'

'Sorry, Kyle.'

A hint of red-faced obstinacy was entering the conversation. 'But I *want*—'

Calmly, Ally turned back to her sandwich assembly line, effectively cutting her son off in mid-flow. When you had a young son, a toddler daughter and a husband to sort out by half-past eight, nothing could be allowed to disrupt the daily routine. Not even your son's favourite underwear. 'Pants,' she intoned with her back

1

to him and just a soupçon of menace. 'Now. Or no chocolate pudding tonight.'

With much muttering, her eldest child shuffled off upstairs, while his three-year-old sister Josie liberally splashed her cereal about, some of which found its way into her mouth but most onto the floor.

It was chaos every morning at number 22, Brookfield Road, but Ally took it all in her stride. Or to be scrupulously honest, she loved it. Some people might accuse her of having no ambition, but this had always been her own personal dream: a husband she loved, a house of their own, and two important jobs – part-time teacher and full-time mum. OK, so a little extra money wouldn't go amiss, and they'd never be in the same social league as her elder sister, but did that really matter? They managed. And she wouldn't have changed places with toffee-nosed singleton Miranda for anything.

Luke Bennett yawned as he entered the kitchen, still pulling on his work shirt, a lock of sandy-gold hair slipping down over one eye. He was quite good-looking really but in a decidedly crumpled way; no matter what Ally did to them, his clothes looked perpetually unironed. Luke was one of those men who could have five o'clock shadow at seven in the morning: no matter how often he shaved, he invariably looked as if he hadn't bothered. Thankfully, outreach workers for homelessness charities weren't generally judged on their personal grooming, and besides, Ally loved him just the way he was. She'd never really fancied the slick, City type; or the 'metrosexual' who was forever pinching his wife's moisturiser, for that matter.

'Hi darling.' He gave Ally a squeeze and a tickly little kiss on the back of the neck. 'What's up with Kyle? He's got a face on him like a slapped backside.'

'Lost underpants.'

'What – again? How can a boy *lose* underpants?' Luke stepped in a puddle of milk and shook his soggy, slipper-clad foot. 'Josie!'

The little girl held up her spoon up to her dad and smiled.

Luke contemplated the sodden remnants of his slipper as Nameless the cat trotted over to lick it clean for him. 'Oh well, never mind. At least it's only milk!'

'And let's try and get some breakfast your tummy please,' instructed Ally (who, like all mums, had eyes in the back of her head). With one deft movement she whisked away Josie's bowl and spoon and handed her some toast soldiers. 'Have some toast instead ... you like toasty soldiers. Kyle! Breakfast. Now!'

Luke extracted a few envelopes from the back pocket of his cords. 'Post's come. Mainly junk mail. Oh – one for you though.' He waved it in front of his wife's face. 'Ooh, look: a Wiltshire postmark.'

Ally groaned. They only knew two people in Wiltshire, and one of them was currently working in Dubai. The other one was Miranda.

'Tell you what, you open it,' she said, adding jam to Kyle's toast as he raced into the room. 'I've got sticky fingers.'

'Coward.'

'Guilty as charged.'

'Is that a letter from Auntie Miranda?' piped up Kyle, his interest peaking. 'Is she coming to see us? When's she coming?'

Oh dear I do hope not, thought Ally, instantly feeling guilty for having such unsisterly thoughts. I don't think my inferiority complex has quite recovered from the last visit yet. But rich Auntie Miranda was always welcome in Cheltenham as far as the kids were concerned. There couldn't be many other kids whose aunties showered them with presents as expensive as Miranda's.

Luke didn't answer. He was too busy reading the contents of the envelope, and chuckling. 'Well, well ...'

'Well, well, what?' demanded Ally, her curiosity aroused.

'What do you reckon to Mr Fancy-Pants then?' Luke handed her a photograph of a dark-haired, lean-jawed, smart-suited guy whose almost peridot-green eyes seemed to reach right out of the picture and draw Ally in. Not classically handsome, that much was true; but striking. And he had that certain magnetic something that made a woman want to look and keep on looking.

She affected an unimpressed shrug. 'He's ... OK I guess. What is he, another one of Miranda's actor-friends or something?'

Luke chuckled. 'Believe it or not, that guy there is a big-time property developer who owns his own polo team. Oh, and he's also the future Mr Miranda.'

'What!' Ally's eyes widened in disbelief. 'She's never ...?'

'That's right, darling, it's time to buy a hat. Your ever-loving sister is finally getting hitched.'

*

3

This was going to be the mother of all engagement parties, and there were hordes of well-heeled, designer-clad clones in the Overbury Suite; but Ally's sister stood literally head and shoulders above the whole lot of them, like a six-foot beacon of loveliness.

Miranda Morris was the sort of woman who glided through a room as though she were on invisible wheels. Endowed with effortless elegance, she was the irritating kind of woman who never tripped over things, ate with the wrong fork or looked anything less than stunning – with or without make-up. The type of woman, as Ally's best mate Zee had once quipped, who'd eat crisps with a knife and fork. Oh, and she had enough of her own money to keep her in Manolo Blahniks for life.

It wasn't too difficult to guess what a bloke might see in her, but all the same Ally couldn't help feeling a wee bit sorry for Gavin. After all, she'd spent all her childhood years sharing a bedroom with Miranda, and it had been . . . well . . . an experience, and not one she'd care to repeat. Gavin Hesketh must be quite a guy if he fancied attempting it on a permanent basis.

After years in her shadow, Ally ought probably to have hated her elder sister, but the curious fact was that nobody hated Miranda. Ally suspected it might be genetically impossible. And yet this was the woman who'd had every damn thing she demanded as a child; never showing a hint of gratitude towards her hard-up parents or her hard done-by sister. Then she'd breezed into medical school, junked it after a couple of years in favour of an international modelling career, and promptly posed and pouted her way to a Coutts bank account that was exponentially bigger and fatter than her über-pert backside.

Nowadays, at the ripe old age of thirty-seven, the girl who couldn't sew a button on or boil an egg was playing at being an interior designer and filling the rest of her time doing 'charity work', which (as Luke had noted) seemed to consist mainly of going to posh dinners with local celebrities. Everything in Miranda's life was so, so easy. Ally wondered if things would be any different for her now that she had somebody else to think about. Knowing Miranda, probably not.

Ally finished adjusting her make-up, straightened up and looked at her reflection in the powder-room mirror. Not too bad for a thirty-year-old mother of two: half-decent boobs, nice shiny golden hair and not too much of a jelly-belly; but all the same it was hard

4

not to feel outclassed when you were wearing last year's skirt and top and everybody else was in this season's Prada. And Ally hadn't quite got to the stage where she was desperate enough to accept her big sister's hand-me-downs. It wasn't only the fact that Miranda was twice as tall and half as fat. It would just have been too much like history repeating itself.

All her life Ally had felt like an afterthought. Her mother and father had been trying for a baby for eight years when Miranda made her dramatic appearance; and right from day one Miranda had always seemed like the 'special' one in the family. It helped of course that she was the most beautiful baby anybody had ever seen, the cleverest child in her year at school, and brilliant at any and every activity she'd ever tried her hand at, from macramé to driving a tank. But most of all, she was the golden child; the baby Maureen and Clive had feared they'd never have.

Not surprisingly, when Ally unexpectedly popped out seven years later, just after her mum had given away all the baby clothes, the excitement was noticeably more muted. It wasn't that there was anything wrong with Ally, far from it. She was healthy, perfectly presentable and above-averagely intelligent. But compared to her big sister she was, well, a bit ... ordinary. How could she be anything else, compared to Miranda?

One final blot of her lipstick, and Ally headed back towards the party. But she'd only got a few yards down the hotel corridor when a voice called out her name.

'Alison?'

Surprised, she stopped and looked round.

'It is Alison, isn't it? I haven't quite got the hang of everybody's names and faces yet.' The tall, dark and kind-of handsome Gavin Hesketh was walking towards her. 'Sorry if I startled you,' he went on. 'I just wanted to thank you for your engagement present.'

Ally fidgeted, curiously uncomfortable in the light from those almost spookily luminous green eyes. They gave her the shivers. Nice ones, though. 'Um. Great, that's fine. No problem.'

'Only I thought Miranda was a bit ... well, let's face it, much as I love her she can be a little thoughtless sometimes.'

Ally raised an eyebrow. Perhaps the beauteous Gavin hadn't been entirely blinded by lust then. Generally, Miranda's besotted suitors didn't take the trouble to figure out the real Miranda until some time after they'd been dumped. 'You think so?' she asked, with a touch of amusement.

He laughed. 'I know so. And you're her sister, so you do too. I'm guessing you've been on the receiving end of Miranda's "directness" more times than you can count. Anyhow, I thought she was very rude about your present. Those hand-embroidered tablecloths are absolutely beautiful, and they must have taken forever to make. Thank you.'

He had hold of her hand, just for a few seconds, and she just couldn't decide if she was desperate for him to let go of it, or desperate for him not to. All she knew for sure was that she didn't dare look him in the face, because then those green eyes might perceive the truth: that she was thinking about him in a way that a future sister-in-law really shouldn't.

'I – I'd ... er ... better go,' she said eventually; and as she looked up their eyes finally locked, and she felt the delicious spark zap between them.

'Yes, I think you had,' Gavin replied after a moment's silence.

And then she knew that he had felt it too.

# Chapter One

Gavin tapped his fingers impatiently on the desktop and tried not to hum along to the tune in his ear. He wasn't accustomed to being put on hold; something he studiously avoided by getting his PA to make his phone calls for him. But not this one. He didn't want Karen knowing, in case she let slip something to Miranda and blew the whole thing. Unfortunately, the old adage was only too true: if you wanted something done properly, there really was no substitute for doing it yourself.

The electronic muzak pinged to an abrupt halt and a disembodied female voice returned to the other end of the line.

'I've spoken to Mr Sallis, sir, and he says wouldn't you prefer a marquee in the grounds? Most people—'

'Yes, but I'm not most people,' pointed out Gavin tartly. 'So please explain again to your Mr Sallis that I have to have that stately home for the entire weekend, or I'll be forced to take my business elsewhere.'

Up in the loft at 22, Brookfield Road, Ally peeled a skein of itchy cobweb off the end of her nose and sneezed. 'Remind me again, Zee, why exactly did I let you drag me up here?'

'Why?' Zebedee Goldman, who sounded a lot more exotic than he actually was, grinned at his best mate through the fretwork of dusty rafters. He looked more like one of Fagin's urchins than a thirty-five-year-old single dad. 'Because you're skint and you can't resist a treasure hunt. Same as me.'

'Treasure?' scoffed Ally. 'In *my* attic?'

7

'Well ... stuff that's good enough to sell at the car boot sale, anyhow. That counts as treasure, doesn't it?'

She evaluated the scene in one sceptical sweep of her rather pale, doll-blue eyes: eyes that had sometimes led people to underestimate her. Men mostly. 'I hate to burst your bubble, love, but this is a 1950s' ex-council house; and the last people who lived here kept chickens in the shed. I doubt anybody's left any Picassos stashed away for a rainy day.'

Zee left off rummaging through a sagging and mildewed cardboard box which seemed to be filled with broken teapots and bits of old Lego. 'Ah, but you'll never know if you don't look. Did you see that programme on Channel Six last week? The one about that woman who found that medieval parchment stuffed down the back of a second-hand bureau? Then there was the guy who found he'd had an icon hanging in his downstairs loo. That could be us, this time next year.'

Ally shook her head and smiled at his childlike enthusiasm. She loved Zee dearly, in a twin-sisterly, co-conspiratorial kind of way; the pair of them had hit it off the very first time they met, at their respective kids' nursery school, and ever since then he had been trying to involve her in his never-ending schemes to make money out of junk. Still, you couldn't help but respect a young widowed dad who'd jacked in a well-paid job as a book designer to make a living doing the odd freelance design job while selling rubbish on eBay, just so that he could spend more time bringing up his daughter.

Over the years, Zee had become a good friend to Luke, too; and it seemed almost comical now that Luke had ever had suspicions about the closeness of his friendship with Ally. Anyone even remotely observant could see that it just wasn't *that* kind of relationship. Besides, as far as Ally was concerned Zee – bless him – was about as sexually alluring as a one-eared teddy bear.

She blew the thick layer of dust off a pile of bundled papers. 'Ooh look, a six-month run of the *Cheltenham Courant*, 1953. And some half-empty tins of gloss paint. All different colours, naturally.'

'No probs,' Zee assured her. 'We'll pour the whole lot into one tin, give it a quick stir and flog it on the stall for 50p a go. Rainbow paint. Very postmodern.'

Ally laughed. She'd allowed herself to believe that this boot sale was a great money-making idea, but it was hard to imagine anyone in their right mind forking out good money for this tat. 'Very bullshit, more like. Still, Luke would approve. Recycling, and all that.'

'What's this?' called out Zee, brandishing a flat, leather-covered box he'd found inside the old linen chest underneath the skylight. Before Ally answered he opened it up and gave an appreciative whistle. 'Hey, these look a bit of all right. Whatever they are.'

'Hang on a minute.' She tottered gingerly along the joists towards him, trying not to recall the moment in her childhood when her dressing-gown-clad father had stepped on the wrong bit of their loft floor and her sleepover friends had been treated to the sight of two hairy legs dangling through the ceiling.

Zee was giving his finds a close inspection. 'I reckon these are solid silver, you know. Bound to be worth something to somebody.'

Gently but firmly, Ally removed the box from Zee's enthusiastic grasp, closed it and replaced it in the linen chest. 'They are,' she replied. 'To my sister.'

'Uh?'

'They're antique ivory-handled caviar spoons,' Ally explained. 'A wedding present from Miranda.'

'Aaah. Right. So you didn't actually go out and buy them yourself then?'

Ally smiled at the ridiculousness of the idea. 'Are you kidding? She spotted them in an antique shop in Geneva of all places, and – get this – she thought they'd "come in really handy". Honest to God, she really did.'

'Caviar spoons?'

'Caviar spoons.'

'I wonder what she thought they'd come in handy for.' Zee scratched at his dusty brown locks. 'And doesn't Luke have a thing about ivory anyway?'

'He doesn't like having the stuff in the house, which is why we hide them up here. And even if he didn't have ethical objections to them, what use would our family ever have for anything that's too small to eat baked beans with? I daren't get rid of them though, so we keep them up here and bring them out whenever Miranda's in the vicinity.'

Zee frowned. 'She'd understand if you sold them though, wouldn't

9

she? What with you having kids and needing the money?'

Ally brought down the lid of the oak linen chest with an emphatic clunk. 'Call me a big fat coward,' she replied, 'but I'm not about to find out.'

Gavin's plans were starting to take shape. By mid-morning he had charmed the owner of Nether Grantley Hall into letting him have it for the entire weekend, plus full use of the private grounds; and all for a third less than he'd been prepared to pay for the privilege.

They could have had a party at home, of course; but it would've had to be a pathetically small affair. The Hesketh eight-bedroom luxury barn conversion would have struggled to accommodate twenty overnight guests, let alone a massive jungle extravaganza for two hundred plus. Besides, it was Miranda's fortieth; it ought to be marked by something a bit special. And if you had money and style, Gavin always argued, you really ought to flash them around once in a while.

All in all it was good that things had worked out so smoothly, since Gavin didn't believe in having a Plan B. That wasn't how he operated. What he did believe in was getting whatever you wanted first time round, because anything else was second best and that just wouldn't do.

It was go-getting philosophies like that which had built up Gavin Hesketh's property-development business from a single terraced house in Swindon to mega-money – all in five years. There were an awful lot of people out there who would have liked to be Gavin Hesketh, but he would never have dreamed of swapping places with any of them. He was having a blast just being himself.

The entertainment agency got back to him on his mobile as he was eating a light sushi lunch at his desk and going through the figures for the new conference centre he was thinking of building. Never do one thing when you could do two, was his motto; and if you could manage three, so much the better. If you didn't leap up and grab the opportunities, some other bastard would.

'Ah, Mr Bergstrom, hi,' he said, tucking his phone under his chin. 'Have you got me my orchestra?'

'I can do you a very nice forties' nostalgia combo, sir. "White Cliffs of Dover", all the old favourites. Good musicians, very tasteful, and all the authentic gear.'

10

'I said twenties.'

'To be completely honest, Mr Hesketh, twenties' acts are a bit out of fashion at the moment. There just aren't the bookings for 'em, see. What about an Elvis tribute act? They always go down well.'

Gavin let out a small groan of exasperation. The world, it seemed, was as full of amateurs as ever. 'Let's not waste each other's time, Mr Bergstrom. I want a full-size twenties-style orchestra for the Saturday night. Plus singers. And dancers. I am prepared to pay for it. For God's sake, fly somebody in from Vegas if you have to.

'And if you can't, find me somebody who can.'

It was a very different world at the offices of ChelShel, Cheltenham's homelessness charity on Henrietta Street, and Luke's middle-aged client was considerably less choosy than Gavin Hesketh. He'd have been happy with any solution that didn't involve spending another night sleeping rough in a smelly shop doorway.

He looked up hopefully as Luke came back into the small office he shared with Chas, one of the other case workers; then his face fell. 'You didn't manage to find me a room for the night then?'

Luke's apologetic expression said it all. 'Sorry, Jake. There aren't many hostels round here, and they're all full.'

'Great.'

'There may be a vacancy for tomorrow night though. So call by in the morning and check again.'

'Don't I always?' Slowly Jake started to gather together his grubby belongings as Luke looked on, aching with sympathy and frustration in equal measure.

'I really am sorry Jake, but you and I both know how it is. You don't fit the stupid rules the authorities make. You're not under sixteen, you're not pregnant or a single parent, or over sixty-five, or mentally ill ... '

'So what you're saying is, because I'm managing to scrape by without slitting my wrists, they can get out of doing anything for me.'

Luke tried not to wince, but it was true. He could have punched the wall in frustration. 'Well ... put it this way, you're not a priority case.'

Jake got to his feet and hauled his rucksack onto his shoulder. 'People like me never are a priority, are we? More of a bad smell in the corner.' As he reached the door, he turned back with the ghost of a smile. 'If you ask me, my son should be working for the housing department. He seems to think the same bloody way they do, at any rate.'

A couple of seconds elapsed as the spring-loaded door glided silently shut, then Luke hissed 'fuck' under his breath and kicked the waste-paper bin across the office. It clattered against the back wall and scuttered to a halt, upside down.

'You know, you're not the world's headmaster,' commented a quiet voice behind him. 'Sometimes you can't force the world to behave like you think it should.'

'Oh really?'

'Take it from me – you know I'm right.'

The words came from a forty-something guy in jeans, steel-capped boots and an old Star Wars T-shirt, who was doing battle with the office's aged photocopier. ChelShel was not the best funded of housing charities. In fact there were whispers that the council liked it that way, if only to keep the spotlight off the town's small but growing homelessness problem. Luke could quite believe it. Anything to avoid frightening away the wealthy tourists who poured into Cheltenham to patronise its plethora of festivals. He had a nasty suspicion that the council spent more on hanging baskets than it did on the sixty or so people who slept rough on its streets every night.

He grunted and sat down. 'Give it a rest, Chas. I suppose you're going to go all holy on me now and tell me priests are always right about everything.'

He chuckled. 'Don't you believe it. They just teach us how to sound as if we are. That way, everybody else gets to feel nice and reassured, and we're the ones left wondering.'

'I wouldn't exactly describe Jake as reassured,' commented Luke. 'I mean, the poor guy's finally got a roof over his head, he's sharing a flat with his son; things are looking up. Then the son moves his new girlfriend in and the next minute it's: "I know you've got nowhere else to stay Dad, but we're having a baby so could you just pack your bags and sod off?" Charity begins at home, eh? Could've fooled me.' He rubbed his stubbly chin as a persistent idea bubbled up again at the back of his mind. 'Maybe I could . . . '

12

Chas silently slipped a mug of coffee in front of him.

'Oh. Thanks.' He looked sideways at Chas. 'You know we do have the boxroom.'

The priest put up a hand to stop him. 'Don't even think about it, Luke. Even you can't house the entire homeless population of Cheltenham in a four-bed semi in Whaddon. And I think the lovely Alison might have a word or two to say about it too.'

Luke pictured Ally's probable reaction on discovering that her boxroom – which they had plans to turn into a study – was about to become an emergency hostel. Perhaps Chas had a point. 'Well I'm not giving up on that guy,' he declared, feeling in his desk drawer for his little black book of useful contacts. 'There has to be somebody in here somewhere I can embarrass or coerce into doing something.'

Chas shrugged. 'Good luck, go for it.'

At that moment, the office phone rang and Chas's hand got to it first. 'ChelShel? Yes, sure, I'll pass you over. Luke, a lady called Miranda for you.'

Chas had yet to meet the divine Miranda or her entourage of beautiful people with huge, empty houses. Boy, did he have a treat in store.

Luke's hand tensed involuntarily as he gripped the receiver. 'Afternoon, Miranda. How's things?'

'Oh you know, busy, busy, busy. The new line of wallpaper is out on Monday and I just don't seem to get a moment to myself, d'you know?'

'Oh, absolutely.' Luke felt an attack of sarcasm coming on. Trouble was, Miranda just brought out the bad side in him. 'Matter of fact, business is a bit busy round here too. Fancy a few lodgers for that third garage you never use?'

'Pardon?'

'Well, the office is absolutely swarming with homeless asylum seekers. You know, I reckon we could fit half a dozen in your garage if I got in a carpenter to put up some MDF partitions ... '

There was a short pause, while Miranda worked out whether or not he was joking; then, having concluded that he must be because he wouldn't be that mean, she giggled like a breathless sixteen-year-old. 'Oh you are funny, Luke. It's amazing how you keep that sense of humour of yours really, working in such a sad place. Listen, I've got some really exciting news for you. Something to cheer you up.'

13

You're moving to the Moon, thought Luke. 'Really?' he said out loud.

'Really! You see, Gavin's organising an absolutely *huge* party for my fortieth next month, only it's supposed to be a secret and I'm not meant to know. So I'm pretending I don't.'

'That's ... er ... nice,' murmured Luke, still scanning the pages of his book of contacts for somebody – anybody – who might owe him a favour. 'So what exactly can I do for you today?'

'Well, you can be sure to tell Alison that you and she and the children simply *have* to be free the *whole* weekend of my birthday, because I've heard a whisper that it's going to be a complete extravaganza, and I'm not going to let you miss any of it!'

'We'll do our best,' replied Luke, who had been hoping against hope for a quick family get-together and then home to watch the football highlights, 'but what with work, and the house, and ferrying the kids round to all their clubs and stuff ... '

'You'll do more than your best, my darling. You'll be there.' Miranda was always at her best when a hint of dominatrix entered her voice. 'And you will do one other thing for me, won't you Luke?' she added in the sweetest of purrs.

'What's that?' he enquired, somewhat fearfully.

'You will wear something ... *nice*, won't you? Just this once.'

'Palm trees,' repeated Gavin, craning his head furtively around the stable door to check that his wife wasn't outside. The coast was clear. 'I want palm trees and plenty of them ... '

'Real ones or plastic ones?' enquired the voice on his mobile.

'Real, of course! What do you think I am, cheap? Native huts, lianas, oh, and some live birds of paradise and that kind of thing.'

'No problem with the trees or the huts,' the voice assured him. 'It just so happens we've got a lot of scenery left from last year's *Tarzan* musical at the Bristol Hippodrome. Might be some trouble with these exotic species of yours though; lot of rules and regulations these days.'

Gavin hummed and hawed, which he seldom did. This had to be right, but ... 'Bloody bureaucracy. Well OK, whatever you can get. You've got the list. Oh, and a tiger cub.'

'A what?'

'You heard. Make sure you get a cute one. My wife adores tigers.'

14

'Er . . . they're a touch hard to come by these days, Gav. Endangered species and all that.'

'I wasn't actually suggesting you go out and capture one yourself. Borrow one or something. Doesn't London Zoo hire them out by the day?'

'I could get you one of Damien Hirst's sharks.'

'A tiger cub. Or you're fired.'

No compromises, Gavin told himself firmly. Miranda's birthday weekend must be perfect, entirely perfect; exactly as if had stepped straight into the pages of her favourite book. And it was going to be that way because he wouldn't allow it to be anything less.

Miranda phoned just as Ally staggered back in through the front door from an afternoon's supply teaching, with Kyle and Josie bickering in her wake and a thousand plastic carrier bags of shopping dangling from her straining arms.

She flung the whole lot onto the kitchen table, dislodging the cat from its usual sleeping place in what used to be the fruit bowl, and made a grab for the wall-mounted phone.

'Hello? Yes?'

'Is that you, Ally?' enquired Miranda's voice. 'What am I saying? Of course it is, nobody has vowels like yours.'

'What?'

'Your vowels. They're very distinctive. You know, very . . . Gloucestershire.'

'What – common, you mean?' Ally stuck her tongue out at her sister down the line. 'Gee thanks. As I recall,' she added, trying to shove maxi-packs of crisps into the kitchen wall cupboards, 'yours were even broader than mine before you did that charity thing with Joanna Lumley.'

Miranda's laughter tinkled like crystal waters down an Alpine mountainside. 'Oh Ally, you're so funny. A real scream.' Right on cue, an ear-splitting shriek threatened to shatter her left eardrum. 'What on earth are those children of yours doing? They're awfully . . . loud.'

'Kids are,' replied Ally, with a glare at her wayward progeny. 'Oh, just normal kid stuff. Fighting with sticks of celery actually.'

'Oh. How creative. Now listen, it's about my party next week.'

'Your . . . *surprise* party?' enquired Ally with a smile. 'The one you're not supposed to know about?'

15

Miranda waved this aside airily. 'Oh, Gav knows I know, and we both want to make sure it's absolutely perfect. Besides, I'm much better at organising functions than he is. So I wanted to let you know about the dress code.'

Ally's jaw dropped. 'What dress code? I thought this was a family birthday party.'

'Well I think it's a little more than that, darling. I'm not forty every year, thank God. In fact next year I think I'll go back to thirty-nine and start counting backwards. Anyhow, it's fancy dress for the Saturday do, but you're not to worry because I'm having something run up specially for you and the kids.'

'What!'

'She's a wonderful designer. You'll love it when you see it, you really will.'

Ally sank slowly onto one of the kitchen chairs, blinking mechanically and craving chocolate. 'Fancy dress?' she repeated faintly. 'But I was just going to pop down to the Matalan sale.'

# Chapter Two

Several people were falling about laughing in the kitchen at 22, Brookfield Road; but Luke wasn't one of them. He was staring at the cardboard box lying open on the table.

'There is absolutely no way on earth that you are going to get me into *that*.' He picked up the fancy-dress costume between thumb and forefinger as though it might go off at any moment. 'I mean, dear God, look at the state of it!'

'But it's great, Dad!' enthused Kyle. 'It's got a sword and everything! Is there a gun, too?'

'I'll have that, thank you very much.' Ally whisked the sword deftly away from her son's eager fingers. There were no limits to what a ten-year-old boy could do to his sister with a three-foot length of pointed silver plastic, and Ally had no desire to put in another family appearance at A&E just yet. They were probably still recovering from last Christmas's bauble-swallowing incident. 'Now, why don't you two go upstairs and wrap up those lovely birthday presents you made for Auntie Miranda?' Ally wondered what her super-chic sister would make of Josie's lopsided cardboard windmill, and Kyle's 'jewellery box' (a corn-flake packet decorated with football stickers). Still, to her credit, however withering Miranda had been about other people's gifts, she'd never uttered a cruel word about the children's offerings, no matter how dire.

'I want to see Daddy all dressed up!' protested Josie.

'Yeah Dad,' chimed in Kyle, 'we want to see you in your soldier outfit.'

'Then you'll wait a very long time,' replied Luke with a withering look at the offending costume. 'I am *not* going to a party

17

dressed like an extra from *Zulu*. In fact, why don't I just not go to the party at all?' he suggested hopefully.

'Daddy will put his costume on for you later,' promised Ally, ignoring Luke's attempts to deny it. 'Now go up and wrap those presents. And don't forget to put them somewhere where the cat can't chew them!' she called up the stairs after them as they ran off giggling.

When she came back into the kitchen, Luke was perched on the edge of the table with a pith helmet two sizes too big obscuring most of his face. 'I always knew your sister hated me,' he commented wryly. 'I just didn't realise how much.'

'Aw come on, it suits you!' retorted Ally.

'Yeah, right!'

'It does! I always knew you'd look good in uniform, and these Victorian ones are well sexy. Besides, it's only a fancy-dress costume. Everybody looks stupid in fancy dress.'

'Ah, so you admit it – I'm going to look stupid!'

She leaned her face close to his and whispered lovingly in his ear: 'Darling, you'll look a whole lot stupider if I have to shove that plastic sword up your arse. Now come on, put the thing on and let's see what you look like.'

Luke heaved a sigh of martyrdom and slid off the table. 'You're a hard woman, Ally Bennett.'

She grinned. 'You'd better believe it.'

He grumbled under his breath as he heaved himself into the tight breeches and red jacket. 'What's Miranda on about, anyway? I thought this thing on Saturday was supposed to be a birthday party, not a fashion show for dead people.'

Ally shook her head and smiled. 'I told you, somebody told Gavin about this amazing "Jungle" party they had at the Hall exactly a hundred years ago, and you know what he's like when something catches his imagination. He decided to hire the Hall and recreate the whole thing, just for Miranda. Isn't that romantic?'

Luke grunted. 'Expensive.'

'So? He can afford it. Now, how are those breeches, Major Bennett?'

'Tight,' he replied faintly.

'I think they're supposed to be.' She ran an appreciative eye over him as he buttoned up the tunic. 'Oh yes, definitely, very nice. You can wear those in bed tonight if you like.'

'Hussy.'

'Complaining?' she enquired archly.

Luke chuckled. 'Hardly. Tell you what ... If we packed Kyle and Josie off to Zee's for the rest of the afternoon, you and I could try out these breeches right now.'

'But what about the ironing?' teased Ally. 'And that lesson plan I've got to do for work tomorrow?'

'Stuff the ironing and come and teach me a lesson,' replied Luke, drawing her into a hungry embrace. He winked. 'And you can take that as an order.'

The following morning, Ally was in more of a rush than usual as she had recently taken on a permanent part-time teaching job at Pussy Willows, a local nursery school. Some day, when the kids were both at big school, she'd probably look around for a full-time teaching job, but for the time being she was happy just keeping her hand in and spending the rest of her time being a mum.

As she sat at the lights in her faithful old Fiesta, she watched the other drivers in their sleek Beemers and Porsches, most of them far too rushed and harassed to notice the double rainbow arching across the sky behind the cemetery gates, or the robin twittering away on a nearby gatepost. The moment the lights switched to red and amber, they stamped on the gas and shot off into the distance like so many greyhounds on a stadium track.

Ally had never felt that way about work – not *driven*, the way so many other women were nowadays. It wasn't that she didn't care about her work; she took pride in being a good teacher. But it was a long way from being the only thing in her life, and she was glad about that – even if her parents weren't.

Naturally, the word 'disappointment' had never actually been uttered – at least not while Ally was around to hear it – but one way or another, Mum and Dad Morris had made it pretty obvious that there was only one big success in the family, and it wasn't her.

When she was a kid, the way her parents idolised Miranda had really hurt. Whatever Miranda wanted, she got. And since the Morrises weren't especially well off, that meant that whenever she wanted something expensive, everybody else went without something to pay for it. And why? Because Miranda was destined for Great Things. They never seemed to notice that their younger

19

daughter was doing equally well at school, but with considerably less of the drama-queen histrionics.

It wasn't until she was in her mid-teens that Ally realised they didn't even know they were doing it. If she'd accused them of favouritism, they'd have been genuinely horrified. Maybe they were right anyway: maybe Miranda did have something she didn't, be it brains, talent, charisma or just the fact that, unlike 99.9 per cent of all women on the planet, she looked irresistibly pretty when she cried. At any rate, from that moment on Ally stopped competing; not because she knew she could never win, but because competing just wasn't her thing. Miranda was welcome to all the glamour she could get her hands on – and the hassle. Ally had everything she'd ever wanted or needed, right here in Brookfield Road.

Mind you, she mused as she pottered along the A road at thirty miles an hour, much to the annoyance of a string of drivers behind her, a bit of Miranda's money wouldn't go amiss. Not with the soaring cost of school shoes and judo lessons ...

Ah, but what about the other fringe benefit of being Miranda: the luscious Gavin?

The very thought of him made her cheeks turn pink. It was so embarrassing. She didn't even fancy the bloke! Of course she didn't. Not really *fancy*. He just had a way of making her go all silly whenever he looked at her, turning her giggly and wobbly-kneed like a fourteen-year-old with a crush on her maths teacher. It was something about those deep, lustrous, masterful eyes ... And it didn't help when other people commented on how much they seemed to 'enjoy each other's company'. That just made her feel as if the whole world was hoping they'd jump into bed together or something. As if that wasn't practically incest!

She was quite sure he had no interest in her either. Why on earth would he, when he had the delectable Miranda?

Nevertheless, it was all so awkward that Ally had taken to hiding round corners when Gavin was in the vicinity. Great, she thought. And now I've got a whole weekend of avoiding him to look forward to. A whole weekend of him being all dark and masterful, Luke being grumpy because I made him wear that uniform, the kids being hyperactive on a diet of fizzy drinks and cake, and Miranda being ... Miranda.

The thought was so alarming that Ally almost missed her turning,

20

and decelerated with such suddenness and squealing of brakes that the manoeuvre unleashed a fanfare of enraged parping from the car behind. I really shouldn't be on the road, mused Ally, not for the first time. I'm never thinking of fewer than two things at once.

As she swung right into the driveway of the Pussy Willows Nursery School, she was doing precisely that. Because even as she ran through in her mind what she was going to teach the children that morning, another part of her brain was thinking about Gavin Hesketh; and wondering.

Was he as apprehensive about Miranda's birthday weekend as she was? Or was she just flattering herself?

By the time Luke got home from work that night, the kids had already been fed, bathed, read to and packed off to bed, protesting that every other kid at their school had a computer, a PlayStation and a TV in their bedroom and stayed up till two in the morning watching MTV. Nameless the cat was asleep on top of the TV, his tail dangling down over the screen; and Ally was sprawled across the sofa in the sitting room, slippers off and helping herself to chocolate Brazil nuts and a clandestine Bailey's.

Nameless had waddled his way into the Bennett family's lives as a tubby eight-week-old kitten, and was now a barrel-shaped, middle-aged moggy who believed in never moving unless it was absolutely necessary. Not that he'd always been quite so inert. On the day he'd arrived, he'd managed to wee all over the new sofa, upset the contents of the kitchen bin all over the floor and had eaten half of Ally's favourite pot plant. When Luke arrived home and asked what on earth had happened, she'd just laughed, pointed to the kitten and said, 'The guilty party shall remain nameless.' And so he had.

Nameless was snoring contentedly by the time the front door banged shut and Luke's footsteps came thudding up the hall. Ally's ears pricked up. She could tell the kind of day he'd had, just from the way he walked – and there was a definite spring in his step.

He was positively beaming as he came into the room and flung his messenger bag onto the nearest chair. 'Hello darling. I'm really sorry I missed the kids' bedtime again. Do I get a kiss?'

'Only if I do too,' she teased.

They had a cuddle and a smooch. 'Did you have a good day?' enquired Ally.

21

'As a matter of fact I did. Remember that guy Jake? The one I told you about whose son evicted him?'

'Uh-huh.'

'Well, I found him a home! And not just a hostel place either. I managed to get him into one of those new low-cost bedsits at the housing project on the Bluebell Estate.'

'Great. But I thought you said the new block wasn't ready for another three months.'

'That is the one drawback. Plus it's a private project, aimed at making a profit, and I'd be happier with a housing association. But hey, it's still good news. Now I just have to find him somewhere to stay until then ... Anyway, how about you – how were the ankle-biters?'

She grinned through a yawn. 'Not too bad, they let me out alive. I think I must be getting old though, I'm knackered. Three choruses of "The Wheels on the Bus" and I'm good for nothing. Or nothing except a nice hot bath and bed.'

'Hm, sounds good to me,' commented Luke, with a suggestive wiggle of an eyebrow.

'Well, it is a big bath,' she confided with mock seriousness. 'I might be a bit lonely on my own.'

'Can't have that then, can we?'

'I was rather hoping you'd say that.'

What Ally wasn't hoping for, at that moment, was a telephone call. And when the damned thing rang, for two pins she'd have pulled the flex out of the socket. But over the years in the ChelShel office, Luke had answered so many telephone calls that it had become an automatic reflex. And before Ally could say, 'Don't answer that,' he already had.

'Maureen, hi, how are you? Yes, fine, fine. No, it didn't turn out to be ringworm in the end, just an allergy or something. Yes, sure, I'll pass you over.' He turned to Ally and stated the blindingly obvious: 'It's your mum.'

Ally had often wondered about her mother's occult powers. She certainly seemed to have an uncanny ability to sniff out any kind of impending intimacy and effortlessly prevent it happening. How else could you explain her arrival on the doorstep with a lamb casserole and some holiday snaps on the night Luke came home bearing gifts from the naughty lingerie shop? Or the time he and Ally were about to get playful in the garden hammock, and she

22

phoned to ask what the children wanted for Christmas? As Luke often said, with Maureen around it was a wonder they'd ever managed to have kids.

Ally took a deep breath. 'Hello Mum, how are you? And Dad?'

'We're perfectly fine, dear. It's you I'm worried about.'

'Me?' Ally's small nose wrinkled in puzzlement.

'Both of you.' Maureen cleared her throat as if she was about to broach a particularly embarrassing subject. 'It's about your sister's birthday do,' she said. 'You're not going to let the side down, are you?'

The telephone receiver slid away from Ally's ear. Just for a few moments, she was speechless. 'Mum thinks we'll let the side down at Miranda's party,' she informed Luke, not bothering to cover the mouthpiece with her hand.

'All right then,' said Luke, with just a little too much eagerness. 'Let's not go.'

Maureen was saying something, but with the phone dangling all Ally could hear was a sort of vague buzzing sound, like a wasp in a jam jar. 'Mum,' she said at last, sticking the receiver back against her ear, 'why on earth should we let anybody down?'

'I know you don't *intend* to,' replied Maureen, 'but with you two being, you know, not poor exactly, but ... well ... I mean to say, presents are so expensive these days, aren't they?'

'Yes,' agreed Ally, sensing that her mother was on one of her fishing expeditions and aiming to pull the worm off her hook. 'So you've got Miranda something nice then? Pushed the boat out a bit?'

But Maureen wasn't about to be derailed so easily. 'What? Yes, of course we have, but that's not the point. What I want to know is, what have you and Luke bought her?'

Ally sighed, glanced at Luke and flashed him a despairing smile. 'Actually,' she replied after an enjoyably long pause, 'we haven't bought Miranda anything yet, have we Luke?'

Luke's 'not really' down the telephone was obliterated by the sound of Maureen having the vapours. 'What? What! My God Alison, if you couldn't afford a decent present why didn't you tell me?'

'I—'

'Right, that's settled. Your father and I will buy something suitable, and then you can pretend you bought it. Dear me though, I do wish you'd said something about this earlier, John Lewis can be hell on a Friday afternoon, and—'

'Yet,' repeated Ally as her mother paused for a nanosecond to breathe.

'Pardon?'

'I said "yet". We haven't bought Miranda anything *yet*,' repeated Ally. 'Relax, Mum. We just haven't got round to it, that's all. But I'm sure we'll find something nice in time for the party.'

'You're sure?'

'Quite sure.'

'She's still your big sister, you know. And she thinks the world of you.'

Oh really, thought Ally as a wave of scepticism flooded over her. This was after all the big sister who'd once decapitated all Ally's teddies and stuck their heads in a row on the school railings, just because Ally had innocently revealed to Miranda's latest beau that the whole family had just had headlice. 'Look, stop worrying Mum. I'm not going to fob her off with something from the Pound Shop.'

But as she replaced the receiver, Ally had the very distinct impression that her mother wasn't convinced.

'Don't laugh!' protested Ally. 'It's not even slightly funny.'

Zee wasn't so sure about that. His shoulders were still heaving with mirth as he went back to the Transit van for the next box of boot-sale bargains. 'Oh come on Al, it's hilarious. My mum hasn't bought presents for me to give to other people since I was about four. And here you are, in your thirties with two kids and a following wind, and yours is still fretting about letting loose with your pocket money.'

Ally threw him what she hoped was a dark look, but it came out looking more like trapped wind. 'You know as well as I do why she's being like this,' she muttered as she hauled a basket of old clothes out of the van and dragged it towards the trestle tables they'd set up in the field.

'Do I?' Zee enquired.

'It's only because it's a present for my perfect sister. I mean, heaven forbid that the Blessed Miranda should be offended by a less-than-gorgeous present. Even though she and Gavin have got enough money to buy his 'n' hers bloody gold mines.'

Zee chuckled. 'You're great when you get angry. Your eyebrows go really weird.'

It was no good thinking murderous thoughts; Zee was perfectly immune to them all. Ally gave a weary sigh. 'Remind me why I'm standing in a muddy field at half past seven on a damp October morning, trying to flog bits of tat,' she pleaded faintly.

'Because any one of these so-called bits of tat here,' Zee swept an arm over the jumble of unwanted artefacts, 'could be our passport to fabulous wealth.'

Now it was Ally's turn to laugh. She picked up a single brown sock between finger and thumb. 'You're an optimist Zee, I'll give you that.'

'All right then, you're here because you want to make a few quid to buy your sister a decent present, and I'm here because I need to pay the gas bill. Now come on, help me get this cloth on the table, let's make it look nice and professional.'

They fiddled about with the plastic tablecloth until it looked reasonable, and then set about decanting about two hundredweight of rubbish onto it. They had the lot: souvenirs from Alicante, nodding dogs with one ear missing, rubber chickens, hideous soup plates, obsolete cameras, a rusty blowlamp and even a picture of Fidel Castro.

'I just wish she wouldn't make it so bloody obvious,' muttered Ally, banging four chicken-shaped eggcups onto the table top.

'What?'

'Phoning me up like that, to check we'd bought a decent present – she and Dad have always been like that. Miranda first. Miranda gets what Miranda wants, and the rest of us just sort of grovel about gratefully in her shadow.' An awkward feeling of self-consciousness crept over her. God, she thought; I sound like a whingeing adolescent. 'I suppose I ought to be immune to it by now,' she admitted, 'but sometimes it just gets to me a bit, knowing that no matter what I do I can never quite match up. Can I help it if I was just an ... an afterthought?'

Zee gave her elbow a companionable squeeze. 'Hey, it's not quite that bad, is it?' Silence answered his question for him. 'Oh. Well, I'm sure they care just as much about you really, they just don't show it very well.'

'Hmm,' replied Ally, non-committally. She stood up, wiping damp hair off her forehead. 'You any good at this selling lark then?'

25

Zee treated her to a grin filled with gleaming teeth. 'Just call me the Donald Trump of the car boot sale.'

'Come on then Donny, get your finger out. I've got a present to buy, and it'd better be a good one or I'm toast.'

'Donald Trump, eh?'

Ally looked across the waterlogged stall at Zee, who was still jigging about under an umbrella, trying to get a signal on his mobile so he could check up on his babysitter.

He looked back at her sheepishly. 'Maybe more of a Del Boy,' he admitted. 'Hey though, we sold that really horrible rug that the dog was sick on! Would you believe they thought the bleach stain was part of the pattern?'

She shook her head and a spray of rainwater came out of her ears. 'There's that much water in my brain,' she replied, 'that I reckon I could probably believe just about anything right now – except the possibility that we might make a profit.'

In the last half-hour or so the rain had really started to set in, and Ally was beginning to see why the kids had been so reluctant to come and spend an 'exciting' day helping Mum and Uncle Zee 'make loads of money'. Clearly they'd been privy to inside information on the true-life horror of a boot sale in the pouring rain.

Ally closed her eyes and fantasised about being back at home, in a nice warm bed, with a nice warm husband. Bit too late for that though. Luke would have set off for football practice by now, via the pub, and the kids would be round at Kerri-next-door's house, playing unsuitable video games and eating everything they could lay their hands on.

'These shoes leak,' she announced with sudden realisation as the cold wetness started creeping up her ankle. 'And I wish I'd sold those bloody caviar spoons now.'

Zee wasn't listening. In fact Zee had disappeared. When he returned, a few minutes later, he looked as if he had just seen the Holy Grail. 'Hey – you'll never guess!'

'You've bought something?'

He nodded enthusiastically.

'Something ... good?'

He nodded so hard his head nearly fell off.

'Wow.' Despite her scepticism, Ally felt a frisson of interest. 'What is it? Come on, show it to me then!'

26

Zee unveiled with a flourish. 'Ta-dah!'

Ally peered at it. 'It's a doll, Zee. A Barbie doll. With no clothes on.'

'Not just any Barbie doll. This is a 1978 limited edition with extra-long hair – *pink* hair! They're ever so rare.'

'Zee, it's only got one leg and somebody's drawn all over the face with green felt pen.'

'Well yes . . . but with a bit of restoration here and there, and a new leg, she could be worth . . . oooh . . . as much as fifteen quid!'

Be still my beating heart, thought Ally. Sorry Miranda, but it looks like I'll be visiting the Pound Shop after all.

# Chapter Three

'Do you really think she'll like it?' asked Ally worriedly, as the Bennett family rust-heap trundled towards Wiltshire through weak October sunshine. It was a nice afternoon, but they'd sort of promised to be at the Hall by lunchtime, so they were probably in enough trouble with Miranda already.

Luke answered without so much as a glance at the gift-wrapped box on his wife's lap. 'How could she not like it?' he reasoned. 'It cost an arm and a leg.'

'Not by Miranda's standards,' Ally pointed out. She lowered her voice, as though that made any difference with all four of them squeezed into a space little bigger than the average wheelie bin. 'You don't think she'll notice, do you? The fact that it's factory seconds?'

'What's factory seconds, Mummy?' asked a small voice from the back seat.

Ally craned round to give her big-eared daughter a tense smile. 'Nothing you need to worry about, Josie,' she promised between clenched teeth.

This might be an adequate explanation as far as Josie was concerned, but Kyle didn't like to let his superior knowledge of life go to waste so he aired it. 'It means there's something wrong with it, so Mum got it cheap,' he explained. 'Basically it's rubbish.'

'Shh!' appealed Ally, though there was nobody else around to hear the dreadful secret. 'There's nothing wrong with it, Kyle . . . well, nothing much. And nothing anybody will notice.' I hope, she thought to herself. 'Now, who wants some more carrot sticks?'

'Why can't we have crisps and chocolate, Mummy?' whined Josie.

'Because carrots are good for you,' Ally replied in a sing-song, adding under her breath, 'and I don't want you dropping bits on your nice clothes.'

Kyle scratched fretfully at his neck, scrubbed squeaky-clean and red under the collar of his cute little Victorian sailor suit. 'Mum . . . I don't have to wear this all day, do I?'

''Fraid so, tiger.'

'But people can see my knees! And it itches!'

'So does mine, mate,' chimed in Luke, visibly melting in his uniform. 'And you wouldn't believe the chafing.'

'Ah, but these costumes are for Auntie Miranda's special birthday. And you want to please Auntie Miranda, don't you?' cajoled Ally, playing her ace. She knew her kids; and they knew how generous Auntie Miranda could be when she was in the right mood. Pure, altruistic love might not make them behave, but the prospect of large and expensive presents almost certainly would.

''Spose,' grunted Kyle, wriggling uncomfortably.

'I like my dress,' declared Josie, a vision in lace and pink frills, with a snowy pinafore on top, Railway-Children style. 'It's pretty. Can I wear it always, Mummy?'

'Er . . . maybe not always, sweetie. We'll see. Now, who wants some dried apricots?'

The occupants of any passing spaceship with an interest in human history might have wondered why a Victorian soldier was driving his equally Victorian family along the Swindon road in a beaten-up, late-twentieth-century Volvo. As did the occupants of several other vehicles, and there was plenty of ironic horn-beeping as the car rattled its way along the leaf-strewn dual carriageway. Ally couldn't remember ever feeling quite so *obvious* in her whole life.

She dearly regretted taking the mickey out of Luke's uniform. He'd taken his revenge by lacing up her all-too-horribly-authentic corset so tight that she was still seeing spots before her eyes, and now her two most prominent assets were making a bid for escape from her plunging décolletage. This may be a genuine period design, thought Ally, but modest it ain't. Maybe we've had the wrong idea about the Victorians all this time . . . or maybe Miranda just sees me as some kind of nineteenth-century hooker. On balance, that seemed more likely.

As though reading her mind, Josie announced with a giggle: 'I can see Mummy's boobies in the mirror.'

29

You and everybody else, thought Ally. Just wait till *I* have a party, Miranda Hesketh. I'll teach you the meaning of embarrassment.

Over at Nether Grantley Hall, the morning mists had cleared, revealing the set from an expensive but sketchily researched period drama. But then Gavin wasn't bothered that the twenties-style dance band was a glaring anachronism amid the aspidistras and antimacassars, or that a DJ was playing chill-out music in a marquee on the lawn. Miranda liked twenties music, and you could hardly dance to Beethoven, could you? Besides, you couldn't expect the younger guests to stooge around in crinolines and false whiskers all weekend without going round the bend. That was why he'd hired the quad bikes and the bungee rig.

He stood on the front steps of the Hall, thumbs tucked into his waistcoat pockets like some prosperous mill-owner, and surveyed his creation. Yes, a bloody excellent achievement, if he did say so himself. And it was the dream setting for Miranda. She looked like something out of a Pre-Raphaelite painting, gliding about with her bosoms out and her hair all flowing. Even when she was disco-dancing she looked elegant. She was an amazingly beautiful woman; almost unreal.

Lord Grantley stood beside him, nibbling on a canapé. 'You're pleased with the old Hall then?'

'Oh yes.'

'You bloody well should be!' the aristocrat pointed out. 'You screwed one hell of a good deal out of me.'

Gavin tried not to look too smug. He had indeed secured the Hall for the weekend at a knockdown price. But could he help it if he was a born negotiator? 'True,' he admitted, 'but like I said, you scratch my back—'

'And this new equestrian centre you're planning ... you say Nether Grantley is definitely your chosen location?'

Gavin tapped the side of his nose. 'At this stage it's strictly between you and me, of course.'

'Well, naturally. Now, about this summer sales conference you were thinking of hol— Mr Hesketh?'

'Hm?'

'The conference. You wanted to talk about it.'

'What? Oh, yes. Right.' But Gavin's gaze was fixed not on Lord

30

Grantley, nor on the lovely Miranda, but on a beaten-up old Volvo that was bumping up the driveway towards them. 'I ... er ... could it wait until later? Only there's somebody I need to see.'

'At last!' said Gavin, gravel crunching underfoot as he strode towards them. 'I ... we thought you weren't coming!'

'Sorry we're late, Gav.' Luke shooed the kids out of the car and locked it – not that anybody in their right mind would want to steal it, but it was a kind of automatic reflex. 'It's all my fault, I was messing about and lost track of the time.'

Ally directed a meaningful stare at her two offspring, and they thought better of grassing up Daddy, who had spent most of the morning trying to make up excuses for not coming at all.

'Anyhow, we're here now,' Ally pointed out breezily as she accepted a chaste peck on the cheek. As ever, she found it ridiculously difficult to look Gavin in the eye, as though there were some guilty secret between them that everyone might see if they dared make eye contact. 'Where's the birthday girl?'

'Miranda? Oh, she's floating around looking gorgeous and having a wonderful time. I'll go and flush her out for you in a minute.'

'We've brought a present,' explained Ally. 'It's not much, just some pretty glassware I thought she might like.'

'Of course she'll like it,' said Gavin firmly. 'You chose it.'

Like some silly fourteen-year-old, Ally felt the warmth of a blush spreading across her cheeks. Fortunately nobody seemed to notice; Luke and the kids were far too distracted by a man dressed as Oscar Wilde, complete with green carnation.

'Hey Dad, isn't that ...?'

Kyle nudged his father's elbow, but Luke had already noticed. 'Oh yes ... you know, I think you're right. The one who played the villain in the last James Bond.' He pointed across the lawn to the marquee. 'And I'm sure that lady over there is off that Australian soap on Channel Six. What's it called? Ally?'

Ally jumped as Luke spoke her name. She'd been caught in a kind of trance, her thoughts floating off into fantasy-land and her power of speech deserting her, the way they always seemed to whenever Gavin was around. 'What did you say?' she asked, slightly shaken.

'That Aussie soap on Channel Six. What's it called?'

31

'Oh, you mean *Return to Wombat Creek*,' cut in Gavin before she'd had a chance to think about it.

Everybody stared. 'You don't ... watch it, do you?' enquired Luke, suppressing a smirk at the prospect of his sophisticated, square-jawed brother-in-law glued to the sofa by cheesy goings-on in the outback.

'Sorry to disappoint you – it's just that our housekeeper never stops going on about it. I think I know more about it than she does by now. And of course, Miranda knows half the cast members. God knows how she does it, but what with all her charity events, she seems to be best friends with just about everybody in show-business.'

'She would be,' murmured Ally to herself.

'Sorry?'

'Oh, nothing. Any chance of stashing this present somewhere? It's a bit heavy.'

'Of course. Follow me and I'll get you both a drink.' Gavin snapped his fingers and a demure-looking Victorian parlourmaid appeared from nowhere. 'This is Kirsty,' he informed the children. 'If you go with her, she'll show you the miniature ponies and the fainting goats. And if you're very good, she might even let you see a *real live tiger cub*! What do you reckon?'

'Wow!' enthused Kyle, his eyes like saucers. 'Can we go? Can we?'

Luke frowned. 'Are you sure it's safe to let them go?'

'Kirsty's a fully qualified nanny. And we've brought in all kinds of amusements especially for the kids. Soft play areas, storytellers, magicians ... Don't you worry about a thing; they're going to have the time of their lives. Now, let's go and get you two a drink before you die of thirst.'

Gavin might know next to nothing about botany, but he certainly knew what ought to be done with a nice bit of exotic foliage. Overnight, the Great Hall at Nether Grantley had been transformed into a tropical jungle.

Real exotic trees and lianas had been shipped in, along with an entire, full-size native village scrounged from a performance of *South Pacific*, a couple of enormous painted wooden idols, some live macaws and a whole menagerie-full of stuffed animals, taking pride of place, next to the finger buffet.

Admittedly it was a little non-specific in terms of location.

Not many jungles could boast a Siberian tiger, a North American totem pole and an African village within spitting distance of each other; but hey, this was Miranda's birthday and she could have whatever she wanted. He had drawn the line at the polar bear, though.

Clive and Maureen Morris sipped at their drinks and listened in rapt attention as their elder daughter told an adoring clique all about her latest interior design project. In all honesty they weren't very interested in interior design – a few rolls of embossed wallpaper and a tin of Dulux were about the limit of their imagination; but they really loved basking in Miranda's reflected glory. It made all those years of scrimping and saving worthwhile. They'd never really stopped to wonder whether Ally felt the same. Ally was just a nice, ordinary girl who'd never been any trouble: a daughter who'd never caused them a moment's worry – but there again, not that many excitements either. Not like Miranda.

'. . . with these darling little glass mosaic tiles carried through into the bathrooms.' Miranda tossed back a glossy mane of chocolate-coloured hair. 'I did consider Moroccan-style tiling for the mezzanine, but one has to be so careful not to make things look too . . . busy.' She beamed at the various murmurs of agreement. 'It's the first time I've done an entire hotel, and I must say I'm rather pleased with it. Any more of that champagne, Russell?'

A liveried footman – rather more eighteenth century than nineteenth, owing to a shortage at the theatrical costumier's – appeared from nowhere to refresh Miranda's glass. The bottle moved on, to hover questioningly over Maureen's drink. 'Madam?'

Maureen hurriedly shielded the glass with her hand. 'Oh goodness me, no thank you! We've already had one glass, haven't we Clive? And we don't really drink, well, only on *very* special occasions.'

'Oh go on, Mum,' giggled Miranda. 'You and Dad should learn to live a little. It's not a crime, you know!'

'Well I don't know dear,' said Clive doubtfully. 'We're not used to the high life like you are. We're very ordinary, you see.'

'Don't be silly Dad, you'll never be ordinary to me.'

'Or me,' echoed a voice from behind a suit of armour.

Heads swivelled to see who the voice belonged to. Ally smiled apologetically, certain they'd been expecting someone more interesting. 'Only me, I'm afraid. Hiya big sis. Just stopped by to wish you a happy birthday.'

'Oh Alison,' her mother sighed reprovingly as she peered into the cardboard box. 'I told you your father and I would get something – you only had to ask. But no, you had to go off and buy ... *that*.'

'What is it?' enquired Clive, taking a peek. 'Oh. How ... unusual.'

'It's a bowl. A glass bowl. From Transylvania,' Ally added wearily. 'I thought the colours were really vibrant and different, but no, you're right; it's crap.' She jammed the lid back on. 'I don't know what I was thinking.'

'Hang on a minute.' Miranda gently moved her mother out of the way. 'Do I get a look at it? After all, it is my present.'

Reluctantly, Ally removed the lid again. 'You'll hate it,' she warned. Just like you've hated every other present I've ever bought you, she added silently. Sometimes she thought it would be easier to buy a birthday present for God than to buy one for Miranda.

Miranda reached into the box and drew out the bowl. 'Hey, you know something? This is really cool.'

Ally blinked. Her mother blanched. 'It is?'

'Oh, absolutely. This rough, slightly unfinished style is just what I've been looking for.'

'Wow. Great.' Ally felt quite faint.

'Yes, it's going to look just fab in the downstairs cloakroom with some pot-pourri in it. Thanks sis, it's really sweet of you.'

Downstairs loo? thought Ally with a silent sob. We spent all that money and it's going in the downstairs loo?

She didn't really have a chance to comment out loud, because Russell the footman had returned, this time looking a lot less composed. 'Is anybody missing a small boy?' he enquired.

Glances were exchanged. 'What do you mean, a small boy? What's going on?'

Russell coughed discreetly. 'From what I understand, he says he's ten and his name's Kyle.'

'Kyle!' shrieked Ally. 'That's my son! What's happened to him?'

Russell's expression settled somewhere between pity and embarrassment. 'Nothing too terrible, madam, not according to one of the guests – he's the local doctor. It appears that your son won't need to go to hospital.'

'Hospital!' Ally almost fainted.

'But apparently he's a little ... erm ... inebriated. He's currently sleeping it off in the summer drawing room.'

'Drunk? You're saying my little boy's drunk?' All the colour drained from Ally's face. 'How? He's only ten, for God's sake! Right, take me there right now, I want to see him.'

As she rushed off after the footman, she just caught her mother's judgmental eye. There wasn't much doubt who Maureen thought was to blame for this whole sorry episode. But then that was no great surprise to anyone; least of all Ally.

# Chapter Four

Luke was seldom if ever inclined to violence, but right now Ally feared he might wrench Gavin's head from his shoulders and drop-kick it through the Orangery windows.

'You said Kyle would be safe!' Luke seethed, backing Gavin up against the wall. 'Perfectly safe, he'll have a wonderful time, that's what you said. All that stuff about him being with a qual-ified nanny —'

'Well he is – was,' interjected Gavin, but Luke wasn't interested in listening.

'And now look at him! Ten years old and he's tipsy!'

Outwardly calm, Gavin gently eased Luke's hand from his throat. 'I know it's a shock,' he said, 'But it wasn't Kirsty's fault. The little . . . er, rascal gave her the slip right after he'd seen the tiger cub.'

'She shouldn't have let him!' If Luke's breath had been fire, Gavin's face would be a charred cinder by now. 'She was supposed to be responsible for him – and Josie.'

'Kirsty did go and look for Kyle the minute she realised he was missing,' pointed out Ally quietly. 'And when she tracked him down she got a doctor there in minutes to check him out. It's prob-ably down to her that he's going to be all right.'

Ally knew she was exaggerating Kirsty's saintliness, but she needed to make Luke calm down. She was upset enough already, without him picking a fight with her brother-in-law. And in any case, it was hardly Gavin's fault, whatever Luke might think.

She laid a hand on Luke's arm. 'Come on, darling,' she urged. 'How was anybody supposed to guess that Kyle would go round drinking the dregs out of all the empty wine glasses? If it's

36

anybody's fault it's mine, for letting him out of my sight.' She sighed. 'After all, we both know what he's like.'

'Then it's *both* our faults,' replied Luke, his anger cooling a little. 'He is a little sod sometimes, isn't he?'

'You said it. Remember when he nearly burned down next door's shed?'

'There you go then,' ventured Gavin, with a look of relief. 'Kyle's just one of those kids who are into everything. I was a bit like that myself. Anyhow, in the end there's no real harm done, is there?'

'No real harm?' Luke could hardly believe what he was hearing. 'My God, it's easy to see you don't have kids. Kyle's only ten! He could've got alcoholic poisoning and died!'

'Yes, but luckily he didn't,' Ally pointed out gently, as much to reassure herself as Luke. 'He's just a bit out of it and tomorrow he'll have the headache from hell.'

'And I bet he won't ever do it again,' added Gavin.

Luke looked from one to the other, as though he suspected some kind of conspiracy, let out an explosion of breath, and sat down on a Queen Anne chair. He wiped the back of his hand wearily across his forehead. 'I get the feeling I'm the only person round here who thinks this is serious.'

'No! Not at all.' Ally put an arm round his shoulders. 'We're all as shaken up as you are, but there's no point in getting angry, is there? Save that for Kyle when he's feeling better.'

'Luke mate, I'm really sorry.' Gavin looked genuinely rueful. 'I didn't mean to sound like I don't care, because I do ... It's just ... I guess I'm used to keeping a lid on my feelings, that's all.'

He held out a hand, and after a moment's hesitation, Luke accepted it. 'Yeah, well, maybe I overreacted a bit. But he's my child, Gavin; and there's nothing more precious in the world than your kids. That's something you just can't really understand until you have kids of your own.'

After Kyle's escapade, it was pretty obvious that he wasn't going anywhere that night. The Bennetts would have to do exactly what they'd planned to avoid: spend the night at Nether Grantley Hall. Still, there were compensations: at least Miranda seemed far too busy with the more important guests to bother much with them.

The rest of the afternoon and evening festivities didn't exist as

37

far as Ally was concerned. She could hear the echoes from the big jungle party in the Great Hall, but it all sounded unreal, like something playing in the far distance on a tinny old radio.

While Luke took charge of Josie, Ally spent a romantic evening sitting on a chair next to Kyle's borrowed bed, holding a bucket for him to be sick into. Foolhardy and disobedient he might be, but it was impossible not to feel sorry for the little guy, and she suspected Gavin had a point about him not doing it again. Alcohol had definitely lost its glamour for one small boy at least.

Maybe when he was a spotty teenager and all his mates were all out binge-drinking and collapsing all over Cheltenham's pavements, Kyle would be the smug one with the orange juice. Maybe. At least Ally had that single positive thought to balance out all the scary ones that kept reminding her how bad things could have been if he'd drunk just a little more alcohol.

I could've lost you, you little devil, she thought to herself as she mopped Kyle's face with a damp cloth. It was a horrible feeling and she never wanted to have it again, though as a mother she knew that she probably would, many times over.

'I don't feel well, Mum,' croaked Kyle piteously.

'I know love. But you'll be better soon.'

'Is Dad really angry?'

'A bit,' Ally admitted. 'And so am I.'

'I didn't mean to.'

'But you did anyway,' Ally pointed out.

'I'm sorry, Mum. Really I am.'

'Well, that's good.'

'I don't like it when you and Dad are angry.'

'Of course you don't!' replied Ally. 'But if we get angry it's for a reason. And anyway, we're not just angry, we're upset. You could've made yourself really, really ill.'

'Mum, I *am* really ill,' Kyle assured her, his blue eyes innocent and round as a cherub's.

Ally chuckled despite herself, and ruffled her son's hair. 'You'll survive, kiddo,' she said. 'As long as you say a very big "sorry" to your dad.'

Kyle laid his head back down on the pillow, and she thought he'd drifted off to sleep. But a few minutes later, he suddenly opened his eyes and sat up. 'What about Nameless? We left him at home and he'll have no food to eat!'

38

'The cat's fine. I rang Natasha from down the road, and she's popping in to feed him.'

'But he's all on his own in the dark.'

'Cats like the dark. He's probably popped out through the catflap to catch himself a snack. Now come on, stop fretting and go to sleep. Things will look a whole lot better in the morning.'

At last there was peace and quiet at Nether Grantley Hall.

Most of the party guests had gone home, and the ones who hadn't had staggered off to their rooms or sweet-talked themselves under another guest's duvet. Kyle and Josie were fast asleep, head to tail in the double bed, and Luke was snoring in an armchair. Ally and Luke had been given a room of their own down the corridor, but neither of them could face leaving the two kids on their own. Not tonight.

Normally Ally could sleep anywhere. In fact she was renowned for it. Buses, cars, trains, floors, sofas, and even on one memorable occasion when Josie had been teething, the one basket only aisle at Sainsbury's: she'd dozed off in all of them. But tonight it wouldn't have made any difference if she'd been curled up in a feather bed with pure silk sheets. She knew she just wasn't going to sleep.

In the end, she decided to go downstairs in search of a kitchen and a mug of tea. Surely they must have tea, even in big posh stately homes like Nether Grantley Hall? Even the aristocracy couldn't spend all day every day drinking Pimm's, though it might account for the red noses and the gout. A biscuit would be nice too, as she hadn't eaten since lunchtime. Her gastric juices encouraged her to think bigger. Maybe she could find a few leftovers from the party and bring them back to share with Luke . . .

She slipped out of the room onto the landing, closing the door silently behind her, and groped for the light switch. One soft click and she was blinking in a wash of sudden brightness. Somewhere on the floor below, a grandfather clock chimed three, making her start. The long, carved wooden staircase stretched down in front of her like something out of a haunted house film. Or one of those over-the-top historical romances. Ally could just imagine it playing host to Rochester pursuing his new bride, although perhaps not in search of a cup of tea.

Five minutes of determined wandering through twilit corridors,

39

and Ally was comprehensively lost. The trouble was, everywhere looked the same: just endless oak-panelled passages lined with paintings of grim-faced ancestors, and the occasional party-popper or discarded beer bottle here and there, as a reminder that somebody had just had one hell of a party. Ally could imagine Miranda stretched out in a four-poster bed in her Agent Provocateur negligee, congratulating herself on the social event of the year while Gavin licked her perfectly manicured toes . . .

Miranda. She hadn't bothered to come upstairs all evening to see if Kyle was all right. Bloody typical.

Ally was walking along another anonymous corridor on the ground floor, thinking mildly murderous thoughts about elder sisters, when she heard something. No, not something: someone.

She stopped. Listened. Was it . . . yes, she was convinced of it. It was somebody crying.

Now, some people might have tiptoed away and left well alone, but not Ally. She just wasn't that kind of girl. No, Ally always barged right in to help and then probably wished later that she hadn't. Once she'd attacked an intruder with a frying pan, moments before realising it was her dad, who'd forgotten his house key. It seemed that she never ever listened to the voice of experience.

She located the sound of crying to a half-open doorway just ahead. All sorts of dreadful thoughts flashed through her mind, and she grabbed a statuette from a nearby table, just in case. Then she took a deep breath, pushed the door a little further open, and peeped inside.

To her relief, the room wasn't full of masked burglars or indeed anything very scary at all. It looked like a library or a study of some kind, and over by the window a woman was sitting at a desk with an empty whisky bottle, head down and sobbing into her folded arms. Ally wondered what had happened to her. Whatever it was, it must have been bad.

'Excuse me.' Ally walked across to the desk. 'Is something wrong? Can I help?'

A moment later, she almost died of shock as the woman raised her tearstained face to reply.

It was Miranda.

Frankly it was a toss-up who was more aghast.

'W-what are you doing here?' demanded Miranda through a

waterfall of tears. 'Why aren't you asleep?'

Ally ignored the question; she felt shell-shocked. The weeping woman in front of her looked like Miranda, even sounded like Miranda, but how could it be? Ally hadn't seen her sister like this since . . . She racked her brains. Since never. The only tears she'd ever wept as a child were when she was told she couldn't have something, which frankly hadn't happened very often. People seldom said no to Miranda.

Ally tentatively laid a hand on her sister's shoulder. 'What's happened? Whatever's the matter?'

'I'm fine, go away,' Miranda answered in a dull monotone.

If her sister hadn't looked so downright miserable, Ally would've laughed at the ridiculousness of the statement. 'Oh. You're fine, are you? Do you actually realise what you look like?'

'I don't care. I really don't care about anything right now. Please, just go away.'

'Have you had a row with Gavin or something?'

Something flared in Miranda's eyes. 'You've got no idea, have you?'

'Pardon?'

There was a hard edge of bitterness in Miranda's voice now. 'I said you've no idea. About me. With your neat little life, two-point-four kids and everything falling into place exactly the way you always planned it. No idea at all.'

That was just plain exasperating. Ally grabbed a chair and sat down. 'No? Well I don't reckon you've got much of an idea about me either, not if you think like that.'

They sat and looked at each other warily across the desk.

'My life's not half as easy as you seem to think,' Ally went on, half to break the uncomfortable silence, half because she felt an irrational need to justify herself, 'juggling the pennies, bringing up kids, worrying twenty-four/seven if you're doing the right thing—'

Miranda stared down at the desktop. 'But it's still easier than looking on and wanting what you can never have.'

Her hoarse whisper lingered in the air like a wisp of woodsmoke in an autumn sky, and something inside Ally knew instinctively that this wasn't one of Miranda's attention-seeking games.

'Miranda, what's this all about?'

Silence. Miranda's hand clenched and unclenched on the

41

desktop, and something on her wrist caught Ally's attention: a bracelet made from garish, plaited plastic strands. She recognised it instantly as the one Josie had made for her auntie the previous Christmas. God God, Ally thought; I never imagined she'd keep it, let alone actually *wear* it.

'You ... could tell me about it,' Ally said hesitantly, half afraid of what Miranda might come out with. As if Miranda had anything serious to be unhappy about. 'If you wanted. But if you'd rather not ... '

Miranda hesitated, then uncurled the fingers of her left hand. What looked like a crumpled piece of thin card fell onto the desk. But it wasn't any old piece of card, it was a photograph.

Ally recognised it before she'd even smoothed it out. It was one of the photos of Josie's christening, all of six years ago now. The one with all the godparents standing around the font with the vicar after the ceremony; and the baby, all swaddled up in Maureen's family's christening gown, yelling for all she was worth as Miranda struggled not to drop her into the water.

Miranda. Holding a baby. It wasn't a sight you saw every day, and there had been plenty of jokes to that effect. Ally looked up questioningly.

'How's Kyle?' asked Miranda.

'He's going to be fine.' Ally's resentment kicked in. 'It would've been nice if you'd asked about eight hours ago, but hey, better late than never. You had a party to run.'

Miranda's pink-rimmed eyes closed, squeezing out a teardrop that quivered for a moment before trickling down her cheek. 'I couldn't. I was afraid.' She swallowed. 'I ... we ... had some bad news yesterday.'

'Oh yes? What kind of news?' Shares gone down a couple of points? wondered Ally. Consignment of Japanese designer wallpaper held up at Customs?

Nothing could have prepared Ally for the shock of her sister's reply.

'We've been having IVF. It hasn't worked.'

Ally's jaw hung open, slack and stupid-looking. 'You? And Gavin? Trying for a baby?' It felt as if the whole universe had just been turned upside down like a giant egg-timer, and everything was now running again, only in the wrong direction. 'A *baby*?'

42

'It was our final go,' Miranda said quietly. 'We've had two failed attempts before. This was our last chance but it didn't work.' She opened her eyes and looked directly at her sister. 'We've been trying since we first got married but ... You have to call a halt some time, or in the end you go mad.'

'You never said. I had no idea ... '

'I didn't want you to. The failing is hard enough, without everybody pitying us as well. Besides,' added Miranda with matter-of-fact directness, 'you all think I'm a selfish bitch who'd make a terrible mother.'

Ally didn't know what to say. She wanted to deny it, assure Miranda that everybody thought she was born to be a parent, but it would only have come out sounding like the lie it was. To be fair, though, she'd always been a decent enough auntie, in a hands-off sort of way.

'To be honest,' Ally said after a few moments, 'I never imagined for a moment that you'd want kids. You always gave me the impression you thought women with kids were thick and unambitious.'

Miranda smiled thinly. 'Never heard of the green-eyed monster, sis? It's not just money that makes people envious you know. And when the whole bloody thing's your own fault that just makes it all worse.'

Questions tumbled over themselves inside Ally's head. 'What do you mean, your own fault? How can it be your fault if you can't conceive? It's just bad luck, surely.'

Miranda ran a fingertip gently over the surface of the photograph that lay before her on the desk. 'Fashion models have to be thin,' she said. 'Thin as in stick insect. So you watch what you eat. Only trouble is, before you know it you've got anorexia and you're eating paper tissues to fill yourself up.

'Back then I never believed it when people said starving yourself could make you infertile. But this time when they tried to harvest my eggs they said they weren't viable. They think I've been going through early menopause in the last year without even noticing. It's ludicrous but when you're used to not having regular periods ... '

'Oh God,' said Ally. 'Look, you can't blame yourself, you weren't to know.'

'Maybe, maybe not. But remember, I'm an obstinate, selfish

43

bitch. Ask anyone. If somebody had told me about the dangers, I probably wouldn't have listened.'

There was a long silence.

'I'm sorry,' said Ally. 'About the IVF. Really sorry. You and Gavin must be ... '

'Yeah.' Miranda shrugged. Her face had dried, accentuating the brightness of the unshed tears in her eyes.

'I wish there was something I could do to help.' It was a platitudinous formula, a very English string of empty words that never led anywhere, but it was what people said when they wanted to be kind and couldn't think of anything more constructive to say. It wasn't as if you'd ever actually be asked to *do* anything. That wasn't the point of the exercise at all.

'There is something,' said Miranda.

'Oh.' Ally started, caught completely off balance. 'Like ... what?'

'There's still a chance for me and Gavin to have a baby.'

'What – adoption, you mean? Or fostering? Well, if you need me and Luke to provide character references or something—'

'Not that. I'm talking about actually having a baby that's genetically ours. Well, Gavin's anyway. And it would be related to me too, so it truly would be our baby. Do you understand what I'm saying?'

Ally had a feeling that she did. But she really, really didn't want to. 'No,' she said. 'I don't. I think you'd better spell it out for me.'

'Surrogacy,' said Miranda, a new light in her eyes. 'Don't you see? It would be perfect. But we need you. Please, Ally. Please think about it.'

A cold wave of realisation washed over Ally. 'I'm sorry Miranda, but I don't think—'

'Please!' It was the first time in her life that Ally had heard her sister beg. 'Ally, please listen to me, you're my only chance. Please be a surrogate mother for my baby.

'If the tables were turned, I'd do it for you.' Ally had always thought her sister was one of the most selfish people she knew, but seeing the desperation in her tear-stained eyes, as she fingered the shiny plastic bracelet her niece had given her, she almost – *almost* – believed her.

# Chapter Five

'I'm sure it was the drink,' said Ally, as Luke scraped stubble off his face the next morning. 'I'm sure she didn't really mean it.'

Luke exchanged glances with her in the mirror through a face-full of foam. He wasn't at his best, having been jolted awake at four in the morning by a wife babbling about mad sisters and surrogate babies; not to mention having to borrow a razor and some 'normal' clothes from Gavin, which made him feel even more conspicuous than the uniform had done. And although he liked to think of himself as pretty unshockable, the look on his face suggested otherwise.

'Hmph. I'm not so sure about that. I wouldn't put anything past your sister.'

Ally perched on the edge of the massive Victorian bath and drummed her fingers on the cast iron. 'Yeah, I know what she's like, but last night she was . . . ' Ally lowered her voice in case the kids were awake and listening in the adjoining bedroom, 'drunk as a skunk.'

'My point exactly.' Luke picked at an in-growing hair on his chin. 'What's that saying? "In vino veritas"?'

Ally wrinkled her nose disgustedly, and teased: 'Hey, don't you lay your Latin on me, kid. We didn't all go to private school you know.'

Luke winced. He never liked being reminded of his secure, middle-class upbringing, however light-heartedly. It wasn't that he was ashamed of his lovely mum, or the father he scarcely remembered, since he had died when Luke was only six; just that he was painfully aware of the yawning divide between him and his clients at ChelShel. And – criminally ungrateful though it made him feel

– he did sometimes find himself wishing he could have bypassed the cricket pitches and crisp school uniforms, and gone to the local comprehensive instead.

'You know exactly what it means. People often come out with the truth when they've had too much to drink.' He tweezed out the rogue hair with a grunt of victory. 'So maybe she did mean it.' Luke turned to face Ally, towelling his shaven face. 'I'm sure she thinks other people are only in the world so they can make sure she has a nice time.'

'She's ... not *that* bad,' protested Ally, very feebly.

'So if she fancies having a baby and she can't manage it herself,' Luke went on, 'it's easy: get one of the minions to do it for her. In case you haven't guessed, that's where we come in.'

'Both of us? I can't quite see where you fit in.'

'You to have it, and me to stand around telling everybody what a great idea it is. Only I'm not,' he added hastily. 'In fact the minute I see the selfish bloody cow I'm going to—'

'Daddy!' Luke and Ally were so deep in debate that they hadn't noticed a little strawberry-blonde head peeking round the bathroom door. They performed a synchronised swivel in the direction of Josie's voice. She was standing in the doorway, cute as a button in her pink monkey pyjamas, and dangling a toy gorilla by its ear. 'Daddy said a bad word!' she declared with a gleeful wag of a small finger. 'He said the B word!'

Ally coughed to cover up a giggle. Luke turned red. 'Um ... did I? Well that was very naughty of me, wasn't it?'

'Now you have to put twenty pence in the jam jar on the fridge, Daddy.'

'Daddy will,' Ally promised solemnly. 'As soon as we get home.' The sooner the better, she added to herself. After Kyle's misadventures and Miranda's emotional outburst, Ally couldn't have cared less if she never saw Nether Grantley Hall again. Which, by all accounts, was pretty much how Luke felt about her sister.

Luke duly agreed to pay up, much to Josie's delight. Both the kids had swiftly backed Ally's idea for a swear-box – perhaps not surprisingly, since they were the beneficiaries. Once it was full, all the money was earmarked for ice creams and outings. Ally sometimes suspected her two offspring spent all day being deliberately infuriating, just in the hope of goading their overwrought parents

46

into a flurry of bad language. It quite often worked, too.

Josie bounded off back into the bedroom, singing 'Daddy said the B word, Daddy said the B word.'

A dreadful, sepulchral voice moaned back at her from the depths of the big feather bed. 'Shut up, Josie. I'm trying to die.'

Ally bit her lip. She hated seeing her little boy suffering, even if it was his own silly fault. And she could see from the expression on Luke's face that this was no easier for him. But he was determined that Kyle had to learn; had to know enough about hangovers to be very sure that he didn't want another one for an awfully long time. In his job he'd seen far too many people's lives destroyed by drink.

'Sorry, big man,' said Luke, peeling back the duvet. 'No dying today. It's breakfast time. And I know how much you're looking forward to bacon, egg, sausage and tomato with a nice big dollop of brown sauce. Not forgetting a nice thick, greasy slice of fried bread.'

Whether Miranda also enjoyed a traditional English fry-up for breakfast, they didn't get to find out. She didn't arrive late. She simply didn't turn up at all. Ally could tell that Luke was annoyed. More than that; he was disappointed. She sensed that he'd been relishing the opportunity to tell Miranda that, for once in her gilded life, she couldn't have every damn thing she wanted.

It wasn't until they were outside the front entrance to the Hall, stuffing bags and children into the old Volvo, that Gavin appeared at a brisk trot, looking like a man who was trying to deal with a thousand different things at once.

'Ally – Luke. Great! I thought I might have missed you.' He paused for breath. 'Miranda wanted to say goodbye and thanks so much for coming.'

'Couldn't she say it herself?' enquired Luke.

Gavin coloured slightly. 'Miranda's feeling a bit . . . fragile this morning.' He eyed the pasty-faced Kyle. 'Looks like she's not the only one, either. How is the little lad?'

'He'll be fine,' replied Ally. 'But I'll get our GP to give him the once-over, just to be sure.'

'Of course, yes. Look – I really am so sorry.' Gavin's gaze captured Ally's with a kind of gentle possessiveness. He had a way, thought Ally, of making you feel like you were the only person in the world who mattered.

47

When Ally looked into that handsome face, she felt all her righteous anger evaporating, and heard herself stammer something about 'these things happening'.

'We're both sorry,' Gavin insisted. 'And I wish I could make this up to you somehow. If I'd had any idea Kyle was going to go off and get himself into that kind of trouble . . . well, I'd have made damn sure it didn't happen.' He pushed a handful of rather soft, silky hair back from his forehead, and those lovely, compelling eyes blazed more strongly than ever. 'Guess I'm not quite as good a manager as I thought I was,' he added, directing a rueful smile at Ally.

There was a short silence. Ally looked to Luke to say something polite and meaningless, but there was an obstinate streak in Luke and he wasn't going to make this easy. Not for a brother-in-law who let ten-year-old boys get drunk and who liked flirting with his wife.

'Just as well you don't have any kids of your own then,' he commented, with just enough emphasis to make it clear that he *knew*, and then banged shut the rear doors of the car. 'Come on, you lot. It's high time we went home.'

All the way home in the car, Ally wondered if Gavin knew about Miranda's emotional outburst the previous night. Maybe he'd slept right through, and hadn't even noticed that she wasn't lying in bed next to him. After all, he'd had a fair amount to drink, too.

As she gazed out at the dripping October landscape, she tried to imagine how she'd feel if she discovered Luke had been dispensing drunken revelations about their marriage. Bad, she decided. Embarrassed, certainly. And even worse than that if he'd dispensed them to somebody like Miranda. Ally put herself in that position, and squirmed at the thought of Miranda knowing her most intimate secrets.

Perhaps that's exactly how Miranda's feeling right now, she mused. About me.

Most probably she was drinking treble Alka-Seltzers and cursing her big mouth as she swore never to have another drink again. Feeling humiliated, and praying for a chance to turn the clock back twenty-four hours, so that she could keep her gynaecological secrets to herself and retain her dignity into the bargain.

They arrived home well before lunchtime, but it was pretty

obvious that Kyle was recovering as he was asking for pizza and chips before they'd even got their coats off.

'You'll be sick!' protested Ally, tripping over the cat as it rushed to wind itself around Kyle's legs.

'I won't Mum, I'm hungry!'

'Hmm. Have a glass of milk and some biscuits, and then we'll see how you feel.'

The phone in the hall rang as she was trying to make a pot of tea, but nobody so much as moved a muscle.

'Anybody going to answer that?' she enquired; waited a few seconds longer, then gave in and went to answer it herself before whoever was calling dropped dead from old age. 'Hello?'

'Ally, it's Miranda,' announced the breathless voice on the other end of the line. 'I've been trying to phone you on your mobile.'

'Have you? Oh, I must've forgotten to switch it on. Is something up?'

There was a pause. 'I need to know, Ally.'

'Know what?'

'I need to know if you've been thinking about . . . what I said. Last night, in the library.'

'Well of course I have,' replied Ally. 'I'd be lying if I said I hadn't. You did drop a bit of a bombshell, you know. And I've never seen you so plastered before in all my life. But don't worry,' she added. 'I know when to keep my mouth shut.'

'You don't understand.' Miranda's voice acquired a note of real agitation. 'I need to *know*. About whether you're going to do it or not.'

Ally did a kind of mental double take. '*Do* it?'

'Please Ally, you know what I'm saying. I need to know if you're going to have a baby for me.'

'A baby?' The directness of the question, at half past eleven on a perfectly ordinary Sunday morning, left Ally reeling. 'You . . . you can't just—', she stammered, the very picture of discomfort. 'Do you realise what you're asking?'

Before Miranda had a chance to reply, Luke seized the telephone receiver from his wife's hand. 'Listen to me, Miranda,' he said firmly. 'I'm sorry if you want kids and you can't have them; that's pretty rough luck. But you are *not* using my wife like . . . like some kind of breeding cow!

49

'It's high time you grew up and realised that sometimes, no means no. Got that? Good. 'Bye, Miranda.'

A couple of days later, Ally found herself enjoying a free pub lunch at Zee's expense, to celebrate his latest eBay coup.

'This is very nice,' she commented, through a mouthful of chicken Caesar wrap, 'but I hope we're not eating all your profits.'

'Actually it isn't costing me a penny,' Zee confessed. 'I fixed the landlord's computer, and he paid me with a free meal for two.' He prodded his fork into a blob of slimy green stuff, and confided: 'If you ask me, he got the better end of the deal. This spinach has been boiled to oblivion.'

Ally nodded and said 'Mm,' not really listening. Her mind kept drifting off – always to the same place: the library at Nether Grantley Hall, at three o'clock last Sunday morning. Try as she might, she just couldn't shake the incident out of her head. Luke seemed to have dismissed it as easily as he had cut Miranda off in midflow; but then Miranda wasn't his sister, and it wasn't his body she had designs on. The very thought of it made her skin feel all crawly.

When eventually she tuned into Zee's monologue again, he was saying something about designer trousers.

'What? I didn't quite catch that.'

'I said, is it really ethical to buy something from a charity shop and then sell it for a profit on eBay?'

'Er. I don't know,' Ally replied lamely. Then fell silent again.

Zee stopped chewing and cocked his head on one side. 'Go on, shoot.'

'Pardon?'

'Tell me what it is that's bothering you. And don't say "nothing". You've been on a different planet for the last five minutes.'

'Oh. Sorry.' Ally felt horribly self-conscious now; she hadn't realised it was so obvious. 'It's just ... Miranda.'

'Ah.' Although he had only met her a few times, Zee had heard so much about Miranda from Ally that he was beginning to feel like an expert. 'I take it the big jungle party wasn't a great success then?'

'I don't know,' confessed Ally. 'We sort of – missed it. Kyle got drunk and it all went downhill from there.'

50

'Kyle? Don't you mean Luke?'

Ally let out a brief laugh. 'I wish I did.' And she explained about Kyle's little adventure, and how she'd spent the evening listening to the festivities from a distance and mopping up the results of his upset stomach.

'So a good time wasn't had by all then?'

'Not exactly. Mum and Dad were their usual selves of course. And then there was Miranda ... ' Ally sighed into the remains of her lunch.

Zee raised an eyebrow. 'Just her usual unpleasantness, or did she excel herself this time?'

'Oh, she excelled herself all right,' replied Ally, 'In fact I'm not sure you're even going to believe this.'

And she recounted the events in the library in all their lurid detail, while Zee's jaw dropped gradually lower until he looked like a startled village idiot.

She finished and looked at him expectantly. He scratched his head. 'Bloody hell.'

'Told you.'

'She really asked you to have a baby for her? You're not having me on?'

'Zee, do you really think I'd joke about something like that?' Before he opened his mouth to answer, she added, 'And just in case I didn't believe her the first time, the minute we got home she phoned me up and asked me all over again. Luke went mental.'

'Luke did? He never struck me as the mental type. But I can see why he might be a bit upset. I take it he's not exactly in favour of the plan then?'

'He told Miranda to get stuffed.' She suppressed a nervous giggle. 'Slightly unfortunate choice of words under the circum-stances. But anyway, he made it quite clear that it wasn't going to happen.'

'But you're not so sure?'

Ally stared at Zee. 'Of course I'm sure! No way am I getting pregnant for somebody else, least of all Miranda.'

'So why do I sense a teensy bit of hesitation?'

Ally was tempted to tell him he was imagining it, but there had never been any secrets between her and Zee. And if she'd lied to him he'd never believe it anyway. Besides, why would she want to? The whole thing was quite clear-cut – wasn't it?

'It's just . . . Luke didn't see her like I did.' Ally twisted a paper napkin between her fingers. 'She was so upset, Zee. I don't think I've ever seen anyone so upset. It was like she was in real, physical pain. I had no idea she wanted a child that much. To be honest, I thought she was one of those women who'd freak out if they got pregnant. Just shows how much I know my own sister.'

'You're not thinking of doing it, are you?' asked Zee, a note of real concern in his voice.

'No, of course not!'

'Are you sure?'

'Absolutely sure. But I just can't help feeling guilty.'

'You've no cause to,' Zee pointed out. 'It's not your fault she can't conceive. In fact, from what you told me it sounds like it's at least partly down to her.'

'I know. But . . . she's my sister.'

'Would she do it for you?'

The question hung in the air between them. They both knew the answer, whatever Miranda might claim.

Zee reached across the table and gently took the shredded remains of the paper napkin from Ally's hands. 'You do realise this is an incredibly dangerous thing you're talking about? I don't just mean the legal implications – and oh boy, you'd need to look into those *really* carefully – it's a complete emotional minefield too.'

'I know that.'

'Ally, I knew a couple once who tried it. The baby was born disabled and it ripped their marriage apart.'

'That's not going to happen, Zee.'

'Can you be sure about that? And you'd be having a baby with a man who wasn't your husband. That baby might be for your sister, but genetically it would be yours. How would you feel about that?'

'Frightened,' confessed Ally. She straightened up and pulled herself together. 'But since I'm not going to do it, there's no problem, is there?'

'Not if you're not going to do it,' Zee agreed; but she could still hear doubt in his voice.

'Look, it's a stupid idea – I know that,' Ally declared. She wondered who she was trying to convince: Zee or herself. 'She's got loads of money: why can't she just . . . buy herself a Chinese

52

orphan or something? Or whatever nationality is in vogue this season. Now, shall we order pudding?'

She dared to make eye contact with Zee, but he didn't look entirely convinced. 'Come on, stop looking so worried,' she urged. 'It's not as if I'm actually going to do it, is it? I'm not *that* stupid.'

Luke was the kind of guy who was never really off-duty.

So when a social worker phoned him about a housing emergency at eight o'clock in the evening, just as he was sitting down to a late dinner with Ally, he didn't think twice. He just grabbed the car keys and headed for the office, to fetch the documents she needed.

Ally was used to it. She'd lost count of the number of dinners that had been left to desiccate in the oven while Luke was out Doing Good. But that was a part of the way he was; she didn't doubt for a moment that without it, she wouldn't love him half so much.

A sleepy face appeared through the banisters at the top of the stairs, just as he was walking to the front door. 'Where are you going, Daddy?'

'Just out, to help somebody. I'll be back soon. Now you go back to bed, Jo-Jo, and be good for Mummy.'

As he drove across town, the darkness softened here and there by ludicrously early Christmas lights, Luke thought about what a lucky guy he was. Two good kids – one of each – and a lovely wife. The perfect family. Sometimes he thought it would be nice to have another one, or even two. An only child himself, he'd always dreamed of having a big family. But he would never try to pressurise Ally. She deserved to have a life too, beyond being a homemaker. Maybe one day she'd get broody again, and come round to the idea of her own accord. But for now, Luke was happy just being the way they were. He saw so many broken families that he was under no illusions: few people had a life as good as his.

He arrived at the office and swung the old Volvo into the car park. To his surprise, there was a light burning in the office window. That was odd; the cleaner had usually finished by seven at the latest. Maybe Chas or one of the office cleaners was working late.

A short flight of stairs took him up to the door of the ChelShel offices. Sure enough, there was no need for his key; it was already unlocked.

'Hello – anyone home?' he enquired as he pushed open the door and strode past the reception desk. 'Don't suppose the kettle's on? I could murder a coffee.'

The only answer was an eerie silence. Had the cleaner left the light on and forgotten to lock up? Or – horrible thought – had they been burgled again? When would the local lowlife realise that there was never any money in the office?

He headed for the main office, anxious now. But he needn't have worried; the only person in the office was Chas, bent over his desk as if he was concentrating very hard on something.

'Hi Chas. Working late?' Luke walked over and laid a hand on Chas's shoulder. It was shaking. 'Chas? Are you all right?'

Very slowly, the priest straightened up and turned to look at him. His face was a mess of tears; his breath came in staccato gasps. 'I'm sorry. I didn't want anybody to see me like this. Priests don't cry, do they? We're supposed to have faith.'

'What on earth is the matter? Has something happened?'

With a trembling hand, Chas held out the photo of his sister's little girl, Maisie, which he kept in pride of place on his desk. She smiled out from the frame, proud as anything in her very first school uniform.

'Th-there was an accident,' he said hoarsely. 'Hit and run.'

Luke's heart was in his mouth. He knew how much Maisie meant to Chas, a man who would never have children of his own. 'Maisie's been hurt?'

Chas shook his head dumbly. He couldn't say the word. But more tears squeezed themselves out from beneath his eyelids.

'Oh God no,' breathed Luke. 'Not . . . dead?'

But he knew instantly that she was. 'Oh Chas, mate . . . ' He put an arm round the priest's shoulders and wished with all his heart that he knew what to say and do. 'I know it's not much consolation but I feel for you, I really do.'

Chas gripped his hand like a drowning man. 'Actually, you'll probably never know how much it helps. Normally I'd talk to God you see,' he explained, looking up with watery eyes. 'Only this time I don't think He's listening.'

'Of course he is, mate; of course he is,' murmured Luke, for all his confirmed atheism praying that he was right. He sat down beside Chas. 'But you can talk to me too, you know.'

It took all his strength to sit there and just be with Chas. Because suddenly, selfishly, all he wanted to do was go straight home, take his own children in his arms, and beg whatever insane God ruled this messed-up world never to steal them away from him.

Instead he sat there beside Chas and let him weep silently into his jacket until he had no more tears left to cry.

# Chapter Six

A few evenings later, Zee picked up Ally in his van, and the two of them set off for the weekly drama group meeting at St Jude's church hall. Tuesday was the one night when Luke had faithfully promised not to work late. Even domestic goddesses needed a break sometimes, and Ally cherished her weekly opportunity to be somebody else for a couple of hours.

Tonight there was going to be a complete run-through of the forthcoming St Jude's Community Players' production of *Oliver* – rather an ambitious undertaking for a company whose previous high point had been *Aladdin*. Zee was still agonising over his lines, while Ally was having serious misgivings about her ability to get up on stage and sing in public. Warbling uninhibitedly in the bath was one thing; actually inflicting her voice on a real live audience was a whole lot more scary. Could she sing? She didn't really know. Why oh why had the director ever imagined she'd make a good Nancy? Quite possibly because she was the only woman member under forty who was slim enough to fit into the costume . . .

But it wasn't stage fright that was occupying their thoughts as the van made its way down to the end of Ally's road, past the local bookie's and the chip shop, and then swung out onto the inner ring road.

'Isn't it awful about Chas Lawson's little niece?' sighed Ally, gazing out of the window at the dark pavements, glossy with rain. 'Luke's been terribly down about it, and as for Chas . . .'

Zee nodded sadly. 'It still doesn't seem possible, somehow. I mean, it's so desperately unfair. Kids aren't supposed to die, are they?'

56

'She was only seven,' sighed Ally. 'Barely a year older than Josie.'

'She was in the same Brownie pack as my Emma.' Zee managed a rather sad little chuckle. 'They hated each other, you know. But you know what little girls are like – next week they'd probably have been best friends.'

Only there's not going to be a next week, thought Ally. She turned to look at Zee and said what they were both thinking. 'Can you imagine if . . .?'

Zee shuddered. 'God, no. I don't want to. Just thinking about losing my Emma . . . No,' he decided with a firm shake of the head. 'I don't want to go there.' He flipped open the glove compartment and pulled out half an enormous bar of chocolate.

'What's that for?' asked Ally.

'Emergency rations. To cheer us both up.'

'We'll get fat,' Ally scolded, breaking off a large chunk. 'And when did you last see a fat Fagin or a spotty Nancy?'

'Exactly!' declared Zee, energetically munching. 'It's going to be a ground-breaking performance. Now, give me another piece of chocolate, and I'll show you my false nose.'


'Read it again, Daddy,' pleaded Josie as Luke reached the end of *Six Dinners Sid* for the third time. 'Please!'

Enough was enough, and there was only so much of Sid that a dutiful dad could take. 'Not tonight, sweetie,' he replied, transforming her protests into giggles with one of his silly faces. 'It's time you got your beauty sleep; tomorrow's a school day.'

Josie wriggled down under the duvet until just her eyes and the tip of her nose were visible above it. 'I don't need beauty sleep,' she objected. 'Granny said I'm beautiful already. And I'd rather be clever anyway,' she added on reflection. '''Cause then I can invent something important and be rich and famous and buy you and Mummy a castle and some ponies with pink manes.'

Luke smiled at the artlessness of it all. 'Ponies?' he enquired.

'You can look after them for me, so I can ride them when I come to stay.'

'Ah, I see. Well then sweetie, it's time to go to sleep and grow an even bigger brain.'

'But Daddy—'

'Sleep.' He kissed his little daughter lightly on the forehead, turned out the bedside light and left her to dream of pink ponies.

A couple of steps down the landing, he put his head round Kyle's door. There was nothing to be seen of Kyle himself, just a mound of duvet and a curious, orange glow like a halo around the edges.

'Kyle, how many times have I told you not to read under the covers?' he enquired, trying to sound stern but not really succeeding. He remembered only too well doing the same thing when he was Kyle's age. 'You'll ruin your eyesight, you know.' God, he thought. I sound like my dad.

The mound of duvet stirred and a dishevelled head appeared. 'How did you know?'

Luke chuckled. 'Duvets aren't light-proof, you know. It was like Blackpool Illuminations in here. Now, get your head down and get some sleep, or we'll both catch it from your mum when she gets home.'

Downstairs, he settled himself in his favourite saggy armchair – which was saggy only because of the number of times Kyle and Josie had used it as a trampoline – and treated himself to a big bag of crisps and a beer. It wasn't such a bad old life, all things considered. In fact, this evening came close to perfect happiness; all it lacked was Ally, and she'd be back home soon.

The TV was on, but Luke found his gaze wandering around the sitting room, taking in things that normally he didn't notice: the dent in the wall by the door, where he'd caught Kyle doing a spot of indoor skateboarding; the stain peeking out from underneath a rug – a reminder of the time Josie had knocked half a tin of emulsion off the window ledge; the upward progression of faint pencil-marks on the wall by the door, chronicling the kids' transformation from bumbling toddlers to half-grown human beings. It was true what his mum had always said: kids aren't kids for long. You have to enjoy them while you can.

His mind flitted involuntarily back to Chas, so devastated and so ashamed of his own despair. Chas, who had chosen a path which guaranteed that he would never have kids of his own. And then, inevitably, he found himself thinking about Gavin and Miranda. Everything about those two annoyed and irritated him. Maybe Gavin wasn't such a bad guy underneath the posh suits and the glamour, but at the end of the day he was married to Miranda, and that spoke volumes.

Or did it? What Miranda had told Ally that night after the party seemed to have thrown everything upside down. All this time, they'd assumed Miranda was too selfish to want kids, and all this time, they'd been completely wrong. Oh, she was selfish all right; but not about wanting children. In fact, from what Ally had said, and the way her sister had behaved on the telephone, there was no woman on the planet who wanted a baby more than Miranda Hesketh.

Luke fidgeted, suddenly not so comfortable any more. He wanted to shut Miranda out of his mind, tell himself that it wasn't his fault she couldn't have children, and that her happiness or otherwise wasn't his responsibility, or Ally's either. But then his mind kept going back to their own two bright, happy, mischievous kids, and reminding him just how much happiness they had brought into his and Ally's lives. Maybe happiness wasn't quite the right word: it was something more complex. Yes, fulfilment, that was a better way to describe it. And he closed his eyes and tried to imagine how he would feel if, one day, a big hand reached down from the heavens and snatched Kyle and Josie away. How he would feel if he and Ally had tried and tried, and never managed to conceive.

The more he thought about it, the more his grudging sympathy for Miranda and Gavin grew. What Miranda was asking of Ally was outrageous, of course it was; yet Luke was beginning to understand how, in her position, he might have asked exactly the same.

'Nancy darling, you're limp; positively *flaccid*!' exclaimed Rupert the director, a bald accountant from Stroud who looked like a nightclub bouncer but sounded more like Noël Coward. All the veins in his bullet head were bulging as he flapped his script around in exasperation.

'Sorry Rupert.' Ally plonked herself down on a chair with a wobbly leg that was standing in for some part of the set or other. 'But I don't really think I'm cut out for all this showing your knickers and singing "Oom-pah-pah" lark.'

Rupert's nostrils flared; always a bad sign. 'I'll not have defeatist talk around here, Ally, you know that. I cast you for this part and I am never, ever wrong. Got that?'

Ally gave him a weak smile. Other cast members muttered and nudged each other; it was hard to tell if they were laughing at

59

Rupert or her; being Ally, she naturally assumed the latter.

'Right then.' Rupert raised his right hand, as ever weighed down by half a ton of bling jewellery, and snapped his fingers to call the accompanist to attention. 'From the top, Monica – and Ally, this time I want to see real Cockney verve. You're an East End tart, not a novice nun.'

Ally felt more like a novice idiot, but dutifully stumbled her way through the pub scene without actually falling off the stage or losing her place in the song. She could see from Rupert's face that he wasn't anticipating any Oscar nominations though.

At last she had a chance to scuttle back off the stage and rejoin the rest of the cast, who were lounging around the hall drinking tea and making up jokes about Rupert's taste in shirts. Somebody handed her a plastic cup and she downed the contents gratefully as she watched Zee getting to grips with his part.

Ah well, at least somebody else was having problems. Ally wasn't sure which Zee was finding more difficult: remembering his lines or stopping his prosthetic nose from falling off. If Ally was strictly honest in her judgement, that nose made him look more like a parrot than a small-time Victorian crime lord. In fact he wouldn't have looked out of place on Long John Silver's shoulder. The make-up girls kept assuring Zee that it was only a prototype, but anybody who'd seen last year's *Aladdin* knew that realism wasn't exactly their speciality.

Or political correctness for that matter, Ally mused. Only the Players, who still dwelt firmly in the 1950s, could ask a Jewish actor to wear a false nose because he didn't look Jewish enough. And only Zee would do it and not be offended.

Ally stifled a grin and wondered why any of them ever did any of this. It must be an addiction; that was the only explanation. Why else would a bunch of apparently sensible adults put so much effort into making themselves look silly in public?

As though reading her thoughts, a voice behind her remarked: 'My God, what a nose. Poor bastard. I hope it's not real.'

Recognising the voice but not quite placing it, Ally looked back over her shoulder. She could hardly believe her eyes.

'Gavin? What on earth are you doing here?'

He glanced back towards the stage, where Zee was marshalling his urchins. 'Didn't you know? I'm a connoisseur of fine theatre.'

'God knows what you're doing here then, mate,' quipped a bloke standing next to Ally.

60

'You're a bit late to audition,' Ally remarked. 'It's only three weeks till the dress rehearsal.'

'God help us,' added the bloke next to her.

Usually when Gavin and Ally met, the banter flew back and forth between them; it was their way of covering up the uncomfortable attraction they felt for each other. But tonight Gavin seemed uninterested in jokey insults and merry quips. In fact he looked downright serious, and that stirred up a warning flutter in Ally's stomach. 'Is something the matter, Gav? Has something happened?'

Gavin didn't answer. He just replied: 'Any chance we could have a chat?'

'Yeah, sure.' Ally checked her watch. 'I've got at least another ten minutes before I'm needed again. So what's this about?' She looked at him expectantly.

Gavin shuffled his feet. 'Actually, I meant ... is there somewhere private around here?'

'Oh.' Ally felt a slight sensation of warmth rise to her cheeks, and hoped that she wasn't blushing crimson. She'd tried so often not to think about being alone in a room with Gavin, and now he'd forced the thoughts right back into her head. 'Well, there's the little office where they store stuff for the mother and toddler group.'

'Whatever.'

She made a half-hearted attempt to put him off the idea. 'It's a bit crammed with stuff – there's not much room in there.'

'It'll be fine. I'd just rather the whole world wasn't listening in.'

He made it all sound so ominous that Ally dared not ask why. She felt totally conspicuous as the two of them walked across the hall, past a man painting flats for the workhouse scene, and through a door with an ancient sign that read: *Please knock and wait*.

'I see what you mean,' said Gavin as the pair of them breathed in to squeeze past stacks of soft play equipment, a portable sandpit and a ball-pool, finally reaching a tiny oasis of space in the far corner of the room.

'What's with the cloak and dagger routine?' demanded Ally, suddenly not sure that she wanted to know.

Gavin perched his undeniably lovely backside on the top of a red and yellow plastic slide. 'Sorry, I didn't mean to be mysterious. I

61

just don't think it's the kind of thing either of us would want to talk about in public.'

'OK, but *what kind of thing*?'

He took a deep breath, looked Ally straight in the eye, and said: 'Surrogacy.'

Subconsciously, she'd been half-expecting something of the sort, but even so it came as a shock. If there'd been room, she would have backed away, but as it was she had a mop-handle sticking in her back. 'So Miranda told you, then. About that night at the Hall.'

'Did you think she wouldn't?'

Ally ran a hand through her tousled hair. 'I don't really know what I thought.' Her eyes met his again. 'Actually I did think you might have put her up to it.'

'We'd talked about it a couple of times,' admitted Gavin. 'But only in a general way. We hadn't talked about you.'

'Well, if Miranda told you what happened, I guess she also told you what my answer was.'

The ghost of a smile flitted across Gavin's lips. 'She did mention something about Luke telling her to fuck off. But that was Luke's reaction. What about you, Ally? What do you think about it?'

She stood and gazed at him, open-mouthed, for a moment. 'I think you've got a cheek, coming here and putting pressure on me when Luke and I have already said no. And before you start with the emotional blackmail,' she continued without a breath, 'yes, of course I feel for you and Miranda. I'm desperately sorry the IVF didn't work. But there are other ways of being parents.'

'Adoption's not the same, you know that,' objected Gavin. 'And what are the chances of getting a baby? Besides, are you telling me you'd really feel exactly the same way about your children if you hadn't given birth to them?'

'I hope I would,' she replied honestly. 'Or I'm not much of a mother. Being a mum isn't just about biology, you know. And even if I did have a baby for Miranda, it wouldn't be her biological child, would it?'

'It would be her sister's,' replied Gavin. 'And mine. And that's enough for us.'

Ally tried not to look into his eyes, because when she did she found it impossible to ignore the deep-down look of desperation. This was a man who wanted a child every bit as much as his wife did. A man who might come across as pushy and demanding but who was in real pain. And she, little Ally Bennett, was refusing to take that pain away. She knew damned well the situation was a thousand times more complicated than that, but that look in Gavin's eyes still made her feel like the most selfish person in the whole wide world.

'I'm sorry, Gavin,' she said softly. 'I just can't do it.'

He hung his head, and for a moment she wondered if he was going to cry. The thought of such vulnerability only made her feel more selfish, and more guiltily attracted to him.

But Gavin didn't cry. He straightened up and reached into the inside pocket of his Armani jacket. 'If it's money . . . ' he began.

Ally stared at him. 'What?'

'I know you and Luke aren't well off, and you've got two kids to support, and if you had a baby for Miranda you might have to stop working for a while.'

Her eyes narrowed. 'What exactly are you getting at?'

The hand emerged from the jacket pocket. It was holding a cheque book. 'I can make things so much easier for you, Ally,' he enthused. 'You and the kids. OK, so paying for surrogacy's against the law, but paying expenses is fine. You can have some of the luxuries you've always wanted, maybe move house so the children have a better school. Just say how much you need, we'll call it essential expenses, and I'll write the cheque right now.'

A wave of disgust washed over Ally, sweeping away the sympathy she had felt for Gavin just a few moments earlier. 'My body may be nothing special to anybody but me,' she said with quiet fury, 'but it's mine and it's not for sale. At any price.'

'Ally, please,' he begged, 'you misunderstand—'

'I wish I did,' she snapped back. 'Because believe me, you're not the Gavin I thought I knew.'

It was late that evening, and the children were in bed. Ally and Luke had flopped down on the sofa in the lounge with the remains of a bottle of unpalatable plonk, and somebody inoffensive was smooching away on the hi-fi. Ally sighed softly as she let her tired head droop onto Luke's shoulder.

Anyone who had peeked in through the door might have described it as a romantic scene; but although Ally and Luke were physically about as close as any two people could get, their thoughts were drifting.

How would I feel? agonised Luke for the thousandth time. How would I feel if my kids were taken away from me? How would I feel if I'd never had a chance to be a father in the first place?

He couldn't get Chas's face out of his mind. In the years he'd worked for charities, he'd seen plenty of grief, but never like that. When he saw Chas's face he found himself thinking about how he'd feel if he couldn't have children. And then he thought of Gavin.

Maybe, he thought, we were too hasty when we turned Miranda down flat. Maybe Ally should think about it some more ...

Beside him on the sofa, Ally kept the secret of Gavin's unscheduled visit to herself. She could just imagine Luke's reaction if she told him that Gavin had tried to buy her services as a surrogate.

Now that she'd had time to think about it and the initial shock had worn off, she wondered if she'd been a little too harsh towards him. People like Gavin – rich people – always thought about everything in terms of money, didn't they? So it was only natural that sheer desperation would drive him to think he could solve this problem in precisely the same way.

He's a good bloke really, she told herself. Tonight was out of character. He doesn't seriously think he can buy a baby for Miranda; he just wants what every couple wants – a chance to have a family. And he can't understand why I won't give them that chance.

I know I'm right to say no. I only wish saying it didn't make me feel so bad.

# Chapter Seven

Ally stared at Luke. 'What did you say?'

Luke didn't turn towards her; he just kept on walking as he spoke, pushing the supermarket trolley down the breakfast cereal aisle, the way he did every Saturday morning while Maureen watched the kids. Ally had the distinct feeling he was too embarrassed to look her in the eye. 'I said, I've been wondering if we maybe ought to give this surrogacy thing a bit more thought.'

'"We"?' enquired Ally, with heavy emphasis.

This time, Luke's eyes did flick across in her direction. 'Yes ... well, you mostly I guess,' he admitted. 'Seeing as you're the one who'd actually be ... you know.'

'Gee, thanks for noticing.'

'But it's something that has to be a joint decision, isn't it?' reasoned Luke. 'Something we'd both have to really want to do. Otherwise it'd be a disaster.'

Ally grabbed a giant box of cornflakes and rammed it into the trolley, trying not to notice the colourful display advertising a new cereal with extra folic acid, 'for mums-to-be who really care'.

'We already made a decision,' Ally reminded him, 'and it was no. In fact, as I recall you made it for both of us.'

'I ... could've been a bit hasty,' admitted Luke, accidentally pushing his trolley into the back of a pair of glamorous ankles. Their owner swung round, spat out a venomous 'Watch where you're going,' pushed past him and disappeared into Cakes and Fancy Biscuits. She didn't look like the kind of woman who'd ever have trouble making her mind up about anything, thought Ally.

'Hasty? Is that what you call it?' Ally felt irritation simmer inside her.

65

'But you did make it pretty clear you weren't keen on the idea either,' Luke pointed out. 'How did you put it – "over my dead body"? Besides,' he went on, 'I just couldn't stand the idea of you being pushed around by your sister. Again.'

'But it's OK if you're doing the pushing around?' enquired Ally.

'Sorry?'

'Oh come on, Luke!' Heads turned and Ally hushed her voice in embarrassment. 'Darling, I know you're upset about Chas's little niece, and we're all shocked about what happened; but her death and Miranda's infertility are two entirely different things. You can't make one thing all right by solving the other.'

'Well – obviously!'

'But I can't help feeling you've got the two things all mixed up in your head,' Ally insisted. 'Miranda could have ten babies, but none of them would be Maisie, would they?'

Luke marched off in search of crisps, but Ally stuck to him like glue.

'One minute you're telling Miranda that the whole surrogacy idea is an insult,' she pointed out, 'and then suddenly you're doing this massive U-turn and practically telling me I should do it!'

'That's ridiculous!' protested Luke. 'I only said we should *think* about it.'

'But we already have – haven't we?' Ally didn't let on that the subject had been gnawing at her thoughts – and her conscience – all week. She paused. 'Or has something changed?'

Luke hesitated. 'I think maybe I have.' He reached down a couple of tins from the top shelf. 'Seeing somebody's grief when they lose a child . . . it kind of makes everything else seem totally unimportant. And then it sets you thinking about how bad it must feel if you can't have kids at all.'

'Like Gavin and Miranda.'

'Exactly. And you know as well as I do how desperate your sister is for a baby.'

Not to mention Gavin, thought Ally, wondering how Luke would react if he knew about Gavin's clumsy attempt at blackmail. Badly, she thought; which was as good a reason as any not to tell him. It had nothing to do with the fact that she liked Gavin; now was simply not the time to start a family feud.

'True,' she agreed. 'But what about how I feel?' Ally side-stepped a zig-zagging toddler pushing a toy pram. 'Or doesn't that matter?'

66

'Of course it does! What you feel matters more than anything.'

This time their eyes did meet. It was a relief for Ally to be able to look deep into her husband's eyes and recognise the love reaching out to her. The love, the warmth, the honesty and the trust that had brought them together and kept them that way for almost a decade.

'So you're not saying I should have a baby for them just because they want one and they're the kind of people who always get what they want?'

'Good God, no.'

'Because that would feel like I was being ... I don't know ... pimped by my own husband or something!'

Luke bent forward and kissed her, lightly but with real passion. 'Sweetheart, please don't think like that. If the idea disgusts you we'll forget it. End of story. Your sister will just have to sort her own life out for once.'

I wish it was that easy, thought Ally as they stood in line at the checkout. Why does everything have to be so bloody complicated? And why can't I seem to think about anything else?

Ten minutes later they were sitting in the supermarket café, drinking lattes and talking about everything except what was really on their minds, when the *Magic Roundabout* theme tune sounded from the depths of Ally's handbag.

'Oh no,' she muttered as she rummaged for her mobile. 'That'll be Mum, wondering why we're taking so long, or Sally's mother, wanting a cake for the PTA sale. Why do I let myself be bullied into these things?'

But it wasn't Sally's mother; it was Gavin, sounding agitated for the first time Ally could recall.

'Ally, is that you?' he gabbled. 'Yes, of course it is, it's your phone. Look – please – you've got to come over. Now.'

'Hey, wait a minute, slow down. What's going on? Has something happened?'

'It's Miranda, she's in a terrible state.'

The word 'Miranda' made Ally's heart sink. Any one of a million small things were capable of rocking her sister's unreal world to its foundations: a bad haircut, inferior champagne, turning up to a charity auction wearing the same outfit as the guest speaker ... It wouldn't be the first time Ally had set off on a wild goose chase to Wiltshire, on her one free afternoon with Luke, only to discover that Miranda's definition of an emergency didn't quite match up to her own.

'Tell me exactly what's wrong,' she probed.

It wasn't like Gavin to beat about the bush, but Ally sensed an unusual degree of hesitancy in his voice, as though every syllable was fighting not to be let out.

'I . . . found her . . . in the bathroom.'

'Go on.'

'Sitting in the middle of the floor. Sobbing her heart out.'

Ally tensed. 'And?' she coaxed.

'I ask her what she's doing, and she says . . . she says,' suddenly it all came flooding out in a single breath, 'she says, "If I can't be a mother, what's the point of anything?" Then she says she wants a divorce.'

'What!' Ally could hardly believe her ears.

'She said if I divorced her, then I'd be free to "get myself a proper wife" who could give me children.'

'Ye gods,' gasped Ally.

'What's up?' demanded Luke.

Ally put a hand over the mouthpiece. 'Miranda. She's . . . very upset.'

'Please Ally, come over,' urged Gavin. 'Miranda's just not listening to me right now. I know you can talk some sense into her.'

Well, I can talk to you, sis, thought Ally as she and Luke hurried back to the car park; but we both know there's only one thing you really want to hear.

'. . . so there we are, trailing all the way back to Cheltenham in the dark with half a ton of defrosted shopping in the boot,' Ally explained, rubbing at her weary eyes. 'And then when we finally get back, the kids are bouncing off the walls 'cause they've been cooped up with Grandma since breakfast time. Hell, what a day.'

She and Zee were taking a quick half-hour out in the brand-new mezzanine coffee bar at Seuss & Goldman. Ally had just done a morning stint at Pussy Willows, and Zee was about to set off for a massive bric-à-brac event in Grantham. They could both use a reviving double shot of piping-hot caffeine.

'Look, I'm sorry if this sounds callous,' commented Zee, 'but all your life, your sister has been a real pain in the arse.'

Ally sighed. 'Believe me, I know.'

'And right now you're feeling sorry for her, but you're my best mate and I'm worried about you. I don't want you thinking it's your responsibility to sort out everything in her life that she doesn't like. She has a husband for that, God help him.'

Ally nodded. 'You're talking a lot of sense, Zee. But if you'd seen the state she was in yesterday ... Honestly, it was enough to break your heart.'

'I know, I know.'

'And it's tough when life turns round and smacks you in the teeth, takes away the one thing that means everything to you.'

Zee looked down into the slow-swirling depths of his coffee-cup. 'Tell me about it.'

Ally mentally kicked herself. 'Oh Zee, I'm sorry. I wasn't thinking.' She reached across the table and curled her fingers around his. 'You still miss Sarah an awful lot, don't you?'

'Every time I look at Emma I see her mother,' replied Zee. 'It's kind of a terrible thing and a wonderful thing, at the same time. Mind you, it's even harder for Emma – because her mum died giving birth to her, she sometimes has this idea that somehow it's all her fault.' Zee returned Ally's hand-clasp. 'How do you explain to a little kid that life is sometimes a complete bastard? At that age, everything is supposed to be butterflies and ice cream and fluffy bunnies.'

'I don't know,' confessed Ally. 'I think you have to let her ask questions and then answer them honestly.' She took a sip of coffee. 'You love her to bits though, don't you?'

Zee's face lit up. 'Along with Sarah, she's the best thing that ever happened to me, you know that.'

'And that's what my kids are to me,' agreed Ally. 'And to just about every parent I know. No matter how hard things are sometimes, no matter how annoying they can be, you'd never, ever want to be without them. Life takes on a whole new dimension when you have children – and so do people. It's like ... like the ultimate stage in growing up.' She laughed. 'God, listen to me – I sound like one of those self-help manuals.'

Zee stopped stirring his coffee and sat back in his chair. 'This has all got something to do with Miranda, hasn't it?'

Ally nodded. 'I can't bear to think that I'm depriving her of feeling all these things I feel,' she admitted. 'Stopping her from being a complete person, if you like.'

69

'Don't you think you're being a bit hard on yourself? I mean, if she's that desperate she could adopt, or find somebody else to have a baby for her ... '

Ally shook her head. 'It's not the same, Zee. It might be for us, but not for her. She needs to feel a connection with the baby. A blood tie.' She looked up. 'Which means ... since I'm her only sister ... ' she swallowed hard, 'that there's only me to do the job.'

Zee choked on a mouthful of biscuit crumbs. 'Hang on a minute, Ally. You're not actually going to *do* it, are you?'

'I'm ... thinking about it.'

He leaned forward across the table and looked at her intently. Ally quailed; Zee knew her too well, he could read her like a book. 'You *are* going to do it, aren't you?' he said softly.

She nodded. 'Yes. I think I am.'

'Does Luke know?'

'Believe it or not, he's the one who persuaded me to consider it.' She met his gaze. 'Do you ... do you think I'm doing the wrong thing?'

'Please!' Zee threw up his hands. 'Don't ask me, I don't have the brain for metaphysics. And this is an incredibly dangerous thing, you know.' He rubbed his chin. 'Have you looked into all the legal aspects, like I told you to?'

Ally nodded.

'*Thoroughly*?'

'Thoroughly. I found this really helpful online site ... '

Zee sighed. 'Well, if you really want to know what I think ... '

'Which I do.'

'I'm inclined to think that creating a life can never be a *complete* mistake.'

Ally brightened. 'Exactly, and—'

'But.' Zee raised a hand and stopped her short. 'That doesn't mean what you're doing won't cause problems. In fact I'm one hundred per cent certain that it will. I admire you Ally, I really do,' he added. 'You're a damned sight braver than I could ever be. But you'd better be ready for a few tough times ahead. Don't forget: it doesn't always work out right.'

'I know, Zee, but—'

'But nothing. I told you about those friends of mine who split up because the baby was disabled?' Ally nodded. 'Well, I also read

70

about a gay couple who lost out because the birth-mother decided to keep the child, and then she—'

'Well *that's* certainly not going to happen to me, is it?' Ally half-laughed at the suggestion. 'I've had my family, I've got my kids. And I'm quite clear in my mind: this baby's Miranda and Gavin's, not mine.'

'I hope so,' sighed Zee, looking more worried that Ally had ever seen him. 'For your sake, I really do.'

The next few days in Ally's life could only be described as surreal. In the past, the details of her conceptions had been a secret between her, Luke and Mother Nature. But this one, it seemed, was going to be arranged by a committee.

The following Sunday Ally, Luke and the kids drove over to Miranda and Gavin's deluxe barn conversion for lunch and 'a little chat' as Gavin had described it. He'd made it sound so informal on the telephone, but the minute she arrived and saw the look of ecstatic excitement on her sister's face, Ally knew there was no going back. If she had any remaining doubts about the rightness of what she was doing, she realised she'd better banish them right now; because there was no way that she could look at Miranda's happy face and think about changing her mind.

'Ally, oh Ally!' Miranda came rushing towards her across the cobbled yard, completely oblivious to Luke and the children. 'Oh Ally darling, I can't tell you ... you've made me so happy!'

A hug from her big sister was something of a novelty in itself; but this hug was a super-strength one, bone-crushingly tight and rather frightening in its intensity. Ally was panting for breath by the time she'd extricated herself from it. 'Hey, don't get too excited, sis, it hasn't happened yet,' she reminded Miranda.

But Miranda didn't want to know about the possibility of failure. Ally could see that, in her mind, the nursery was already finished, and the baby was contentedly gurgling away in an antique bassinet. What Miranda wants, Miranda gets – as usual, thought Ally with a brief flash of resentment. Then she felt guilty, and reminded herself that Miranda was only asking for something that other women took for granted: other women like Ally.

Gavin was something of a amateur chef and lunch was delicious, but only Kyle and Josie really enjoyed it. While they were shovelling down seconds, everybody else at the massive farmhouse table

71

was pushing minute quantities of pasta around the plate, waiting for this interminable ritual to be over.

After a Sussex pond pudding so enormous that it would have fed the Bennetts for a week, the children started squirming restlessly in their seats and glancing longingly out of the kitchen windows.

'Mum, can we go out and play?' wheedled Kyle.

'That's a good idea,' chimed in Miranda eagerly. 'Why don't you go and find Charlie, and ask him if he'll show you round the stables? Uncle Gavin's just bought two new polo ponies,' she added by way of an incentive.

Not that the kids needed encouraging. They loved Charlie, who was in charge of Gavin's many horses. He smelt of animals, always had a pocketful of Mint Imperials, and had a gift for telling the kind of grisly stories that terrified parents and fascinated children.

'Can we, Mum?' pleaded Josie.

'Go on then. But make sure you put your coats on, it's cold out there.'

Kyle and Josie vanished in a miniature stampede. As the back door banged shut behind them, a tense silence descended over the kitchen.

'This is nice,' commented Luke, sounding as if it wasn't.

'Yes,' agreed Gavin, twirling the stem of his wine glass.

There was a long silence, punctuated by the laborious ticking of the grandfather clock in the corner. Then Ally and Miranda started talking at the same time:

'Shall we—'

'Do you think we ought to—'

They both stopped in mid-sentence and looked at each other. Then Miranda giggled. 'Are you as nervous as I am?'

'Twice as nervous,' replied Ally. 'I don't know what to say.'

Gavin and Luke felt the focus of attention shifting to them. 'I guess there's ... stuff that needs discussing,' advanced Luke. 'Like ... er ... when and where.'

'And how,' added Gavin.

Everybody looked at him. 'What?'

'Surely there's only one way to do it?' puzzled Miranda.

Ally was appalled. 'One way? Look, nothing personal Gavin, but I am *not* doing *that*!'

'Doing what?'

She reddened to the roots of her hair. 'You know – sleeping with you.'

Gavin looked thunderstruck. Miranda started giggling again. 'Oh you are funny Ally, I didn't mean that! I meant, you know, the thing with the turkey baster.'

'Oh.' Ally wasn't sure it sounded much better. 'I read in a magazine about some woman who did it that way,' she recalled with some trepidation. 'The bloke handed her a yoghurt pot full of ... you know ... in the street, and she ran into this café and sat with her feet up in the ladies' loo for half an hour.' She looked imploringly at the others. 'Please tell me I don't have to do that.'

'Of course you don't. And I wouldn't let you anyway.' Luke took her hand and gave it a protective squeeze. 'There are private fertility clinics where they specialise in this kind of thing. I think we should leave it to them – don't you?'

Everybody around the table nodded and looked relieved.

'How about the one we used when we had IVF?' suggested Miranda.

'Good idea,' agreed Gavin. 'Why don't you give them a call tomorrow morning and make an appointment?'

Ally couldn't think of any real reason why not. So that was that. She could hardly admit that she was terrified and leg it, could she?

'I guess that's all sort of settled then,' she said, feeling far from settled herself.

Gavin's eyebrows arched in surprise. 'But what about the contract?'

This was the cue for startled expressions all round. 'The what?' gaped Ally.

'The legal agreement.' Gavin clearly couldn't believe nobody had thought about this before. 'You know, in case of any ... disagreements. As a matter of fact, I asked a lawyer friend to rough something out.'

'What disagreements?' demanded Luke, sensing the beginnings of a personal insult. 'Why should there be any disagreements?'

'Oh, I'm sure there won't be,' replied Gavin, smooth and unruffled as ever. 'But sometimes things do go wrong with these arrangements, you know, and it's best to be prepared in advance. People refuse to hand over babies, or—'

'I'd never do that!' exclaimed Ally, horrified at the suggestion.

'Of course you wouldn't,' agreed Luke, the scent of battle in his nostrils.

'Or else there's something wrong with the baby and nobody wants it,' Gavin went on.

Now it was Miranda's turn to be horrified. 'As if we'd reject a baby just because it was sick or disabled!' she exclaimed.

'Yes, yes, I'm sure you're right darling, but—'

Luke looked as if he was about to thump Gavin, but Ally spoke up first. 'I really don't see there's any need for a legal agreement,' she said calmly. 'We're a family. If we can't work things out without a contract, it's pretty pathetic. Don't you think, Miranda?'

'Absolutely.' Miranda directed a hard stare at her husband. 'Sometimes, darling, you can be an insensitive pig.'

'Only sometimes?' murmured Luke, just loudly enough to be heard.

'Hey, I'm only trying to—'

'Don't you think we should be celebrating this, not arguing about it?' cut in Ally. 'It's a baby, not a business deal!'

There was a brief hiatus. Everybody looked embarrassedly at their feet.

'What about that lovely case of Mouton Rothschild?' prompted Miranda, slipping an arm through her husband's and kissing him lightly on the cheek. 'The one your uncle gave us for a wedding present. I think this might be just the moment to sample some of it.'

Gavin looked as if he might be about to pursue his argument; then his features relaxed into a smile. 'You're right. I'll go and fetch a bottle.'

Gavin disappeared for a moment and returned with a very dusty bottle of red wine. 'I guarantee you've never tasted anything like this,' he declared, rubbing the cobwebs off on his sleeve. 'We've been saving it up for a special occasion, and Miranda's right: they don't come more special than this.'

He started pouring some wine into Ally's glass; Miranda put her hand over it. 'I'm not sure you should be drinking any more alcohol, Ally,' she counselled. 'Not in your condition.'

'But I'm not pregnant!' protested Ally.

'Not yet,' conceded Miranda. 'But who knows ... in a week or two? And I do so want everything to be right for this baby. Incidentally, I assume you'll be giving up work straight away?'

74

Ally stared back at her sister. 'Then you assume wrong! Teaching's a big part of my life, and it took ages to get the job at Pussy Willows.'

'But ... ' Miranda was clearly troubled. 'Look, if it's the money, we're happy to help you out.'

'For the last time, sis: this is not about money! Why does everything come down to money with you? I like teaching, I worked right through my other two pregnancies without any problems whatsoever, and I'm going to do exactly the same this time round.'

'Oh,' said Miranda, investing the lone syllable with a whole world of meaning.

'And by the way,' added Ally, 'before you ask, I'm not giving up my drama group either. In short, either I'm doing this my way, or I'm not doing it at all.'

'I can see there's no arguing with you,' commented Gavin. Ally caught his eye and could have sworn he was trying not to laugh. 'Just like your big sister, eh Miranda?'

Miranda pouted. 'Well, the very least you can let us do is buy you a new car,' she declared. 'I am *not* having my unborn son or daughter chauffeured in something that looks like a rusty skip on wheels.'

As the others argued the toss about paying for new cars and home improvements, Ally gazed glumly at the trickle of wine in her glass. Oh well, she thought as she downed the small mouthful and drank to the fertility of her insides: it's starting already. And it's not going to stop until my non-existent bump turns into a real live dream come true.

Later, as Luke was rounding up the kids' stuff and Ally was checking that they were securely belted into the back of the car, Miranda and Gavin canoodled on the driveway and rhapsodised about their future son or daughter.

'It's going to be so loved and adored,' gushed Miranda. 'And we're going to make sure it never wants for anything, aren't we, darling?'

Gavin kissed her affectionately on the forehead. 'It'll have everything a baby could ever want or need,' he promised. His eyes looked deep into Ally's. 'And it's all down to this wonderful sister of yours. How can we ever thank you, Ally?'

At that moment Luke returned with Josie and Kyle in tow, mud-

75

spattered and thankfully too tired to be any trouble on the way home. 'Ready for the off?'

As the beaten-up old Volvo drove away from Miranda and Gavin's house, considerably improving the view, Ally's thoughts turned to Zee. Now there was a man whose love for his daughter meant far more to him than his own life. Zee had hardly any money, and couldn't buy her any of the designer clothes or expensive toys the other kids had, but Emma didn't care. Why? Because her dad filled her life with fun and laughter and love.

Ally knew Gavin and Miranda were full of good intentions, determined to give their child a good life. And doubtless they would. But could they really give it as much as Zee gave Emma?

That remained to be seen.

# Chapter Eight

Over the next few weeks, as Christmas approached, Miranda was on the phone to Ally almost every day. Was she eating properly? Taking her folic acid supplements and her iron tablets? Had she tried out that new prenatal exercise DVD Miranda had got her from America? It was all so wearing that Ally was sorely tempted to tell her sister that she'd taken up smoking, developed a serious gin habit and taken to eating nothing but Big Macs. The trouble was, Miranda would probably believe her and go into hysterics.

Luke, for his part, was admirably calm about the whole thing. Not many husbands, Ally figured, would be so sanguine about the prospect of their wife having another man's baby; or having to accompany her through all the morning sickness and the piles, without the pay-off of being able to keep the baby in the end. He was, she decided, quite simply a saint.

Naturally things weren't happening quickly enough for Miranda, who'd have liked the entire baby-making process to last about two days; but Ally was more than happy to take things slowly.

'I'm not sure it's really sunk in yet,' she admitted to her friend Eve, a nursery nurse from Pussy Willows, on a pre-Christmas shopping trip to the huge April Glade shopping mall. 'It still feels like it's all happening to somebody else.'

Eve gave her what could only be described as a funny look. 'Not sunk in? Blimey Ally, you could be pregnant by the end of next week – and that definitely won't be happening to anybody else!'

Ally winced. 'Yes, I know.'

'There's still time to change your mind.' Eve poked her in the ribs. 'And stop pretending you're interested in those jumpers. You've picked up the same one three times.'

'Have I?' Ally hadn't even realised. 'Sorry, I was miles away. What did you say?'

'I said you can still change your mind if you want. God Ally, you can't let yourself be pushed into doing something like this, it's way too serious for that.'

'I'm not being pushed,' protested Ally.

'So you're sure you're doing the right thing then?'

'Yes.' Ally felt like a hapless contestant on the sort of game show where you have ten seconds to give the right answer or lose a million quid. 'No – I mean yes! I'm just a bit . . . scared, I think.'

'Not half as scared as I'd be,' declared Eve. 'You wouldn't get me doing it, not for anything. Ooh, thirty per cent off.' She held up a hot-pink halter top. 'What do you reckon?'

'I'm not sure about the colour. It reminds me of . . . prawns.' Ally went back to rummaging in the bargain bin. 'Well, I'm doing it and I'm glad I am,' she continued. 'But it takes some getting used to. I mean, personally I've never bothered much about how my insides work, but suddenly half of Gloucestershire knows all about my ovulation cycle!'

'Creepy,' agreed Eve. 'Tell you what though, from what you've said that brother-in-law of yours is a bit of all right. I reckon you should skip the fertility clinic and go for a good old-fashioned roll in the hay.'

'Eve!'

'Ha! You're blushing. I knew you fancied him.'

Ally didn't bother denying it; she knew she'd only dig herself a deeper hole. When all was said and done, Gavin was very fanciable – in an abstract sort of way. It wasn't as if she'd ever dream of actually *doing* anything, perish the thought. And he'd probably laugh in her face if she ever suggested it.

She seized upon something black and sparkly from the bottom of the display bin, and pulled it out. It was a really pretty, low-cut little cocktail number, a lot more glamorous than her usual party outfits but at a knockdown price. 'Hey Eve, look at this.' She held it in front of her and savoured the way it sparkled in the mirror. 'I could wear it for Christmas and then save it for the next time Miranda throws one of her glamorous midsummer dos.'

'It's great.' Eve nodded appreciatively. 'But aren't you forgetting something?'

'Like what?'

'Like the fact that by next summer you'll almost certainly be the size of a bungalow. You're going to be pregnant, remember?'

Ally remembered. In fact, the idea really hit home for the very first time.

'Now come on girl,' breezed Eve, 'let's find the café – you look like you could use a shot or two of caffeine . . . while you still can!'

A couple of days later, Ally and Miranda were summoned to the Havelock Ellis Fertilty Clinic, ushered into a comfortable room with armchairs and jolly, sperm-shaped light fittings, and presented with cups of tea and expensive biscuits.

'It's all perfectly simple,' said the nurse with the soothing voice. 'We'll send you home with five free ovulation kits today, and as soon as we get a clearer idea of your cycle we'll be able to plan the best day for your insemination. You will be free to come in at short notice, I take it?'

'Of course she will,' replied Miranda breathlessly, 'won't you Ally?'

'Er . . . yes,' replied Ally, trying not to think about what excuse she was going to give the head teacher at Pussy Willows if she had to rush to the clinic at five minutes' notice to be impregnated. It was, after all, only the first in a long line of awkward questions and potentially embarrassing situations. 'Do I have to take any pills or anything beforehand?' she enquired.

'I'm sure that won't be necessary, dear. Not if you're ovulating normally, and I'm sure you are. Now, let me see . . . ' The nurse consulted her clipboard. 'The donor is . . . ?'

'My husband,' cut in Miranda.

'Ah yes, Mr Hesketh. A *very* satisfactory sperm count, I'm happy to say. We'll get him in beforehand to, you know, do his thing, and then everything will be ready and waiting for you on the day. Do you have any questions?'

Ally and Miranda looked at each other, silently daring one another to ask something. It was Ally who broke first. 'Um . . . how do you actually . . . er . . . you know, get it in?' she asked, feeling very stupid.

'The sperm? We inject it into the uterus through one of these.' The nurse slid open a drawer and took out a thin plastic tube. 'Not very romantic, I'll grant you,' she said with a smile, 'but effective.'

'And ... painful?' wondered Miranda, sounding almost eager.

'No, no, not at all,' replied the nurse. 'Or at least, not in most cases. About ten per cent of our ladies have menstrual-type cramps for a little while afterwards, but that's all. And of course, we wash the sperm thoroughly before injection, just as a precaution.' She answered the next question before it was asked. 'In some cases, placing neat sperm into the uterus can cause severe pain and fainting,'she explained cheerily. 'But that's not something you'll need to worry about.' She stood up, smoothing down her skirt. 'Now, shall I show you round the insemination suite? I'm sure you'll be terribly impressed.'

From that moment on, Ally sensed Miranda watching her like a hawk, almost as if her sister was trying to guess when she was ovulating. At first she thought she was imagining it, but hardly a day went by without a phone call or even a visit. And then the kids started to ask questions.

'They keep asking why Auntie Miranda's always round at our house,' Ally told Zee as they did their make-up for the first performance of *Oliver*. 'I mean, you can see why. As a rule it's only on high days, holidays, the kids' birthdays and whenever she needs to have a good moan. At the moment she's there so often I'm thinking of making her up a bed.'

'So what do you tell them?' Zee enquired, fiddling with Fagin's mighty beak of a false nose.

'Well, last time I said she was really interested in seeing what we've done with the back garden ... but I'm not convinced they believed me.'

Zee let out a chuckle that made his nose wobble. 'I'm not surprised! Have you actually done *anything* with the garden? Last time I saw it, it still looked like a bomb-site.'

'I planted a rose bush last week, and Luke power-washed the patio,' protested Ally. 'But yeah, you're right. It does still look like Beirut on a bad day. I think I need some new excuses.'

'Actually,' replied Zee, contorting his face as he glued on his tatty grey beard, 'I think you'd be better off practising telling them the truth.' He dropped his voice in case anyone else heard. 'If the insemination works first time, you're going to have a lot of explaining to do.'

Ally closed her eyes and forced herself not to hyperventilate.

'It's tomorrow,' she said, almost inaudibly.

'What?'

'Tomorrow,' she repeated, more loudly. '*It* looks like happening *tomorrow*. The clinic rang just before I came out. I need to phone in my temperature in the morning, just to make sure I'm ovulating, but apparently tomorrow should be just about perfect.'

'Oh. Wow.' Startled, Zee almost drew a line down his cheek. 'So ... I guess that's a relief then, actually having something happen?'

Ally laughed at the ludicrousness of it all. 'Zee love, I can't move for things happening. I've got *Oliver* all week, then it's Christmas, and after that we're all supposed to be traipsing up to Leeds to see Luke's mum – and while that little lot's *happening*, I'm trying to get myself pregnant by my brother-in-law!'

At the word 'pregnant', ears pricked up all over the dressing room and Mr Bumble dropped his top hat.

They looked at each other's faces, half made-up and harassed, and both burst out laughing. 'By the way, Eve thinks I'm crazy,' commented Ally.

'Well you probably are,' Zee pointed out. 'Tell you one thing though.'

'What's that?'

'Bet you're so worried about tomorrow, you've got no room for first-night nerves. You're going to steal the show.'

And he was right.


Luke gripped Ally's hand very tightly as she walked up the steps to the Havelock Ellis Clinic. 'Are you sure you don't want me to come in with you?'

She shook her head. 'This is something I have to do on my own, sweetheart. Gavin's done his bit and now I must do mine.'

'I don't understand.'

'I'm not quite sure I do either,' she confessed. 'But having you there with me while it was happening ... it'd make me feel as if I was doing something wrong somehow. And I couldn't bear that.'

She walked up to the door at the top of the steps, her arms and legs shaking. Then Luke called out to her: 'You were wonderful in the show last night, really wonderful. Everybody said so.'

Ally turned and smiled nervously at him. 'Really?'

'Really. Didn't it say so in the *Courant*?'

'Luke, I don't know if I can do this ... '

'You can do anything, Ally. Anything you set your mind to.'

Then she drew herself up straight, threw her shoulders back and walked in through the front door of the clinic.

Now, there really was no going back.

Confirmation of Ally's home test result came through on Christmas Eve, as Ally was making mince pies in the kitchen, to the accompaniment of a cheesy carol CD and the sound of Josie and Kyle squabbling in the lounge.

'Oi – shush! Or there'll be no presents,' she yelled through the doorway as she wiped her hands and lunged for the telephone on the kitchen wall. 'Hello?'

'Mrs Bennett? It's the clinic here. I'm really sorry, but—'

She replaced the receiver silently, calmly. The kids were still fighting in the next room but she was oblivious to them. It wasn't so much the shock – the home test had indicated that she wasn't pregnant – but the knowledge of what it meant. She was going to have to wait a month, or maybe two given it was the holidays, and then go through the whole thing all over again.

# Chapter Nine

Christmas in the Bennett household was pretty much like Christmas in every home with kids: initial hysteria, followed by too much chocolate and far too many presents, culminating in the mass boredom and family arguments that set in on Boxing Day.

Ally had imagined that Miranda and Gavin might want to spend Christmas along with them this year, what with their newfound closeness. But in view of the results from the clinic, maybe it wasn't so surprising that they'd chosen to spend the holiday at one of Gavin's luxury hotels up in Scotland. Besides, as Miranda had said, she needed the time to think about whether or not to continue with the surrogacy.

As for Ally and Miranda's mum and dad, as usual they had ummed and aahed about which daughter to spend Christmas with, and ended up deciding to stay at home instead: 'Well, we wouldn't want to upset either of you, dear, would we?' Obviously this wasn't strictly true; they'd far rather have stayed with Miranda, except for the fact that she always insisted on cooking Christmas lunch . . . and if there was one thing Miranda really couldn't do, it was cook. The indigestion was just too high a price to pay, even if the champagne was real Veuve Clicquot, and not supermarket plonk like they got at Ally and Luke's house.

Luke only had one close relative: his mother, Shirley. Since his father had left when he was three, and Shirley had lost her only other child on Christmas Eve, it was perhaps not surprising that she preferred to avoid Christmas altogether.

So – apart from the aunts, uncles, cousins and friends who made flying visits and left stuffed with mince pies, there were just four people sitting around the Bennett family turkey. Not that anybody minded. In some ways it was nicer, thought Ally, just being together with Luke and the kids, and savouring the fact that they had created a family of their very own. Something strong and enduring, built on love.

Luke seemed to have read Ally's mind.

It was after Boxing Day lunch. The kids were riding their bikes up and down Brookfield Road, working off the last of the Christmas pudding, while Luke tackled a mountain of greasy washing-up, up to his elbows in a tsunami of bubbles that threatened to escape from the sink. 'You know, I'm glad your folks didn't come to stay,' he remarked. Then he thought for a moment. 'God, that sounds terrible, doesn't it?'

Ally deftly caught a dripping plate as it slipped through his fingers, and set about drying it. 'You're only saying what I'm thinking,' she replied. 'They're not the easiest of people, are they?'

'Unless your name's Miranda.'

'Maybe I should change mine,' quipped Ally. 'Besides, Miranda's adamant that she doesn't want them to know anything about the surrogacy arrangement until there's a baby on its way – not that there will be unless she changes her mind about trying again.'

'It's your father's farting I didn't miss,' declared Luke. 'He's a one-man brass band when he's had Brussels sprouts.' He chuckled to himself. 'Parents, eh?'

'Hey, do you remember the time we had my lot and your mum over for Kyle's christening?'

'How could I ever forget? They practically started a punch-up in the vestry. And all because of that bloody christening robe. Told you we should just have dunked Kyle in the bath and left it at that.'

Ally giggled at the memory. It hadn't seemed funny at the time, but with hindsight ... 'Oh yes ... that robe. Mum bought Kyle that microscopic antique christening robe, and she kept telling everybody he must be obese, because he wouldn't fit into it.'

'And then my mum said it was no surprise he wouldn't stop crying, because the damn thing was so tight he couldn't breathe.'

'Well, she was right! So Kyle ended up getting christened in his second-best Babygro. Do you think they'll ever forgive us?'

'Shouldn't think so. And anyway if they did start approving of us, I think I'd start to worry in case we were turning into them!'

84

Amused by this hideous prospect, Ally stacked her plate in the rack and started on another. 'Of course, Miranda wouldn't have any of that trouble. She'd just get Vivienne Westwood to run her up a made-to-measure christening robe. And there'd be no pork pies and crisps at the party either, you can bet on that.'

'I know we're not rolling in money like your sister.' Luke turned to look at her over his shoulder. 'But we do have good times, don't we?'

'The best.' Ally abandoned the plate and snuggled up behind him, her arms wrapped tightly about his waist. There was just the faintest hint of love handles there, and for some reason that made her love him all the more. 'I wouldn't swap what we've got for anything of Miranda's.'

'Not even Gorgeous Gavin?' joked Luke.

It was meant in fun, but just for a split second it brought Ally up short. Then she laughed with him. 'A man who's so vain he spends a hundred quid on a haircut? A man who has pedicures? Give me a break! I like my men *real*.' And she nibbled affectionately at his shoulder.

'Didn't you have enough lunch?' he enquired.

'I'm always hungry for you, darling,' she purred, only half-jokingly.

'Your timing's a bit off though,' Luke pointed out, turning round and embracing her with soapy arms. 'We can hardly have an early night at half past two in the afternoon!'

'Spoilsport.' They cuddled rather damply as the washing-up water cooled in the sink. 'Do you think Miranda and Gavin will make good parents?' Ally wondered aloud. 'Assuming they, you know, go ahead.'

Luke shrugged. 'As good as any, I should think. I mean, in the end it's all about muddling along and following your instincts, isn't it?'

'I guess.'

'As long as they love the kid, they can't go too far wrong. And they both seem really up for it.'

'You're right,' agreed Ally. 'But my not getting pregnant the first time ... it seems to have really knocked Miranda back. She's got this crazy idea that if it didn't work the first time, it won't work at all.'

'Well, it might not,' Luke pointed out. 'I did think she was being a bit over-optimistic before.'

'I can see why she's undecided,' conceded Ally. 'I mean, what's it going to do to her if I try and fail again – and then keep on failing?'

Luke's expression grew more serious. Taking a step back, he held her by the shoulders and fixed her with his wise brown eyes. 'I don't want to hear you say that word ever again, Ally. You have not failed, and you are not to think that way, do you hear?

'You're doing something wonderful for Miranda, something nobody else could or would do for her. And if it doesn't work out in the end, it's Mother Nature who's at fault, not you.'

He put a finger under her chin and tilted it gently upwards. 'I love you, you know, Mrs Bennett.'

Then he silenced her reply with a kiss; and a shrill young voice piped up from the kitchen doorway: 'Eugh, gross! Don't look, Josie, Mum and Dad are *snogging* again.'

A little while later, during the slow days between Christmas and New Year, Ally was out with the children, trawling the sales for cheap school clothes, when she got a call on her mobile – from Gavin.

'Ally, is that you?'

'Gavin? Josie, put that back at once! Sorry, I've got the kids with me. Is something up?'

'No, nothing in particular. Miranda's still rather down, of course ... hasn't quite made up her mind yet, I don't think – which is why I thought it might be a good idea for us to meet up and talk things through.'

'All four of us?'

'Well ... I don't think there's any real need for Luke to put himself out. He's said himself he doesn't want to be too closely involved with the gory details. But I do think it would be useful for the rest of us to get together. You know, just to chat about where we go from here.'

'OK then. Kyle, don't touch that! Somebody has to eat it. Sorry Gavin, what did you say?'

'How about tomorrow evening, at that new café-bar in Montpellier? The one they've done out to look like a church? What's it called ... Vespers? That's the one. Around seven? Got to rush I'm afraid – business meeting in five minutes.'

Before she'd had time to explain that Luke was working late

again, and it might not be possible unless Zee or Kerri-next-door could babysit, Gavin had rung off.

She wasn't particularly surprised that Gavin had suggested meeting up to talk things over, or even that he'd said Luke didn't really need to be there; but all that changed when she got to the Vespers café-bar and found that there was no sign of Miranda either.

Gavin greeted her with a smile that could weaken knees at fifty paces, and stood up eagerly to make room for her at the corner table. 'Ally, darling! It's good of you to come.'

'Where's Miranda?' she asked, avoiding a kiss on the cheek; she was more than a little uncomfortable in the unexpectedly lone presence of Gavin the love god, minus his attendant goddess. She suspected Luke wouldn't have been particularly happy either if he'd known she was alone with Gavin – assuming you counted a heaving bar on a Friday night as alone. Had Gavin engineered this tête-à-tête for some nefarious reason? Or was she just being silly?

When he heard the tone of Ally's voice, Gavin's radiant smile faded by a few kilowatts.

'Miranda, um, didn't really feel up to coming,' he replied. 'As I told you, she's quite down at the moment.'

'All the more reason for you to have brought her then,' suggested Ally, avoiding the softly cushioned seat next to Gavin. It was ridiculous, but she felt happier opting for the bum-numbing salvaged pew opposite instead. Safer, even. 'She needs people to tell her that whatever happens, it's all going to be all right.'

'Er ... yes.' Eyes fixed on the table top, Gavin fumbled with his bottle of *bière blonde*. Something was definitely up.

'There's something you're not telling me,' said Ally. 'Isn't there?'

'Only that ... ' Gavin looked up. 'Actually, Miranda doesn't know I'm here. I thought it might be better if I saw you on my own.'

'Oh, great!' Ally pushed back her chair. 'In that case I think I'd better go, don't you?'

He looked genuinely mystified. 'Go? Why?'

Men, thought Ally. Or at least, some of them. If they had brains they'd be dangerous. 'What do you imagine Miranda's going to think when she finds out you're having clandestine trysts with me while she's back home, sobbing her heart out?'

87

'This isn't a tryst!' snorted Gavin.

'No, too right it isn't. But if you're not careful, it's how she'll see it,' retorted Ally. 'Any woman would. And right now, Miranda's feeling pretty fragile.'

'Oh hell, you're probably right.' Gavin scratched his head, somehow managing to do so without disturbing a single, immaculately groomed hair. 'I didn't think of it that way.' He looked genuinely crestfallen. 'All I'm trying to do is help.'

'By going behind her back?'

'No, of course not. I just thought we could talk more freely if she wasn't here, what with her being so ... highly strung at the moment.' Gavin heaved a sigh. 'Look, I'll go and phone her now and tell her I've met up with you but I'll be home soon, would that be OK?'

'I ... guess.'

Ally watched him step outside to get a better signal on his mobile. A few minutes later he returned, his beaming self again. 'All done, she's fine about it.'

'You're sure?'

'Of course I'm sure. Now, can I get you a drink?'

A youth in a red cassock served him an overpriced glass of house white and a blueberry juice and passed them over the stone-topped bar, along with a dish of crispy snacks that bore an unpleasant resemblance to Communion wafers. Ally had already made up her mind by the time Gavin returned with the drinks: this was definitely the silliest and least tasteful theme bar she'd ever been in – not that she'd had many boozy nights out since she had the kids. The Friday-night crowd of students and office workers seemed to be lapping it up, though.

'Penny for 'em?' ventured Gavin, returning to his seat opposite her.

'Oh, just thinking how different life is when you're young and unattached. All that freedom and no responsibility ... it's so long ago I can hardly remember the last time I was drunk!'

'You *are* young,' Gavin replied with a reproving wag of the finger. 'And you look it too. Nobody would ever think you had a ten-year-old son.'

Ally shrugged off the compliment, though secretly flattered. 'Oh, I sometimes think it's the kids who keep me that way. When you've got children, you have to live at their pace, be enthusiastic about the things they like, you know, generally run around and be a bit crazy.'

'Go on, tell me. Tell me about it.' There was so much eagerness in his eyes.

She smiled. 'Let's see . . . playing football on Weston mudflats in the rain, in wellies and a swimsuit. Dressing the cat up as Father Christmas. Making a full-size Dalek out of egg-boxes—'

'And that's exactly the kind of stuff I want to do too,' cut in Gavin, alight with enthusiasm. 'I can't tell you how much I want to be a father. I want my own little son to have a kick-about with, I want to take him to places and show him the things I loved when I was a kid, teach him to make paper planes and sail a dinghy, make him laugh—'

'Hold on!' she laughed. 'Babies do come in two varieties, you know.'

'Varieties?'

'What happens if you have a girl?'

'Oh, a girl. Yes, of course. Then I guess Miranda will do all the girly stuff with her.'

'I bet she'd love to have a little girl to dress up,' reflected Ally, recalling instances in her childhood when Miranda had done the very same thing to her, not always with attractive results. Particularly the time she'd had her hair 'restyled' with the garden shears. 'It'd be a dream come true for her.'

Gavin's face fell. 'That's the problem,' he said. 'And that's why I wanted to talk to you alone. I don't honestly think she knows what she wants any more. She was so sure it was going to work first time, and when it didn't . . . it's like the bottom has fallen out of her world.'

'Miranda's not used to failing,' said Ally. 'I don't think she's ever failed at anything before, and it probably terrifies her. Just imagine how much it must hurt when you're desperate to be a mother and it's the only thing you can't get right.'

'She keeps talking about giving up, Ally,' said Gavin, a note of desperation in his voice. 'I – we – can't let her. We've got to keep on trying.'

Ally felt weary and beleaguered. 'Look Gavin, like I told you on the telephone, if Miranda really doesn't want to go through it all again, you have to respect her wishes. Maybe she just needs a few months off, to think about something else, then she'll change her mind and we can try again.'

Gavin shook his head. 'No, if she gives up now I'm convinced that'll be it. Full stop.' He seized Ally's hand. 'Please help me persuade her, Alison. Underneath she's so desperate for a child, it's just that she's so mixed-up and upset that she's not sure about anything any more. Will you talk to her? I know she'll listen to you. Will you? Please?'

She could have refused; told him that this mad surrogacy plan had put enough strain on them all already. But in all honesty, only someone with a heart of stone could have said no to the look of sheer desperation in Gavin's eyes. Behind the public façade of a business tycoon, in total control of himself and everything around him, lay the look of a small boy, helpless to prevent his dream being stolen away.

'I'll talk to her,' she said finally. 'But you have to understand: that's all I can do.'

Miranda was having a bad day. In fact, contrary to the normal course of her life, rather a lot of her days had been bad lately, ever since she'd let that ill-advised chink of hope into her childless life and it had promptly gone sour on her.

Suddenly everything from her domestic plumbing to her sex life seemed to be catching the fallout from this sudden attack of luck failure. Gareth was convinced that she was projecting her own stress onto the world and if she started 'thinking lucky', everything would be return to normal.

Much as she would like to believe his theory, Miranda wasn't so sure. How could negative thinking alone hold up a consignment of wallpaper at a customs post in Taiwan? It wouldn't have been so bad if it hadn't been specially designed and commissioned wall-paper for a cabinet minister's country house, which of course had resulted in a series of increasingly unpleasant phone conversations with senior civil servants.

And then there was the charity gala concert and fireworks display that Miranda was organising. Or rather, there wasn't. Because with less than a month to go before the big night, they'd lost the venue and the bill-topping soprano had gone down with shingles. And the whole thing had been cancelled. She was begin-ning to wonder if the Mayor's charity evening, in a few months' time, was going to be any more successful.

Each new mini-disaster seemed to outdo the last in horribleness, and doubts were creeping insidiously into Miranda's mind like wily cat burglars, insinuating themselves into cracks in her self-esteem which she'd never even suspected were there. Have I lost my golden touch? she asked herself. And she caught herself wondering: What will be the next thing to go – my irresistibly gorgeous husband? Or worse, my looks?

Is every bit of this somehow my fault?

That was a ludicrous idea, of course, but Miranda had never bothered much with logic. Luck had always been her guiding light.

Miranda Morris Designs had its headquarters in the sleepy but appropriately snooty market town of Beeston Parva, a short drive from Gavin and Miranda's Wiltshire home. An old stone-built cottage had been converted to form a small and exclusive ground-floor showroom, with a design studio up above, at the top of a wrought-iron spiral staircase which had claimed many a stiletto heel and wrenched ankle.

On this grey and drizzly January morning Miranda was up in the studio, making herself feel better the only way she knew how: by being unpleasant to a junior member of staff.

'Jesus, Emil,' Miranda whisked a set of designs off the young designer's drawing board, 'what the fuck are these supposed to be?'

The bespectacled twenty-two-year-old, fresh out of St Martin's with a critically acclaimed graduation show under his belt, did his best to fight his corner. 'It's an abstract interpretation of a traditional floral pattern, using the interplay of—'

'No Emil, it is a mess. A MESS!' Miranda flung the sheet of paper into the air and left it to flutter down onto the floor behind her. 'You are not Celia Birtwell, Emil. Or the ghost of Laura bloody Ashley. You do not do "mystic daisies" on pretty frocks. You are supposed to be designing sophisticated wallpaper for very rich people. Do you really think they want to look at their walls and see something that looks like a hippy's acid trip?'

A residual spark of self-esteem prompted Emil to protest: 'Miranda, I really don't think—'

But Miranda was onto him faster than a Jack Russell onto a lame rat. 'No, Emil, you don't. And that's the problem. But you had better start, because there are plenty of other young designers out there who'd be quite happy to take your place'

There was a knock at the door, and the tirade froze into a tableau as Angela, the manageress from the floor below, stuck an apologetic head into the design studio. 'Sorry to bother you, Miranda, but you've a visitor downstairs.'

'I told you expressly not to disturb me! Can't you see I'm in the middle of something!'

'I thought you'd want to know,' replied Angela, who was one of the few people totally unbothered by Miranda's overdramatic moods. 'It's your sister.'

Five minutes later, Emil had been kicked out of the studio to fetch coffee and sandwiches for everybody, and Ally was sitting on the Philippe Starck sofa bed which Miranda fully expected her designers to sleep on rather than go home and leave a key project unfinished.

Up till now, Ally had always half assumed that Miranda's interior design business was just one of those expensive, self-indulgent hobbies enjoyed by wealthy wives who didn't much care if they never made any money. If this was the eighteenth century, she'd always thought, Miranda would be Marie-Antoinette, milking cows on her pretend farm and letting everybody else eat cake.

But that was before she saw – and heard – Miranda wiping the floor with Emil. Ally revised her opinion. Not so much Marie-Antoinette, more Genghis Khan. She wasn't looking forward to this conversation.

'It's nice to see you,' said Miranda, though it clearly wasn't. 'But things are a bit hectic at the moment.'

'I'll go if you like,' suggested Ally, perhaps a little too eagerly. 'This is obviously a bad time.'

Miranda rubbed her eyes. They were rimmed with pink and looked weary, like the rest of her. 'No, don't be silly, you've come a long way. So it must be something important.'

'I ... um ... ' Shit, thought Ally. I had this all thought out and now I can't think where to start. 'It's about ... well ... babies.'

'Right.' Miranda reacted coolly. 'Did Gavin send you?'

'Sort of,' admitted Ally.

'I thought so.'

'But I only said I'd come because I thought it was a good idea too,' Ally added hastily. She certainly didn't want her sister thinking she took orders from Gavin. 'He told me you were still talking

92

about giving up on the surrogacy idea, and that seems like such a pity to me.'

Miranda sank back into her executive chair, with a long, slow sigh. 'I'm tired,' she said. 'And . . . a bit scared.'

'Why scared?' enquired Ally. 'Of failing, you mean?'

'That, yes. But it's more than that – it's the way the whole thing makes me feel. I really want a baby but I'm so scared it's never going to happen.'

'I know it's stressful, sis, but—'

'I'm simply not used to it, Ally. All that emotion, surging about all over the place. I'm used to having everything under control – especially me. The funny thing is,' she added, with a hint of shame in her voice, 'I've never felt so control of myself as I did when I had anorexia. Every little aspect of my life was so beautifully ordered.' She looked her sister square in the eye, practically demanding condemnation. 'That's a pretty terrible thing to say, isn't it?'

Ally shrugged, trying hard to look and sound more matter-of-fact than she felt. She was terrified of saying or doing the wrong thing. 'You feel the way you feel. Look, I don't know much about anorexia. When I was a kid and you were away being a model, I was so naïve I just thought you were, you know, naturally skinny. But from what I've heard, lots of people feel that way.'

'But it's because of starving myself when I was a model that I can't control my body now, isn't it? If I'd been *normal* like you,' she made it sound like something slightly grubby, 'I'd have been popping out sprogs like I was shelling peas.'

'You don't know that for certain,' argued Ally.

Miranda leaned forward, eyes blazing. 'Maybe you don't, but I do. And now I'm expected to cope with this . . . this bloody roller-coaster – backwards, forwards, upside down. It was bad enough going through IVF, and now it feels like I'm back to square one again. I'd psyched myself up just enough to get through one cycle, and when it failed . . .' She flopped back into her chair, a picture of angry misery.

'You thought, "Right, that's enough, I'm not doing that again"?'

'Give that girl a prize.'

Ally thought about her sister for a moment; about all the things she had done in her life, all the adventures she'd had, the people and the situations she'd commanded. And then she took a chance.

93

'Some people might say you were a coward,' she said softly.

The angry glint returned to Miranda's eyes. 'You mean *you* think I'm a coward. Like you know anything about infertility.'

'I know what it feels like to want a baby more than anything else in the world, and I can imagine what it feels like if you can't have one,' Ally countered. 'And I also know how strong you are. If anybody can do this, you can.'

Miranda shook her head. 'You're right, I am a coward. I think about the next cycle and all I can imagine is failure.'

'You don't *do* failure, Miranda. Sometimes I wonder if that's the real reason you chucked in medical school – you were afraid you weren't going to make the grade.'

'You cow!' snapped Miranda, rising to the bait. 'You know damn well I've never run away from anything, and the only reason I quit as a medical student is because I had the chance to earn ten times more money doing something a hundred times more glamorous!'

'You're running away from this, though,' pointed out Ally. 'Nobody else is. Gavin wants to go ahead, I'm here to do my bit, even Luke's right behind it. But you'd rather run away than try the one thing that could bring you the baby you've always wanted.'

'I thought I understood you, Miranda. Even when we were kids and you bullied me I admired you for your strength. But I guess I was wrong about that.'

Ally retrieved her handbag and stood up to go. Miranda was still sitting in her chair, motionless except for the fact that, almost imperceptibly, her hands had started to shake.

Ally was halfway to the studio door when Miranda finally spoke.

'Don't leave me, Ally,' she said suddenly in a tiny, little-girl voice. 'Please don't leave me. I can't face this on my own.'

After all Miranda's umming and aahing, it was too late to try again in January, and everything seemed to slow down to an imperceptible crawl. It was late February when Ally finally made a return trip to the Havelock Ellis Clinic.

The routine was the same as before, only this time she wasn't alone; Miranda was with her. Despite the embarrassment, the uncomfortable intimacy of it all, Ally knew she had to share this experience with her sister. Realisation had finally hit home: if a baby was born, it wouldn't be hers and Luke's; she would just be a kind of antenatal nanny, looking after it until Miranda took over. So it simply wouldn't be right for Miranda not to be there at the moment its life began.

And – miraculously – it did.

Miranda didn't just come to the clinic. She was there too when Ally got the telephone call from the gynaecologist, confirming the result of the pregnancy test. But the two of them already knew it was positive, because they'd done two home tests in Ally's bathroom, sitting side by side on the edge of the bath and chewing their nails as they waited for the endless three minutes to elapse. They just needed somebody official to tell them they weren't imagining things.

'Oh God, oh God!' gasped Miranda as Ally put down the phone. 'I'm going to be a mother! I have to phone Gavin right now – I'm going to be a mother!'

Ally laughed and danced round the bathroom with her sister, sharing in her excitement. But deep inside she was already wondering: if Miranda's now a mother-to-be, what does that make me?

It was a question that would take some answering.

# Chapter Ten

When Ally saw Zee five minutes before the drama group's AGM, he guessed that she had something special to tell him before she'd so much as opened her mouth.

'Don't tell me – let me guess,' he pleaded, tapping his forefinger against his cheek reflectively. 'I know, a New York theatrical agent was so impressed by your Nancy, he's signed you up to play the part on Broadway!'

Ally threw back her head and laughed so hard that the sound echoed right round St Jude's church hall and everybody turned to look at her in surprise.

'Well if he has,' she replied, 'he hasn't bothered telling me about it yet. Perhaps the letter's stuck in the post.'

Zee stepped back and looked her up and down. 'There's something different about you,' he remarked, almost accusingly. 'You're all giggly and excitable, like when you've been on the booze.'

'Haven't touched a drop,' promised Ally, solemnly crossing her heart for good measure. 'In fact, between you and me I've given up the hard stuff altogether.'

Zee's eyes narrowed. 'You haven't given up soft cheese as well, have you?'

'As a matter of fact I have. And cleaning out the cat's litter tray.'

'You're up the duff!' exclaimed Zee, clapping hand to his mouth.

'Shh, keep your voice down,' urged Ally, 'It's really early days yet. The only other people who know so far are Luke, Gavin and Miranda.' She glanced around her. 'Or they were, until you decided to broadcast the news.'

'Oh, I'm sure nobody heard. They're all far too busy bitching about each other and deciding who to vote off the committee.' Zee nodded towards a gaggle of middle-aged thespian wannabes, heads together in a corner like Macbeth's witches. 'Are you really? You're not having me on?'

She shook her head and ran a hand lightly over her stomach. 'I don't feel any different yet, mind. But I'm sure the morning sickness will kick in soon. When I was expecting Josie, I lived on dry biscuits and weak tea for the best part of two months.'

'Wow.' Zee shook his head as though he couldn't quite make up his mind whether his best mate was very brave or very mad. 'I take it the lucky parents-to-be are a bit pleased?'

'Put it this way, Gavin's still in orbit, and suddenly overnight Miranda's a childcare expert. She phones me every evening at ten o'clock, to check that I'm having an early night!'

'Ah, bless her.' Zee stretched out a sneaky hand to the table spread out with the half-time refreshments, and helped himself to a plate of biscuits marked '10p each, 3 for 50p'. 'Peckish?'

'Don't mind if I do. You know, I'll probably be eating these with Marmite on in a month or two,' mused Ally as she bit into a chocolate one and savoured its squishy yumminess. 'Might as well enjoy them while they still taste normal.'

'What about Luke?' asked Zee.

'Oh, he's pretty normal too, thanks.'

'Come on, you know I didn't mean that!' Zee pointed, charades-style, at Ally's stomach. 'How is he, you know, about you being you-know-what?'

'Oh.' There was just the merest hint of hesitancy as she replied, 'He's fine. Really good about it.'

'Sure?'

'Of course I'm sure! He's the one who persuaded me to do this, remember? He's still getting used to the idea, that's all – just like the rest of us. If anybody's having trouble adjusting, it's me.' She glanced around and lowered her voice. 'Sometimes I catch myself thinking: this isn't my husband's baby, it's Gavin's – and then I start feeling as if I've been, I don't know, having an affair with him or something!'

'That's just plain silly.'

'I know.'

Zee gave her a suggestive wink. 'Unless of course you'd actually

97

*like* to have an affair with Gavin . . . '

Ally swiped him with her handbag. 'Wash your mind out with disinfectant! Of course I wouldn't!'

'All right, don't hit me, it was only a joke!' Zee put up his arms in mock defence. 'Well, as long as everything's pretty much OK.'

'It will be.' Ally pulled a face. 'Once I've thought of a way to explain this to the kids. Don't suppose you have any suggestions?'

'You're kidding aren't you? I tried explaining the facts of life to Emma once, and she ended up thinking we were all descended from bumble bees.'

Rearranging the biscuits to disguise the absentees, Zee replaced the plate on the table and wiped a hand on the seat of his jeans – drawing Ally's attention to the fact that they were not his usual pair of ten-year-old, falling-to-bits Levis. 'New strides?' she enquired. 'That's not like you.'

Zee turned coy. 'Well, I wanted to look half-reasonable for later on,' he confessed. 'I'm going out for a drink.'

'What, with Brillo and Grouch?' Ally couldn't imagine anybody making an effort to look good for Zee's dishevelled mates-cum-occasional business associates.

'No! I'm sort of . . . seeing somebody.'

'Aaaah – a female somebody?' Ally beamed. 'I'm really pleased for you. Who is she, what's she like?'

'I don't really know yet,' Zee admitted, 'this is our first date. She's one of the mums from Emma's gymnastics club.' He fidgeted in schoolboy embarrassment.

'Well, I hope she turns out to be really nice.' Across the hall, somebody shouted, 'Can you take your seats please, we're starting in five minutes.' 'Better sit down, I guess, or we'll get detention for talking at the back.'

It took an eternity to get everybody settled, read through the minutes of the last meeting and list all the apologies for absence. By the time the committee had meandered its way through half of the agenda, Ally could feel her eyes closing. It had been a busy day at Pussy Willows, with several new children to settle in, and she could just go for a nice little sleep in a comfy chair . . .

A couple of minutes later, Zee woke her with a razor-sharp elbow to the ribs. 'Ow!' she squeaked, throwing him a filthy look.

'What was I supposed to do? You were snoring!'

98

'I so don't snore!' she hissed back.

'Hah!'

Fortunately Zee's timing was perfect, as it was finally time for the interval, complete with builders' tea and overpriced biscuits. 'Quick cuppa and I'm off,' confided Ally to Zee as they made a beeline for the man with the kettle.

'But it's only half-time. We haven't even got to "Election of Officers" yet.'

'If I have to sit through another hour of Madam Chairman's thoughts on the cultural relevance of Alan Ayckbourn I won't just be snoring, I'll be comatose! No, I'm definitely going home, and if I were you I would as well.' This time it was her turn to make with a theatrical eyebrow-wiggle. 'You don't want to keep your lady friend waiting.'

As luck would have it, just as Ally put her cup down and stuck one arm into her coat, Madam Chairman herself – the formidable Doreen Grey-Burroughs – cut a swathe through her acolytes and headed right for her. Oh no, thought Ally; either she's going to propose me for treasurer again, or she's found out why Bill Sykes' dog was sick all over Oliver on the opening night . . .

'Alison, my dear,' boomed Mrs Grey-Burroughs, 'surely you're not leaving already?'

Ally mumbled something vaguely credible about being let down by the babysitter, making sure not to catch Zee's eye as she did it.

'Oh, that's a pity. I was hoping to persuade you to stand for the committee this year. Never mind though, at least I can give you this before you leave.'

Ally looked down at the substantial tome that had just been shoved into her hands. 'What's this?'

'The score of *The Sound of Music*, of course! You haven't forgotten, have you, dear? We're thinking of doing it for our autumn production. I know we won't be starting rehearsals until after the summer break but I just wanted to know I could count on you for Maria.'

'Oh shit!' The words escaped from Ally's lips faster than her brain could censor them, producing a momentary flicker of distaste on Madam Chairman's face. 'Sorry. Yes, you're right, Doreen, I did say I *might* audition for the part.'

Doreen wagged a reproving finger. 'If you recall, I think it was a little stronger than *might*,' she teased. 'And with your lovely, pure soprano voice and your slim, youthful figure . . . '

Beside her, Ally heard Zee choke as he struggled not to laugh. There's really no way out of this, she thought, except to tell it like it is. So she did.

'I'm really sorry, Doreen,' she began quietly. 'I would have loved to play Maria, but just between you and me, I'm afraid I've just found out that I'm . . . um . . . pregnant again and I'll be having the baby right in the middle of the Autumn season.'

Doreen Grey-Burroughs' features hovered between annoyance and benevolence. Perhaps surprisingly, benevolence won out. 'You're expecting another baby? Oh that's splendid! Congratulations, my dear. Your husband must be thrilled.' There was a short silence, while Ally worked out how best to respond to this most awkward of statements. Something inside her screamed to tell them the whole truth about the baby and be damned; but she felt bad enough about letting out the secret of her pregnancy before she'd even told the kids, or her own mum and dad.

'Well, you know,' she said with an awkward smile. 'Anyhow, I'm really sorry about Maria, but it just can't be done.' She turned away, had another thought, and turned back again. 'Er . . . about the baby. I'd be awfully grateful if you could keep it to yourselves just for a little while. It's very early days, you see, and you know how it is: anything could happen.'

The following morning, when Luke tramped wearily into the ChelShel office, weighed down by the day's mail, he found Chas already at his desk, stoically working his way through a list of telephone numbers, and as usual trying to find homes for the un-homeable. 'Strewth, you're keen. How long have you been here?'

'Oh, only a couple of hours,' Chas replied with his usual diffidence. 'When you're trying to house people, there just aren't enough hours in the day.'

'Any luck?'

'Hm, sort of. That new Church housing association in Gloucester says it might have a vacancy in a couple of months' time.' Chas sighed. 'Which isn't a whole lot of use when you've got people sleeping in shop doorways right now.' He glanced up at Luke's morose expression. 'You don't look like you're having a good day, either – and it's only just started.'

100

'Oh, sorry; I didn't realise it was that obvious.' Luke dumped the pile of mail onto his desk. 'It's nothing really. Just, you know, the usual.'

'The baby, you mean? Is something wrong?'

Luke shook his head. 'No, not really. Not with the— not the way you mean.' He realised with a start that he couldn't bring himself to say the word 'baby'. 'Ally accidentally told some busybody at her drama club she's pregnant last night.'

'She's pregnant?' Chas's face registered mild surprise. 'I thought whenever it happened you were going to wait until three months.'

'We were.' Luke sighed and sat down. 'It wasn't Ally's fault; she didn't have much choice. She was pestering her to play the lead in *The Sound of* sodding *Music* – in October.'

'Oh, I see. And she actually told her about the surrogacy arrangement?'

'No, she didn't go that far,' admitted Luke. 'Thank goodness. I mean, we haven't even told the family yet.'

'Hm.' Chas put down his pen and sat back in his chair. 'It's only putting it off though, isn't it? And you won't be able to do that forever.'

Luke shifted uncomfortably on his rickety chair. 'Yes, yes, I know it's stupid trying to keep things under wraps, seeing as pretty soon *everybody*'s going to know about it.' A note of slight irritation entered his voice. 'I'd just like a chance to get my own head round it first.'

'I'm sorry you're having a hard time coming to terms with it,' said Chas. 'Truly I am. And you know if there's anything at all I can do to help ... '

Luke nodded. 'I appreciate that, mate; thanks. But you still don't agree with it, do you? The whole idea of it, I mean.'

'Surrogacy?' Chas rubbed his furrowed brow. 'Well, let's say the Church's position on it is ... not entirely consistent. On the one hand there's no doubt that your wife's creating a life for the purest, most altruistic of reasons, and that's a wonderful thing. Plus, some would argue there is a Biblical precedent: Abraham in the Old Testament has a baby with his serving girl, with his wife's agreement. But on the other, if I was wearing my dog collar I'd be expected to warn you that surrogacy is interfering with God's will. That it offends the child's dignity, interferes with the mother–child relationship, damages the sanctity of marriage ... '

'Great,' said Luke bitterly. 'So you do something wonderful and you go to Hell for it?'

'I don't think it's quite that simple, Luke. In fact I'm sure it's not. All we can do is have the best heart we can, and listen to what it tells us. God knows, I've had my own dark moments these last couple of months. I won't try to pretend my faith hasn't been tested.'

The two men sat in silence for a few moments.

'I don't believe it can be a bad thing, I just don't,' Luke said finally.

'Neither do I,' replied Chas. 'Not in my heart.'

There was another short silence, then Luke's gaze drifted to the office clock. At the periphery of his consciousness, two telephones started ringing simultaneously. They would wait.

'It's nearly lunchtime,' said Luke. 'Don't suppose you fancy going for a drink?'

Chas already had his coat on. He grinned. 'I thought you'd never ask.'

# Chapter Eleven

Bent over the downstairs toilet at 22, Brookfield Road, Ally gave a final heave and wiped her mouth on a square of tissue. Ah, good old morning sickness; somehow the memory of it faded between pregnancies, so that when it happened again, it invariably came as a nasty surprise. And just to add insult to injury, it wasn't even morning.

Still, never mind. What was it her mum was always saying? 'The sicker you are, the more secure the pregnancy is, dear.' Rationally, Ally was quite sure that was complete bollocks, but she clung to it as a comforting thought.

Outside the door, she could hear Josie giving her father a loud news bulletin.

'Mummy's face went all yellow, and she put her hand over her mouth, only the sick sort of squished its way out through her fingers—'

'It was gross,' agreed Kyle, with the kind of relish that only a small boy can muster up. 'Some of it went on the carpet,' he added as a delicious afterthought.

A swiftly-stifled curse hinted to Ally that Luke had just found the vomit on the carpet – with his foot.

'And then Mummy ran in the toilet and she bolted the door, and we could hear her being sick,' Josie prattled on. 'She's been sick every day this week, Daddy. Is she going to die?'

That, thought Ally, is my cue to face the world again. I may look and feel half dead, but I don't want to be buried just yet.

She slid back the bolt and stepped out into the hallway. 'There'll be no dying in this house,' she announced firmly.

'Oh good,' beamed Josie. 'Can we still have chocolate muffins for tea then?'

The mere thought of muffins, chocolate or otherwise, sent Ally's stomach plummeting back into the queasy vortex, but she swallowed hard and got on with what had to be done.

'I expect so,' she breezed. 'But first, you two come and sit in the lounge. Daddy and I have something we'd like to tell you, haven't we, Daddy?'

Luke's mouth flapped open. Grabbing Ally by the arm, he marched her round the corner into the kitchen and started speaking in a kind of *sotto voce* hiss. 'We haven't even told your mum yet!'

'Or my dad.'

'Oh, he doesn't matter, he just goes with whatever she says. But if she thinks we told the kids before we told her, she'll go mental!'

'And you don't think she's going to go mental when we tell her anyway?'

The logic of this point left Luke powerless to respond. All he could manage was a nod of resignation and a quiet groan to himself. Then he and Ally went into the lounge.

The kids, being kids, were busy trying to guess what Mummy and Daddy were about to tell them.

'We're getting a pony,' decided Josie. 'A pink one.'

'There's no such thing as pink ponies!'

'Yes there are! Or a guinea pig,' she added moments later. 'Guinea pigs are nice too but I don't want a pink one.'

Kyle rolled his eyes. Little sisters: all they ever did was have ridiculous fantasies and generally get in the way. 'No, we're in trouble,' he informed Josie in a voice that bore witness to years of experience. 'They only make us go in the lounge when it's something really serious.'

Luke and Ally came in and sat down on one of the two sofas which faced each other across the rather battered but cosy Bennett living room. The other was occupied by Kyle and Josie, Kyle looking like a prisoner in the dock who couldn't quite remember why he was on trial.

'You're not in trouble,' announced Luke. 'We've just got something important to tell you, that's all.' Hard swallow. 'Mummy's having a baby.'

Kyle and Josie looked at each other. Kyle shrugged. 'Whatever.'

Josie looked rather less pleased. 'Is it a girl baby or a boy baby?' she demanded.

'We don't know,' Ally answered honestly. Miranda had made

the decision that she didn't want to know before the birth, so nobody else was going to, either. 'And right now, it's just a tiny little blob in my tummy.'

'The thing is,' Luke went on slowly, picking his way through the minefield, 'this baby's a little bit different.'

Kyle's ears pricked up. 'Is it a mutant?' he asked hopefully.

Ally tried to keep a straight face. 'No love, it's not a mutant. It's just a baby. But this baby isn't like you or Josie. It's not your mummy and daddy's baby. It's Auntie Miranda and Uncle Gavin's. Mummy's just taking care of it for them.'

This clearly stretched juvenile understanding beyond breaking point.

'Why can't Auntie Miranda look after it?' Josie wanted to know. 'She's got a much bigger house than we have.'

'Weeell,' explained Luke, 'it's all because Auntie Miranda was poorly a long time ago, and now her tummy can't take care of a baby while it's growing. So your Mummy said she would look after it in her tummy until it's born. Isn't that kind of her?'

'Oh. OK.' Kyle thought for a moment. 'Is that it?'

'What?'

'Is that all you were going to tell us, 'cause if it is can I go back out with my skateboard before tea?'

Ally looked at Kyle's little sister, who was still wearing an expression of extreme scepticism. She was quite obviously worried or annoyed about something. Perhaps I should have read this up in a book, or gone to see a child psychologist, anguished Ally, her heart beating faster as she thought of all the myriad psychological defects her kids would probably develop now that she'd done it all wrong.

Josie piped up: 'Mummy.'

'Yes, sweetheart?'

'The baby.'

'Yes.'

'It's not coming to live here with us is it?'

'No Josie, it's Miranda and Gavin's baby, so it's going to live with them in their house.'

'So if it's a little girl I won't have to let her share my bedroom?'

Ally almost laughed with relief. So that was it. Josie had only just had a grown-up bedroom makeover, and it was pretty obvious that her cool new boudoir was a privilege she wasn't going to share without a fight.

'No, sweetheart. You won't have to share your bedroom. I promise.'

'Well, I suppose it's all right then.' Josie's demeanour brightened considerably as she hopped off the sofa. 'Mummy.'

'Yes?'

Josie looked up at her mother with an angelic, dimpled smile. 'Can I help you make the chocolate muffins now?'

A couple of days later, Ally took a few hours off and accompanied Zee to the advance viewing for an auction on the outskirts of Cirencester.

'Posh people,' Zee informed her when she wondered aloud if the trip was really worth it. 'There's loads of them round Cirencester, with pots of dosh – Royals, even. Bound to be one or two forgotten gems in amongst the tat.'

As they drove along the winding road, Ally related the awkward conversation she and Luke had had with the kids. 'I told them I was looking after Miranda's baby in my tummy. Do you think that was OK? I mean, they seemed all right with it, but—'

'Good God, Ally, of course they're all right. Kids are amazingly adaptable, you know. Anyway, what else would you have told them?'

'How do you mean?'

'Well, I take it you weren't thinking of going into all the ... ahem ... ins and outs of artificial insemination?'

'Hm,' acknowledged Ally. 'You have a point there. They may want to know more, though. Kyle's already done a little bit on sex education at school.'

'Then I guess you'll just have to sit back and wait for the questions.' Zee hummed along to a track on the radio. 'Mind you, that's easy for me to say. I don't have to answer them.'

'You've done your bit,' Ally reminded him gently. 'When Sarah died ... '

Zee sighed. 'I suppose it's good really that Emma never got to know her mother. If she had, she'd miss her as much as I do.'

They sat in companionable silence for a little while, Ally reflecting that life was bloody cruel; but that even so, Emma was a lucky little girl. Zee made a better mother than a lot of real ones.

Eventually Ally broke the silence. 'Unfortunately it's not just the kids who'll be asking questions,' she said ruefully. 'Luke's mum's

106

bound to be cool with the whole surrogacy thing – she's often said she'd have given it a try herself if she'd had the chance – but God only knows what my mum and dad are going to make of it all.'

Zee flashed a startled stare at her. 'They don't know? I thought you were planning to tell them first.'

'We were. But we wanted to wait a while before we told anybody, just to be on the safe side. Then there was that business at the drama club, and just when we thought we'd handled that neatly, the kids started noticing me throwing up most mornings, so we didn't have much choice but to tell them.' Ally quailed at the thought of the coming weekend. 'Miranda and I are going over to see Mum and Dad on Saturday.'

'That'll be . . . fun.'

'Look on the bright side. If you hear an explosion, at least you'll know where it's coming from.' Ally wriggled restlessly in her seat, discomfited by the thought of Saturday's inevitable inquisition. That was quite enough of that. 'Tell me something nice,' she demanded. 'Something nice that's happened to you.'

Zee rubbed his nose thoughtfully. 'Well I must say, Kate and I are getting on very nicely at the moment.'

'Kate? The one you took out for a drink? Hey that's great! I didn't dare ask. Heck but I'm hungry,' she added, rummaging in her bag for something to eat and producing half a fluff-covered Wagon Wheel. 'Must be empty after all that puking. Ah well, waste not want not.'

'Ewww.' Zee averted his eyes as she bit into the unsightly biscuit.

'Go on,' urged Ally. 'You were telling me about Kate.'

'Let's just say we've been out twice more since that first drink, and last night she, um, invited me in for coffee.'

Ally giggled delightedly. 'Zee, you sly dog!'

'I know, I know.' Zee blushed with embarrassment. 'Normally, it's one date and they can't wait to get away. But for some reason, Kate actually seems to enjoy spending time with me. Baffling, I know.'

'Mystifying,' agreed Ally with a twinkle in her eye.

'Believe it or not, even her little girl seems to think I'm all right – and that's a first. I've lost count of the number of sprogs I've been loathed by. Even Emma thinks Kate's nice, and you know how difficult to please she is.'

'Well, don't knock it,' advised Ally. 'Just enjoy your good luck while it lasts. At least you know Kate's not a gold-digger,' she added. 'Seeing as you haven't got any gold to dig.'

'Only until I unearth the big find that makes my fortune,' Zee reminded her firmly.

'Zee love, you've been saying that for years now, and the best thing you've ever found was that first edition of a 'Mr Men' book. That's hardly going to fund a jetsetting lifestyle, is it?'

Zee sniffed. 'Oh ye of little faith. You just wait. This auction's going to be a good one, I can feel it in my bones.'

Ally swallowed her final mouthful of furry biscuit. 'Are you sure that's not rheumatism?'

'Oh, shut up, pie-face.'

Saturday came with the kind of grim inevitability usually associated with Monday mornings.

Just after nine am, when half of Brookfield Road was still prising its eyelids open after a heavy night on the beer, Miranda's shiny new 4x4 slid up to the front gate of number 22, announcing its arrival with a loud parp of the horn.

Luke tailed Ally to the front door. 'You don't have to go on your own. I could come with you.'

Ally was oh so tempted. But she knew she had to turn the offer down. 'It's sweet of you, darling, but this time I think Miranda's right. It's best if just the two of us do this.' She managed a little laugh. 'Me and Miranda versus the parents: now there's a novelty!'

The horn sounded again. Luke stuck his head out of the door and waved to Miranda to hold on a minute.

'I love you, you know,' Ally said with a smile. And they kissed.

'Me too. Now get in that car, and go and tell your ma and pa what's what.'

Never had the trip across Cheltenham seemed longer. A journey which usually took ten or fifteen minutes appeared to have somehow been stretched to incorporate as many red lights, roadworks, old ladies on bicycles and slow-moving tractors as possible. Ally twisted the strap of her handbag round her fingers, willing this to be finished and hoping she wasn't going to come over all nauseous in her sister's new car; while Miranda went on endlessly

108

about nursery furniture and how much she was hoping that Gavin would be a 'hands-on' father.

'I must send him round to you,' Miranda declared as they neared their parents' house.

'Gavin?' Ally nearly fell off her seat. 'What for?'

'Some parenting practice, of course! Between you and me, I don't think he's had much experience of babies.'

'Then again, neither have you,' Ally pointed out.

'True,' conceded Miranda. 'But I'm a woman, so all that mothering stuff comes instinctively, doesn't it?'

Ally wondered if Miranda was serious. Perhaps she ought to mention the rush of undiluted panic she'd experienced, the first time she was left alone with baby Kyle. There hadn't been much instinctive about the way she'd tried to put his nappy on the wrong way round; that was for sure. But no; it could wait. Soon enough, Miranda would discover that every parent had all the answers, that they were all different, and all equally wrong.

In any case, it was too late to have a conversation with her sister. The 4x4 was already turning into the drive of Farfrae, Maureen and Clive's neat little semi-detached bungalow. And worse: the two of them were standing at the lounge window, waving them in.

'This is all very unexpected, dear,' commented Maureen as she took Miranda's coat and hung it in the hall cupboard. 'And you've brought Alison with you.'

The way she said it, it was hard to make out whether she was pleased, horrified or just plain perplexed.

'You should have given us more notice,' she added reprovingly. 'Shouldn't she, Clive? I haven't even had time to make scones.'

'Never mind love, they're here now.' Clive gave both his daughters a hug. 'And I'm sure they haven't just come here for your baking.' He caught his wife's eye. 'Excellent though it undoubtedly is.'

Maureen relaxed into a beatific smile.

'As a matter of fact we've come to tell you something,' announced Miranda as the four of them sat in the lounge, drinking weak, milky coffee out of the same 'best' bone-china cups Ally remembered from her childhood.

'Really dear? What's that then?'

'Gavin and I are having a baby.'

109

Ally nearly choked on her biscuit. Maureen merely looked as if she might explode with pride, while Clive smiled and nodded like the dog on the back shelf of Ally's old car.

'Oh Miranda, that's *wonderful*!' gushed Maureen. 'I've been hoping for so long . . . but I kept thinking "no, she's too busy with her career to disrupt it by having children".'

'Er . . . Mum—', cut in Ally, but she was just getting into her stride.

'You won't believe this,' laughed Maureen, 'but when the two of you walked in here, I thought to myself: "My, but Alison's looking peaky. I bet she's got herself pregnant again." And instead, it turns out to be you!'

Maureen paused for breath, and Ally seized her opportunity to get a word in edgeways. 'Actually Mum,' she said, 'you were right first time. I'm the one who's pregnant, not Miranda.'

'Don't be silly dear, that doesn't make sense. How can Miranda be having a baby if you're the one who's pregnant?'

It was the moment of truth.

'Because Miranda can't have babies of her own,' Ally replied, more calmly and quietly than she felt. 'So I'm having one for her.'

Clive took off his glasses and rubbed them vigorously on his woolly cardigan. Maureen's jaw dropped. She stopped fussing around looking for the sugar tongs, and flopped back into her armchair. 'You? You and Luke? You're having a baby and giving it to Miranda?'

'Not exactly,' replied Miranda. 'Gavin's the father.'

Maureen's eyes widened in speechless horror. Clive started humming distractedly to himself, the way he did whenever a sex scene appeared on TV. It was patently obvious what was going through their minds.

'Hold on a minute!' Ally leapt in swiftly. 'Before you start thinking *that*, Mum, no we didn't! We went to a proper clinic. It was all very . . . clinical. And professional. With test tubes and stuff.'

'Dear God,' said Maureen faintly. 'I don't believe I'm hearing this. When—?'

'Well, I'm only about six weeks gone. The baby should arrive in late November or thereabouts,' replied Ally. 'Not that long before Christmas.' And a little shiver ran down her back. Putting it into words made it all feel extremely real and imminent, as if

110

someone had just set the timer on a bomb and it was now rhythmically counting down to the big explosion.

'Gracious me,' said Clive, pouring himself a cup of black coffee and downing it in one. Maureen merely stared at her two daughters, as though she had just realised that she'd given birth to aliens.

Miranda leaned forward and took her mother's hands. 'Aren't you excited, Mum? You're going to be a granny again!' She paused. 'Are you all right, Mum?'

Maureen shook herself. 'Yes dear. I'm perfectly fine. You'll just have to allow me a little time to get used to this. I haven't had such a shock since we found out your Great-Aunt Ethel's boyfriend was in the SS.'

'But this is a *nice* shock,' Ally pointed out. 'Isn't it?'

'Yes dear, it's all very lovely, but ...' Maureen rubbed her temples fretfully. 'It'll be a baby with two mothers. How can that possibly work?'

'It won't have two mothers,' Ally assured her. 'The baby might be growing inside me, but I've known from the start that it's not mine. It's Miranda's.'

'Then what will you be?'

It was a question that had exercised Ally a great deal lately, and she hadn't yet found the right answer, but Miranda and her mother didn't need to know that. So she smiled confidently. 'I'll just be its ... special auntie.'

Miranda slipped an arm through Ally's and drew her close. Closer than they'd been in years, thought Ally. Maybe closer than they'd ever been. It felt strange – but good.

'A *very* special auntie,' Miranda declared. 'Ally's one in a million, Mum. She really is.'

Ally was determined not to take Miranda's gushing too seriously – after all, it couldn't last – but even so, this fleeting experience of sisterly solidarity brought a lump to her throat. For once, she thought, I'm not the inconvenient spare part.

Her mother was still staring at her, wide-eyed and struggling to accept the reality of what was happening. Clive had vanished altogether, doubtless to panic in the comforting surroundings of his garden shed.

'I just don't understand, Alison,' Maureen said softly, shaking her head.

111

Ally perched on the arm of her mother's chair. 'Understand what, Mum?'

'You ... doing all this. For Miranda. You really want to go through all this sacrifice so your sister can be a mother?'

Ally nodded. 'I had to think about it for a while,' she admitted. 'But how could I say no? She's my sister. And it means everything to her.'

Maureen turned her face away, sniffed discreetly and deftly wiped away a tear, but not before Ally had seen it sparkling on her cheek. 'Are you OK, Mum?' she asked.

'Of course I am!' Maureen fanned herself with an embroidered napkin. 'It's just far too hot in here; your father's obviously been fiddling with the central heating again.'

It was freezing in Maureen and Clive's front room, but nobody contradicted her.

'You're very pale, Alison,' Maureen announced, snapping back into Efficient Mother mode.

'I told her that,' agreed Miranda.

'I'm naturally pale, Mum.'

'Too pale.' Maureen's eyes narrowed. 'Are you taking your iron tablets?'

'Yes, Mum.'

'And what about constipation?'

'Mum!' pleaded Ally, half laughing.

'A regular digestive system is very important,' Maureen scolded. 'Your cousin Deirdre's friend got so constipated that everything got pushed out, and they had to sew six inches of colon back inside her bottom. You don't want to get like that, do you?'

'No, Mum.'

'Don't worry Mum,' cut in Miranda. 'I'll be keeping a very close eye on her. She's going to give up chips and take a half-hour walk every day, aren't you Ally?'

'What is this?' Ally protested, only half jokingly. 'Pregnancy boot camp? I told you, sis – I'm doing this my way, remember?'

But deep down inside, she didn't really mind. It was nice to feel that they cared; even if it was more about the baby than about her.

At that moment Clive reappeared in the doorway, carrying a dusty wine bottle festooned with bits of old cobweb. 'Anyone for a small glass of peapod and dandelion 1983? Not for you Ally, of course.' He ignored his wife's protests. 'I know the sun isn't over the yardarm, dear, but I rather think this counts as a celebration.'

A couple of weeks later, Ally and Miranda were standing by Ally's dining-room window, cups of coffee in hand and gazing out onto a balmy late-April morning.

In the garden of number 22, Gavin was kicking a ball around the rough, weedy turf with Luke and Kyle – and proving that being a polo-playing toff didn't necessarily mean you couldn't also bend it like Beckham. Or, mused Ally, look fantastic in a pair of tight tracksuit bottoms. More fantastic than any bloke over thirty had a right to look . . .

She shook herself. Honestly Ally, she scolded herself; and you a respectable married woman! A moment later, Miranda's voice bored its way into her consciousness: 'I said, are you awake?'

Ally started. 'What? Sorry, I was . . . thinking.'

'He's doing well, isn't he?' Miranda beamed through the glass at her beautifully muscled husband. He wasn't even perspiring, Ally noted; whereas poor Luke was bent over with his hands on his knees, panting like an overheated greyhound. 'Natural father material, if you ask me. Still, I sensed deep down that he would be.'

'You know, I honestly thought you were joking!' commented Ally. 'About this "parenting practice" thing.'

'Ah well,' replied Miranda, 'that's where you went wrong. I *never* joke about anything.'

Except when you're laughing at some poor minion's expense, thought Ally, but this wasn't the time for a bout of sisterly bickering. 'Well, you certainly caught me on the hop,' she admitted. 'I open my front door to bring in the milk, and you're standing there with Gavin, announcing that you've brought Gavin for his first lesson!'

'Yes, well, I'm sorry I didn't give you more notice, only Gavin got an unexpected window in his diary. It's normally chocker on a Saturday. Nice pyjamas, by the way.'

Ally reddened. 'It's a good job it's not summer yet – I might not have been wearing any!'

This didn't seem to bother Miranda very much. Clearly she couldn't envisage her trophy husband being driven into a frenzy of lust by the sight of Ally, with or without her pyjamas on. Probably she was right.

'Parenting is a very serious business,' declared Miranda, as if it was something very new and exclusive, which Ally knew nothing about. 'And Gavin and I want to be really good at it.'

'It's not like passing an exam, you know,' cautioned Ally.

'Of course it isn't! But there are so many mistakes that can be avoided, aren't there? You only have to watch those reality TV shows with the hideous families where they eat nothing but burgers and even the dog's got an ASBO. Oh, and by the way, I want you to teach me everything you know about reusable nappies.'

'Er . . . not a lot,' confessed Ally. 'I always used the disposable ones.'

Miranda looked utterly scandalised. 'Oh Ally, how could you? Don't you realise what they do to the environment?'

'Yes,' sighed Ally. 'But there are only twenty-four hours in a day.'

'Well!' sniffed her sister, obviously unimpressed, 'our baby's bottom's having nothing but the finest Egyptian cotton next to it.'

'Good for you.' You're right of course, thought Ally. But I bet you come down off the moral high ground when you've got a week's worth of steaming nappies strung across your dream kitchen 'I suppose you could always use one of those expensive nappy services,' she conceded. 'After all, you can afford it.'

She and Miranda wandered out into the garden just as the kick-about was coming to an end. Gavin and Kyle seemed to be getting on like a house on fire, or at least there was a lot of air-punching going on, which in Kyle's world amounted to much the same thing. He didn't do air-punching with Luke, Ally reflected. Or with her. Only with other boys, and cool people. And nobody could say that Gavin Hesketh wasn't cool.

'I scored three goals,' Kyle announced proudly.

'Great,' enthused Ally.

'Two of them should've been disallowed though,' remarked Gavin.

'Shouldn't!'

'Should! You practically picked the ball up and ran with it!'

'No I didn't!'

The two of them threw insults back and forth until finally they fell about laughing. Luke wiped his sweaty face on the sleeve of his jumper. 'I think I'm getting too old for this,' he commented.

'Any chance of a cup of whatever you're drinking?'

Ally was alone in the kitchen, making more coffee and a hot chocolate for Kyle, when she heard footsteps behind her.

'I hope you haven't got muddy feet,' she warned.

'No miss, I wiped them on the mat before I came in.'

It was Gavin's voice. Ally swung round. 'Oops sorry, I thought you were Luke.'

'Sorry to disappoint you.'

Ally's mouth was suddenly dry. 'Oh, I wouldn't say that.' God, listen to me, she thought; he'll think I'm flirting. Anxiously trying to think of something sensible to say, she tripped over the corner of a mat and splashed half a carton of milk all over the worktop. 'Oh ... *bugger*!'

Gavin caught her as she stumbled forward, almost cracking her head on the corner of the fridge; and she found herself in his arms, gazing up into his eyes like in some love scene from a cheesy rom-com. 'Are you OK?'

'Fine, thanks,' she gasped, wriggling free and readjusting her cardigan to cover a little more of her burgeoning chest.

'Quite sure?'

'Positive.'

'Can't have you injuring yourself,' commented Gavin, pulling lengths of kitchen towel off the roll by the sink. 'Or that little one in there.' Ever so gently, he touched her belly, and she felt a shiver pass right through her.

Their eyes met. 'Does it feel strange, being pregnant?'

'Not the being pregnant bit. Just ... the circumstances.'

'You do realise how grateful I – we – are?'

Ally looked away. 'There's no need, really. Here, give me that kitchen towel and I'll mop up this milk.'

'No you won't, I'm not having you exert yourself.'

'Oh. OK then.'

Ally watched, entranced, as Gavin made a first-rate job of mopping, washing and even drying the worktop; then put milk in all the mugs, switched the kettle back on, and sat her down by the kitchen table. 'Sit there, and don't do anything,' he instructed. 'I'll make the drinks.'

'I'm not ill.'

Gavin's eyes crinkled at the corners as he smiled. 'Of course you're not. But you're a very special lady, and I want to look after you. I'm sure Luke does, too.'

As he got the drinks ready, Ally watched him. It was no hardship; Gavin Hesketh was more than easy on the eye. Fit and lithe, he moved like liquid gold, with just a hint of muscle suggesting the hidden strength in his slender body. Ally desperately forced her attention onto something else.

'You're enjoying being with Kyle, aren't you?'

'Very much. He's a great kid. I've always wanted a son, you know. A boy to do all those father–son things – take him to the match, teach him to row and ride a horse, maybe go rock-climbing—'

'But what about Josie?' cut in Ally. 'She's been up in her room all morning.'

'I guess she just didn't fancy a kick-around in the mud with the boys.'

'Girls play football too, you know.'

Gavin grimaced. 'Not very well though.'

'That's debatable! Zee's daughter's fabulous at it. And I know Josie plays at school sometimes. But anyway, you'll be doing something nice with her this afternoon, won't you?'

Gavin's brows knitted. 'Sorry?'

'What if this baby's a girl? Miranda doesn't want to know the sex till it's born, so it'll be a mystery right up to the last minute. And if you're going to have a daughter you're going to need some practice. You told me yourself, you don't know much about girls.'

'Well ... no,' he conceded, looking uncomfortable. 'But that's what an all-boys' public school does for you.'

'Yeah, so Luke's told me. But hey, all the more reason to practise!'

He scratched his ear. 'Yes, I guess you're right. But what do I do with her? I haven't a clue what little girls do for fun.'

'Easy!' Ally slid open the drawer in the rickety kitchen table she'd inherited from her mother's last clear-out, and pulled out a sheaf of leaflets. 'Hang on a mo. There!' She pulled out the one she wanted and thrust it into Gavin's hand. 'That's what little girls do for fun.'

Gavin gaped. 'Pink Pony World? What the *hell* is Pink Pony World?'

'Don't worry, Josie will tell you all about it. It's every little girl's favourite TV programme and now there's a theme park as well. It's only about half an hour by car, and she's been desperate to go for months.'

'Do I ... oh Jesus, can't I take her somewhere else? The pictures, or fishing or something?'

'Pink Pony World,' Ally repeated firmly. 'If you want to make a little girl very happy, that's where you're going this afternoon.'

'Well,' replied Gavin, pocketing the leaflet with a sigh, 'OK. I'll probably have nightmares about pink ponies for weeks afterwards; but if it makes *you* happy, it's worth it.'

# Chapter Twelve

The next time Ally met up with Zee, they were sharing the touch-line at an end-of-season football match in the North Gloucestershire under-nines' league, while Molly – Zee's beloved mongrel – charged about adding vocal encouragement.

'She's quite a girl, your Emma,' commented Ally appreciatively, as a blue and white blur zipped down the right wing with the ball at its feet.

'Certainly is,' agreed Zee, eyeing his daughter's ball-control skills with fatherly pride. 'She reckons when she grows up, she's going to be the first woman player in men's professional football. And knowing her, she will.' He smiled to himself, just a little wanly. 'She's totally pig-headed, just like her mother.'

'You can be pretty obstinate yourself,' Ally reminded him. I reckon most people would have given up the bargain-hunting business by now, but not you. It's a good job you still get some design work to pay the bills, or you'd probably be one of Luke's clients by now.'

Zee chuckled. 'Emma would never forgive me if I gave up. And believe me, you don't want to be on the wrong side of my daughter.'

Ally shuffled her feet, grateful that she was watching rather than playing. She needn't have turned up this week, as Kyle was only on the bench; and she'd certainly have preferred a day out with Luke and Josie. But Zee didn't know the first thing about football, and she knew he liked to have someone to talk to while he pretended to understand what was going on, and jab him in the ribs when it was time to jump up and down and make excited noises.

'Kate couldn't come today then?' she enquired.

Zee shook his head. 'She did a night shift at the General and she's sleeping it off at hers. That's the trouble with bank nursing, you just have to take what you're offered. But there aren't any permanent jobs going at the moment.'

'Still, she's not been in Cheltenham long, has she? Something'll turn up. After I had Josie, it took ages to get the job at Pussy Willows. Good nursery teaching jobs are a bit thin on the ground.'

'So what do they reckon about the latest Ally Bennett production?' Zee pointed to Ally's stomach.

'Actually they've been great about it. Very, well, modern. Believe it or not, the mums all think I'm some kind of saint. Silly, isn't it?' She watched Emma thunder towards the opposing goal, liquid mud dripping from her socks. 'Come on Emma, go for it, you can do it!' It was time to nudge Zee, who promptly joined in with some shouting and an enthusiastic wave of his scarf. A murmur of interest swelled through the assembled parents and hangers-on, and then ... 'Aw, bad luck. Good shot though, Emma.'

'From what Luke told me, it sounds like Gavin's pretty impressed with you too,' remarked Zee. 'What's all this I hear about tickets to the opera?'

Ally reddened. 'He just got a couple of freebies, that's all. And Miranda *loathes* opera. She thinks it's just a load of fat people shouting at each other in Italian.'

'You mean it isn't?'

'Oh no,' replied Ally with a grin. 'Sometimes they shout in German. Anyhow,' she went on, 'I happened to let slip that I've always wanted to go to the opera, and he reckoned I could do with a treat. Only problem is, Luke hates opera too, so he won't go with me. I was going to tell Gavin to forget it, and then Miranda volunteered him to go with me instead. Poor bastard.'

'Hm.' Zee rubbed his chin. 'Sounds more like he wins on all counts to me.'

'How do you mean?'

'Well, he gets a trip to the opera and he doesn't have to go with Miranda. Now that's what I call a result.'

Ally choked on a laugh and it turned into a cough. Out of the corner of her eye she noticed that Emma's team seemed to have gained an extra player. 'Er ... Zee.'

He was rooting in the pockets of his voluminous vintage over-coat for another Mint Imperial. 'Yeah?'

Over on the other side of the field, the referee's whistle was shrieking itself to death. All along the touchline, parents and siblings were falling about laughing. 'Don't look now Zee, but I think Molly's—'

Something big and hairy came lolloping across the field and proudly deposited something mud-smeared, shapeless and more than a little chewed at her beloved master's feet.

Zee looked up. 'Molly's what?'

'Stolen the ball.' Ally stooped to retrieve the deflated object, watched by twenty-two baleful eight year-olds. 'Do you suppose they carry a spare?'

It's only a night out in Birmingham, Ally chided herself a few weeks later, as she scrutinised her reflection in the cheval mirror one last time. It's hardly in the same league as Covent Garden, is it? And why are you worrying about it anyway? You're not going on a hot date; Gavin's your brother-in-law.

All of which was true; but of course everything was so much more complicated, now that the baby was on the way. Not just *the* baby, she reminded herself; *our* baby – mine and Gavin's. She corrected herself: Miranda and Gavin's. I'm just the means to an end. The problem was that it didn't always feel that way. How, she wondered, were you supposed to divorce yourself from the growing life inside you; spend nine months and a bit taking meticulous care of it, while all the time being careful not to become too attached – as though it were a trainee guide dog and you were a puppy walker?

I wonder what you'll be like, she pondered, looking down at her stomach: at four months beginning to swell, hinting at the complete miniature person developing inside. Who will you be? Will you grow up to be like me, or Gavin – or Miranda? Or someone who surprises us all?

Maybe Gavin was asking himself the very same things.

She grabbed her coat and headed downstairs. Gavin and Luke were sitting in the lounge, about as far apart as it was possible for two people to be in one small room. Luke was slumped in his usual armchair, dressed in his old tracksuit bottoms and a shapeless T-shirt, looking pale and utterly exhausted. Gavin on the other hand looked – as usual – as if he had just walked off the set of a menswear fashion shoot. He was perched on the edge of the Bennetts' lumpy cat-hair-encrusted sofa, clearly wondering just how much of its encrustations had already adhered to the seat of his charcoal-grey trousers. It was a look of such discomfort that Ally couldn't help but smile.

As she came into the room from the hall, both men looked up. Gavin's expression visibly brightened. 'Ally, you look gorgeous. Doesn't she, Luke?'

'She always looks gorgeous,' replied Luke, the last two words turning into a yawn. 'Sorry love, I'm a bit buggered after last night.'

'I can't say I'm exactly surprised,' commented Gavin. 'Walking the mean streets of Gloucester at two in the morning, looking for down and outs, is my idea of hell.'

'Just as well you're not the one doing it then, isn't it?' replied Luke, with a glance that indicated more irritation than bonhomie. He turned back to his wife. 'Have a great time, love. Sorry I'm not coming, but you know what I'm like with opera. If I can fall asleep in *Cats*, imagine what I might do in *The Magic Flute*.'

'That's OK, I understand.' Ally shrugged her arms into her coat. 'Make sure you check on Kyle, or he'll be on that computer all night – and if Josie can't sleep, read her—'

'I know, I know. The story book about the pink ponies.'

Gavin groaned. 'God, not more pink ponies. You know, I swear those three hours at Pink Pony World were the longest of my entire life.'

Ally laughed. 'That's funny; Josie wanted us to take her back there again the next day! That's little girls for you.'

Gavin pulled a face. 'What age do they grow out of the bloody things, anyway?'

'Oh, about the same age they start getting interested in boys, I should imagine,' replied Ally. 'So we've got that to look forward to, haven't we darling?'

'Quite,' agreed Luke. 'All those sleepless nights, sitting up waiting for them to come home. All the arguments about unsuitable boyfriends. When you look at it like that, pink ponies aren't all that bad.'

'Hm.' Gavin didn't sound too convinced. 'Thank goodness for boys, that's what I say. I know where I am with a kid who likes paintball and motorbikes. I'm not even sure Josie likes me, you know ... '

'Don't be silly,' scoffed Ally. 'You're her uncle, of course she likes you. You know,' she went on, 'Zee's little girl wants to be a car mechanic when she grows up – if she can't be a professional footballer.'

'A mechanic? God help us. Before you know it she'll be painting all the hubcaps pink, and trying to change spark plugs with two-inch stick-on fingernails.'

Ally thought this was a bit over the top and was about to say so, but Luke beat her to it. 'I didn't realise you were an old-fashioned sexist, Gavin.'

'Sexist? Don't be ridiculous! I employ lots of women.'

'As car mechanics?' enquired Luke.

'No – but only because I've never met one that could do the job properly,' retorted Gavin. 'It was a joke, Luke – a *joke*! Honestly, you can't say anything these days without being grabbed by the PC police.'

Ally could see that Luke wasn't about to let this drop, and felt a surge of irritation. OK, so Gavin's humour was a little off the mark, but he was a nice guy all the same, and besides, this was supposed to be her special night out, not an excuse for two alpha males to lock horns in her front room.

'Oh, Luke knows you didn't mean it, don't you Luke?' She directed a look at him which left no room for misinterpretation.

Luke let out an exasperated breath and capitulated. 'Yeah, sure. Whatever.'

But Ally could tell from the look in his eyes that the chance of him and Gavin ever being best buddies was fast approaching zero.

Ally's eyes were sparkling as she and Gavin shared an interval drink in the theatre bar.

'Orange juice,' she pouted. 'I'd love a glass of wine.'

'Uh-uh.' Gavin wagged an admonitory finger. 'No alcohol for you, it's bad for ...' he paused, 'our baby.'

'Not even a teeny-weeny little bit?' she pleaded, half-jokingly.

Gavin relented. 'Well, maybe just one sip. A small one,' he added firmly. He lifted his glass to Ally's lips and watched her savour one tiny, delicious drop of the chilled liquid. 'You really miss wine, don't you?' he remarked.

122

'Hey, that makes me sound like an alcoholic!' she protested, giggling. 'I think I only miss it because I know I can't have it. I'm sure Miranda would be horrified if she knew I'd even *thought* about drinking.'

'I wasn't actually talking about Miranda,' admitted Gavin. 'I meant you and me. This is *our* baby, yours and mine. It is, isn't it?'

Ally felt a hot flush climbing her cheeks. 'Er ... technically, I suppose,' she said lamely. 'Biologically. But I'm having it for Miranda, remember.'

'Yes, of course. All the same,' Gavin stretched out a hand and stroked her burning cheek, 'it means there's a very special bond between you and me, and I think there always will be.'

A delicious shiver ran down her spine. 'I ... guess.'

He gazed deep into her eyes. 'Never underestimate yourself, Alison. You're a very special person. You know, it's a pity Luke couldn't come tonight. Sometimes I wonder if he really appreciates you.'

Ally didn't admit that, just occasionally, she wondered that herself. Or the fact that since she'd become pregnant this time around, she'd been feeling less appreciated rather than more. 'Oh, he works hard; he gets tired,' she replied. 'And opera really isn't his thing. Or anything on the stage, really.'

'You don't mean he really did fall asleep in *Cats*?'

Ally nodded.

'Good God, if he can sleep through that racket he could sleep through the end of the world!'

'He'd been up for thirty-six hours straight,' Ally explained, sipping at her orange juice. 'That's the nature of the job. Occasionally, if there's some kind of crisis, I don't see him for a couple of days.'

Gavin shook his head. 'I don't know how he can do it,' he declared. 'If you were my wife I'd want to come home to you every night.'

Ally didn't know where to look, or whether to be flattered or embarrassed; so she quickly changed the subject. 'Thank you so much for bringing me tonight; I'm having a brilliant time.'

'My pleasure. Can I get you another drink?'

She shook her head. 'Better not. Pregnancy's playing hell with my bladder, and I don't want to have to sneak out in the third act.

But I wouldn't say no to to one of those amazing ice-cream sundaes.'

'Eating for two?' he enquired with a smile.

'No, just being a pig,' she replied cheerfully, and they laughed together.

As the five-minute bell went and everyone threw the remains of their gin and tonics down their throats, Ally cast a little side-long look at Gavin. God but he was handsome. And intelligent. And interested in all the things she was interested in. It's a good job we're both taken, she thought to herself as they headed back to their seats; because tonight is starting to feel dangerously like a date – and I'm loving it. Instantly a backwash of shame engulfed her. What kind of woman are you, Ally Bennett? she scolded herself. You're pregnant, for God's sake – you're supposed to be all pure and serene, not lusting after other people's husbands! Especially when they belong to your own sister.

'It was wonderful,' Ally enthused as she and Luke stripped wall-paper in their bedroom the following evening. It had been crying out for redecoration ever since they moved in, but somehow there had always been something more important to do; and now, five years later, the walls still boasted the same two, hideously clash-ing patterns, glaring at each other across the double bed. Miranda had frequently offered to send along some of her minions to take care of the job, but they'd always resisted. They didn't mind accepting donations of posh paper and paint, but this was their home and Ally in particular wanted to feel that they'd created it themselves, wonky wallpapering and all.

'Good,' said Luke, his face a mask of grim concentration as he hacked away at five layers of wallpaper, sandwiching a coat of purple gloss paint. 'I'm glad you enjoyed it.'

'Gavin knows such a lot about opera,' Ally went on, filling up the steam stripper from a watering can.

'I bet he does,' muttered Luke, almost inaudibly.

Ally straightened up. 'Sorry?'

'I said, I'm sure he does,' Luke replied, raising his voice. 'Anyhow, you had a nice time and that's what matters.'

'I'd have had a nicer time if you'd come too.'

Luke pulled a face. 'I very much doubt it. For one thing I don't

124

look half as good as Gavin in a penguin suit, and for another, I'd either have been asleep or insane with boredom after the first ten minutes.' He threw Ally an apologetic look. 'All that screeching in Italian – it's just not for me, love.'

'It was in English actually.'

'So was *Cats*,' Luke reminded her. 'Let's face it, when it comes to things theatrical, I'm a complete dud.'

Ally could have reminded him of all the times she'd endured cricket matches and marched in public demos for his sake, but she wasn't into that kind of mean-spiritedness. He had allowed himself to be dragged along to see her in *Oliver* but only under sufferance. It was slightly sad really. Sad that this was something they could have shared, but he didn't want to try.

She decided on a different tack. 'Gavin's ever so excited about the baby.'

'I should bloody well hope he is!' exclaimed Luke. 'After the sacrifice you've made for him.'

'You don't like Gavin, do you?'

Luke groaned. 'Gavin's fine. Top guy. What do you want me to say?'

'Just that you like him.'

'All right then, I like him.'

'You don't though, do you?'

'What!' Luke threw down his scraper in exasperation. 'What did I just say?'

Ally picked it up and started on the same section of wall. 'Ever since I got pregnant, you've been funny about him. What's the matter? Is it jealousy or something?'

Luke opened his mouth as if to say something cutting, then closed it again. Stepping gingerly over the steam stripper, he put his arms round Ally's waist and drew her towards him. 'Why on earth would I be jealous of Gavin? I've got something he can never have.' He kissed her on the nose. 'You.'

Ally smiled and nuzzled a kiss into the crook of his neck. 'The kids are both tucked up in bed at their grandma's,' she murmured in his ear. 'Why don't you and I have an early night?'

'It was as if I'd just told him I was infectious,' lamented Ally, gazing sorrowfully across the café table at Zee. 'The minute I suggested an early night, it was "Oh, sorry, I'm really tired – and

125

besides, this wall really needs scraping." Like it hasn't already waited five years!'

'Oh dear,' sympathised Zee. 'So you think he's gone off you-know-what then, do you?'

'I don't think, I know. Since I got pregnant he barely wants a cuddle any more, let alone sex.' At the word 'sex', several heads turned; Ally stuck her tongue out at a seedy-looking bloke who was eyeing her over the top of the *Racing Post*. She lowered her voice and leaned forward. 'All I can say is it wasn't like this when I was pregnant with Kyle and Josie – quite the reverse.'

'So it's something to do with the fact that it's not his baby?'

Ally gave a non-committal shrug. 'Well . . . it certainly looks like it. But can I get him to admit it?' She stabbed her spoon into the rock-hard mound of brown sugar in the stainless steel bowl before her. 'Anyway, it looks like I've got another five months of celibacy to look forward to.' She eyed Zee critically. 'Why are you laughing? It's not funny!'

'I know, I know.' Zee fought off an attack of the giggles. 'It's not you I was laughing at, it's the situation. There you are, unable to, you know, get any; and here I am, hiding from Kate in a grotty café—'

An enormous woman in an apron swung round, almost decanting a plate of all-day breakfast into Zee's lap. 'Did you say my café was grotty? Because if you did, you can pay up and get out!'

'No, of course I didn't,' pleaded Zee. 'I love it here. These Spam fritters are delicious, really they are.' He forced a beaming smile as he swallowed down a big, greasy forkful. Once the enormous café-owner had grudgingly retreated behind her counter, Zee drank half a mug of tea in a single gulp. 'Oh God, got to get rid of the taste. Now, where was I?'

'Hiding from Kate in a *really nice* café,' Ally prompted him. 'But why?'

'Because, between you and me,' Zee glanced dramatically to left and right and lowered his voice to a whisper, 'she won't leave me alone.'

'How do you mean?'

Zee rolled his eyes ceiling-wards. 'Do you want me to draw you a picture, love? She can't get enough of me. It's all night every night, and all day as well if she can get the time off work. I'm completely exhausted!'

126

'And you're complaining?'

'Only a little bit,' Zee admitted. 'But I can see I'm going to have to start taking ginseng or something. I've never been irresistible before.'

'Well don't look at me,' sighed Ally. 'If you want to avoid having sex, maybe you should take some lessons from Luke. Though I suppose Gavin has had more practice at being irrestistible ...' she added without thinking. Try as she might, she couldn't tear her wandering mind away from her delectable brother-in-law, with the hard body, the soft voice and just a hint of Mr Darcy.

'What's this? Lusting after your sister's bloke? Tut, tut, Ally, and you a respectable mother of two – and a half!'

She waved away his teasing comments. 'Don't be silly. He's good-looking, yes, but he's absolutely not my type.'

'Added to which, he's extremely spoken for,' Zee reminded her.

'Quite. So you can wipe those disgusting thoughts right out of your mind!'

Zee smiled and nodded, and Ally imagined that she'd said enough to convince him. But words aren't always the most eloquent way to get a message across, and Zee was far from stupid.

He couldn't help noticing the way her eyes sparkled whenever she mentioned Gavin. To his way of thinking, that could only bring trouble.

Ally didn't really know why she did it. There was no need whatsoever for her to go and thank Gavin in person for their night out. She'd already sent him a thank-you card and spoken to him on the telephone; any more than that was overkill.

But the moment she heard from Miranda that Gavin was going to be in Cheltenham all day, she knew what she would be doing on her afternoon off. And it wasn't wallpaper stripping.

As she neared the front entrance to Napier House, where Gavin was working that day, Ally's nerve started to falter. She couldn't bring herself just to march up to the front desk and ask for Mr Hesketh. Fumbling in her handbag, she took out her mobile and started texting:

JUST PASSING, U FREE 4 COFFEE?

Her thumb hovered for a few seconds, then pressed 'send', and the message was gone. Ah well, if Gavin didn't reply at least it wouldn't be as embarrassing as asking for him and being told he was too busy to see her. That was what she told herself anyway.

In what seemed like the blink of an eye, a little envelope popped onto her screen.

ALWAYS FREE 4 U, BE DOWN IN FIVE. X

As she gazed at Gavin's message, everything came sharply into focus, her knees started to buckle and she almost fled. Thus far, it had all been a harmless fantasy, but now she was making assignations that she hadn't even told Luke about. Not that Gavin would misconstrue her meaning, she was sure about that. He knew perfectly well that this was exactly what it purported to be: two friends meeting for coffee. He couldn't possibly think she was interested in more than that.

Could he?

# Chapter Thirteen

'This feels so strange,' commented Miranda, sitting on the edge of Ally's bed while her sister finished getting changed into her comfy exercise gear. 'Here I am, expecting a baby in less than five months' time, and you're the one who gets to have the bump.' She eyed Ally's belly wistfully, though to the impartial observer it was barely any larger than normal. 'It doesn't seem quite fair, somehow.'

Ally pulled on the hideous jogging pants that had served her so well through her last set of prenatal classes. 'Don't forget I'm the one who gets the morning sickness and the constipation as well,' she reminded her. 'And even bumps aren't all they're cracked up to be, you know. Imagine trying to buy those chic designer clothes of yours with a big blobby belly. And think of the awful stretch-marks.'

Miranda acknowledged the truth of this with a rather sad little nod. 'All the same, I still wish it was me. And the sweetest little boutique's just opened in Stow-on-the-Wold, selling designer maternity wear.' A glint appeared in her eye. 'I could take you there if you like, buy you something ... decent to wear?'

Ally scrutinised her reflection in the cheval mirror. Her jogging pants were saggy around the crotch, with an indelible stain on the left knee, and she'd had the sweatshirt since her student days: the faded writing across the back read HOCKEY FIRST XI. 'I know I look a bit scruffy—' she began.

'A bit!' A peal of laughter rang round the bedroom. 'Ally love, if you were a tramp they'd sack you for letting the profession down.'

'But scruffy suits me,' protested Ally. 'It's comfy. And believe

129

me,' she added, 'once you're a mum you'll know how much that means. Look at Zee – he's a parent and he doesn't bother about fashion, does he?'

Miranda shuddered. 'I sometimes wonder how that best friend of yours can bring himself to leave the house. The last time we met, I seem to remember he was wearing pink moon boots, horrible old cords and the sort of jacket even a scarecrow would baulk at. I mean – *why*? The man could look almost human if he made an effort.'

'That's parenthood for you! The moment the little darlings pop out of the womb, all fashion sense goes out the window. Unless you're one of those yummy mummy types I guess ... and you don't see many of those down our local supermarket.'

'Hm,' replied Miranda. 'Well if I ever dress like you, you have my permission to shoot me. Oh go on, Ally, let me buy you some nice clothes – it'll be fun!'

Fun for whom? wondered Ally, who'd never been much of a shopaholic even when she had the money. But then she remembered her resolve to involve her sister as much as possible in the pregnancy, and relented. She knew it must be hard for Miranda to stand on the sidelines while her husband and sister got on with producing a baby on her behalf. 'All right then,' she conceded. 'But nothing silly, OK? Remember those orange jodhpurs you bought me? Kyle was so embarrassed he refused to let me pick him up from school.'

This small objection was waved away like a slightly annoying fly. 'He's a boy, Ally. Boys have to be taught how to be stylish. All except Gavin, of course – he's a natural.'

'Yes, he would be,' murmured Ally.

'He looks good in anything, but I think he's at his sexiest when he's in his polo gear. What do you think?'

Ally almost choked. She was feeling bad enough already about the close bond that was building up between her and her sister's husband, to say nothing of the couple of times they'd met up for coffee and not bothered mentioning it to anybody else. The idea of judging Gavin's sexiness was just a bit too much. 'I don't know,' she eventually forced out. 'Like you say, he looks good in anything.'

'Yes, you're right. And of course, you don't look at him in that way, do you? He's more like a brother to you. Silly of me to ask really.'

Ally consulted her watch. 'We should go, or we'll be late.'

Miranda looked surprised. 'We've got ages yet. Plenty of time for another coffee and a chat.'

'No, really, I think we should get going now,' urged Ally. The last thing she wanted was an extended tête-à-tête with her sister. 'The traffic might be bad. Come on.' She picked up her towel and pillow. 'Time for you to learn about the miracle of childbirth.'

The antenatal classes had formerly been held at the Cotswold General, in the Mildred McNulty Maternity Wing; but funding cuts and staff shortages had driven them across the road, to St Jude's church hall.

It didn't bother Ally – one floor was much the same as another, and the course tutor was a nice, down-to-earth midwife with lots of experience – but Miranda was incensed: 'They can't expect mothers-to-be to come here – where's the soft lighting and the comfy chairs? There isn't even a coffee bar!'

Several expectant mothers overheard this and fell about laughing. 'When's the last time you used the NHS, love?'

'Twenty years ago,' she replied proudly. 'And it was ghastly then. But this!' She shuddered and turned to Ally. 'I really think you should take my advice and go private.'

'But I don't want to go private.'

'I told you, I'll pay for everything.'

'Blimey, if somebody else was paying I'd go for it, love,' cut in the woman who'd burst out laughing.

'It's not about money,' Ally tried to explain. 'It's the principle of the thing. Besides, I know the staff at the General. They were great when I had Kyle and Josie.'

'Ah, but that was before they cut the funding and sent half the midwives to Gloucester,' remarked one of the other mothers-to-be, a lady so obese that even at nine months gone it would be hard to tell if she was pregnant or not. 'It's not what it was,' she added wistfully.

Miranda gave Ally a meaningful look, but she stood her ground. She'd always felt uncomfortable with private health care, private education – in fact, anything that meant there was one law for the rich and another for everybody else. If that made her old-fashioned, she didn't care. 'No,' she said firmly, and she threw an exercise mat at her sister. 'Here, lie down on that and behave yourself.

131

'Charming!' Miranda sniffed the mat. 'Ugh. How many other people have used it?'

'Don't even think about it love,' advised the large lady. She eyed the pair with interest. 'You two *together*, are you?'

'Yes,' replied Miranda.

'No,' Ally cut in hastily. 'Not the way you mean. She's my elder sister.'

'Oh.' The fat woman looked disappointed.

'Sorry.' Ally shrugged apologetically.

'Together? What's she on about?' demanded Miranda, straining to look over her shoulder as Ally dragged her away to a bare bit of floor.

'Just lie down and listen to the midwife, will you? I for one could do with a good relax.'

As the talk progressed from breathing exercises to pictures of dilated cervixes, Ally's mind wandered while Miranda frantically scribbled notes and asked complicated questions. I was right to bring her, thought Ally. It's all new and exciting to her. This way, she feels properly involved – even if she does come across as the class swot. Maybe I should take this thing one step further . . .

The midwife's soothing voice instructed them all to stretch out comfortably on their mats and imagine themselves on a faraway beach, lying on warm sand, listening to the waves swishing to and fro. It was the most delicious part of the class, the bit Ally had been waiting for; but she just couldn't get her body to relax. It was no good, her mind was too active. There was something she had to say before she could let go.

She rolled onto her side to deliver her momentous decision to Miranda. 'I think . . . I'd like you to be with me when I have my baby. In the delivery room.' She paused, waiting for Miranda's reaction. But nothing came. So she prodded Miranda in the side.

But the only sound that came out of her was a softly sonorous snore. Miranda was fast asleep.

While Miranda was enjoying a nice sleep on the floor of the church hall, Gavin was busy being the perfect uncle; at least in Kyle's eyes. Unfortunately, as he complained to Ally at their next coffee date, he was not having quite the same degree of success with Josie.

'I did try to think of her ... being a girl and all that – I did!'
His expression was so wounded-looking that Ally couldn't help
laughing. 'It's not funny you know!'

'I know, I know.' Ally wiped a tear from her eye. 'But did you
really think tickets to a football international at the Millennium
Stadium would be Josie's idea of the perfect present?'

'No, of course not! That's why I thought she might like a riding
lesson while Kyle and I were at the football. She is obsessed with
ponies after all,' he pointed out.

'Pink ones,' Ally reminded him.

'Pink, brown, orange – what's the difference?' Gavin threw up
his hands. 'Anyway, how was I supposed to know the damn thing
would bite her? The instructor swore blind it had a "lovely way
with children". And now Josie thinks it's all my fault.'

He looked up to see Ally smiling – not unsympathetically –
through his gloom. 'You think it's all my fault too, don't you?'

'Oh, I just think it might have been better if you'd thought of
something all three of you could do together. I mean, would you
like being sent off to do something else while your big brother got
to go out with your uncle and do something exciting?'

'But she hates football!'

Ally wondered how someone so smart, charming and intelligent
could be so thick. 'I'm not talking about football! You need to
think of something that both she and Kyle would enjoy.'

'Well Kyle refuses to go anywhere near Pink Pony World, so
that's right out. Thank God.'

'He does like animals though. And Josie's mad about anything
with fur.'

'I don't think a day out looking at my polo ponies is going to be
that exciting for them, do you?'

'Stop playing stupid, Gavin,' advised Ally.

Gavin looked like a crestfallen schoolboy, a lock of hair slipping
down over his forehead and just begging to be gently stroked away.
'Aw. But I like playing stupid with you – you make me see the
funny side of things. Even bloody ponies,' he added darkly. 'Life's
too serious sometimes, don't you think?'

Ally nodded. 'Sometimes. It certainly is for Luke. I mean, I care
about people too, but it's like he cares enough for twenty people –
and then some more. Just occasionally, it wears me out.'

'Miranda goes all serious on me sometimes,' remarked Gavin.

133

'Miranda, serious?'

'I know, I know. But it's that silly interior design business of hers – I thought it was just a hobby, but she's turning it into an obsession. As if she needs the money!'

'And then there's you,' pointed out Ally. 'You can get pretty intense about your work.'

'True,' he admitted. 'And when Miranda gets that way at the same time ... well, it's not exactly a recipe for sweetness and light.' He smiled at Ally. '"Sweetness and light", that's nice. It's exactly how I think of you.'

Ally's latte went down the wrong way, and Gavin had to pat her on the back, which if anything only added to her confusion. 'About this day trip,' she said, pulling herself back together.

Gavin raised an eyebrow. 'What do you suggest?'

'The zoo. There's a really fabulous one called the Animal Experience, and it's only a few miles out of Cheltenham, so nobody will throw up in your car.'

'I should damned well think not! That's real leather upholstery, you know.'

Ally laughed. 'I'd expect no less from you.'

He pouted. 'Are you saying I'm a snob?'

'Let's just say you appreciate the finer things in life.'

'Like you.'

Ally swallowed hard. 'Pardon?'

'You heard. Like you – and Miranda. My two ideal women.' He toasted them both in mocha. 'You know,' he added with a twinkle in his eye, 'it's a pity I can't have two wives.'

'If I didn't think that was a joke,' Ally said slowly, 'I would have to pour that vase of flowers over your head.'

He winked. 'I've told you before, Ally Bennett: I never joke.'

Now that Ally's pregnancy was progressing, she felt she was seeing babies everywhere. In fact, half the women she knew seemed to be pregnant. Even Ally's post-menopausal mother had put the fear of God into Clive by taking down all the old baby clothes from the attic and cooing about how she'd never really completed her family, and that nice doctor in Italy who could make you have a baby at seventy.

Ah well, thought Ally, patting her blossoming belly, at least I'm in fashion.

As was her old college friend Jude, mother to a six-month-old Churchill lookalike called Zak, whose current hobbies were eating, farting, filling his nappy and looking cute. Jude lived and worked on the other side of Oxford, and didn't often come over to Cheltenham; but the sensational news of Ally's surrogacy exploits had brought her up the A40 faster than a mouse after Gorgonzola.

'I can't believe this!' she squealed, laying a hand on Ally's stomach. 'And after all you said about never having another baby!'

'But I'm not really,' argued Ally. 'It doesn't count if it's for somebody else, does it?'

Jude wagged a gorgeously manicured finger that marked her out as a paid-up member of the yummy mummy brigade. 'Ah, but will you feel that way in a few months' time?'

'Of course I will.' Ally felt a tad uncomfortable under Jude's searchlight gaze. 'I have thought this out, you know.'

'What about Luke?'

'It was Luke who persuaded me to do it.'

'Good God, he really is a new man!'

'Yeah.' Ally felt a sudden urge to pour out all her misgivings about Luke and their lack of closeness, let alone a sex life; but it wouldn't do. It wasn't the kind of thing she could tell Jude. Ten years ago, sure; but they just weren't that close any more. She wondered what Jude was keeping from her for the same reason. 'So how's motherhood?'

'Completely wonderful, actually. And the university has even got a crèche now, so I can take Zak to work with me and breast-feed him at lunchtime! Can't I, sweetie?' She rubbed noses with her plump first-born, who gurgled appreciatively.

'I thought Seamus was going to stay home and take care of him?' Ally knew she'd said the wrong thing the minute the words left her lips.

'Er . . . I've been meaning to tell you but I wanted to do it when we met. Seamus and I aren't together any more.'

'Oh. I'm sorry.'

'Don't be.' Jude tossed her dark, bohemian locks in an ostentatious, see-if-I-care kind of way. 'Seamus turned out to be a grade A bastard – he was knocking off students right, left and centre and I never had a clue until I walked in on him in one of his "private tutorials".' She lowered her voice, although there was nobody else to hear. 'And you know some of them weren't even girls.'

'Oh God, that's awful. What did he have to say for himself?'

'Some crap about really loving me and Zak, but being "powerless to deny his fundamental sexuality". In other words, he wanted to have his cake and eat it. He hasn't seen Zak since he moved out. And I'm beginning to think it's good riddance.' She calmed down, slicked her hair back behind her ears and smiled. 'Is there any of that tea left? I'm parched.'

Ally was on the way back to the kitchen with the teapot when the doorbell rang.

'Hello,' said the beautifully groomed figure on the doorstep. 'Gavin's away and the design studio's closed for redecoration. So I thought I'd come and see you. Did you know you're pouring tea onto the doormat?'


'Gosh, this is exciting!' enthused Jude. 'Finally I get to meet Ally's famous sister!'

Miranda preened herself with obvious pleasure, crossing her legs elegantly on Ally's distressed sofa, and blissfully unaware that she was sitting in a big patch of Nameless's discarded fluff. 'Oh, not that famous,' she said with a smile. 'Not these days, anyhow.'

'Of course you are!' insisted Jude. 'First an international catwalk model, and now your own interior design company – your cushion covers are absolutely fab, by the way,' she added by way of an aside. 'And the vice-chancellor's wife swears by your hessian wall-coverings.'

'Ah, but I've got a new challenge awaiting me now, haven't I Ally?' Miranda looked to her sister for loyal support. 'I'm going to be a mother at last – the most important thing I've ever done!'

Ally knew that Miranda meant every word of that from the bottom of her heart, but she still managed to make it sound as cheesy as a Miss World contestant wishing for world peace. The habit of speaking in soundbites died hard.

'Isn't Zak a gorgeous baby,' purred Miranda, wiggling a finger in his gurgling face.

'I suppose you must be getting in lots of practice looking after babies,' beamed Jude, bouncing little Zak on her knee. 'You know, ready for the big day.'

'Well, er ... I'm going to the antenatal classes with Alison,'
replied Miranda. 'I'm sure that will stand me in good stead.'

'I think you might need a bit more than that, sis,' Ally hinted,
not for the first time.

'Oh yes, motherhood's absolutely overwhelming to begin with.
Then again, nothing can really prepare you for that, can it, Ally?'

'There you are then,' declared Miranda. 'Anyway, I'm sure I'm
a natural. Can I hold him?'

'Of course! Zak's such a sociable baby, he loves being cuddled
by everybody. There you go, darling, be good for Mummy.'

As Miranda took Zak in her arms, Ally saw something in her
eyes that she had never seen before: a joy and a light that seemed
to illuminate her whole body. And in that moment, Ally knew for
sure that what she was doing was right. Whether you liked her,
loved her or loathed her, this was a woman who wanted a child
more than anything else in the world, and it would have been
wrong to deny her that chance.

'Oh, he's just perfect!' crooned Miranda. 'Look at his little
fingers and his little toes, and ... ew! My skirt's all damp!'

Ally cringed. Jude laughed happily. 'Oh, has Mummy's little
darling wet himself then? Don't you worry, Mummy will soon
have you all lovely and clean and dry again.' She rummaged in her
changing bag for a spare nappy as Miranda held Zak at arm's
length, worriedly inspecting the damp patch on her Prada.

'I could change him for you if you like,' volunteered Ally, glad
of an opportunity to escape if Miranda was going to start moaning
about her skirt.

'No, no, I'll do it. Wait a minute though.' Jude giggled and put
her hand to her mouth. 'I've just had a much better idea. Miranda
can change him! Go on,' she urged, 'it'll be wonderful practice.
And it's so easy, isn't it Ally?'

Oh definitely, thought Ally. Not a recipe for disaster at all.

Much to his surprise, Gavin was not experiencing a disaster at the
Animal Experience. Quite the opposite. The zoo was brilliantly
laid out, there were loads of cute little fluffy baby animals for Josie
to drool over, and plenty of big scary ones for the boys to admire.
And they even managed a glimpse of the park's latest acquisitions:
a breeding pair of incredibly rare Javan yellow skunks, together
with their tiny, spiky baby.

With Kyle walking beside him, and Josie's small, sticky hand in his, Gavin felt for the first time like a proper uncle. After a few false starts, he at last had the feeling he was getting the hang of this. If parenthood was anything along the same lines, he might turn out to be quite good at it after all.

And then they came to the deer enclosure, complete with one very tiny, spotty faun, tottering behind its mother on fragile, spindly legs.

Josie was instantly entranced. 'Look, Uncle Gavin – Bambi!'

Hope and relief soared in Gavin's heart. At last: a subject he and Josie were both interested in. Deer! He liked deer; he had a big herd of them on his land. 'That's right, that's a baby deer. You like deer, don't you?'

Josie nodded emphatically. 'They're pretty. Can I stroke one?'

Gavin recalled some of his own less pleasant experiences. 'Better not – they'd probably just run away, but they might bite.'

This was music to Kyle's ears. 'Yeah – you stick your fingers out and they bite them all off,' he told Josie with gruesome delight. 'Then your hand, and then they swallow up your whole arm, until there's nothing left!'

Josie looked up at Uncle Gavin for reassurance. 'That's not true, is it, Uncle Gavin?'

'Of course not. Kyle, stop frightening your sister.' Hey, thought Gavin, now I'm really starting to sound like a parent! I'm the main man! 'I've got some deer at home on my land, haven't I, Josie?'

She nodded. 'Yes, I've seen them. Are they all your pets?'

'Not exactly,' admitted Gavin. What did they say: honesty was the best policy? 'I ... um ... turn them into venison.'

'What's venison, Uncle Gavin?'

Kyle stuck his face in front of Gavin. 'Dead deer, that's what venison is! He turns them into dead deer!'

Lower lip quivering, Josie put her hands over her ears. 'No he doesn't! I'm not listening!'

Kyle prised one hand away. 'Yes he does, yes he does! And then people eat them!'

'No, no! Uncle Gavin, tell him it's not true!'

Gavin threw Kyle a look of weary displeasure, then squatted down beside Josie with a sigh. 'Kyle didn't say it in a very nice way, but he's right,' he admitted. 'Lots of animals are kept for meat – cows, pigs, sheep, all kinds. And deer are the same. They

138

taste very nice,' he added as an afterthought. 'And they're very good for you.'

He should have known from the look of traumatised horror on his niece's face that he'd pushed the truth far enough. But being Gavin, he took it just one step further. 'You like venison too,' he said with a smile.

Josie's eyes bulged. 'No I don't!'

'Yes you do,' he reminded her gently. 'Remember that lovely stew you had at our house, the one you said was like beef only better?' He swelled with pride. 'That was venison from our very own herd.'

The awful wail that emitted from Josie's mouth caused a stampede in the deer enclosure, and the lion keeper came charging out of the zoo's kitchen block, convinced that somebody had just set off one of the emergency alarms.

'You killed Bambi!' squealed Josie. Then she kicked the squatting Gavin so hard in the shins that he toppled over backwards. 'You killed Bambi and then you made me eat him!'

Then she took to her heels.

As he lay on his back on the tarmac, with a giraffe looking down at him, he knew he'd been right all along. He really was never going to understand the fairer sex.

I shouldn't be surprised, Ally told herself. Why shouldn't Miranda be good at changing a nappy? I'm not going to be annoyed with her just because it took me a whole packet of the damned things to get it right when I first took Kyle home. I'm not that immature. Really I'm not.

It was vexing though, watching her totally inexperienced sister dealing with little Zak as though she'd been wiping babies' bottoms all her life. She seemed to have quite got over the damp patch, and was happily answering Zak's gurgles with baby-talk he seemed to find utterly fascinating as she lifted up his little legs and whisked away the dirty nappy from his little pink bum.

A good wipe, a little powder, a kiss on the tummy and he was lying on a nice fresh nappy.

'Bravo, most impressive!' exclaimed Jude.

'I told you I was a natural!' declared Miranda happily as she prepared to stick the nappy into position. 'All you have to do is – aagh!'

139

'Oh look, bless him, he's christened you!' giggled Jude as Miranda spluttered and wiped the wee off her face. 'That happens to everyone at least once, doesn't it Ally?'

'Oh, at least,' agreed Ally, not bothering to mention that actually, it had never happened to her. Suddenly, she felt a whole lot better.

# Chapter Fourteen

Gavin had more than a few things on his mind; and they weren't all connected with the challenge of impending fatherhood. Or the fact that Josie now regarded her Uncle Gavin as a serial killer of cute and cuddly animals. The truth was that, even with his life in a state of flux, Gavin's considerable business interests had to be kept going.

Others might have taken the opportunity to delegate; but there was quite simply nobody Gavin trusted enough to do his job for him; not even his long-suffering PA Karen, who had been known to travel up to Manchester with an ironed shirt at five minutes' notice.

Which was why he was standing in the conservatory at midnight, in his silk robe and slippers, having a heated conversation on his mobile.

'Listen, Grantley,' he seethed, 'when I bought that land from you, you swore blind there was outline planning permission for an equestrian centre – and you certainly never said a word about any rare bloody orchids! I'm going to have to consult my lawyers about this.'

An apologetic voice on the other end of the line babbled something about being every bit as surprised as Gavin.

'Surprised? How can you be surprised? According to the nature conservation bloke who contacted me, the damn things have been growing wild on your land since God was in short pants. And now I'm being threatened with an environmental assessment study before I can start building.'

He stopped for breath and Lord Grantley took the opportunity to get his side across.

'Extinct?' A note of wary relief entered Gavin's voice. 'You're telling me nobody's actually seen one of these things in the last twenty-odd years?' A glimmer of hope appeared on the horizon. 'Are you absolutely sure?'

'Well ... no,' admitted Lord Grantley.

'Idiot!' Gavin roared in frustration and flung his mobile into a heap of cushions on the rattan sofa, imagining it was Lord Grantley's head. He would have thrown it at the wall, but it was an expensive model and he didn't want to damage it.

For the first time in a long while, he felt distinctly stupid. He'd been so sure he was making a shrewd deal, but here he was, stuck with a piece of land that was worth precisely nothing if some no-account little weed decided to poke its leaves above ground when the environmental assessor came calling. By all accounts, the sheep's tongue orchid wasn't even pretty. It certainly didn't sound it.

Hm. He rasped a hand across his stubbly chin. If turning up these orchids on the land spelled disaster, somehow he was going to have to make sure the assessors didn't find any. But how?

When he returned to the bedroom, he found Miranda no longer asleep, but sitting up in bed reading *The Happy Little Baby Book*. He groaned. 'Don't you ever put that thing away?'

She frowned at him reprovingly. 'Just doing my homework, darling. It wouldn't do you any harm to read this, you know. It's full of practical baby-care tips.'

He kicked off his slippers and threw his robe over a genuine Biedermayer chair. 'Why would I want to know all that stuff?' he demanded.

Miranda looked at him as if he was mad. 'I'd have thought that was obvious! We're having a baby, darling, or have you forgotten?'

Gavin slid beneath the crisp cotton of the duvet cover, and sank into his wife's warmth with a sigh of pleasure. 'Of course I haven't forgotten! But so much of this parenting lark is instinctive, isn't it? You said so yourself.'

'Well, yes,' Miranda admitted. 'But there's all sorts of practical stuff we need to know as well – feeding, burping, nappy-changing—'

Alarm registered on Gavin's handsome face. 'Nappy-changing? Hang on, isn't that what nannies are for?'

This produced a look of intense disapproval from Miranda. 'Just because you had a nanny and your parents swanned around all day being terribly posh, that doesn't mean we're going to do the same,' she told him firmly. 'Alison and I didn't have a nanny, and ... well ... I turned out all right, didn't I?'

'No nanny?' The full implications percolated down into Gavin's consciousness. 'But that's impossible! Unless you're thinking of giving up your business?' he suggested hopefully.

Miranda was aghast. 'Don't be ridiculous, Gavin. We'll employ a couple of day-nannies, of course we will. But we'll have to manage on our own at night. I'm not having my child growing up thinking Nanny is its mother – like your friends all did. Actually,' she added, closing the book with a yawn, 'I'll probably get a manny.'

'A what?'

'A male nanny, Gavin, don't you know anything? One of those nice, healthy Australian boys who bring children up without giving them complexes. He'll be a nice substitute father-figure when you're away on business. Unless,' she added sweetly, 'you're thinking of giving up your business?'

'I'm not having some young hunk in my house when I'm not here!'

'Don't be so Neanderthal, darling – if they want to be nannies they're probably mostly gay anyway.'

'And I am not having a gay role model for my son!'

'Or daughter,' Miranda reminded him.

'Whatever.' Gavin flopped back onto his pillows. 'Why can't you just stay at home and be a proper mother, like Alison?'

Miranda's eyes narrowed. 'Alison doesn't stay at home, she goes out to work.'

'Yeah, but only for a couple of days a week. And she'd give it all up at the drop of a hat if the kids needed her.'

'Are you saying I'm going to be a bad mother because I'm not old-fashioned like my sister?' There was a warning flash in Miranda's eyes and Gavin wasn't about to ignore it.

'Of course not,' he answered with a wistful sigh. 'I guess I'm just a bit old-fashioned at heart, too. Sometimes I think I'd love to come home and find you in an apron, baking a cake.'

'Oh really?' Miranda seemed almost amused. 'So you'd rather come home to that than ... this?'

143

She pushed back the duvet and deftly unfastened the tiny pearl button holding her filmy negligee across her breasts. It fell away, exhibiting the kind of body women everywhere dreamed of achieving, and men of possessing. Gavin was no exception; in fact, where Miranda's charms were concerned he was a complete pushover.

'God, Miranda, you're irresistible.'

'I know,' she smiled, doing the button back up and rolling onto her side, with her back to him. 'Night, darling.'

And with that, she clicked off the bedside light, leaving Gavin feeling like he'd never sleep again.

It was another bright July morning and Ally was giving the whole house a really good clean. She was no housework fanatic (a quick glance at the inch-deep fluff behind the washing machine was enough to establish that); but there was something exhilarating about a proper cleaning session: something that had a lot to do with life and hope.

On the whole, Ally liked her life. There was enough teaching in it to keep her brain from going soggy, and enough time with the kids to reassure her that they wouldn't feel neglected. She was happy to have Luke too, even if his fluctuating moods did sometimes drive her mad. He was a good husband. She even liked being pregnant, despite all the petty ailments, annoyances and inconveniences.

The only thing she really didn't like was not knowing how to behave. This baby inside her: was it hers, or Miranda's, or hers and Gavin's, or somehow a part of all three of them? And if it wasn't hers, should she be forming any kind of bond with it? If I talk to you, she found herself silently addressing the foetus, the way I talked to Kyle and Josie, will you get too accustomed to my voice and come to think of me as your mother? Worse, will I come to think of you as my child? Is it better to try and cut myself off from you altogether – as if you're somehow not really there at all?

But a baby-bump wasn't something you could just ignore, like a verruca or a piece of irritating lift music. As the baby inside the bump grew, so did its presence, its pervasive personality. Already she sensed that it was dangerously close to becoming a person, especially now that it had begun to move inside her.

She was still deep in thought ten minutes later when the phone

144

rang. Duster in hand, she made a grab for the receiver. 'Hello?'

'Alison dear, it's Doreen,' boomed a voice that carried like a foghorn across the Severn estuary. 'Doreen Grey-Burroughs.'

'Doreen. Hi. Lovely to hear from you.' Ally's brain worked feverishly, trying to recall what she was supposed to have done but hadn't. Whatever she'd forgotten, Doreen clearly hadn't. Elephants looked like amnesiacs compared to the chair of St Jude's Dramatic Society.

'Just called to see how you are, dear.'

'Oh. Very well, thank you.' Alison relaxed a little. Stop being paranoid, she scolded herself. Doreen's not after you for anything; it's just a nice friendly chat.

'Excellent, excellent!' There was a small hiatus, and then Doreen added: 'Actually, I did ring up to ask you something as well.'

I knew it! thought Ally. 'What, exactly?' she enquired.

'Well, to paraphrase the, er, musical score itself, we're not entirely sure how to solve a problem like Maria. Eleanor Bassenthwaite's let us down by moving to the Isle of Mull, which leaves us without a soprano lead. And as you know, rehearsals start at the beginning of September – that's barely a month left to reorganise everything!'

'If you're asking what I think you're asking, the answer's no,' declared Ally. 'I told you, I can't possibly play Maria if I'm eight months pregnant!'

'No, no, dear,' soothed Mrs Grey-Burroughs. 'I wouldn't dream of asking such a thing.'

'You wouldn't?'

'Of course not. But I did wonder if you could help us out just a teensy weensy bit.'

'By doing what?' demanded Ally, expecting an invitation to paint scenery or search Cheltenham for plastic edelweiss.

'Playing the mother abbess.'

'What!' Ally was too stunned to laugh. 'Doreen, a massively pregnant nun is even worse than a massively pregnant governess! Besides—'

But Doreen had an answer for everything. 'We can do such a lot with costumes, dear. Under a really voluminous habit nobody will be able to tell. And it would help us so much. Our current abbess could sing Maria for us and as you have such a gorgeous singing

145

voice, you could step in and take her place. Perfect!'

'Except I'm not doing it,' replied Ally.

'Just think about it dear,' urged Doreen, not in the least daunted. 'You'd be helping to save the entire production, and you have such a wonderful talent ... '

'It's very nice of you to say so,' Ally replied firmly, 'but the answer is definitely no.'

All the same, as she replaced the telephone receiver she had the feeling she hadn't heard the last of it.


That afternoon, Ally was all set for a couple of hours' lesson preparation when the doorbell rang. Typical! Just when she was trying to concentrate.

To her surprise, it wasn't Zee but Gavin standing on her doorstep.

'Can I come in?'

'Of course you can.' She looked him up and down. There was a definite woebegone air about him. 'Something wrong?'

'Oh, not really,' he replied, in a voice that implied the opposite. 'I could just use some sensible company.'

Ally sat him down in the kitchen, at the ancient table with one leg propped up on two copies of the *Reader's Digest*. He looked desperately out of place amid the debris of bog-standard family life: a stripped-down lawnmower on some newspaper by the back door; two small pairs of muddy Wellingtons; a fridge almost entirely obscured by children's paintings; and a tatty cat curled up in the fruit bowl, fast asleep. Even so, he seemed to relax the minute they started chatting over a pot of builders' tea.

'I'm completely convinced now,' he announced between mouthfuls of home-made biscuit. 'I really am utterly useless with the female sex.'

The concept was so laughable that Ally rolled her eyes. 'Oh come on,' she retorted; 'whatever gave you that idea?'

'There was that trip to the zoo, for a start-off.' Gavin winced at the memory. 'I've still got the bruises you know,' he confided, hitching up the leg of his Hugo Boss trousers.

'Well if you will go telling six-year-old girls that they've been eating Bambi's relations ... '

'I thought you were supposed to be honest with kids. I was just telling it like it is. Nature red in tooth and claw, and all that. Girls! I'll never understand them.'

146

'Honest?' Ally shuddered. 'Gavin love, if parents were totally honest with kids all the time, they'd have absolutely *no* respect for us at all, *ever*, instead of just not much.'

'You reckon?'

'Parents are supposed to be able to do anything, right? Anything and everything. How's a kid going to feel if its parents start going on about all the things they can't do? Or admitting that they're terrified of spiders, thought GCSEs were a total waste of effort and failed their driving test ten times?'

'I suppose you do have a point there,' conceded Gavin. 'But it's not just Josie ... even Miranda's being funny with me at the moment.'

'Funny?' Ally looked at him over the top of her mug of tea. Gavin looked deeply uncomfortable, almost squirming with embarrassment. 'It's OK, you don't have to tell me.'

'I want to,' insisted Gavin. 'It's since ... you know ... the baby.' He nodded towards Ally's stomach. 'Now she knows it's on the way, it's the only thing she ever thinks about or talks about. Well, that or her precious business.'

'That's not so surprising is it?' ventured Ally. 'I mean, you have been trying for a baby for years. You must think about it a lot, too.'

'Yes, of course I do, but ...' Gavin really did squirm now. 'She just doesn't seem very ... interested in me any more. You know,' he swallowed, 'sexually.'

'Oh.' A hot flush rose up Ally's cheeks. 'I see.'

'It's like, I don't know – like I've done my job and now I'm surplus to requirements. She actually turned her back on me in bed last night,' he added morosely.

Their eyes locked. At that moment, a huge wave of understanding seemed to pass between them. The next thing she knew, Ally heard herself murmuring: 'Yeah. Me too.'

Gavin's eyes widened. 'You mean you and Luke – you don't ...?'

'Hardly at all. Not since I got pregnant. It feels almost like he doesn't want to touch me any more.' Ally felt a tear prickling the underside of her eyelids. 'But it was all his idea, Gavin! He thought it was such a great thing to do – and now this!'

Hesitantly, Gavin extended a hand across the table top. 'I'm sorry,' he said. 'I didn't know it was so difficult for you too. Still,

147

I guess things'll get back to normal once the baby's born.'

She looked into his eyes. 'Do you think so?'

He paused. 'I don't know.'

'You see, I don't know how much of it I can take,' Ally confessed. 'This horrible distance that I can feel opening up between me and Luke. You know something?'

'What?'

'I realised this morning that I talk more to you than I do to my own husband. And ... ' She forced herself not to look away. 'You're more supportive, too.'

'Really?'

She nodded. 'Really. You're the only person who makes me feel like a woman. You make me feel desirable, not just a big fat pregnant blob that nobody in their right minds would want to even cuddle, let alone have sex with.'

'I don't think any man in his right mind could feel that way,' said Gavin firmly.

'Well I'm sure Luke does.' She sighed. 'You know, I'd do anything for him to give me a proper hug.'

'To me, you're stunning; more beautiful than you've ever been,' Gavin declared. 'And any time you want a hug, you just go ahead and say so. OK?'

His hand slid a little nearer, and just for a few seconds, she took it. Then the moment was gone, and she was on her feet again. 'Fancy another cup of tea, or are you in a hurry? Luke should be back soon. I'm sure he'll be pleased to see you.'

Luke stared at his wife in disbelief. 'The mother abbess? She actually wants you to play the mother abbess?'

Ally nodded and turned the page of her trashy bedtime novel. 'Yes, I was a bit surprised too.'

'Surprised? It's the most ridiculous thing I've ever heard!' Luke buttoned up his pyjama jacket and flopped into bed beside her. 'Of course, you're not doing it.'

Up to that moment, Ally had had absolutely no intention of taking to the stage as the world's first pregnant mother abbess, with or without a voluminous habit. But if there was one thing she really couldn't stand, it was being told what she could and couldn't do. 'I can if I want to,' she replied with all the calm defiance of a hormonal fifteen-year-old.

148

Luke drew back and stared at her. 'I hope that's a joke.'

'Why should it be?'

'Why? Because you're a pregnant woman with responsibilities, and you're old enough to know better! I'm not having my wife endangering her health for the sake of some stupid play.'

Again, he had said precisely the wrong thing. Ally's hackles bristled. 'It's not stupid, and it's a musical, not a play. You know how much I love acting,' she added, giving voice to a long-dormant grievance. 'Why do you always have to run it down?'

'Oh Ally. Come on, love. You know I didn't mean that.' He tried putting his arm round her, but she shook it off.

'Yes you did. You think everything I do is stupid. Just because I'm not out there changing the world, like you think you are. Honestly, the way you go on, anybody'd think you were a super-hero or something.'

Luke was aghast. 'I don't go on!'

'Oh yes you do. And half the time you're not home in the evenings anyway, so you won't even notice if Kerri from next door is here instead of me, will you?'

Luke's expression grew positively grim. 'For the last time, Ally, you are not doing this ... musical.'

'Because you say I can't?'

'No, because you've got more sense. Or at least I hope you have.'

Seething with righteous indignation, Ally threw back the first thing that came into her mind. 'I bet Gavin doesn't try to tell Miranda what to do.'

'What the hell does it matter what those two do or don't do?' he snapped back at her. 'They're a waste of space, the pair of them, with their fancy-dress parties and their personalised Porsches.'

'What!'

'He seems to think about nothing but making money, and as for your sister – the only thing she's any good at is organising charity lunches for bored rich women. God only knows why I thought they'd make good parents.'

Angry tears stung Ally's eyes. 'In case you've forgotten, this pregnancy was your idea! It's a bit late to change your mind now!'

The words hung in the air between them, like an accusing sword.

'It's late,' muttered Luke, rolling over and switching off the bedside light. 'We can talk about this some other time.'

The following morning, Miranda and Gavin were facing each other as usual across the elegant breakfast table that had been especially designed and built for them by one of the minor Royals. Over the years, their careers had brought them into contact with a lot of rich, famous and influential people – a factor which certainly hadn't done their respective businesses any harm. And now, as Gavin saw it, it was time to call in a favour or two.

Miranda almost choked on her glass of lemon-infused hot water as Gavin told her about the great sheep's tongue orchid fiasco.

'You mean to tell me these things have been growing on the estate for years and nobody bothered to tell you?'

Gavin had to admit, with a glum face, that this was so. 'And the way the contract's worded ... let's just say we can't really get out of it. It's going to cost us a packet if I can't get permission to build on the land.'

Miranda let out an impatient 'hmph'. 'Well thank you for the brilliant business advice, darling. As I recall, you told me it was a guaranteed no-risk investment.'

'It is!' Gavin lobbed a dollop of marmalade onto his toast. 'As long as I can get past this stupid bloody environmental assessment thing.'

'That's really going to happen, isn't it?' Miranda pointed out with heavy sarcasm. 'I mean, the minute the guy spots one of these incredibly rare orchids he'll be on the phone to the Natural History Museum and that'll be that: no building for the next thousand years.'

'Unless ... '

'Unless what?'

Gavin leaned across the table and took his wife's hand. 'You know one or two government types, don't you?'

'I may have decorated the odd cabinet minister's country house. Why?'

'I need a bit of favourable consideration. Maybe someone who can send us down a ... sympathetic scientist to do the environmental impact assessment?'

An amused smile twitched the corners of Miranda's exquisite mouth. 'Darling, I hope you're not thinking of bribing anybody.'

'Perish the thought.'

'Good. Because I wouldn't want Miranda Morris Designs dragged through the mud on account of some scandal or other.'

'Remember,' Gavin reminded her, 'if the equestrian centre does get built, your company gets the contract to furnish the visitor centre and the VIP areas.'

'Well.' Miranda spooned pomegranate seeds onto her fresh blueberries. 'I *might* know someone you could talk to, I suppose. But nothing more than that.'

'Actually,' confessed Gavin, 'I was sort of hoping you could talk to him – or her – for me.' He took her hand, raised it gently to his lips and kissed it. 'You have such a wonderful way with people.'

# Chapter Fifteen

As July marched on towards the school holidays, the days were not so much balmy as blisteringly hot, filling Cheltenham's parks and gardens with bright-red necks and peeling shoulders. In the heart of town, Seuss & Goldman sold out of designer bikinis and the windows of all the travel agents screamed with Dayglo advertisements for last-minute package deals to Tenerife. Bumble bees bumbled; the municipal tennis courts filled up with Wimbledon wannabes; and passers-by either smiled or sweated and cursed, depending on how they felt about the heatwave.

Alas, the generally sunny outlook hadn't penetrated the walls of the ChelShel offices. Inside, Luke was listening with growing despair as Jake coughed his way through a tale of woe.

'And that's when they gave us all one of these,' he said, pausing to cough and spit something into a grimy handkerchief; then producing a crumpled sheet of paper and handing it to Luke.

Luke read it and passed it to Chas.

'Can they do this?' Chas wondered aloud.

'Can they really throw us all out like that?' echoed Jake.

'I'm afraid they can,' replied Luke, anger fizzing inside him. 'It's a private housing company, remember. Not a housing association. Under the contract you signed, all they have to do is give you one month's notice to vacate your flat, and that's what this letter is doing.'

'But why?' Chas ran a hand through his thinning hair. 'Why would they suddenly evict all their tenants?'

'Because,' Jake coughed and wheezed like a punctured accordion, 'they've had an offer for the building and it's too good to turn down. At least that's what the word is.'

'An offer?' Luke frowned. 'Who from?'

'Some big money-man. You know, one of these local developers with a finger in all the pies. Smarmy git. You know the sort.'

'Yeah,' said Luke, thinking of Gavin. 'Actually I do.'

Jake looked him straight in the eye. He was thin, yellow-skinned and his chest rattled with every painful breath. 'So what do I do now, mate? Go back to sleeping in doorways?'

'I think you should be in hospital,' said Luke.

'Already tried that. They gave me some antibiotics for the shadow on my lung and told me to go home. Home – good one, eh?'

Luke held out a hand as Jake wearily headed for the door. 'We'll do our best for you, I hope you know that.'

Jake nodded, but there was little energy in the gesture. 'Sometimes people's best isn't enough though, is it?' he said with a sigh. Then he stepped out onto the street and melted into the passing crowds.

For several minutes Luke sat slumped over his desk, head resting on his folded arms. 'Sometimes,' he declared in a muffled monotone, 'I hate the world and everybody in it.'

Chas came across and laid a hand on his back. 'We all have moments like that.'

Luke sat up and stretched back in his chair. 'This isn't a moment, it's a lifetime.'

'This isn't just about Jake, is it?' Chas dragged his chair up to Luke's desk and sat down. 'You've been looking miserable for weeks. Do you want to talk about it?'

'No,' replied Luke. His shoulders sagged. 'But if I don't, I think I'll go mad.' He looked across at Chas. 'I still don't think I'm coping very well. With Ally and the baby.'

'You're worried about her? Well, that's only natural.'

'That's not it.' Luke hung his head under the weight of guilt. 'It's like I told you before – the whole idea of her being pregnant, and it not being mine. I know it's stupid,' he added hastily, 'but – oh hell, I can't say this.'

'I used to be an army chaplain, Luke. Believe me, I'm pretty hard to shock.'

'I keep having this really crazy feeling, as if I've been ... betrayed.'

'By your wife?'

153

He nodded. 'I know, I know, it's insane. Ally's done absolutely nothing wrong, it's all me. And just to make things worse, I'm the one who made her feel bad when she said she didn't want to go through with the surrogacy. But I can't help it. Every time she wants me to make love to her all I see is the baby, and then I see Gavin – and then I feel sick.

'And now she says she wants me to be with her and Miranda for the birth. Not Gavin though, thank God. And I understand why she wants me there, Chas, I really do. It was my idea and I should be supporting her, not shying away. So how can I explain to her that I'm not sure I can bring myself to do it?'

Zee woke late; very late. A bleary glance at the bedside clock told him it was past ten in the morning. He wondered fleetingly why Emma hadn't woken him, then remembered that she was over at a friend's house for a birthday sleepover. Kate must have switched the alarm off, bless her, to make sure he got a decent night's sleep after all the long and lustful nights the two of them had spent together over the past couple of months.

That was just like her: not just sexy, but sweet and thoughtful too. For the first time since his wife's death, he really felt he had met someone he could get close to. He didn't want to jump the gun of course; but Kate might even be if not The One, then at least someone he'd like to spend an awful lot of time with . . .

It took a few more drowsy seconds for Zee to realise that Kate wasn't in bed beside him. She must have gone downstairs to make breakfast. Her scent was still fresh on the sheets though, and he rolled over to bury his face in her pillow.

That was when he found the envelope.

It was tucked under Kate's pillow, with just the corner peeping out. Puzzled, Zee slid it out. On the front it said simply 'Zee', in Kate's familiar rounded, almost childlike handwriting.

He tore it open, unfolded the single sheet of white paper, and read the few lines it contained.

Then his world fell apart.

Ally was humming maniacally to herself as she attacked the housework, overtaken by one of the periodic cleaning frenzies that gripped her whenever she was pregnant. If the vacuum cleaner hadn't become got clogged with one of Kyle's socks and promptly sputtered to a standstill, she probably wouldn't even have heard the frantic hammering on the front door, interspersed with staccato bursts on the doorbell.

Trotting downstairs to the hall, Ally squinted through the spyhole in the door. A huge, distorted eye stared back at her, and a familiar but frantic voice shouted: 'Let me in Ally, oh God please don't be out! I have to talk to you right now!'

She opened the door and, before she had a chance to say 'What's going on?' Zee was dripping sweat onto her hall carpet and babbling frantically about Kate and babies and being used.

'Good grief, Zee.' She ran a finger across his forehead. 'You're soaking!'

'Car wouldn't start,' he panted, still getting his breath back. 'Ran all the way here.' He started babbling again.

'Hey, hold on just a minute,' urged Ally, tucking a hand under his arm. 'Come into the kitchen and I'll make you some tea. Maybe then you'll make more sense.'

Ten minutes later, they were drinking extra-strength tea at the kitchen table, and Ally was gazing in shock at Zee across the ex-fruit bowl, which as usual was tastefully tenanted by a snoring cat.

'Well, I was wrong,' she admitted. 'Even now you've told me, it still doesn't make sense. Why would Kate want to leave you? I thought you were getting on so well together.'

'So did I,' Zee moped. 'I even thought we might be falling in love.'

He blew his nose loudly, but Ally knew it wasn't a head cold that was making him sniffle. He looks awful, she thought; and a surge of protective anger rose up inside her. Zee was like the brother she'd never had but always wanted, and when he was hurt, she felt hurt too. It was almost impossible to believe that the last time she saw him he'd been on top of the world, happier than he'd been in years.

Ally ate half a plate of chocolate biscuits without really noticing. She still couldn't quite get her head round this. 'You're saying she left you because she's pregnant?'

'Exactly.'

'But why would she do that? Most women would want to get closer to the father of their baby . . . wouldn't they?' She tried not to think about Gavin as she said it. That was different. Completely

155

different. A thought hit her. 'Unless ... it's not your baby.'

Zee laughed sadly. 'Oh, it's mine all right. I mean, hey, we've been shagging all day and all night for months – she wouldn't have had the time or the energy to two-time me. The thing is, she's got what she wants now, and it seems I'm surplus to requirements.'

'What she wants? The baby, you mean?'

'Apparently it struck her the first time we met that I'm good breeding stock. Not too stupid, not too fat, and with the same colouring as her little girl. Since Dad number one wasn't available to father child number two, I got the job. It seems she just omitted to tell me.'

'My God.' Another chocolate Hob-Nob disappeared. 'I've heard of women doing that kind of thing – stringing blokes along just to get them pregnant – but it's trashy magazine stuff. Not real life. Oh sweetheart.' She squeezed Zee's hand with chocolate-smeared fingers. 'I'm so sorry. What are you going to do?'

Zee looked at her blankly. 'Do? What can I do? She's gone: wham, bam, thank you Zee, and now I never want to see you ever again.'

'But you've got rights! You're that baby's father.'

'Yeah, in theory. But Kate's made it pretty clear she doesn't want me around. She says she's even moving to a different part of the country, so the three of them can have a "fresh start". What's the use, Ally? I've been a complete idiot – and what child wants a sad loser for a father?'

That made Ally even angrier. She gripped his hand so tightly that her knuckles turned white and he winced. 'Listen to me, Zee: you are *not* a loser. Ask Emma; ask anyone who knows you. *Really* knows you. You're kind, generous, a great dad – and you can't just let this woman walk out of your life and take your child with her!'

'But I don't even know where she's going' lamented Zee.

'Then find out. Correction: *we'll* find out.'

'How?'

'I don't know! But we'll think of something. Look, I don't like it when people hurt my friends, especially my best friend of all; and I'm not going to let her get away with it.'

This was a strange time. It felt to Ally as if everything in the world had something to do with babies. Every advertisement had a baby

156

in it; every shop window seemed to be full of baby clothes and cots; and every conversation she had with Miranda centred on Ally's growing belly.

'Baby' might be Miranda's current favourite word, but by contrast, every conversation Ally had with Luke seemed to be characterised by a complete lack of it. Whenever she attempted to introduce the subject of her pregnancy, Luke contrived to steer things in a different direction, and now she even found herself avoiding the topic herself. Ally's baby was like the elephant in the corner of the room: glaringly obvious to everybody, but steadfastly ignored.

Consequently, when she tried to kiss Luke goodbye at the front door on that particular weekday morning, and yet again his lips dodged hers at the very last moment, neither of them alluded to Ally's hospital appointment later that day. Neither of them could break through the wall of embarrassment, and that hurt more than a little. Ally knew all of this was proving difficult for Luke, but she longed for him to be there for her, in all the little ways he'd been there for her in her previous pregnancies. Sometimes she wondered if he was punishing her: but why would he punish her for something that was at least partly down to him? None of it made any sense.

Ah well, at least Miranda was supportive. Tiresomely so on occasion, if Ally was honest with herself. It wasn't that she didn't appreciate the daily phone calls, the vouchers for luxury prenatal massages and the gifts of relaxing aromatherapy candles; the pampering sessions were most acceptable, but Miranda's constant concerns about the state of her bowels and exhortations to ingest ever-weirder food supplements did sometimes get a bit much to take.

All the same, it was impossible not to feel a little warm inside whenever Miranda was talking about the baby. No matter how preposterous she was sometimes, no matter how plain daft some of her ideas were, there was no mistaking the look of pure joy that sparkled in her eyes when she talked about being a mother after wanting to for so long.

And today was the day Miranda had been going on about incessantly for the past fortnight; the day when everything would become dazzlingly real: Ally was having another scan – and this time the baby was going to look like a baby, not an amorphous, flickering blob.

157

As she and Miranda sat in a draughty corridor at the General, pretending to read five-year-old copies of *The People's Friend*, there was no denying the fact that Miranda was an awful lot quieter than usual; Ally doubted that it had anything to do with the scary sister who glowered at anybody who blew their nose too loudly.

'Are you OK?' she asked.

'No,' admitted Miranda in a tiny voice. 'I'm scared, Ally.'

Ally looked at her in surprise. 'Hey, it's only another scan. You've had loads of scans before.'

'It's not *only* anything! Besides, this is the first one Gavin's been able to come to. What if the baby's not all right?'

It was a question every mother-to-be asked herself ten times a day, but that was no reason to upset Miranda. 'It will be.'

'But what if it isn't?' Miranda insisted. 'I mean, there's nothing hereditary in the family or anything, but these things can happen out of the blue, can't they? Not that I'd love it any less or anything, but all the same ... you worry, don't you?'

'We'll deal with that if and when it happens. Which it won't. There's no point torturing yourself, you know.'

Miranda knew. 'But I can't help it,' she explained. 'Babies are so tiny and fragile, and there's nothing I can do, only be a kind of useless spectator, and get you to eat the right things. I think I might feel differently if I was carrying the baby inside me,' she added. 'I just hate being – you know ...'

'Powerless? Yes, I do know. I felt like that when I was stuck in labour for hours and hours with Kyle, with nothing happening, and they threatened me with an emergency Caesarean.'

'And you didn't want that?'

'Of course not. He was my first, and I was so determined it was all going to be natural. You know, in the end I think I pushed that baby out by sheer force of will. It's not surprising he shot out like a bullet. The obstetrician caught him like a rugby ball.' She saw the look of horror on Miranda's face. 'Sorry, childbirth's so ghastly that you have to make jokes about it.'

'I don't care how horrible it is,' sighed Miranda. 'I still wish it was me.' She reached across and placed a hand on her sister's stomach. 'I'm never going to feel what it's really like, am I? Never go through what other women do.' Her eyes met Ally's. 'Will I still feel like a proper mother?'

'You *are* going to be a proper mother,' replied Ally firmly.

158

'This little one's mother. The fact that you didn't actually give birth to him or her won't make the slightest difference.'

'I hope you're right.'

'I'm always right. Except when it comes to choosing curtains.'

'And fashion. You're hopeless at fashion.'

Ally laughed. 'I'm a frumpy old mother-of-two. I don't *do* fashion. Just saggy old joggers, remember.'

They sat there in silence for a while, lost in their own thoughts, as trolleys rumbled back and forth down the corridor. Ally wriggled on her seat, desperately trying not to think of waterfalls and running taps. What sadist had decreed that you had to have a bursting bladder in order to have a scan?

Miranda's eyes kept flicking across to the clock on the wall opposite.

'Where's Gavin? He promised he'd be here!'

'He will be.'

'He should have been here twenty minutes ago.' Miranda gripped Ally's wrist. 'I need him here.'

'No you don't. You've got me. Besides, I'm sure he'll be here in a minute.'

Something had better happen in a minute, mused Ally. Because if it doesn't, there's going to be a flood round here.

Fifteen minutes later, with still no sign of Gavin, Ally was lying on a trolley as a technician smeared freezing-cold jelly over her stomach.

'That's it, Mrs Bennett, now you lie still and we'll take a look at what's going on in your tummy, shall we?'

The probe slid over Ally's bump, producing a snowstorm of black and white fuzz on the screen. Miranda's grip on Ally's hand was tighter than a tourniquet. 'Where is it? I can't make anything out. Which bit is the baby?'

'Just hold on a minute. Let me try this . . . ' The technician tried a slightly different angle, and the fuzz began to resolve itself into something. Something recognisably baby-shaped. 'There!' she declared, tilting the screen towards Ally and Miranda and pointing at the screen. 'See that little black bit there, sort of . . . winking at you? That's the heart.'

'Oh my God,' whispered Miranda, reaching out and touching the screen. 'That's my baby. My baby!'

'Is everything OK?' asked Ally.

'Looks absolutely fine from where I'm standing. Have you already been told the sex?'

Miranda leapt in instantly. 'No, no, don't tell me! I don't want to know before the big day.' Her fingers spread out on the screen of the scanner. 'Oh God – is that bit there its head?'

The technician nodded. 'That's right. And you see there – the legs and arms? And if you look closely you can even see its little fingers.' Her brow furrowed. 'Are you OK?'

Miranda raised her head, smiling through a cascade of tears. 'Of course I'm all right!' she laughed. 'I'm more all right than I've ever been in my whole life before.'

When they emerged from the scanning room, Miranda clutching the first precious image of her child-to-be, she almost collided with Gavin. Out of breath and perspiring, he looked considerably less debonair than usual.

'Where were you?' demanded Miranda. 'You promised!'

'There was an accident,' he gasped. 'On the M5. Big pile-up.'

'Oh no.' Ally noticed a slight graze on the side of his face. 'You're all right, aren't you?'

'Oh, fine. The Porsche had a bit of a bump, but the man in the breakdown truck got me here as quickly as he could.' His eyes sought out the envelope in Miranda's hand. 'Is that . . .?'

A secret smile began at the corners of her lips and spread all over her face. 'Our baby, yes!'

'Well?'

She whisked out the scan and he took it eagerly. 'We're having a baby, Miranda. We're really having a baby!'

'I know, isn't it wonderful!'

Ally stood there feeling almost left out – an outsider at her own pregnancy. It was one of the oddest feelings she had ever had. 'We should probably go,' she said gently. 'The car parking ticket's only good for another ten minutes.'

'Bollocks to that,' declared Gavin. 'If you get a ticket, I'll pay.' He couldn't take his eyes off the scanner image. 'Go on then, tell me,' he said expectantly.

Miranda and Ally eyed each other questioningly. 'Tell you what, darling?'

'What is it? A boy or a girl? I've been biting my nails all day.'

160

'I've no idea,' Miranda replied airily.

'What?'

'I didn't ask.'

'B-but ... then go back in and ask now!'

'I think Miranda wants to keep it a surprise,' hinted Ally.

'Oh my God – Miranda, I thought we'd agreed that that was a stupid idea!'

'No darling; you said it was a stupid idea, and I didn't say anything.' She stood on tiptoe and planted a kiss on the end of her husband's startled nose. 'I'm afraid we'll both just have to wait until the big day!'

Gavin let out some kind of inaudible oath. 'Women!' He threw up his hands. 'What is it with women and surprises?'

'What is it with men and impatience?' Miranda retorted. And the three of them headed back to the car park, one at least ill-temperedly pondering the completely illogical nature of the female sex.

# Chapter Sixteen

Luke couldn't remember the last time he'd been asked to put on a suit and look smart. Unless you counted that ludicrous costume he'd had to wear to Miranda's birthday party, which hadn't been so much smart as paramilitary. It was almost as if Ally's sister enjoyed making him wear things she knew he'd feel profoundly uncomfortable in. If he was right, it wouldn't surprise him one bit.

And now she was telling him to drag his one good suit out of the wardrobe and come to another party. Admittedly it was a different kind of party – the Mayor's Charity Music Night, a fundraising musical soirée in aid of Cheltenham's local charities – but Miranda had organised it, which meant it would be full of the kind of people who gave to charity for the simple reason that it made them feel less guilty about being filthy rich.

Frankly, Luke really didn't understand the mentality of it: why didn't Miranda just scrap the party, have a whip-round among her well-heeled mates and shell out the money to the charities? No overheads, no middle man, no administration costs. He laughed to himself at the thought. He knew exactly why she didn't: because without a party nobody would give a penny. Charity dos weren't about being generous; they were about being *seen* doing it. And nobody was better at getting her parties into the pages of *Gloucestershire Life* than Miranda Hesketh.

'Oh no, sweetheart! Not the horrible elastic one.'

Caught in the act, he turned round and realised Ally was standing right behind him, arms folded across her rounded stomach, looking faintly amused but fierce.

'You know I can't tie a real one,' he protested, easing the elastic bow tie over his head. 'Anyway, who the hell's going to know? Or care?'

'I'll know. And you look so smart in a real one. Come here.' She fussed around him, confiscating the elastic impostor and producing a proper bow tie – the one with the instructions that might as well be written in Egyptian hieroglyphics for all the sense they made. 'That's it, chin up.'

'Do I have to?' he asked, without much hope of reprieve.

'Yes you do, and stop pulling that face.' She giggled. 'The wind might change and then you'll stay like that.'

'Great. I quite fancy being northern Gloucestershire's answer to Quasimodo. I've already got the temperament for it, after all.'

'You can say that again.' Ally took a step back to survey her handiwork. 'Hm, not perfect but it'll do. And believe me, those types are so posh they can spot a fake bow tie at fifty paces.'

'Thanks love.' He wriggled a finger around the inside of his uncomfortably snug wing collar. 'I still wish you were coming,' he lamented.

'I know, I'm sorry. But you know it's rehearsal night, and there's not long to go before the show now.' She gave Luke's tie a final tweak to make sure that it was straight. 'There. How about a thank-you kiss?' She presented her soft, pink cheek to his lips, and for a fleeting moment Luke wanted to turn away. What's wrong with me? he asked himself as the feeling ebbed away and he kissed her. She's beautiful and kind, I love her to bits and God knows, nobody could have a better wife. So why do I find it so hard to touch her any more?

And what happens if this feeling never goes away?

The Mayor's Charity Music Night was exactly as Luke had imagined it: the great, the not-so-great and the self-important, all crowded together in Pittville Pump Room and pretending to adore each other, while hapless local musicians tried to make themselves heard over the inane jabbering. If I was playing that cello, mused Luke as the girl on the stage sawed away unheard, I'd smack that guy in the second row over the head with it. Rude git. But of course, I'm forgetting: having decent manners is sooo lower class.

Still, at least the food was good, if pretentious; and so far he had managed to spend most of the party lurking at the back by the buffet tables, snacking on absurd little Yorkshire pudding canapés,

163

and cocktail sausages that you dipped into hot mashed potato. As far as he could tell, nobody had even noticed he was here. With a bit of luck he might be able to down his own weight in sausages, say a couple of quick hellos and then slope off early, to check on the nightly soup round.

Perhaps his thoughts were a little too loud; or maybe Miranda had developed telepathic skills since their last meeting. At any rate, mere seconds later she was at his side, sliding a bejewelled arm through his. 'Luke darling! I'm so glad you decided to come. And you're looking so smart! But why are you hiding yourself away in the corner like this?'

Luke slid a finger under his collar, easing his constricted neck. 'Oh, you know me, I'm not really a party person.'

Miranda gave him a dimpled, rather pitying smile. 'Well we shall have to make you one. Mingling, that's what it's all about, Luke. Mingling with the people who matter. Come along, I'm going to introduce you to some friends.'

A horrible weariness washed over Luke. 'God, Miranda, do we have to? You know I'm crap at all this social niceties stuff. The sooner ChelShel can afford a proper public relations officer, the better.'

But Miranda was already towing him towards her target: a cluster of well-oiled businessmen guffawing over the top of a delicate rendition of 'Le Cygne'. 'Well it can't yet, so for now you'll just have to do the meeting and greeting, won't you?'

'I still don't see the point of it all, you know.' With one sweeping gaze he took in the crowded room, the braying guests, the tinkling glasses and the ignored musicians. 'All this ... partying.'

Miranda frowned. 'It's an event. A *charity* event.' She poked a gorgeously lacquered fingernail at his chest. 'To raise money for charities like yours.'

'Yes, I realise that ... ' Luke could feel himself digging a hole big enough to fall into several times over, but he'd never been good at hiding the way he felt. 'But why does it have to be a party? Why waste all this money?'

'To bring in more.' Miranda was clearly piqued. 'Have you any idea how much work it takes to organise something like this?'

'Have you any idea how many people I could house if I had the money you spend on all your fancy soirées and star-studded charity concerts?' he snapped back.

Miranda gave him a long and very unimpressed look. 'If it wasn't for people like these,' she said, 'you wouldn't have any money at all. Now.' She drew herself up to her full, magnificent height and gripped his arm so firmly that her long fingernails dug through his jacket. 'See that multi-millionaire over there? Do you want him to make a donation to ChelShel, or not?'

While Luke was rubbing shoulders with northern Gloucestershire's fattest cats, and the kids were tucked up in bed, Ally was playing host to an unexpected visitor.

'I'm really sorry to bother you this time of night,' began Zee, 'but Emma's at a sleepover tonight and I just needed to talk.'

Ally took one look at his anguished face and got the best chocolate biscuits out of the top kitchen cupboard. 'Come on, Zee, you're my best mate. Do you really think I mind?'

As Ally bustled around making tea, Zee paced back and forth across the kitchen. He looked, thought Ally, like an abandoned mongrel with nowhere to go. 'I've never felt so used in all my life, Ally. Never! And all that time I thought she really liked me. I just can't get my head round it.'

Poor Zee, thought Ally. Of all the people in the world who deserved to be treated badly, he was bottom of her list. This was a man who had to have the same plastic tree every Christmas because he thought cutting down live Christmas trees was cruel; he was vulnerable, gentle and just a little naïve. Why did fate have to bring Kate into his life, only for her to lay waste to it and then promptly walk out again?

'I think she did like you, Zee,' said Ally after a moment's consideration. 'Whenever I saw the two of you together, she seemed to be genuinely having fun. It's just that you, well, didn't feature in her future plans.'

Zee wilted and just stood there, in the middle of the floor, head down and hands thrust into the pockets of his worn-out cords. 'Oh sweetheart.' Ally put her arms round him and gave him a big bear-hug. 'I know it's horrible. But you have to focus on what you're going to do about it.'

'Like what?' Zee stared morosely at a cracked floor tile. 'I've asked all the people I can think of who knew her, and nobody knows where she's gone. She really doesn't want to be found. Maybe I should give up.'

165

'It's your baby, Zee,' Ally reminded him.

'Ah, but people keep telling me it might not be ...'

'Then they're just stirring it, Zee. We've been through this already. You know Kate wasn't cheating on you with anyone else. You were a hundred per cent sure until people started all this malicious whispering.' Ally's fingers crossed furtively behind her back. Hell, she thought; I hope I'm right. 'You have to stop listening to nasty people who pretend to be your friends. Folk just love putting the boot in when they sense that somebody's down.'

'I suppose,' Zee conceded.

'So – is that really what you want?' Ally demanded. 'To give up?'

'No,' he admitted with a sigh. 'But—'

'No buts.' Ally banged a mug of strong tea on the table. 'Drink this and let's have another think about it. I'm sure we'll come up with something.' She glanced at the clock. 'It's not as if I've got anything else to do.'

Zee drew out a chair and sat down, expertly avoiding the one with the wobbly leg. 'Luke working late again?'

'No, actually he's at one of Miranda's black-tie charity dos.'

'Black tie? Luke?' Zee actually raised a chuckle.

'Quite. You should've seen the face on him. But that's Luke all over. He never could hide his feelings ... ' A wave of melancholy invaded her and she felt her shoulders droop.

'Things still not right between you two, then?' guessed Zee.

Ally shook her head. 'He keeps making excuses for not touching me, but he's the worst liar in the world.' She looked up. 'I think he finds me repulsive, Zee. I really do.'

'Oh come on, Ally. Surely it's not that bad.'

'Believe me, it is. Since I got pregnant he's acting like I've been having an affair or something. Sometimes I wish I had,' she admitted. 'At least then I'd have had some fun.'

Zee reached across the table and they clasped hands in solidarity. 'What a pair we are,' he commented with a little laugh. 'Still, things can only get better, eh?'

'Yeah. Too right.'

Ally smiled back at him, but in her heart she wasn't convinced.

One person noticeably absent from Miranda's party was Gavin, who was otherwise occupied in a rather delicate business transaction.

166

It might still be summer, but it was surprisingly dark and cold in the stables where Gavin kept his string of polo ponies. He'd been standing there in his short-sleeved shirt, getting goose bumps, for a good quarter of an hour, and he was beginning to wonder if he'd been taken for an idiot when finally he heard a car engine and headlights swept across the yard. At last.

He walked across to the 4x4 just as its occupant was getting out. 'Mr Hesketh, I presume?'

Gavin nodded. 'You found it OK then.'

The man smiled at him in the murky glow from the one light on the stable wall. 'It's my job to find things. Unless of course I have a good reason not to.'

That was Gavin's cue to produce the brown envelope. It was a very well-stuffed brown envelope, and it hurt to part with it; but if things worked out the way they were supposed to, he could regard it as a kind of investment.

'Here's your reason,' he announced, hoping the other man hadn't noticed the way his hands were shaking. He'd never done anything like this before. Dodgy things, yes; but nothing as bad as this. 'Make sure you don't find anything.'

The envelope disappeared into a briefcase with a short, sharp click.

'Trust me, Mr Hesketh. I'm a professional.'

Miranda was seldom if ever on the back foot, but tonight had caught her completely off-balance.

She stood in the ladies' powder-room at the Pump Room trying to reapply her mascara, which was no easy task when you were hyperventilating and your hands were shaking. How could she have placed the wrong order for that wallpaper – and worse, had the whole consignment delivered without even checking it first? She would never do anything like that. Not until now. Miranda cringed at the memory of the cabinet minister's wife, buttonholing her by the rum punch, no doubt with the express intention of embarrassing her in front of everybody. Well, it had worked.

I'm slipping, she thought with a frisson of horror. I've taken my eye off the ball and it's not the first time. God knows how many other mistakes I've made.

It was all down to the baby, of course. And she wasn't even carrying it! But how could she go on giving everything to the business when such a huge part of her was hopelessly in love, besotted with the little life growing inside her sister's belly? Her entire perspective on the world was changing, and the baby hadn't even been born yet.

It was a frightening realisation. Please don't let me turn into my sister, she begged silently. Maybe Gavin would be pleased if she spent less time and energy being a businesswoman and more on trying to be the perfect hausfrau, but to Miranda the prospect was downright terrifying. I've always been in control, she thought: of my emotions, my career, my money, even my men. But now something stronger than anything else has come along, and it's taking over, turning everything upside down.

It wasn't fair. Everything had been planned out so perfectly. Nothing was supposed to change. The baby was supposed to fit into her ready-made life, but already it had become the centre of her universe; nothing else stood a chance alongside her overwhelming desire to be a mother. And she could feel the control ebbing away from her, breaking down, causing her to make mistakes she never would have made before.

She had never been so scared in all her life.

Mascara and lipstick touched up, she straightened up and took a good hard look at herself in the mirror above the washbasin. Come on Miranda, she scolded herself. It was just one silly mistake that anybody could have made. A nice bouquet and a ten per cent discount will sort it all out.

A head appeared round the door of the ladies' room. It was Gilly, one of Miranda's trusty lieutenants. 'Oh, you're in here, I've been looking everywhere.'

Miranda turned round. 'Something wrong?'

'Kind of. It's time for the charity auction, but the celebrity auctioneer hasn't turned up.' She paused. 'You did check that he was coming, didn't you? What am I saying, of course you did – you're so efficient.'

Oh shit, thought Miranda with a rapidly sinking heart. Oh shit oh shit oh shit.

Then, just when it counted, inspiration struck. She knew somebody here who'd be sure to help – in return for a good report of his behaviour to Ally. Someone who could organise Christmas for a hundred down-and-outs in a church hall, without a single fight breaking out. The perfect candidate! Donning her

168

most intimidating smile, Miranda shimmied across the hall to a lone figure by the buffet table.

'Luke darling.'

At the word 'darling', Luke's blood froze. 'What?'

She laid an exquisite hand on his shoulder, and he knew he was doomed. 'I've got a little job for you.'

A short while later, on her way to work, Ally got a call on her mobile from Gavin.

'Fancy meeting up for lunch? My treat.'

Ally hesitated. Till now, it had just been the odd cup of coffee and one of those slightly flirtatious chats where neither person says what they're really thinking – exciting, but essentially harmless. Maybe she was reading too much into this invitation, but somehow lunch seemed like a step further into alluring but dangerous territory. No, no, that's silly, she scolded herself. It's just the hormones playing games with my mind, making me have these weird, unsuitable fantasies. Or maybe it was just that she was feeling so fat and unattractive, and needed someone – anyone – to hold her and tell her that she was beautiful? 'Will Miranda be there too?' she enquired.

Gavin cleared his throat. 'You know Miranda, always busy with one thing or another.'

'So she won't, then?'

'Er, no.'

A little thrill of anticipation ran through Ally's body, raising goose bumps all over. It took a massive effort of will for her to make herself reply: 'Then maybe I'd better say no.'

'It's only lunch, Ally.' He said it in a way that made it sound as if it promised so much more.

'I know.'

'So say yes. You can't leave me to celebrate on my own.'

That caught her by surprise. 'Celebrate? Celebrate what?'

'It looks like my planning permission's going to go through without a hitch. I got a letter this morning. The new equestrian centre could be up and running as early as this time next year. I don't think I've ever felt more relieved.'

'Oh. Yes, I'm sure. But what about the – what's it called? – sheep's tongue orchid?' puzzled Ally.

'Guess what – you'll never believe this. The chap came down

169

from London to do the environmental impact assessment, like I told you, and do you know, he didn't find a trace of the leafy little buggers.'

'Nothing! But I thought—'

'So did we all. But it looks as if it was all one big false alarm after all.'

# Chapter Seventeen

It was a hot, sticky night and Ally was sitting up in bed, arms straining round her bump to encircle her knees, her thoughts far away.

'Have you seen my blue boxers?' Luke had to repeat himself twice before the question penetrated her consciousness.

'What?'

'Boxers. Blue. The ones I wear in bed.'

Ally collected her thoughts. 'Oh. I think they're still in the tumble dryer,' she admitted. 'I forgot to bring them up.'

'Great. Well I'm not traipsing downstairs to fetch them. Suppose I'll just have to go commando.' He didn't sound too keen.

Ally's only response was a faint murmured 'Mm.'

Flinging back the duvet, Luke slid into bed beside her. 'Shall I switch off the light?'

No response.

'Is something wrong?' he asked after several moments' silence. 'Are you feeling ill? Have I pissed you off or something?'

Ally shook her head. 'Sorry, I was just thinking.'

Luke groaned. 'You're not fretting about Gavin's bloody riding centre again?' His voice softened. 'You know you can't do anything about it, love. If he wants Nether Grantley to be a posh people's adventure playground, it will be. Guys like Gavin always get what they want.'

Ally sighed. 'Maybe. I'm just a bit sad because I used to take my class there for nature walks round the lake. It was so ... untouched. And now it's going to be just another boring riding course.'

'That's the way it goes, unfortunately,' grunted Luke. 'Take the charity housing project I was telling you about. Everything's fine until some rich bastard developer like Gavin shows up and throws so much money at them that they can't refuse.' His brows knitted. 'In fact I wouldn't be at all surprised if it *was* Gavin.'

'You don't really think that,' Ally told him. 'I know I'm being silly too, though. I expect it's the pregnancy hormones making me all soppy.'

What she didn't say was that Nether Grantley made up only a small part of the way she was feeling. How could she admit to Luke that Gavin was occupying her thoughts in a quite different way? That ever since their quiet, intimate lunch a couple of weeks ago, she couldn't get him out of her head? Or that he'd called her up that very afternoon and asked if they could do it again? Like he said, it was only lunch ... but if that truly was all it amounted to, why was Zee the only person she felt able to let in on the secret?

Zee was right. She ought to have told Luke the first time she and Gavin met up for coffee. But if she had, there'd have been an enormous argument over nothing, and that would have upset the children. Or was it nothing? The question tormented her.

All the same, why shouldn't she have lunch with whoever she pleased? It wasn't as if Luke was around much at the moment, and even when he was, they had so little physical contact that it was as if the two of them were encased in transparent but impenetrable bubbles.

I'm lonely, she lamented. All I want is a hug or two and some decent conversation about things I'm interested in, she told herself. Luke never wants to talk about fun things any more. Just an opportunity to relax and laugh for an hour or two. Surely there's nothing wrong in that.

But as Luke turned away to switch off the bedside light, Ally wondered exactly who she was trying to convince.

Kyle was not the kind of boy to run away from confrontation. Even so, five against one, that was just unfair.

'Stop saying bad things about my mum!' he shouted as they backed him up against the playground wall. He glanced to right and left, but there was nobody around to fight his corner. Everybody else was on the playing field on the other side of the school buildings.

'Your mum's a dirty whore,' sneered the greasy-haired ringleader, two years older than Kyle and about twice as wide. 'My mum heard Trevor's mum telling Tracey from the corner shop.'

Kyle wasn't one hundred per cent certain what a whore was, though he had a fairly good idea, but he knew it was something exceptionally bad, which had something to do with the baby his mum was having for Auntie Miranda. And he *definitely* knew that his mum wasn't dirty, in any way you cared to look at it.

'Shut up!' he spat, scared but furious.

The other boys and the lone girl fell about laughing. 'Shut up, oooh, shut up! I'm sooo scared.'

'Make me,' invited the ringleader.

The gang closed in on Kyle and he had nowhere left to run; so he did the only thing he could do: he drew back his fist and smashed it with all his strength into the ringleader's face.

His nose exploded in a shower of crimson, and he yowled like an alley cat on hot bricks. It was a satisfying moment; but it was only a brief respite.

Kyle swallowed hard. I'm too young to die, he thought to himself; although under the circumstances there wasn't an awful lot he could do about it.

The Pleasure Garden was Cheltenham's newest and most chi-chi restaurant, and it was way out of Ally's league. It felt completely unnatural, walking up to the reception desk and not asking for the Family Special with extra fries. This is all wrong, she told herself; I don't belong in a place like this.

'You came!' Gavin's handsome face lit up with delight as the waitress showed Ally to his corner table. He sprang to his feet to place a kiss on her cheek, but she shied away. 'Is something wrong?'

'I very nearly didn't come,' she confessed. 'I don't like secrets.'

'Neither do I. But we both know what Luke would be like if you told him we were having lunch together. He'd completely over-react – like he did when you first got to know Zee.'

'I think you make him feel insecure,' said Ally. 'And angry. He's got this idea that you're some kind of Victorian moustache-twirling villain, buying up Gloucestershire just so you can evict widows and orphans on Christmas Eve.'

'Pardon?'

'There's this other developer,' Ally explained. 'He – or she –

has bought up the private housing project where some of Luke's clients have been living. I think he suspects it's you.'

'Me! What would I want with a housing project?'

'It's on a prime site.' Ally looked at him directly, pleadingly. 'It isn't you, is it?'

Gavin let out a small explosion of breath. 'No, Ally. It's not me. Though I don't suppose that'll convince Luke.' He raked a hand through his glorious mane of glossy black hair. 'Look, I'm not saying I haven't done the odd dodgy deal over the years—'

'Nether Grantley Hall, for example?'

He ignored her pointed suggestion. 'Like I said, the odd dodgy deal – if I hadn't, I'd be in the gutter by now. It's all one big power-game, you see. But I swear I've never even evicted a spider, let alone helpless orphans.' Gavin gave a half-smile. 'That husband of yours certainly has a vivid imagination.'

'He's only trying to protect people who can't protect themselves.'

'And keep tabs on his lovely wife?'

'Well ... possibly,' Ally conceded.

Gavin sat back in his chair. 'Don't get me wrong, I don't blame him. It's different with Miranda though,' he added, sitting back down at the table. 'She doesn't care what I do.'

The waiter pulled out a chair and Ally sat down, embarrassed by the luxurious surroundings but unable to deny the surge of joy she had felt when she saw Gavin sitting waiting for her. 'I'm sure she does, you know.'

Gavin shook his head. 'No, it's the baby she cares about, not me. I think she's even beginning to lose interest in her own business – she's been making a few bad mistakes lately, and that's not the Miranda I know.'

'No,' agreed Ally, who had also noticed the change in her sister. From entrepreneur to mother-in-waiting, the scale of the transformation had taken her by surprise; but then again, whatever Miranda did, it had to be done properly, to the point of excess. 'But I think she's just turned into a different kind of perfectionist. She's determined to be the best mother in the world.'

'She can't possibly be. That's you.'

It was the cheesiest line Ally had ever heard, but Gavin spoke it with such warmth and sincerity that she hadn't the slightest doubt he meant it. She forced an awkward laugh. 'I don't think so! Ask

174

Kyle and Josie – sometimes they think I'm the Wicked Witch of the West.'

'They don't, you know,' Gavin disagreed. 'When I take them out to places, they tell me stuff they wouldn't tell you.'

Ally helped herself to an olive from the dish on the table. 'Such as?'

'Such as the fact that they think you're great, and they'd much rather be out with you than with a rubbish uncle like me! And before you tell me I'm not rubbish,' he added as Ally opened her mouth, 'remember I'm the guy whose niece thinks he's a serial Bambi killer.'

Ally nearly choked with laughter. 'Oh, I think you just need a bit of practice when it comes to girls. You're fine with Kyle,' she reminded him.

'Ah well, when I was away at boarding school girls were an alien species.' Gavin's gaze locked with hers, and she hadn't the will to look away. 'You're very beautiful for an alien, by the way. Pregnancy suits you.'

'Is this National Flattery Day or something?' enquired Ally.

'Not at all. I just think somebody needs to tell you how great you are, because sometimes I look at you and Luke, and you seem so sad I could scream. Doesn't he realise how lucky he is to have you for a wife?'

Gavin's smooth, sonorous voice was making Ally feel dizzy. She swiftly replied: 'Don't you realise how lucky you are to have Miranda for a wife?'

There was just the faintest hiatus in the conversation, and then Gavin said: 'Of course I do. But that doesn't stop me caring about you too.'

'Please.' Ally's eyes beseeched him, though her body yearned for him to take her in his arms. 'Please don't.'

His hand stretched across the snow-white tablecloth, seeking out hers. 'You're very special to me, Alison. And . . . and I think you feel something for me, too. Otherwise, why would you be here?'

'Gavin!'

With a soft sigh, Gavin drew his hand back. 'I'm sorry. I didn't mean to frighten you.'

'That's OK. You didn't.' Ally fought to control her breathing.

'Do you want me to go away and leave you alone?'

She knew she had to say 'yes', but it came out as 'No, please don't.'

175

And Gavin smiled at her. 'Hey, well there's another thing to celebrate. Look, here's the waiter. Shall we order?'

Why do I have to like you so much? agonised Ally, deliberately eating her dessert slowly so that these moments in Gavin's company would last longer. Why do I have to feel as if I'm on fire whenever you so much as look at me? I'm five months pregnant, I'm not supposed to feel this way! Luke makes me feel warm and secure – or he used to before he started ignoring me – but you make me feel so ... alive. If you ever kissed me ...

No. I mustn't allow myself to think that way. 'It's been lovely, but I really ought to be going,' she said out loud. 'I know it's the end of term, but I've still got to prepare some lessons for work tomorrow.'

'Still determined to keep on working? There's no need to, you know. You've nothing to prove.'

'Stop it, Gavin. You're starting to sound like my sister. I mean it, I really should be going.'

'Are you sure you're not just running away from me?'

'Of course not,' she lied. I can do this, she told herself. All I have to do is walk away and not look back.

She was about to suggest that they ask for the bill when her mobile trilled, somewhere in the depths of her handbag. It wouldn't have been quite so embarrassing if Kyle hadn't changed her ring-tone to the latest novelty Number One.

'Oh shit,' she muttered as everybody in the restaurant turned round and glared. 'I thought I'd turned it off.'

'Sod 'em,' advised Gavin, meeting the glares with an icy stare of his own as Ally rummaged frantically. 'Take your time.'

At last she extracted the phone from several archaeological strata made up of tissues, sticking plasters, Calpol, toy cars, the leg off a Barbie doll, and an emergency bar of fruit and nut chocolate. 'Hello?' she hissed into it, making more noise being quiet than if she'd just spoken normally.

'Ally, it's Zee. You sound ... funny.'

'Well you sound drunk!'

'That's 'cause I am. I'm a bit excited, see, and I wanted you to know 'cause you're my very very bestest friend.'

'And you're mine, but I'm in a restaurant right now, and—'

'I've got it,' cut in Zee.

'Got what?'

'The Big One. The one that'll make my fortune. Little blue and white thing, fifty p on the Cats' Protection League stall in Stroud market. I reckon ... are you still there?'

'Yes, I'm still here.'

'I reckon it's really, really, really old, see.' There was the sound of a muffled hiccup. 'Woo-hoo, lots and lots and lots of money!'

'That's really good Zee, and I'm very happy for you, but I can't really talk right now—'

'I've found her,' Zee said, suddenly sounding sombre, even lucid. 'Kate.'

'Oh my God, you haven't! How?'

'Remembered her ex-landlord, didn't I? People can be very, very cooperative when you buy them a lot of drinks, you know. Nice man, very helpful. He gave me her new address – the one she gave him for forwarding her security deposit.'

'That's great,' enthused Ally, but there was only a crackly silence on the other end of the line. 'Are you OK, Zee?'

'No,' replied a very faint voice which promptly dissolved into drunken sobbing. 'I don't think I am. What do I do next, Ally? What am I going to do?'

Moments after Ally had reassured Zee that they'd talk soon and rung off, her phone trilled into life again. This time, the looks she received could have melted concrete, and she answered with a furtive half-whisper. 'Hello? I'm afraid it's not very convenient, I—'

'Mrs Bennett? This is the headmaster's secretary at St Olaf's.'

Ally's excuses dried in her throat. A call from the children's school was never good news. 'W-hat ... has something happened?'

'Mr Collins would like to see you after school this afternoon, if that's possible,' replied the secretary, somewhat coolly Ally thought. 'It's about your son Kyle. I'm afraid he's been in a rather serious fight.'

177

# Chapter Eighteen

'It's hopeless,' Luke declared, throwing down the phone. 'If there's no publicity in it, nobody's interested in helping out the homeless.'

Chas raised his head from the monthly accounts. 'Unless it's Christmas,' he reminded his colleague. 'And then every well-meaning middle-class person for miles around wants to spend Christmas Day at the temporary shelter, doling out plates of turkey and Brussels sprouts.' He shook his head is sorrowful disbelief. 'It's as if they think homelessness only exists for one week a year.'

'Yeah. Like when Christmas is over, we pack all the homeless people back in a box until next year, along with the Christmas decorations.' Luke chuckled at the black humour of it; then the wave of depression hit him again. 'What are we going to do about it, Chas? The housing project's closed its doors and all of a sudden we've got another dozen rough sleepers – not to mention the Eastern Europeans who came all this way and then couldn't get a job.'

'I could suggest praying,' observed Chas. 'But since you're a confirmed atheist, I won't. Besides, prayers aren't always answered the way you expect.'

'How do you mean?'

Chas laughed. 'Oh, they're always answered. It's just that sometimes He says no.'

'Fat lot of good that is, then,' commented Luke. 'I guess that means I have to go grovelling again. At least the MDs of a couple of local firms have agreed to talk to me.'

'It's a start,' agreed Chas. 'When are you seeing them?'

'First one's this afternoon – but I must leave time to go and see Jake. Poor bastard.'

'Oh, I don't know. If you ask me, hospital's not such a bad place for him to be right now. At least there's a clean bed and three meals a day.'

'*If* he gets over this bout of pneumonia.'

'He will, Luke. I'm sure he will.' Chas looked at him over the rims of his reading glasses. 'I know you particularly like him, Luke, but you have to remember he's just one client among many.'

'I know, I know. You don't have to lecture me. Ally does enough of that.'

'Oh?' Chas threw him a questioning look. 'Still a bit of tension at home, is there?'

Luke took a deep breath and let it out slowly. 'Things will be fine once the baby's ... out of the way,' he said firmly, realising almost as he spoke the words just how cold and detached they sounded. But he'd discovered that was the only way he could cope with the situation. If he gave in to his emotions, he'd be a puddle on the floor.

The office phone rang again and the two men looked at each other.

'Let's ignore it,' said Luke.

'Sure?' Chas's hand hovered over the receiver. 'It might be someone offering us money. Or free accommodation.'

'Yeah, yeah, like hell it is. Oh – go on then, darn you.'

Chas picked up. 'ChelShel, can I help you? Yes of course, just one moment.' He held out the phone to Luke. 'It's for you. Your wife.'

Slightly surprised, Luke took the receiver. Ally hardly ever phoned him at work. It had been different in the early days of their marriage, but that felt like a long, long time ago. 'Ally? Everything all right?'

'Not really,' replied Ally. 'I've just had a call from Kyle and Josie's headmaster. Apparently Kyle's been fighting.'

Luke's eyebrows arched. 'Fighting? Kyle? I thought he was the cheeky-wisecrack-and-then-run-away type.'

'So did I, but according to the head's secretary, he broke another boy's nose.'

'Good God. Then he must have been provoked.'

'I don't know. Anyway, we have to go up after school and see Mr Collins, so maybe he'll be able to fill us in on what happened.'

'After school, you said?'

'That's right. The same time I normally pick up the kids.'

Luke's face registered dismay. 'Today?'

'Yes Luke, today! Are you going deaf in your old age or something?'

'Er ... no. I—'

Before Luke had found the words to explain, Ally guessed what he was about to say: 'You're going to tell me you can't come, aren't you?'

'It's just really difficult at short notice, love. I've got a meeting with a possible sponsor this afternoon.'

'So there's money in it, is there? Oh well, that's *definitely* more important than sorting out your son's education!'

'Ally, don't!' he pleaded. 'The thing is, after that I said I'd go to the hospital to visit one of our clients – Jake. You remember Jake, don't you? He's in with pneumonia, poor guy.'

There was an impatient outrush of breath at the other end of the line. 'I'm really sorry Jake's ill, but he's not going anywhere, is he? Why can't you visit him tomorrow?'

'I kind of ... promised.'

'I see. So you're going to leave me to sort this out on my own, while you're off playing Florence Nightingale?' The tone was flat, beyond bitterness. 'Well thanks Luke. Thanks for letting me know.'

And she put the phone down on him.


Just before four o'clock that afternoon, Ally arrived at the school, checked Kyle over for bruises and left him and Josie sitting in the corridor outside the head teacher's office.

She was a bag of nerves, but at least she wasn't alone. Miranda was with her, summoned at short notice from the beauty parlour by an incoherent phone call. 'I'll call it parenting practice,' she assured Ally when her sister apologised for dragging her across the county.

'Kyle won't say anything about the fight,' fretted Ally as they waited in the anteroom outside Mr Collins's office. 'Why won't he say anything?'

'You're the authority on kids, sis,' replied Miranda, gazing around the room as though this was the first State primary school she'd ever seen – which, if you didn't count her own, it probably was. 'But I'd say he's either trying to avoid getting himself into a deeper mess, or he's protecting somebody else.'

Ally pondered for a moment, recalling the time Kyle had taken the rap for Josie's attempts to redecorate the bathroom with their poster paints. But why would he want to protect the boys he was fighting? Unless he'd started the fight – and that just wasn't Kyle at all.

At last the waiting was over and Mr Collins called them into his office, away from the snooty gaze of his secretary.

'Ah yes, Mrs Bennett.' He shook her hand, as warmly as could be expected under the circumstances. Then his eyes travelled slowly, all the way from Miranda's Christian Louboutin heels to her low-cut Gaultier top – where it lingered. 'And this is?'

'Miranda Hesketh,' Miranda replied promptly, redirecting his attentions to her large and glossy-red mouth. 'I'm Ally's sister. Don't take any notice of me, I'm just here for moral support.' She gave her sister's shoulder a squeeze of encouragement as they sat down on the other side of the head's desk.

'What's all this about a fight?' demanded Ally, before Mr Collins's bottom had even touched the seat of his chair. 'Kyle's never been in a fight before! And as for injuring some other boy ... '

'I'm afraid there's no doubt that he did break the other boy's nose,' replied Mr Collins, sitting back in his chair with his finger-tips pressed together in a steeple.

Ally's heart sank. 'Oh.'

'But there is also no doubt that Kyle didn't start the fight,' he went on.

'Did Kyle tell you that?' asked Miranda. 'Because he wouldn't tell us anything.'

'Er, no. It's fortunate that the head of sixth form happened to be wheeling his bicycle to the bike sheds at the time and managed to see the whole thing. Plus, of course, we do have CCTV footage nowadays.' He sighed. 'Sad sign of the times, I'm afraid.'

Ally wasn't particularly interested in the head's views on contemporary social trends. 'If he didn't start it,' she insisted, 'then who did – and why?'

'It appears that four older boys and one girl were involved, with one of the boys acting as the ringleader. My colleague clearly heard threats of violence being made, along with ... taunts. I am quite sure that these taunts were what drove Kyle to strike out.'

'What kind of taunts?'

181

'Well, they were of a highly ... personal nature.' Mr Collins gave a little cough of embarrassment, but it was clear from the look on Ally's face that she wanted him to go on. 'Regarding ... um ... you.'

'Me!'

'Yes. You and your unborn baby, and the, er, baby's father.' His face was growing pinker by the minute. 'Without going into detail, it seems they centred on certain allegations of an ... illicit relationship.' By now, Mr Collins's whole head was pink, and his ears were turning the colour of goji berries.

Miranda's jaw dropped. 'Ally and Gavin? An affair, you mean? The lying little bastards! I'd laugh if it wasn't so preposterous!'

She turned to Ally for her agreement, but Ally was just drooping in her chair, looking as though all the cares of the world had been dumped upon her shoulders. 'The baby again,' she murmured. 'More trouble. Why is it that you try to do something good, and all it does is cause pain?'

Luke braked so hard outside St Olaf's primary that only his seat belt saved him from flying through the windscreen.

He was late. Very late. But with luck not *too* late. He just hoped Ally had waited for him.

But as he was hastily locking his car, he saw Ally and Miranda walking out through the school gates, with the kids trailing behind, looking unusually glum. Damn. They must already have been in to see the head. He was in big trouble now.

He hurtled across the intervening road, narrowly avoiding being run over by a lorry, and reached them just as they were about to climb into Miranda's Chelsea tractor.

'I'm sorry,' he panted. 'I kicked the hospital visit into touch, but the meeting ended late. What happened?'

'Not now, eh?' suggested Miranda gently; and only then did Luke realise that Ally's face was all damp and swollen.

'Ally?' His heart was in his mouth. 'Ally, what's wrong? Why are you crying?'

She just looked at him with eyes that were sadder than anything he had ever seen, and said: 'I don't want to talk about it.'

Then she buried her face in her sister's shoulder and sobbed her heart out.

\*

182

When she woke up the next morning, Ally felt almost as if the previous day had been an unpleasant dream. Everybody carried on the way they always did: the kids spilling milk and cereal all over the place, Kyle remembering at the last minute that he was supposed to take his PE kit for an annual sports day practice, and nobody – absolutely nobody – alluding to the fight. Luke seemed affable, easy to please, even apologetic. When he left for work, he lingered on the doorstep long enough to say goodbye with a proper kiss.

'I'll try not to be too late tonight,' he promised; 'but I'd better call in at the hospital on my way home, just to see how Jake's getting on.'

She managed a smile and a wave back, and thought that maybe Luke was right: it didn't really matter what people said, or thought. All that really counted was what you knew to be true; that, and the love of the family around you.

That carried her through a noisy and chaotic end-of-term session at Pussy Willows, and by the time she'd picked up the kids from school, driven them home and cooked their tea, she was absolutely knackered – but in a good way. She even got out her *Sound of Music* score and hummed her way through 'Climb Every Mountain'. If she really was going to be Gloucestershire's fattest mother abbess, she had to start somewhere.

After that, she still had enough energy to phone her sister about Zee. Normally, Miranda wasn't exactly the first person who'd have sprung to mind, but unusual circumstances called for unusual measures.

'You know my best friend Zee, don't you?'

Miranda did. 'You mean the boot sale king? Bit ditsy, looks like he gets dressed in the dark?'

'Yes, that's the one. Well, he's going through a bit of a rough patch at the moment, and what with a little girl to bring up on his own, he doesn't have a penny to his name most of the time. Anyway, he's picked up a bit of china he thinks might be worth something, and seeing as you know about antiques, I thought ... '

Miranda laughed. 'Me? Ally darling, all I know about is finding cheap smashed-up bits of furniture in junk shops and tarting them up as "designer's pieces". I don't know my Limoges from my Meissen.'

'But you know somebody who does,' Ally reminded her. 'That

bloke you went out with before you met Gavin. The hairy one, with the really long arms. He was into china, wasn't he?'

'Dirk de la Bedoyere? My God Ally, you've got a long memory!' Miranda shrieked with laughter. 'Yes, you're right, he's an expert in early English porcelain, one of the best. Works for one of the big international auction houses. So, you're asking me to call up an ex-boyfriend I dumped years ago, and get him to look at Zee's pot?'

'Yes please,' Ally confirmed. 'I'd be ever so grateful, and I know it would mean a lot to Zee.'

'Hm,' grunted Miranda. 'Good thing I'm a shameless hussy then, isn't it? Now, where's that little black book of mine?'

Half an hour later, Ally was stretched out on the sofa with a cup of tea, with some mindless music playing in the background, when the front door banged shut and Nameless came shooting into the living room like a bullet from a gun, leapt onto the back of the sofa and disappeared behind the curtains.

Ally sat up just as Luke walked into the room. He looked terrible. 'Hello love, bad day?'

'You could say.' He threw his messenger bag and coat over the back of the nearest chair.

'I've made a pie – it's still warm in the oven.'

'I'm not hungry.'

'Cup of tea then?'

He nodded. 'OK.'

When she came back with it, a few minutes later, he was still sitting in the same position, elbows on knees, chin resting on his hands, staring at the blank television screen.

'Here's your tea.' He took it. 'Did you pop into the hospital then?'

'Yes.'

'How's Jake?'

He turned his head to look at her, and she saw that his eyes were red-rimmed and sore. 'Dead.'

Ally sat down heavily. 'Dead? Are you serious?'

A note of bitterness entered his voice. 'How much more serious than dead can you get?'

'But he only had pneumonia, you said.'

'He had a bad strain of it, the doctor told me, and they got to it too late for the antibiotics to work. And what with being thrown back onto the streets ... He had nobody, Ally. Even his own son deserted him. There was nobody. Only me.'

She knew what he was saying. 'And you could have gone to see him yesterday. Only I said wait, because of Kyle.'

'It's not your fault,' he said flatly. 'And it wouldn't have made any difference. Not really.'

But in her heart, Ally knew he didn't mean that. It would have made all the difference in the world to Luke; and now it was all her fault.

# Chapter Nineteen

In a quiet corner of a Wiltshire country pub, Dirk de la Bedoyere was holding Zee's future prospects in the palm of his hand.

Despite the agonies of suspense, Zee found himself fascinated by the porcelain expert; he was the hairiest man he had ever seen. His forearms looked as though he had strapped hearthrugs to them. Even his ears were hairy. He found it incredibly difficult to imagine Miranda ever going out with a bloke who looked like a gorilla, even if he did have a certain rough charm – and pots of money. Still, as long as the guy knew his stuff . . .

De la Bedoyere held the small blue and white bowl up to the light and subjected it to minute scrutiny. 'Ah yes,' he concluded.

'Yes?' Zee and Miranda looked at each other. 'Yes what?'

'Yes, I was right. It's worth ten, maybe as much as fifteen.'

Zee's heart soared. 'Fifteen thousand?'

This raised an amused smile. 'Er, no. Fifteen pounds. It's quite a nice fake, otherwise it wouldn't be worth more than fifty pence. Anyone fancy another drink?'

'So much for my "find of a lifetime",' commented Zee as he and Miranda walked back across the pub car park to her 4x4. 'I feel a right pillock.'

'Dirk did say it was a mistake any amateur could make,' Miranda reminded him. Zee winced. 'But then I guess you weren't exactly happy at being described that way.'

'I must admit, after five years of buying and selling . . . well, I thought I knew a bit about antiques. Just goes to show it takes more than a copy of *Miller's Guide* to turn somebody into an expert.' He aimed a kick at a small stone – and missed. 'No fool like an old fool, eh?'

'You're not old!' laughed Miranda.

'I *feel* old. And extremely stupid. Suddenly I see how ridiculous I've been, expecting to stumble across some fabulous treasure that'll sweep away all my financial problems and take Emma through college. I'm sorry I've wasted your time,' he added, shamefacedly trailing in Miranda's wake.

'You haven't.' Miranda stopped and waited for him to catch up. 'I don't let people waste my time. Whatever I do with it, it's my decision. And besides, it doesn't feel as if it's been squandered – I know you've had a disappointment, but I'm actually rather enjoying myself.'

'Really?' Zee was taken aback.

'Really. It's nice to do something different once in a while, and it does get awfully tedious sometimes when Gavin's off wheeling and dealing and I'm left all on my own.'

As they approached the jeep, Molly the mongrel awoke and started barking with frantic joy, leaping about and trying to eat her way through the metal grille that separated her from the front of Miranda's car. 'At least somebody loves me,' commented Zee ruefully as Miranda released the locks and Molly leapt into his arms, covering his face with sloppy kisses.

Miranda watched the display of mutual adoration with a smile. 'It's nice to meet somebody who's as crazy about their dog as I am. Gavin gets rather irritable when I let Toby and Ben sleep on the bed, and of course Mum thinks it's unhygienic, but they're like family to me. I'd have cats too,' she added with a laugh, 'only Ben would probably eat them.'

Zee nodded his understanding. 'Do you think things might change when the baby arrives?' he wondered.

Miranda was shocked. 'Good grief no! That would be like ditching my first two children because the third one was a newer model! Animals and kids – it's my dream combination.'

'Me too,' agreed Zee as they climbed back into the car and Molly settled down on the back seat. 'Mind you, I'd kind of like another grown-up person in the equation, too. Life does get lonely sometimes. Then again,' he reflected, 'if recent experience is anything to go by, maybe I'd best not bother ... '

They headed off at speed down the country lane, the sudden

187

acceleration throwing Zee back in his seat like the G-force in a fighter plane. Miranda loved to drive – fast.

'Yes,' she said, neatly negotiating a series of Z-bends that left Zee's stomach behind, somewhere in a nearby field. 'Alison told me about your, er, problem with your ex. She's really worried about you, you know.'

'Pity Kate isn't,' replied Zee morosely.

'Perhaps she is, but she's just really good at hiding it?'

Zee laughed. 'Somehow I don't think so. I tried writing to her new address, but she sent the letters back with "get out of my life" scrawled across the back of them.'

'Ah,' said Miranda. 'I see what you mean. Tell you what,' she said as they approached the gates of the Hesketh residence, 'let's have a nice afternoon and forget about other people for a while. Why don't we take the dogs out for a walk in the woods? We go there every day. Molly will love it – it's a dogs' paradise in there.'

For once in his life, Zee didn't hesitate. He was supposed to be attending a sale that afternoon, but somehow he just didn't have the heart for it after being on the receiving end of Dirk de la Bedoyere's sarcasm. And Ally's sister was turning out to be much more human than he'd thought. 'You're on,' he declared.

He was feeling better already.

Miranda had always avoided Zee in the past; she'd never had much time for big, floppy-haired, gormless men. But she was beginning to wonder if she'd been a little unfair to him. Big and floppy-haired he might be, but there seemed to be quite a serviceable brain inside that untidy head, even if it could use a little reorganisation. And there was no doubt that he was a member of a scarce and dying breed: a genuinely decent bloke.

That was probably why women walked all over him, reflected Miranda as she fetched the dogs' leads from the utility room. In her experience, the human race consisted mainly of bitches and bastards, and consequently anybody else was in for a bad time. All Zee needed was a little toughening up, she decided; but then again, wouldn't it be a terrible shame to eliminate the source of his charm?

As they laughed and chatted together, and the two black Labs checked Molly out, Miranda wondered why she was expending any thought on him at all. Why on earth should she give a damn about

188

a man whose idea of haute couture was probably the British Home Stores sale? Then again, why not? I'm going soft, she decided, surprised but not annoyed by the realisation.

It was a hot day in late July, and the ancient woodland adjoining Miranda and Gavin's house provided welcome shade from the unforgiving sun. As soon as they were under its leafy canopy they let the dogs off the leash, and watched them chase each other among and around the trees.

'You're right,' commented Zee. 'It is a dogs' paradise. Look at Molly go!'

'It's not bad for humans either,' said Miranda. 'Very peaceful and calming. I always come here when I'm fed up, or if I've had a row with Gavin.'

'You and Gavin have rows? I can't imagine that. You two always seem so . . . perfect.'

Miranda chuckled. 'You wouldn't say that if you saw us arguing about who left the top off the toothpaste. Everybody has rows, Zee. Every couple in the world.'

'I guess.' Zee leaned his back against an oak tree. 'But my wife and I weren't together long enough to find that out – before we'd been married a year, she was dead.' He shook himself. 'I'm sorry – here we are, supposedly having a nice time, and I'm depressing you with my hard-luck story.'

'That's OK, you can't depress me. Not when I'm here.' Miranda closed her eyes, tilted her head back and enjoyed the sensation of the leaf-filtered sunlight on her face. 'Nothing could bring me down today.'

The sound of barking made her open her eyes, and she turned towards the source of it. Then came a sharp yelp.

'That's Molly,' said Zee, the smile falling from his face. 'Oh hell, I hope she hasn't cut herself on some wire or something.'

Crashing through the undergrowth, they reached a small clearing where some Victorian benefactor had built a little drinking fountain and a wrought-iron seat. However that wasn't what drew their attention.

Ben and Toby, the two Labradors, were still barking furiously, but Molly wasn't making a sound. She was stretched out on the ground, foam flecking her lips and her back stretched into a weird arch. Every muscle in her body seemed to be in spasm, making her twitch uncontrollably.

189

'Oh God,' gasped Zee. 'She's having a fit. What do I do? This has never happened before. Miranda?'

But Miranda was on her knees beside the dog, murmuring, 'No, oh God no. Not that.'

He grabbed her by the shoulder. 'What the hell is it, Miranda?'

She looked up at him with frightened eyes, set in a face drained of all colour. 'I ... I think it's poison,' she said, pointing to the chewed remains of a piece of steak by Molly's head.

'What!'

'Some bastard's put down poisoned meat. How fast can you carry Molly back to the house? If we don't get her to the vet right now, I don't think she has a chance.'

Zee gabbled a message into his mobile as Miranda put her foot down. By the time they hurtled through the doors of the veterinary surgery, at least they were expected.

'Quickly – bring her through into the surgery,' instructed the vet, a girl who looked far too young and far too beautiful to know how to save a sick dog's life. 'That's it, lay her on the table. Poisoned meat, you say?'

Miranda handed over the remains of the steak, wrapped in her discarded cardigan. 'This is what's left. What do you think it is?'

'Looks like strychnine – rat poison. I'll have to work fast.' She opened the surgery door. 'Now, if you don't mind, can I ask you two to wait outside?'

'But ...' protested Zee.

Miranda gently took his hand. 'Come on,' she urged. 'Let's get a coffee from the machine, and let Keira do her job. There's nothing we can do in here.'

It was outside normal surgery hours, and the waiting room was completely empty save for the two forlorn figures sitting opposite the surgery door, and the two black Labradors lying at their feet.

'This coffee's horrible,' observed Miranda.

'Yeah.'

'Fancy another one?'

'Go on then.'

They sat there, side by side, drinking the sludge-coloured liquid and straining to hear the slightest sound from inside the surgery.

190

One of the nurses went in but didn't come out again; and nobody answered any questions.

'It's too late, isn't it?' said Zee. Ben nuzzled at his hand, as if he understood. 'She's going to die.'

'We don't know that.'

Zee got up, sat down, got up again and paced the floor. 'What are they doing in there?'

'I don't know, Zee. Making her vomit, maybe. I think they give activated charcoal sometimes, to absorb the poison. All I know is there's no antidote.'

Zee's head sank into his hands. 'Then that's it.'

'No, I didn't mean that. I meant ... I think it's just a question of waiting.' Miranda twisted the ends of her silk scarf around her fingers. 'Molly's special to you, isn't she?'

'Sarah and I chose her together.' Zee choked back a sob. 'I know it's stupid, and she's only a dog, but Molly and Emma – they're all I have left. Oh God. What am I going to tell Emma?'

'It's not stupid at all,' said Miranda. 'The only stupid person around here is me. I should never have taken you into those woods.'

'You weren't to know some nutter was going to—'

'I think that poison was meant for Ben and Toby.'

'What? Why?'

'Gavin's made a few enemies around here,' she said slowly. 'You know what people are like about developers. And one or two people in the village are really heated up about Nether Grantley – some of them even accused Gavin of paying somebody to get rid of the rare orchids!'

'Might he have done?' asked Zee.

'I suppose he might – but he didn't! I know my husband, and he's far from perfect but he just wouldn't do a thing like that. That hasn't stopped the locals though. We've had one or two anonymous threats, some nasty things pushed through the letter box, that kind of stuff.'

'Threats to poison the dogs, you mean?'

Miranda shook her head. 'No, nothing as specific as that. Just: "watch your back, we're out to get you".'

'Then it's not your fault at all, is it?'

'Even if it feels that way?'

This time it was Zee who reached for Miranda's hand and gently squeezed it. 'Blaming yourself won't help,' he said. 'Why don't you take your dogs back home? There's no point in us both sitting here.'

'No way.' She planted herself squarely on her seat and picked up a magazine. 'I'm going to see this through with you: end of story.'

Luke yawned into his third mug of coffee. He was sure they didn't put as much caffeine into it as they used to; either that, or he was just more tired these days.

His body had never been partial to burning the candle at both ends, but in his line of work you had to be available any time. What with emergencies, office administration, food runs, regular visits to rough sleepers and poor Jake's funeral, Luke had been even busier lately. Added to which, now that Ally's pregnancy was advancing she was finding it harder to sleep – and there was nothing like an insomniac for keeping the other person in the bed wide awake too.

He knew that the way he felt about Ally was unfair, that his resentment was corrosive and unjust. But knowing that and actually feeling different were two wildly divergent things. So he drank a lot of coffee, avoided spending much time alone with his wife, and kept on repeating his silent mantra: everything will be OK once That Baby is part of somebody else's family. If it ever is . . .

Chas arrived back from a meeting with his bishop just after lunchtime, and found Luke fast asleep with his head in the in-tray. It seemed a pity to wake him, but Chas had news.

'Wakey-wakey for Uncle Chas,' he teased, accompanying this with a firm poke in the ribs.

Luke grunted and growled to himself and then awoke with an 'Ow – get off!'

'Sorry mate, but you were spark out and there are five messages on the answerphone.'

'Aw . . . shit.' Luke rubbed his eyes. 'Bloody coffee didn't work then.'

'Maybe you should try sleeping a bit more at night.'

This was greeted with hollow laughter. 'No time for that – the day's too short as it is.'

'Well then,' announced Chas, perching on the edge of Luke's

192

beaten-up old desk, 'I've got news for you.' He grabbed two pencils and executed an impromptu drum-roll.

'Go on then, amaze me.' Luke tilted back his chair in anticipation.

'I had a nice little chat with my bishop, and you know we've been trying to get the Church to sponsor a part-time administrative assistant for this office?'

'With about as much success as I've had losing these,' retorted Luke, prodding his small but obstinate love handles.

'Well you never know, maybe your wobbly days are over – because the bishop just said yes!'

Luke could not have looked more stunned if Chas had metamorphosed into a Venusian with five legs and three heads. 'You're having me on.'

'Cross my heart, etc., etc. I promise you it's true. It appears somebody donated some money to the bishop's charity fund, and now he reckons they can afford to fund an assistant, two days a week to start with then they'll see how it goes.'

A broad smile spread across Luke's face. 'You mean I won't have to spend all day doing paperwork any more? I can actually get out there and do my job? When's he starting then?'

'Next week – and it's a she. There's only one problem: where are we going to put her? There are only two desks in this office and it's full already,' Chas pointed out.

'Looks like one of us might have to move into the outside toilet – and I vote it's not me!'

Chas laughed. 'Don't panic. We'll just have to sling all that rubbish out of the storeroom at the back. You weren't planning anything this weekend, were you?'

Hours later, Zee and Miranda were still sitting in the vet's waiting room, awash with vending-machine coffee and able to recite all the articles from *Country Life* practically word for word. Afternoon surgery had come and gone; now it was just down to them again.

'Keira said we might as well go home,' Miranda reminded Zee as he stared vacantly at the floor.

'Can't,' he replied with a firm shake of the head. 'Anyway, I've already phoned a neighbour to pick up Emma from her nan's.'

'No, me neither,' admitted Miranda.

'Not until I'm sure, one way or the other.'

193

'At least she's managed to stabilise Molly,' pointed out Miranda. 'And she did say the first few hours would be critical.'

'That's what the consultant said,' recalled Zee.

Puzzled, Miranda cocked her head on one side. 'What consultant?'

'Sarah's. After she had the baby.' He didn't mean to tell Miranda, but suddenly the whole sad story spilled out of him, borne on a wave of pent-up anger he had carried inside him for the last eight years. 'He was so cocky about it all – even told me to pull myself together! And then he told me to go home and get some sleep, because "nothing was going to happen" that night. And all the time, while he was parading about chatting up the nurses, my wife was dying.'

'That's terrible,' said Miranda. 'Did he get struck off for negligence?'

'You're joking. Swift rap on the knuckles, that's all, and an out-of-court settlement for me. I could have taken it through the courts, but what was the point? I might have landed a big payout, but all I wanted was my wife back.' He looked towards the closed door opposite. 'And now I want Molly back, and I'm not leaving until I know something for definite. You understand, don't you?'

'Of course I do,' said Miranda. To her considerable surprise, she really did.

# Chapter Twenty

A few days later, Zee and Ally were chatting in Ally's back garden while Nameless snoozed on the seat of Josie's swing, and Molly lolloped around the overgrown flower beds like an overgrown puppy.

'I'd never have believed it, you know,' said Ally, pouring Zee another glass of home-made iced coffee. 'When you told me what had happened, I was sure that was the end for Molly. And now look at her!'

Zee tossed Molly's well-chewed Frisbee into the air and the dog galloped after it with a bark of joy – straight through the fish pond. 'Poor Miranda,' he said. 'She's still convinced it was all her fault; but the fact is, if she hadn't stayed with me that day, I think I'd have gone crazy.'

'Well *I'd* go crazy if people started putting death threats through my letter box,' replied Ally. 'Why the hell didn't she tell me?'

'What I don't understand is why she isn't putting pressure on the police to get to the bottom of it. I mean, I don't know her that well, but she strikes me as the kind of woman who makes things happen.'

'Oh believe me, she is.'

'So I was wondering.' Zee ran a finger round and round the rim of his glass. 'Do you think she's worried something might come out about Gavin – you know, dodgy deals, that kind of thing? Something he'd rather people didn't know about?'

Ally sipped her coffee reflectively. Privately, she'd been asking herself that very question, and she still wasn't entirely sure she wanted to know the answer. 'Who knows? Miranda reckons not, but I guess all businessmen have a few skeletons in their cupboard

... and he's definitely not Mr Popular around Nether Grantley, that's for sure.'

'I suppose not. But it seems unfair that it has to rub off on Miranda.'

Ally smiled at his earnest expression. 'Hey, you don't by any chance fancy my sister, do you?'

'Of course not!' replied Zee indignantly; then he realised what he'd said. 'Well – yes, of course I do. Any man would, but that's got nothing to do with it. I'd just like to be able to thank her for what she did. She paid the vet's bill without telling me, did you know that?'

'Seems only fair under the circumstances,' reasoned Ally. 'Molly did get poisoned on Gavin's land.'

'All the same, I'll have to have words with her. Oh yes: she's offered to give me some advice about my business, too.'

Ally was quietly impressed. Miranda was not the sort of woman who offered help to all and sundry. At school, while other kids helped each other out where and when they could, Miranda had turned her gift for maths into a playground homework business. There was even a sliding scale of charges, according to how hard the sums were.

'If she's offering advice, I'd take it,' advised Ally. 'Miranda and I may not always see eye to eye, but she's no fool. She's making a real success of that interior decorating business of hers. And she knows all the right people. Another biscuit?'

She offered Zee a groaning plateful of home-made goodies and was pleased to see him take a second handful. With the children on holiday and work at Pussy Willows over for the summer, she was making time to do the simple, domesticated things she really enjoyed, like baking sessions with the kids. Time she would have savoured, if things hadn't been so awkward between her and Luke.

'These are something else,' Zee sighed approvingly through a big mouthful of crumbs. 'Wish I could cook properly. But a gourmet meal round our house means eating off a plate instead of straight off the microwave tray.'

'Well,' confessed Ally, 'it's not all Nigella Lawson round here, either. To be honest I can't remember the last time all four of us sat down to have dinner together. If Luke's not working late – just for a change – the kids are off doing out-of-school activities or I'm at a rehearsal with you.'

196

'Are you and Luke, you know, getting on any better?' ventured Zee.

Ally shrugged. 'Don't ask me, I hardly see him. And when I do, he has hardly anything to say to me.'

'Maybe you're both just tired.'

'Sure.'

But they both knew there was more to it than that. So, thought Ally, did Luke. The question was, who would have the guts to come out and say so? And what – if anything – were they going to do about it?

'Psyche,' repeated the girl with the elfin features and the shiny mane of emerald-green hair. 'Psyche Stevens. But you can call me Psycho. Everybody else does.'

'That's not very kind of them,' observed Chas, taking the proffered hand and finding its grip surprisingly strong. 'Luke,' he called over his shoulder. 'Our new colleague has arrived, and she's called Psyche – sorry, *Psycho*.'

Luke emerged from the tiny kitchen, wiping his hands on his jeans, saw the newcomer – five foot nothing in an orange tunic and black lacy leggings – and joined in the ritual of handshakes and introductions. 'Psyche? That's an unusual name.'

'Dad's a classics professor,' explained the girl, as embarrassed as if she'd been admitting to a lifelong love of the Smurfs. 'I'm the lucky one though. My brother's called Cupid. Now, where do you want me to start?'

Luke had been eagerly anticipating the arrival of the new office dogsbody, simply as a means of dumping his admin and getting more time to do the things he really cared about. But Psyche was more than merely useful: she was a breath of fresh air. And by coffee-time, when Chas went out to check on a local soup kitchen, Luke realised he'd talked more to her in the previous two hours than he had to anybody else in weeks; Chas and Ally included.

It wasn't a happy realisation, but he did feel comfortable with this tiny twenty-two-year-old. It wasn't just that she was easy to talk to, and he certainly didn't feel any physical attraction towards her; but he couldn't help recognising something of himself in her. Or at least, something of the twenty-two-year-old self that had long since faded away. He wondered how all his crusading fire and boundless enthusiasm had somehow been transformed into bitter cynicism, somewhere along the way.

'Don't ever change, will you?' he said, out of the blue.

Psyche looked up from her desk in the old storeroom, where she was busy stuffing leaflets into envelopes. 'Pardon?'

'Sorry, I was just thinking aloud. Remembering how I used to be like you – I was going to change the world, too.'

'How do you know you haven't? It might have been completely different if not for you,' she pointed out.

'Well if I have, I haven't made a very good job of it!'

'I was wondering,' she said a little while later. 'Is there any chance I could have next Friday off?'

Here we go, thought Luke. She's only been here five minutes and already she wants a day off. Serves me right for being too enthusiastic about her. 'I don't know about that,' he replied. 'You're down to work on Fridays, and what with Chas's outside commitments and mine . . .'

'I know, I'm sorry for asking.' She did look genuinely sorry, thought Luke.

'Why did you want the time off?' he asked, intrigued.

'Oh, nothing that important. Just a demo.'

His ears pricked up. 'Friday? Not the big Water-Aid march down in London?'

'That's the one. Are you going then?'

'Wish I was,' he replied wistfully. 'I've marched against everything from apartheid to animal experiments in my time, and Ally, that's my wife, she used to come along with me. But you know how things change. You get older, you get more responsibilities, then the kids come along . . . '

'Oh yes, did I hear somewhere that you and your wife are expecting another baby? You must be really excited.'

She looked at him with such open, smiling eyes that he was quite sure she wasn't trying to wind him up; she really didn't know. 'Actually it's a bit more complicated than that,' he said; and then proceeded to tell her exactly why.

After a few seconds of stunned silence, Psyche uttered just one word: 'Wow.'

'Wow?'

She laughed. 'Yes Luke, wow! It's just . . . incredible!' Pure excitement danced in her eyes. 'What a wonderful, caring thing to do.'

198

'Well, I—'

'I've always thought it takes a very special kind of person to have a baby for somebody else. And your wife . . . Your wife must be truly *amazing*.'

'Yes,' said Luke, painfully aware that Psyche was right. 'She is.'

After that, he felt a desperate need to change the subject. 'What are you doing for lunch?' he asked.

Psyche held up a little paper bag. 'Sarnies.'

'There's a nice new organic café just round the corner. Do you fancy trying it out with me? I can't ask Chas, 'cause he's only into fry-ups.'

'OK, why not?'

Her smile made his day; but he still felt like the worst person in the world.

'Gavin!' Miranda shouted after him as he strode off towards the stables.

'Later,' he called back over his shoulder. 'I need to get some air into my lungs.'

'Gavin, it's important!' She ran after him and caught up with him just as he reached the stable yard. 'We have to talk.'

'Whatever it is can surely wait, can't it? I'm only going out for a ride.'

Miranda didn't waste time answering the question. 'Have you done something stupid, Gavin?'

He laughed. 'Now there's a question.'

'All these threats, Zee's dog, the horrible things people are saying in the village . . . '

'The police will catch whoever's behind it, darling.'

'Maybe, but why are they doing it? Why do they hate you so much? Is it because what they're saying is true?'

Gavin set off across the yard to Black Thor's stable. 'Come off it, Miranda – you're an intelligent woman. You can't possibly listen to a load of inbred yokels with a chip on their shoulder!'

At this, one of the stable lads cast a less-than-friendly look in Gavin's direction, but he didn't notice.

'Did you pay somebody to sort out the Nether Grantley business?' Miranda shouted after him. 'Because when you asked me to introduce you to somebody who could help, that was definitely not what I had in mind! Well, did you?'

199

Just as he reached the stable door, Gavin stopped, turned and gave Miranda an almost pitying look. 'Darling, this is the modern world and we're in business. What do you think?'

And with that, he left Miranda to think whatever she chose.

With Josie at a play scheme and Kyle enjoying the final week of a summer football school, Ally had a final few days to savour before the school holidays came to a close and summer officially ended.

Gavin had texted her earlier in the day, wondering if she wanted to come out for lunch; but for once she'd told him no, she had other plans. It wasn't an easy thing to do, knowing that Gavin would have made her laugh and sent her home feeling warm and worthwhile and appreciated. But deep down, Ally knew that something had to give – and soon. She couldn't go on having cosy little secret lunches with Gavin and hardly exchanging a civil word with Luke.

Either she and Luke had to start talking like grown-ups, or . . . or something nasty and definitive was going to happen to their marriage. And would Gavin be there to pick up the pieces? She didn't even want to think about it, or about what might happen to the kids.

So today she'd decided to make the first move. She'd made a mountain of sandwiches, baked a home-made cheese and bacon pie (Luke's favourite) and some cakes, and crammed the lot into a basket along with half a bottle of wine from the back of the fridge. The sun was shining, and there was a nice shady spot by the lake in the park, just waiting for them. This was going to be a surprise picnic to remember.

Parking the car a couple of streets away, Ally grabbed the basket and headed for the ChelShel office. She must have been around fifty yards away when she saw him emerge from the front door. He turned back, talking to somebody inside the lobby. Ally was about to shout to him to wait for her, when a second figure came out of the building.

This time it was a girl. A tiny, slender wisp of a thing with bright green hair and garish clothes. The new office assistant? Must be. She was just a kid though. Substitute green for red, thought Ally with a start, and that could be me, fifteen years ago.

She was near enough to call out to them, but she didn't. Because she was also near enough to see the way they smiled and laughed at each other, and then set off down the road together as though they had known each other for years. They looked so bloody happy. That was bad enough; but when two of them disappeared into that new organic café Luke had been promising to take her to, Ally knew it was time to give up.

As if in response to some celestial stage direction, a fat grey thundercloud drifted across the sky, obliterating the honey-yellow sun.

A couple of minutes later, Ally was inside the ChelShel office.

'Surprise – I've brought you some lunch,' she said, thrusting the basket into Chas's arms. 'Enjoy.'

'Thanks. Shall I tell Luke you called?' Chas asked as she turned to leave.

'Please yourself,' she replied flatly. 'But between you and me, I doubt he'd be all that interested.'

The weather was definitely on the turn. The late August sky had turned from blue to a leaden grey, and everywhere felt heavy and airless and headachey.

As Zee parked the old van in his driveway that evening, he felt the first fat drops of rain on the back of his head. He could feel thunder in the air, too, and a hot wind began lashing at his face. 'Come on,' he chivvied Emma. 'Let's get you and Molly inside before the heavens open. I reckon there's a storm on the way.'

By the time the three of them were sitting in the kitchen drinking cola, with Molly contentedly gnawing at a rawhide chew under the table, thunder was rumbling in the distance, and the rain was positively hammering down on the glass roof of the lean-to. The forecasters had predicted storms for tonight, mused Zee; and it looked like they'd got it right for once, the bastards. So much for that evening visit to the cinema he and Emma had been planning.

'One, two, three, four, five,' counted Emma, measuring the distance between the last flash of lightning and the next thunderclap, 'six! The storm's six miles away, Dad. Is that a long way for a storm?'

'I don't know,' he admitted. 'But frankly I'd rather it went somewhere else altogether. If it gets next door's wonky chimney, we can wave goodbye to our greenhouse.'

'The lightning's pretty though,' argued Emma. 'Look, it's all purple and yellow. One, two, three . . . '

'Supper, then bed,' decreed Zee, flinging whatever he could find into the well-loved family frying pan.

'Can't I stay up a bit, Dad? To watch the storm?'

'Well ... '

'I couldn't *possibly* sleep with all this noise,' Emma pointed out.

'Hmm. Just a little while then.'

'Yeah! Can I phone Kyle, Dad?'

'Yes – er, no!' Despite his complete lack of scientific knowledge, Zee had a vague notion that using the telephone during a thunderstorm was tantamount to sticking one's finger in an electric socket. 'Better not. Here.' He tossed her a potato. 'You peel that, and I'll try to make chips without burning down the house. Deal?'

About an hour later, when the storm was only four miles away and the sky had darkened to the colour of pewter, someone rapped on the front door. Zee felt like the butler in a Hammer horror film as he opened up and peered outside.

'Miranda? My God, the state of you!'

She blinked at him through a curtain of wetness. 'There's a bloody tree down on the bloody A417, and I bloody drove right into it. Bloody thing.'

'Good grief! You weren't hurt or anything ... ?'

'And just to make my day complete, Ally's not answering her bloody mobile so she must be out. It's a good job I remembered that you live round here.'

He dragged her indoors out of the rain, and called to Emma to bring a towel. 'No, second thoughts, better make that three. And my bathrobe. The thick one. You've never walked all the way here from the A417?'

'Breakdown truck couldn't get out for God knows how long, because of the blocked roads – it's horrible over the other side of the county, apparently. So I thought, who do I know who lives around here? Sorry,' Miranda added, gratefully accepting a towel, 'I seem to have soaked right through your doormat.'

'Hey, don't worry about it. Here, put this on.' Zee fumbled and fussed with the bathrobe.

'It's upside down, Dad. Give it here.' Emma wrapped it round Miranda's shoulders. 'Would you like some chips?' she enquired politely. 'We've got some left over, and they're only black on one side.'

'Now that's the best dinner invitation I've had all week,' smiled

202

Miranda, kicking off her shoes and squelching down the hallway. 'Looks like Gavin'll be eating on his own tonight. Bugger. I'd better phone and tell him to cancel the dinner guests. Don't suppose you know anywhere round here where I could stay overnight?'

'Certainly do,' replied Zee, thrilled to have an opportunity to display his gallantry. 'You can have my room and I'll take the sofa downstairs. And for once,' he added before Miranda could get a word in, 'I'm not taking no for an answer.'

It was the first time in weeks that Luke had made it home before eight pm. Josie was sound asleep, Kyle was staying over at his mate's house, and the scene couldn't have been better set for a romantic evening à deux.

But as the gods hurled furniture at each other across the heavens above Cheltenham, and all the roads turned to quagmires, Ally and Luke gazed at each other miserably across the dinner table.

'This is nice,' said Luke, poking at his almost-untouched dinner.

'Then why haven't you eaten it?' flung back Ally.

'I'm not hungry.'

'No, of course you're not; you had lunch with that young girl from the office, didn't you? In that café you were going to take me to, but I don't suppose you remember that.'

'Of course I do,' protested Luke. 'It just seemed like the right place to take her – it was only her first day, I was trying to make her feel at home. Anyway, lately you haven't wanted to go anywhere much.'

'I'm pregnant, Luke, in case you hadn't noticed. I've got swollen ankles and backache and God knows what else. I'm too knackered to go anywhere most evenings.'

'Unless it's a rehearsal for that stupid musical,' snapped Luke. 'Or a visit to your new best friends – Gavin and Miranda.'

Ally's face burned with anger. 'Well, it is nice to go somewhere just occasionally where people actually talk to me instead of avoiding me and making me feel like the least desirable woman on the planet.'

'Oh, so Gavin makes you feel desirable, does he?'

She yearned to spit 'Yes!' back in his face, but something restrained her. 'Don't be so stupid and childish, Luke. Ever since you persuaded me to have this baby, you've regretted it and you've .

203

been punishing me for it. You can do what you like to yourself. Just don't take it out on me, or Miranda, or Gavin.'

There was a brief silence, punctuated only by the drumming of rain on the roof of the lean-to. Outside, the storm seemed to have abated to a steady torrent, with just a glimmer of brightness at the corners of the sky, suggesting that it might all be over soon. Unlike the tension between Luke and Ally.

Luke shoved his plate away, got up from the table and walked to the window, turning his back to his wife. 'All right then – yes, it was my mistake. I didn't know how it was going to make me feel. There, I've said it. Is that what you wanted to hear?'

'All I've ever wanted to hear is "I love you",' she replied, very softly.

'I do. You know I do,' he replied without turning to face her.

'I used to. Now I'm not so sure.' A long silence followed. Ally was convinced that Luke must be able to hear the thump-thump-thump of her racing heart, even above the heavy thunk of the grandfather clock in the hall. 'It's Josie's birthday in a few weeks' time. And then Kyle's not long after.'

'Yes, I know.'

'Are we going to do something special? We ought to be thinking about it, Luke. Things take time to organise.'

He turned round slowly, visibly calmer. 'I know, Ally. It's just ... there's so much going on right now. I can't seem to think straight, let alone organise anything.'

'OK then, let's involve Miranda and Gavin,' Ally suggested. 'She's great at organising things, and he's got quite close to the kids – well, Kyle anyway.'

A warning flame flared in Luke's eyes. 'Gavin again, bloody Gavin every time!'

Ally's patience snapped. 'Why not? Let's face it, Luke, the kids have seen far more of him in the past few months than they have of their own father.' She took several deep breaths to calm herself down. 'Why do you hate him so much, Luke? Is it jealousy?'

'Why the hell should I be jealous of him? You know money doesn't interest me.'

'I'm not talking about money; I'm talking about the fact that he's the father of this baby.' She cradled a protective hand across her stomach. 'You just can't handle that, can you? Or the fact that we get on well together.'

Luke's eyes narrowed. 'Just how well *do* you get on with him?'

'What!'

'You know what I'm saying, Ally. Do I have a reason to be jealous?'

She felt all the colour draining from her face. Could he hear a trace of uncertainty in her voice as she answered: 'Of course you don't!'?

'Are you quite sure about that?'

She glared back at him, putting all her willpower into not flinching from his gaze. 'You're really glad he's been getting threats, aren't you?'

'Now who's being stupid?'

'You *are* glad. The only thing that upset you was Zee's dog. Apart from that you thought it was funny.' She paused, then said what had been on her mind for some time. 'Is it you, Luke? Are you the one who's been sending them?'

'What the hell—'

'Is it some kind of sick joke to take the wind out of Gavin's sails, or what?'

Luke stared at her, eyes wide, so shocked he was hardly breathing. Very close by, a massive thunderclap was followed by the ominous creak of falling timber.

'How can you say that, Ally?' he whispered. 'How can you even *think* it?'

'If I'm wrong, Luke, I'm sorry, but—'

'I thought you knew me better than that Ally, but if you think that about me, you really don't know me at all.'

She took a few steps towards him. 'Luke, I'm sorry. But the way you've been ... it could have been you. I had to ask, don't you see?'

Ally reached out to touch him but he stepped away. 'Leave it.'

Like a sudden cloudburst, tears flooded Ally's eyes, and all vestiges of outward calm vanished. 'Luke please, all I want is for things to be right between us. Please, just hold me. That's all I ask.'

He hesitated, and for a moment she thought he was going to take her in his arms; but then he turned away. 'I can't. Ally, right now I can't even bear to look at you, don't you understand?'

'Oh, I understand all right.' Cold, agonising anger washed over her, turning her resolve to steel. 'I'm your wife, you persuaded me to have a baby, and now you find me repulsive. So I'll just get right out of your life, shall I? Make things easier for you?'

'For God's sake don't be so dramatic. I'll just take the spare bed tonight, things will look different in the morning.'

Ally grabbed her coat from a hook on the back of the kitchen door. 'Maybe they will, maybe they won't,' she replied. 'But I won't be here to find out.'

Pure blind anger kept her going for the first few miles, then Ally started to feel the fear. When she left the house it was just rain: heavy rain, admittedly, but nothing more than that. Then the storm had returned, turning everything into a nightmare. She'd never driven in weather like this, never in her life before. It was dark and wet, the air was full of debris whirled up by the wind, and the car felt as if it was being tugged towards the edge of the road by invisible forces.

She had to find somewhere safe to sit this out. But she sure as hell wasn't going back home. No use going to Zee's house. He'd said something about a cinema visit and then staying overnight at Grandma's, wherever that was. Diana or one of the others from Pussy Willows? Oh God no, they'd dine out for a year on the kind of gossip her moonlight flit would generate. A hotel? Too soulless and lonely – and expensive.

Ally needed someone to talk to, and with Zee unavailable there was only one place she'd feel secure: Miranda's house. True, Gavin might be there too, but that was all right. As long as her sister was there, nothing untoward could possibly happen, could it? And Miranda was sure to bring everything back into proportion, make her see that things weren't really that bad.

She tried phoning ahead to let Miranda know, but the network was down, no doubt because of the weather. Ah well, it didn't really matter. All Ally had to do was concentrate on getting there without crashing, and everything would be fine.

She was feeling better already.

Gavin finished off a lonely supper of cheese, crackers and yesterday's leftover risotto, and poured himself a glass of port. It was a pity Miranda was stuck in Cheltenham, but at least she hadn't been injured in the accident, and the car repairs were just a nuisance.

He was feeling a bit lonely though. Ever since the age of seven, when his parents had packed him off to boarding school, he'd had a secret horror of abandonment. He'd even been known to spend time with people he couldn't stand, rather than be on his own – not that he advertised the fact. It didn't accord too well with his image. One thing was for sure though: that queen-sized bed upstairs was going to feel mighty big and cold tonight without Miranda to warm it up.

When the doorbell sounded he almost didn't answer it. It was late, he was alone, the weather was apocalyptic out there, and with all the threats doing the rounds, it might be safer not to. But curiosity got the better of him. And as he squinted through the peephole, he had the shock of his life.

Ally!

Wrestling with the bolts and chains, he wrenched the door open.

'Ally, what the hell are you doing out on a night like this?'

She looked up at him, shivering despite the hot night, wet clothes sticking to her, and more than a little tearful. 'P-please can I c-come in, Gavin?'

'Of course you can.'

'And p-please c-ould I have some t-tea or something? I'm a bit c-cold.'

'You can have as many cups of tea as you want,' he promised, gently but firmly ushering her inside and closing the door behind her. 'But first we're going to get you dry and you're going to tell me exactly what's happened to get you into this state.'

Half an hour later, showered and towelled dry, Ally was sitting on Gavin's sofa, trying to explain to him what had possessed her to drive off into the middle of nowhere, during the worst summer storm for decades.

'I know it was a stupid thing to do,' she said, 'and right now I feel like a complete idiot, but it's just . . . I couldn't stand being around Luke a minute longer. Can you understand that?'

Gavin nodded. 'Of course.'

'You see, sometimes – this'll sound crazy but I mean it – sometimes it's as if we just can't stop wanting to hurt each other.' She hung her head. 'It never used to be like that. Not until – you know.'

'The baby, you mean?'

Ally answered with a silent nod.

Gavin poured Ally a second 'medicinal' cognac from the bottle on the table, handed the glass to her and perched himself on the arm of the sofa. 'Please try not to feel bad about it,' he urged her. 'We've all done it, deliberately lashed out at somebody to make them feel bad. Hell, teenagers do it all the time.'

'But they're just kids,' reasoned Ally. 'We're supposed to behave like adults.'

'We're all little kids inside.' Gavin laughed softly. 'I know I still am. Look – I know it's not for me to takes sides or criticise or whatever, but it seems to me you've had enough provocation to send anybody over the edge.'

'I'm sure I've not been that easy to live with myself,' she hedged, instinctively defending Luke though she wasn't sure why.

'Oh come on, Ally! All you've done is be a fantastic wife, mother, sister, teacher, friend – and what's Luke doing while you're wearing yourself out? Stamping around like a toddler who doesn't want to share his toy-box, that's what.'

'It's hard for him,' she protested lamely.

'It's a lot harder for you.' Gavin put down his own drink, took the glass from Ally's hand and set it down on the coffee table. The faintest gasp of breath escaped from her lips as his fingers curled about hers. 'He doesn't appreciate what he has, Ally. You know that. And it's a crime.'

Ally dared to turn her head and look directly at Gavin. There was an urgency in his voice, an intensity in his expression that she found almost frightening ... yet profoundly exhilarating too. Those eyes. How often had she stopped herself from gazing too long into them, somehow sensing that danger lurked in those cool blue depths? And now she was doing that very thing she had denied herself for so long: wilfully losing herself in Gavin's beautiful eyes, letting his melodious voice wrap itself around her, sending a thrill through her whole body, making every tiny hair on the nape of her neck tingle to attention ...

And it felt so good.

'Have you any idea how special you are to me?' he asked. 'Have you?' She froze, unable to answer yet desperate to know, to hear that this man she had yearned for for so long really did see her as more than his exquisite wife's plain sister. 'Oh Ally,' he murmured, 'I wish I could find a way to show you just how much you mean to me.'

208

'Gavin, I'm your sister-in-law. And I'm pregnant – *very* pregnant.'

'You think that makes me feel any less for you?'

Or me for you, thought Ally with a shiver.

His fingers tightened around hers and he bent towards her, his parted lips only inches from hers. The kiss was inevitable, unstoppable and utterly insane. And Ally wanted it with every fibre of her being.

Luke had spent the first half-hour after Ally's explosive departure comforted by a kind of incredulous numbness. Ally hadn't really told him to go to hell, had she? She hadn't really slammed the door on him and roared off into the night, without the faintest hint of where she was going?

The minutes ticked by and there was still no sign of Ally. Well, perhaps she had gone after all; still, she would be back in a minute, because there was a storm raging out there and she was a sensible woman, and she wouldn't want him worrying, and besides, they weren't the kind of people who had dramatic fallings-out.

But as the sky grew darker still, Luke's numbness turned to alarm. What if something happened to her? What if something already had? No, no, he was overreacting. She'd just have driven round to a friend's house to sit things out and then return home when passions had died down a bit. He grabbed the phone book and started calling everybody he could think of: starting of course with Zee.

But Zee hadn't seen Ally – only Miranda, who, for some reason Luke's brain couldn't adequately grasp, was spending the evening at Zee's house; so Ally couldn't be at her sister's house either. None of her other friends had anything to report either. It was as if she'd disappeared off the face of the earth.

Luke was on the point of phoning the hospitals and the police station when the phone rang. He grabbed the receiver as though his life depended upon it. But it wasn't Ally; it was just about the last person in the world he wanted to speak to.

'Luke? Gavin here.'

'Oh.'

'Ally thought you might be worried about her, so she asked me to phone you and tell her she's fine.'

Luke's brain struggled to comprehend this scenario. 'She asked *you*? Why?'

A slightly exasperated intake of breath sounded at the other end of the line. 'Because she's here.'

An icy hand gripped Luke's heart. 'With you?'

'That would seem to follow.'

Luke's hackles rose. 'Don't you get sarky with me, mate. I want to speak to my wife.'

'She's asleep.'

'Then wake her up!'

'With an attitude like that, I'm not surprised she ran out on you.'

'She has not run out on me! Listen Gavin, I *need* to speak to Ally. Now.'

'Sorry Luke, but she's worn out and she needs the rest. I'm sure she'll phone you in the morning and explain. In the meantime, you sound like you could use some sleep yourself. Have you been drinking?'

'No I bloody well haven't! But what the hell business of yours is it if I have?' demanded Luke, and he slammed the phone back onto its stand. Then he sat down in the armchair with the sagging springs, and did something he hadn't allowed himself to do for a very long time.

He wept.

And although she didn't quite know why, the little girl peeping through the banisters at the top of the stairs felt like crying too.

# Chapter Twenty-One

What a difference one night could make.

As Ally's eyelids fluttered open, she realised that all the crashing and pounding of the thunderstorm had faded away, to be replaced by the gentle twittering of birds in the trees outside the bedroom window.

Birds? Trees? Something didn't quite compute. Heavy-headed and with the taste of last night's alcohol stale in her mouth, Ally forced herself into consciousness. There aren't any trees outside our bedroom window, she reminded herself. And if there were, you wouldn't be able to hear the birds because next door have got the builders in.

She propped herself up in bed on one elbow, squinting painfully in the streaks of sunlight filtering through aubergine and silver brocade curtains, and realisation stabbed her as viciously as the shard of pain in her head.

Oh God, she thought as panic overcame her. Where did I spend last night?

It was Saturday, and for the first time in weeks Luke didn't get up early and go to the office, to see if he could make work for himself. He hadn't the heart for it, and even if he had, how could he? With no Ally, he was the only one around to get Josie dressed and fed, pick up Kyle from his mate's house and then, worst of all, answer their questions.

Not that there were many different questions in the car back home, just the same ones over and over again: 'Where's Mum gone?'; 'Why did she go?'; and 'When's she coming back?'. It was just that Luke couldn't find acceptable answers to any of them.

Around mid-morning, he plucked up the courage to phone Gavin's house, but there was no answer and his imagination almost had him climbing the walls. He thought about calling Miranda's mobile and putting her in the picture, but malice wasn't really his game, she'd know soon enough anyway, and besides: what picture, realistically, did he have? Just a few lurid lines sketched out by his imagination.

And all the time, a question of his own kept coming back to taunt him, again and again: 'What if she doesn't come back? What if Ally doesn't come home at all?'

It was just before noon when Ally parked her car and walked very slowly across Brookfield Road to number twenty-two.

Her head was still pounding, and after last night's cognac she wasn't at all sure she ought to have been driving; but accepting a lift from Gavin was out of the question, so she'd taken the chance. It wasn't the drink that was making her shake though, or making the palms of her hands perspire.

Reaching the front door, she counted to ten before taking her door key out of her bag. But before she'd inserted it into the lock, the door was wrenched open from inside and Luke flew out.

'Ally!'

She'd half expected him to be furious, but frankly he looked even more terrified than she was.

'Hello Luke.' There was an endless pause. Nobody moved a muscle. 'Can I come in?'

'What? Oh. Yes, sorry, whatever.'

Luke stepped back to let her pass, and she walked through into the front room, where Kyle and Josie were squabbling over the games console.

'I told you not to do that! Now you've lost all my settings.'

'It was *you* that made it crash!'

'Only because you jogged my elbow.'

'No I never!'

'Yes you did. Little girls can't play video games, they're too stupid.'

'Just 'cause you're a boy, doesn't mean you know everything, Kyle Bennett. I'm going to tell Dad you're being horrible to me.' Josie turned towards the door to yell up the stairs. 'Dad! Kyle said—'. Her eyes widened. 'Mum! Hey Kyle, Mum's back!'

She flung herself at Ally, while Kyle hung back pretending not to be that pleased really. At rising eleven, he had an image to maintain.

'Where did you go, Mum? We missed you. Was it nice? I've got two loose teeth, does the tooth fairy give you more money for big ones?'

As she hugged her daughter, Ally looked over her head at her husband. Luke's face was a horrible grey colour, his eyes filled with the apprehension of things as yet unsaid. Things that, perhaps, ought not to be said at all. She sensed that this was not the time to fall apart. This was the time to hold everything together with at least a show of normality – if not for their sakes, then for the kids'.

'Well, I don't know what you two are doing vegging around in here,' she declared breezily, thanking her lucky stars for ten years' experience of amateur dramatics. 'It's a gorgeous day outside. Much too nice to stay indoors. I think we should all go for a swim. What do you reckon, Daddy?' she appealed to Luke.

'Much too nice to be inside,' he agreed after a moment's hesitation. 'Come on kids, grab your cozzies and let's go down the Lido.'

By the time Miranda made it back home, in the courtesy car she'd blagged from a susceptible garage mechanic, it was well into Saturday afternoon and the sun was, if not actually over the yardarm, then as near as made no difference. Miranda needed a nice big drink.

'Gavin?' she called out as she walked in through the kitchen. 'Gavin, I'm back. And we need to talk.'

He shouted something inaudible back, and she tracked him down to the utility room where, to her surprise, he was stuffing bedding into the washing machine. 'My God, Gavin, doing the washing? Have you had a personality transplant?'

'Only trying to be helpful darling,' he replied with wounded dignity. 'We had a house guest last night, so I thought it'd help you if I washed the bedlinen and made up the bed.'

'A house guest?'

'Your sister. She had a bit of a row with Luke last night and needed somewhere to stay for the night. I was hardly going to send her back out into that bloody awful storm, so I put her in the guest bedroom.'

'Ally!' Miranda was stunned. 'Oh no, I knew they were having a few problems over the pregnancy, but,' a dreadful thought struck, 'she is all right, isn't she?'

'She's fine.'

'And the baby?'

'Yes, the baby's fine as well. Everything here is fine, OK?' Gavin straightened up, pressed the button on the washing machine and looked his wife up and down. 'The question is, are you OK too?'

'What do you think?' retorted Miranda, her former irritation returning. 'My meeting's cancelled, then I drive the 4x4 into a tree during a thunderstorm, some of my favourite clothes get so soaked they dry out looking like corrugated cardboard, and if it hadn't been for Ally's friend Zee I'd probably have spent the night in a ditch. Or a Travelodge, which isn't much better.'

'Pretty tough luck,' agreed Gavin.

'Ah, but that's not the end of it. Because just to make my joy complete,' she went on with a hard stare, 'I find out one of my cheques has bounced because *somebody* has had all the money out of the bloody joint account! I wonder who that somebody could be?'

Gavin winced. 'There may have been a few extraneous expenses,' he admitted, 'relating to Nether Grantley, in the main.'

'Darling, you have skip-loads of money of your own – why did you have to torpedo the joint account, for God's sake?'

'Sometimes expenses crop up, you know,' he replied with obvious discomfort. 'Things you might not want to show up in the books of the business. One-off cash payments, you know the sort of thing.'

'One-off *bribes*, for example?' enquired Miranda.

For the first time, a note of anger entered Gavin's voice. 'Oh, so now you've decided I'm definitely a crook, have you?'

'I don't know what to think,' confessed Miranda. 'But I'd like that cash back right now, please. Now I'm going for a nice long bath,' she called back over her shoulder as she walked towards the stairs. 'If you're a very good boy, I'll let you bring me a double vodka and soap my feet.'

Zee had plenty of food for thought.

For one thing, he realised that he'd grossly misjudged Miranda

214

Hesketh, which when he thought about it was quite silly. For all her airs, affectations, designer clothing and intimidating beauty, Miranda was still Ally's sister; which was a pretty solid indicator that, underneath it all, she had a heart of gold.

Maybe he was biased. He was prepared to admit that. She was after all the most gorgeous woman he had ever set eyes upon, and even better, she appeared not to hate the sight of him; and that in itself was a double he'd never had any realistic hopes of achieving.

But Miranda wasn't the only woman on his mind. There was Ally too, of course: his dearest friend and the closest thing he would ever have to a sister. Zee was becoming seriously worried about her, but was at a complete loss to know what to do about it.

Every instinct told him that her cosy, secret encounters with Gavin were a bad idea, but if Ally insisted that they were harmless opportunities for conversation, who was he to come over all Victorian on her? Besides, he was pretty sure that for Ally they were harmless encounters; it was Gavin he was less sure about. And the thought of coming up against a man like Gavin Hesketh in any way, shape or form, filled him with nameless terror.

Then there was Kate. The very thought of her filled Zee with gloom and foreboding, just as powerfully as it had once filled his dreams with 3D images of Technicolor lust. A small part of his heart had been hoping never to succeed in tracking her down; at least that way, since he had tried to find her, his conscience would be clear and his future life free of complications. But deep down, he had known all along that he would never be able to rest until he and Kate were in the same room together, having a grown-up discussion about the new life he had unwittingly helped her to create.

From now on, he'd told himself grimly, it's triple-strength condoms or a cold shower; and nothing in between.

And now there was this.

As Emma, his little girl, played upstairs in her room, Zee sat on his battered sofa trying to work out what to do. It wasn't a complex dilemma, just an unpleasant one. He was still shaking from the phone call, the strident sound of Kate yelling at him down the line that it was all his fault; that she'd miscarried *his* baby because of *his* harassment; that, in effect, he was some kind of cold-blooded child murderer.

215

To crown it all, she wanted to see him.

He could refuse, of course he could. He was under no obligation to show up just so that she could hurl more unwarranted abuse at him. But something told him he would turn up anyway. Maybe she was right. Maybe it was all his fault.

Yes, he was sure he'd go. The question was, should he take somebody with him? Normally he'd have taken Ally, but with all the trouble from Luke, she had more than enough to think about right now. Which left ... well, nobody really. Zee had plenty of acquaintances, but he didn't go in for legions of close friends.

Then a thought popped into his head. Miranda.

But if he asked Miranda, was there any reason to think she would come? She'd be more likely to blow him out. After all, after years of vague acquaintance he still hardly knew her, not properly. So how come he felt as though he'd known her all his life?

While Zee was trying to decide if he was brave enough to make that crucial phone call, the Bennett family were experiencing the Saturday afternoon from hell.

Ally knew she and Luke had to talk, *really* talk, and she could sense that he did too; but so far all they'd done was snap at each other and the kids, and find things to do that kept them as far apart as possible. It was a childish way to behave, but there was more than just anger or tension in the air: this was fear – of what would be said on both sides once somebody made the first move.

That was why Ally was on her knees in the kitchen, with her head and shoulders inside the cupboard under the sink. It was damp, slightly mouldy and redolent of forty years of cleaning products, but clearing it out was a great way to hide.

'Can I—' asked a small voice behind her.

'No,' she replied, without bothering to turn round. 'Go and play in your room.'

'But Mum—'

'Room. Now.'

Small, dispirited footsteps trailed away and Ally felt like the meanest mother in the world. Poor Josie, she thought with a pang of guilt. It's not your fault your mum and dad have chosen today to behave like sulky two-year-olds. You ought to be outside playing, not cooped up in your room, but Luke's out in the garden and although you don't know it, I'm worried what he might say about last night ...

216

This is stupid, she decided. I have to talk to him like an adult before his imagination runs away with him.

Heavier footsteps clumped towards her across the kitchen floor. She froze.

'Done the grass,' muttered Luke.

'That's good.'

'Might go out for a bit.'

'Fine.'

'Should you be doing that in your condition?'

'God knows.'

There was a kind of flat pause; and then, just as Ally thought he was going to go away again, the veil dropped and Luke fired the first salvo in the war Ally had been dreading: 'Don't want to do anything that might upset darling Gavin, do you?'

Ally's heart pounded against her ribs and she fought to control her breathing. 'Gavin is not my darling,' she said, as coolly as she could.

'Oh really?' Luke's voice dripped with a cheap sarcasm she'd never heard him resort to before. 'But you thought you'd spend the night with him anyway – I mean hey, why not?'

Furious and afraid, Ally jerked upwards and hit her head on the underside of the sink as she wriggled backwards out of the cupboard. 'For God's sake, Luke, I never thought you were the kind of guy to make sweeping assumptions. Ever thought of checking your facts first?'

'I might. If you gave me any. For fuck's sake Ally, will you stop playing games and tell me what's going on? Or is the first I hear of it going to be a letter from the bloody solicitor?'

She stared at him with horror and pain. 'Please Luke, stop this. Just let me explain.'

'Mum.'

Shocked by the sudden interruption, Luke and Ally swung round. Kyle was standing in the door to the hall, gaming joypad dangling from one hand, his face white and his eyes wide.

Ally struggled to force a smile onto her face, but sensed it was probably more of a grimace. 'What's up, love?'

'Go and play for a bit, eh?' suggested Luke, his voice much softer now. 'Mummy and Daddy are having a . . . discussion.'

'You were arguing,' said Kyle, in a way that brooked no denial.

'People do argue sometimes,' said Ally gently. 'Even parents.'

217

'Tim Preston's parents used to argue all the time. They're divorced now.' The large, wide, frightened eyes moved from mother to father and back again. And then he added, in a voice barely louder than a whisper, 'Are you and Dad getting a divorce?'

The words knifed through Ally's soul like tempered steel. She didn't know what to say; but she knew this was no game. When she glanced towards Luke, she saw that he was gazing fixedly back at her. All the anger had left his face, leaving only a kind of questioning fear.

Look how low we've sunk, Ally thought with shame as she recalled how happy they'd been together, just a few months before. It's got so bad we've even made the children afraid. Is it too late to have that talk?

Is it too late to tell you I still love you?


Miranda was a revelation to Zee. Not only had she agreed to come with him to see Kate, she'd actually turned up at his house less than an hour after his phone call, armed with a big box of cream cakes and a comedy DVD.

'I think we could both use a bit of light relief,' she said, draping her gorgeousness across Zee's dog-chewed sofa.

'Things not too good at home?' enquired Zee tentatively. He didn't want to interfere and spoil their budding friendship. On the other hand, any suggestion that Miranda and Gavin weren't getting on too well filled him with a shameless excitement.

'It's not Gavin's fault,' Miranda assured him. 'Well, not really. But he's got so much on with all his business deals that I hardly see him any more. And between you and me,' she confided, 'I think he may have one or two reservations about the baby.'

'Really?' This was news to Zee and, he guessed, probably to Ally as well. 'What sort of reservations?'

Miranda back-pedalled. 'Oh, I don't know, I'm probably imagining it. You know what men are like – they just don't go all goo-goo over babies the way women do.'

'I do,' protested Zee. 'I'm hopeless. I could make silly faces at babies all day.'

Miranda laughed. 'I shall have to remember that when the little one's born and it's driving me mad.' She settled herself down next to Zee on the sofa, and nudged the cake box towards him. 'Go on, help yourself.'

He looked at her in surprise as she selected the biggest cake in the box. 'Cream buns?' he marvelled. 'Do models eat cream buns?'

'I'm a *retired* model now, Zee.' Her tone grew more serious. 'When I got over, you know, the anorexia, I decided that I was going to eat at least one really naughty thing every week and not feel guilty about it. So you see,' she raised the cake to her lips and took a big bite, 'this isn't a cream bun, it's therapy.'

They were halfway through the box of cakes when the phone rang. Zee answered with a mouthful of bun. 'Hello? Sorry? I didn't quite catch your name.'

'Ellen Parks,' repeated the middle-aged female voice. 'I'm Kate's mother.'

'Oh!' Zee nearly fell backwards in alarm. He'd never even considered the possibility of Kate having a mother, let alone met her. He put a hand over the mouthpiece of the phone and hissed to Miranda, 'It's Kate's mother!'

'What does she want?' Miranda mouthed back.

Zee replied with a 'beats me' shrug and returned to the conversation. 'Um . . . Mrs Parks. Hello. What can I do for you?'

'It's about my daughter. I believe you and she had a . . . relationship?'

'Er . . . yes. But she—'

'It's quite all right, you don't need to explain. I know all about the pregnancy and the fact that she left you suddenly. And the fact that you're planning to meet up again. That's why I feel it would be useful to talk. You and I.'

'Go ahead.'

'Not on the telephone. It's rather complicated and I'd find it easier to explain things to you face to face. I wondered if you'd mind coming to see me.'

'Oh. Where?'

'Northampton.'

Zee put his hand over the phone again. 'She wants me to go to Northampton!'

'Where's that?'

'I have no idea! Do you think it's a trap? You know how much Kate hates me.'

'Who knows?' Miranda shrugged. 'Go ahead, tell her yes. But I'm coming along too, just in case.'

*

After Josie and Kyle had gone back upstairs, Ally and Luke sat opposite each other at the kitchen table, over a pot of stewed tea.

'You mean ... you *didn't* spend the night with Gavin?'

Ally shook her head. 'Not in the way you thought. Luke – it's a seven bed house. I slept in one of the guest rooms.' She hesitated, then steeled herself to look Luke full in the face. 'I'm not saying I wasn't tempted – especially after seeing you looking so happy with that new girl from your office.'

'What – *Psycho*?' Luke gaped in disbelief. 'You thought ...? But she's just a – a kid!'

'And then Gavin made it pretty clear he was up for it.'

'I knew it,' muttered Luke. 'Bastard.'

'But to be fair, when I said no he didn't push it at all. I explained to him that I just couldn't do that to you, and he kind of shrugged and left it at that. It was almost as if he expected me to turn him down.'

Luke's fingers stroked Ally's, so very lightly that she was only just aware of the sensation. 'Why?' he asked. 'Why couldn't you do it?'

'Because I love you,' she replied simply. 'OK, sometimes I feel like I could punch you into the middle of next week, but I still love you in a way I couldn't love any other man. You're ... the one. Did you really think I'd throw that away – and mess up my sister's marriage – for a quick fumble with Gavin?'

Luke didn't answer straight away. That hurt a little, because Ally knew that was exactly what he'd thought. Then again, if she'd been drunk, or just a fraction angrier with Luke, mightn't she have yielded to Gavin's bait? There was really no way of knowing.

'I'm sorry,' Luke said softly. 'But I was so afraid you were never coming back.'

'We have a lot of talking to do,' Ally commented.

Luke nodded. 'And I think we need to get away for a few days. Just the two of us. Does that sound like a good idea to you?'

'Of course it does. I could ask Zee to take the kids and—'

Before she'd got the rest of the sentence out, the telephone rang. 'Oh shit.'

'Ignore it,' advised Luke. Then: 'On the other hand ... it might be something important.'

Cursing under her breath, Ally got up and answered it. 'Hello?'

'Ally darling, you're sounding tired. You've not been eating enough green vegetables, have you?'

There was no mistaking that voice: it belonged to Maureen. Mind you, a call from Ally's mother was no great surprise really. Her mother had always had the worst timing of anybody Ally knew.

'Hello Mum. I'm fine, how are you?'

'Oh, you know how it is. Your father's driving me to an early grave as usual with his silly fancies: now he wants us to take up line dancing. Line dancing! Can you imagine, at my age?'

An image of blue-rinsed elephants dancing in stetsons and high-heeled boots promptly popped into Ally's mind, and despite her rather sober mood she had to make an effort not to laugh. 'They say it's very good exercise, Mum. Cardiovascular and all that.'

'I don't care if it is. I can get all the exercise I need chasing my grandchildren around Gloucestershire. Speaking of which, your father and I thought we'd come and see you next week.'

'Next week?'

'Just for a few days. Or a week maybe. After all, it is Kyle's birthday the following week, dear. We really must stay on for that. You haven't forgotten have you? I know pregnancy hormones can affect short-term memory.'

'My own son's birthday? Of course I haven't forgotten!' Oh marvellous, thought Ally. Just when the one thing Luke and I need is precious time alone together, we get time with my mother. 'Are you sure you wouldn't like to come a bit later?' she hinted. Like about ten years later, she added in the privacy of her thoughts.

Maureen snorted. 'Good heavens no! Your father's having his prostate tinkered with in a couple of weeks.'

Ally blinked. 'He is?'

'Oh, nothing to worry about dear, apparently it's just like when the Dyno-Rod man unblocks your drains. Anyway, after that's over and done with it'll be just about time for me to start making my Christmas puddings.'

'It's only September!' protested Ally.

Maureen tutted. 'How often do I have to remind you dear? It's never too soon to plan your Christmas – especially when there's a baby due less than a month beforehand. Anyway,' she went on, radiating motherly goodwill, 'your father and I can make life a little easier for you while we're here, can't we?'

221

'I guess so,' capitulated Ally, who couldn't bring herself to say that actually they'd probably make it a lot harder.

'And you can tell those two little imps of yours that Granny and Granddad are coming, so there's going to be a lovely big family birthday party, with cake and candles and everything. I've already spoken to Gavin, by the way—'

'What! Why?'

'And he says we can have the party at his and Miranda's house. Isn't that kind of him?'

# Chapter Twenty-Two

It might only be the middle of September, but already Ally was feeling the strain of the autumn term. Back home, things had been easier with Luke since their big crisis talk, but the air still crackled with electricity whenever Gavin or the baby was mentioned.

Then there was the weight of Ally's ever-expanding girth.

'I'm sure I was never this big with Kyle or Josie,' she commented to Miranda as they had tea together at Zee's house. 'You know, I reckon there's half a dozen babies in there, all hiding behind each other.'

Miranda's eyes sparkled at the thought. 'The more the merrier!'

Zee bent down and put his ear to Ally's stomach. 'Oh yes, you're right,' he announced. 'I can hear them arguing in there. They must all be girls.'

'Cheek!' protested Ally.

'Better *not* all be girls!' declared Miranda. 'Or Gavin will have a heart attack.' She was laughing, but – to Ally at least – it didn't sound much like a joke.

Zee gave her an uncomprehending look. 'He's not really that fragile, is he? What is he – girl-phobic?'

'Hardly.' Miranda flashed a smile enhanced by several of Harley Street's finest cosmetic dentists. 'Before he met me, he was all over the gossip mags with a different one every week.'

'Between you and me, I think he's still in shock after that visit to the Pink Ponies,' said Ally. 'That and being kicked in the shins by Josie.' She yawned and readjusted her ungainly mass as it sprawled across several sofa cushions. 'Why am I so *tired*? I don't understand it. It's not as if I'm even teaching full-time. I must be getting old.'

'Perhaps you've been sleepwalking without realising,' suggested Zee helpfully.

Ally considered this. 'Somebody'd have to roll me out of bed first. Look at the size of me.'

'Sleepwalking? Sleep-eating more like,' declared Miranda. 'Look at this big fat belly, Mrs Bennett!' She gave her sister's tummy an affectionate poke. 'How much of it is baby and how much is lard, that's what I want to know.'

'Don't you dare be rude to me, Miranda Hesketh!' Ally stuck out her tongue. 'This is your beloved first-born I'm carrying in here, remember! I'm just keeping it nice and warm and cosy for you. On the subject of pregnancy,' she added, 'what's all this about Kate's mother making you go to Northampton?'

'It's a long story,' warned Zee, and proceeded to tell it in loving detail. 'So you see,' he concluded, 'this woman phoned me up completely out of the blue and to be perfectly frank, I don't know a thing about her – I don't even know if she really is Kate's mother!'

'When he told me, I thought it all sounded highly dodgy,' remarked Miranda. 'And that's why I agreed to go with him.'

'To Northampton?'

'That's right.'

The suddenness of this revelation completely knocked the wind out of Ally's sails. 'I see. When?'

'The day after tomorrow.'

'Oh. Right.'

'I'd have asked you, Ally,' said Zee hastily, 'only I thought . . . at the moment, what with the baby and Luke and everything . . . '

For a fleeting moment, Ally felt a little sad; dispossessed, even. She wasn't used to finding things out at second hand. She'd always been Zee's right-hand woman and trusty sidekick, and now she found herself being ousted by her impossibly glamorous sister – just like when they were kids. Talk about history repeating itself.

On the other hand, she might not like it but she knew Zee was right. She was in no state to squeeze into his van for a trip to wild and woolly Northampton, and with her parents about to descend on them at any moment, the Bennett household was going to need all hands on deck. If nothing else, the coming week held the promise of some lively discussions. Ally hardly dared imagine how her mother might react when she found out about Ally's forthcoming role in *The Sound of Music* – not to mention her ever-fussing sister . . .

Yes, one way or another, Ally had her work cut out.

'You did right,' she told Zee. 'You don't want to be held up by a big fat pregnant woman who needs the loo every five minutes. Just you look after him though, sis,' she warned Miranda. ''Cause Zee's my best mate and I'll rip you limb from limb if you don't!'

As she entered the final months of her pregnancy, Ally was beginning to find driving uncomfortable, and on that particular day Miranda had offered to drive her to and from Zee's house. She soon found out why. On the journey back to Ally's house, Miranda set about giving her the third degree.

'What's all this about you and Luke having a big bust-up?'

Ally slipped down several inches in her seat, wishing it would open up and swallow her whole. 'It wasn't a big bust-up. It was only a little one.'

'You can't have a little bust-up,' retorted Miranda. 'All bust-ups are big, it's the nature of bust-ups. And when Josie was over at our place on Sunday, she said you and Luke had given her and Kyle a little talk about the big D-Word.'

Ally frowned. 'The what?'

'Divorce, numbskull!'

Ally wriggled back upright in her seat, her heart beating jungle rhythms. 'Miranda, we are *not* getting divorced! It was just a little . . . explanation. What on earth has my daughter been saying?'

'Relax!' Miranda shot her a worried look. 'And for God's sake don't go into labour, I've only just had this car valeted. I know you're not getting divorced. But frankly, the very fact that you had to explain that to Josie and Kyle worries me a bit.'

Ally wilted under Miranda's searchlight gaze. 'The kids overheard Luke and me having an argument about . . . the night I was over at your house.'

'Ah.' Miranda swore as the traffic lights ahead turned to amber and she had to slow to a halt. 'The night you and Luke had the *really* big bust-up and you legged it to my house to see me, only I wasn't there but Gavin was?'

Ally nodded.

'Let me guess. Luke can't cope with the idea of his wife being

225

alone all night with a man, even if that man is her sister's husband and his wife is so pregnant that even the idea of rumpy-pumpy exhausts her?'

'Er ... something like that.'

'Talk about ridiculous. God Ally, I never had your Luke down as a Neanderthal.'

'Nor did I,' murmured Ally. But inside she was begging Miranda to change the subject; squirming with shame that felt all the worse when her sister so obviously trusted both her and Gavin implicitly.

Ought I to tell her? she agonised. Oughtn't she to know that her beloved husband made a pass at me, even if it was a half-hearted one? Even if it means admitting that I was tempted to respond? That I've been flirting with him in cafés for God knows how long? That this baby inside me strengthened the weird, irresistible attraction that has been pulling us closer and closer together?

On the other hand, why tell her to salve her own conscience, when all it would do for Miranda was hurt her? Why upset her when the weird spell had already been broken, and nothing like that was ever going to happen again? But Ally kept on wondering. If she decided to keep her mouth shut, was it to protect Miranda's feelings – or herself?

She tuned back into Miranda's monologue as they neared Brookfield Road. 'Don't worry,' Miranda was reassuring her. 'Pregnancy does funny things to men – makes them behave in ways they never would otherwise. He'll be fine.' Having read every mother and baby book on the market, Miranda now considered herself an expert.

It does funny things to women too, mused Ally; which is one reason why I'm never ever getting pregnant again. Still, at least Luke and I are being honest with each other now. A little bit of time together, a few quiet nights in without distractions, and things would begin to rediscover their old, sweet tranquillity.

She felt quite sunny inside by the time they reached number 22. Then she spotted the metallic brown Mondeo in the driveway, with the nodding dog on the back window ledge, and knew that Somebody Up There really didn't like her.

'Oh look!' Miranda exclaimed with genuine enthusiasm. 'Mum and Dad have arrived early! Isn't that great?'

*

While Maureen and Clive were deciding how much the children had grown, and whether Ally and Miranda were too fat or too thin, over at the offices of ChelShel, Psyche was also making her presence felt.

'I've completely overhauled the filing system,' she announced when Luke and Chas came back from a pub lunch.

Chas was panic-stricken. 'But that's *my* system,' he protested. 'I'm the only person who understands it!'

'Exactly,' said Psyche with a note of triumph in her voice. 'But not any more. Now, anybody could walk into this office and locate a document within minutes.'

At least Luke was enthusiastic – admiring, even. 'Good work. What's next on your list?'

'A proper computer database of housing providers. I thought I'd get started on it this afternoon, if that's all right with you?'

'Fine by me; just shout if you need a hand with anything.'

Chas whimpered into his pile of old-fashioned paper invoices. 'You do realise I'll never get the hang of it, don't you? You know me: I still haven't got over the demise of the quill pen.'

'That's all right mate,' replied Luke, patting his colleague on the back like an ancient donkey. 'You can sit in the corner doing cave paintings while we surf the information super-highway.'

Chas's response was a very rude and not at all priestly gesture. 'Well you'll be doing it on your own,' he announced, 'because I'm off to see the bishop this afternoon, remember. It's money-scrounging time again,' he explained to Psyche.

'Oh. You mean money to fund my working here? Do you think I'll be able to stay here a bit longer?'

'All depends on how much is left in the pastoral kitty,' replied Chas, 'and which charity is flavour of the month. But I hope so.'

'Yes, I hope so too,' agreed Luke. He realised that he really, really did. Apart from Chas, Psycho was the nearest thing he had to a friend right now; and he needed all the friends he could get.

Gavin had an important meeting that afternoon, too; but not with the bishop. His was with Montague J. Anstruther, a solicitor whose wits were as sharp as his suits. Monty Anstruther had advised him throughout his career, from his first small business selling replica watches to the multi-million-pound development projects he was currently masterminding.

When it came to legality, Gavin wasn't afraid to sail close to the wind – he didn't need to be, because nobody knew better than Monty how fine to cut things and still get away scot-free.

This was a slightly different matter, though. Something of a rather more ... personal nature. A letter he'd received the previous day.

Gavin sat on the other side of Anstruther's desk, fiddling with his diamond cufflinks as he watched the lawyer read through the letter a second time. 'Well, Monty? What do you think?' he demanded when the waiting got too irksome.

Anstruther pushed away the letter, took off his spectacles and rubbed the lenses on his handkerchief. 'The woman who wrote this,' he said. 'You definitely had a relationship with her?'

Gavin nodded. 'Oh yes. If you can call three or four dates a relationship. It was a long time ago.'

'Indeed. Seven years or thereabouts, to judge from the age of the child. And you say you had no idea that the child even existed?'

'None whatever. Here Miranda and I are, trying like crazy for a baby. And then suddenly, out of the blue, I get this letter that freaks the hell out of me ... telling me I already have a son. It really knocked me sideways, I can tell you.'

Montague Anstruther sat back in his chair, rotating it to one side so that he could glimpse the mellow autumn sunshine playing on the rooftops of Gloucester. 'I have to tell you, Gavin,' he said slowly, 'It wouldn't be the first time a woman has tried to obtain money fraudulently by leading an ex-lover to believe that her child was his.'

'Yes, yes, I know all that. But I'm sure he is mine – look at the photo.' Eagerly, Gavin jabbed a finger at the snapshot Grace had enclosed with her letter. It showed a boy, tall for his age, with dark hair and striking eyes. 'He's the image of me, Monty.'

'Possibly.' Monty scratched his chin. 'But that's what DNA tests are for. Tell me: have you answered this letter, given the lady any ... undertakings?'

Gavin shook his head. 'Not yet, no. What do you suggest?'

Montague fixed him with a direct look. 'Proceeding slowly,' he replied. 'Have you told your wife about this?'

228

'Are you crazy?'

'I'll take that as a no. And if this boy did turn out to be your son, how would you feel about it?'

A huge smile spread across Gavin's face. 'Absolutely bloody marvellous,' he replied.

The bishop was an imposing man: six feet four of ex-prop forward in a purple cassock, with a broken nose that made him look like a hired assassin. As he strode about his office the wooden floor quivered beneath his feet, and Chas did much the same.

'Father Malone, money, as I am sure you are aware, does not grow on trees.'

'No, Bishop Hanlon,' agreed Chas.

'I cannot simply dispense grants to all and sundry, on demand.'

'No, Bishop. But—'

The bishop's eyes blazed out from beneath lowering black brows. 'But what, Father Malone?'

'ChelShel is a very worthy cause, Bishop. It has done a great deal of good work with the homeless over the past year, and with the addition of a part-time admin person like Psyche—'

The bishop waved a hand to shut him up. 'Yes, yes, Father, I know all that. It's what every single charity in the diocese says whenever they want funding. However.' He spoke the word slowly, placing emphasis on the final two syllables. 'It just so happens that one of our major private donors has a special fondness for ChelShel, and has provided a substantial sum specifically to help you continue your work.'

Chas was stunned. 'Somebody wants to help us? Who?'

The bishop raised a formidable eyebrow. 'Donations are supposed to remain anonymous,' he reminded. 'But between ourselves ... ' He beckoned Chas closer, and scribbled a name on a scrap of paper.

Chas's eyes widened. 'No!'

'Wonders will never cease, eh? Now, get out of my sight and tell that improbably named office girl of yours that her job's safe for another year.'

'Good grief Mum, what on earth is it – one of those Swiss exercise balls?'

Ally watched open-mouthed as her mother unpacked the enor-

229

mous cardboard box she and Clive had brought with them.

'Don't be silly dear, it's a Christmas pudding.' Maureen lovingly placed the foil-wrapped sphere on the kitchen table; but the tabletop sloped slightly and the pudding promptly rolled off, narrowly missing the cat, trundled across the lino and came to rest by the pedal bin, where Maureen retrieved it. 'You're having a baby in a few weeks' time – you won't possibly have time to make your own puddings.'

Ally decided this was not the moment to confess that, actually, she never made her own puddings anyway, just roughed up a bought one a bit and stuck some holly on the top. 'Well I'm sure it'll come in very handy,' she said, envisaging a new career for it as a doorstop.

'It's lovely to see you again, Mum,' gushed Miranda, 'but wouldn't you rather come and stay at our place? It's awfully cramped for you here, and I should think Ally needs plenty of rest.'

'It's very kind of you to ask, dear,' replied Maureen, 'and you know normally we'd much rather stay with you,' (gee thanks, thought Ally) 'but we're here to help Alison in the house, aren't we Clive darling?'

Clive beamed and nodded his agreement.

'And we're here for Josie and Kyle of course,' she added, spotting the children walking past the kitchen door and lavishing bone-crushing hugs on them before they could escape. 'But as soon as the baby's born we'll come straight to you and help you out.' She clasped her hands excitedly. 'It's so many years since I had a little baby girl to look after ... '

Miranda and Ally stared at their mother. 'Pardon?' asked Ally.

'What did you say?' demanded Miranda.

'I said, it's a long time since I had a little baby girl to look af—'

'A baby *girl*?'

Maureen seemed untroubled by the looks on her daughters' faces. 'What? Well, I'd had enough of all that nonsense about waiting until the birth to find out. So I went across the road to see that lady I know who's a midwife, and showed her Alison's scan. She was ever so helpful. Told me straight away. Isn't that lovely?'

*

230

Ally found her sister alone upstairs, sitting cross-legged on Josie's little single bed with a huge stuffed rabbit in her arms. She looked absolutely petrified.

'Hey, I've been looking for you all over. Are you OK?'

Miranda looked at her fearfully. 'The baby's a *girl* Ally.'

'If that friend of Mum's is right.'

'I'm sure she is.'

'OK.' Ally shrugged. 'So Mum went and let the cat out of the bag. Well, never mind.'

'No, you don't understand. Gavin's got his heart set on a boy, you know he has.' Miranda hunched over the stuffed rabbit. 'What's he going to say, Ally? What's he going to *do*?'

Ally sat down on the edge of the bed. 'I expect he'll be just like any other new dad,' she replied, as encouragingly as she could. 'So excited that he's got a baby at all that he hardly notices which sex it is.'

Miranda shook her head. Her voice quavered. 'He's going to leave me, Ally. He is, isn't he?'

'Don't be silly, of course he isn't. Why on earth would he do that when he loves you so much?' As she said that, she loathed herself and Gavin for every clandestine cup of coffee they'd enjoyed together. 'Anyway,' she went on, 'why's he so set on the baby being a boy? That's what I've never understood.'

Her sister twisted one of the rabbit's ears round her finger. 'He said something to me once,' she replied. 'About him having a little sister, only there was something really bad wrong with her and she died when she was just a toddler.'

Ally's stomach turned over. 'Something bad? Like what?'

'Nothing that could be passed on, he made absolutely sure about that.' Ally murmured 'Thank God,' under her breath. 'Just one of those million-to-one tragedies. But I don't think his mother was ever quite right after that.' Miranda looked up. 'She killed herself, you know.'

'Oh God, no. Really?' Ally felt as if every fresh revelation was another blow to her punch-drunk brain. 'But all the same ... '

'I know, it doesn't make sense. And he won't talk about it.' Miranda reached out a hand and laid it on her sister's belly. 'Do you really think it'll be all right?'

'Of course it will.' Ally caught her breath. 'There – did you feel that?'

Miranda's face filled with wonder. 'Was that the baby kicking again? It feels so strong!'

Ally nodded. 'Certainly does. She's saying "hello Mum" to you. Just hang in there, sis, and in a few weeks' time you'll be Mum and Dad for real. How could Gavin be anything other than thrilled?'

# Chapter Twenty-Three

Ally was so taken aback that she dropped the potato she was peeling into the kitchen sink. A half-finished Hallowe'en lantern glowered at her disapprovingly from the draining board.

'What do you mean, you've asked her round for dinner tomorrow night?'

Luke's face took on the expression of a man realising he has just achieved the exact opposite of what he'd intended. 'I thought if I brought Psyche home so you could actually meet her, you wouldn't, well, have so much of a problem with her.'

Ally very nearly picked up the potato and threw it at her husband's head. 'For the last time, I do not have a problem with . . . whatever her name is!' she lied, somewhat ineptly.

'Psyche. Her dad's a classics professor.'

'I don't care if he's a binman,' declared Ally. 'She's welcome to come round – but not at five minutes' notice! Didn't you think to ask me first? I've got my mum and dad here—'

'Oh, we don't mind, dear,' cut in her mother, so sweetly that Ally wanted to strangle her.

'No, not at all,' echoed her father. 'It's always nice to meet your friends, love.'

'And I'm working tomorrow, and then I've got a dress rehearsal for the show, which is on in one miserable week's time, in case you'd forgotten – and then a technical rehearsal the day after – and if I hadn't, I'd probably be going to Northampton with Zee and Miranda.' She paused for breath. 'So when exactly am I supposed to cook dinner and roll out the red carpet for an extra guest?'

'Er, three extra guests actually,' admitted Luke. 'I sort of told Psyche she could bring someone. And I invited Chas too. I'm really sorry Ally,' he added sheepishly as he followed Ally into the dining room. 'Things have been so difficult for us lately, and I know I've contributed to that. I just wanted to make things right.'

She halted, turned and looked her husband up and down. He had the look of an embarrassed fourteen-year-old, all sincerity and angst, and her feelings towards him instantly softened. 'What am I going to do with you, Luke Bennett?'

'Hit me on the head, drop me in the wheelie bin and wait for the Thursday rubbish collection?' suggested Luke.

'Fat lot of good that would do,' snorted Ally, 'they'd refuse to take you.'

'You could always bribe them.'

Their eyes met and, at first hesitantly and then, uncontrollably, they both burst out laughing.

'I'll tell Psyche dinner's off then,' said Luke as the hilarity faded, blowing his nose loudly.

'No, hang on.' Ally thought for a moment. 'What about Thursday? That gives me more time and there's no evening rehearsal. Could you manage then?'

'I think so. Oh. Wait a minute, I sort of said I might visit that new night shelter on Alstone Lane and ... ' His voice trailed off.

Ally's heart sank. So, things weren't different at all; they were just the same as they'd always been. Luke was never around when there was something more worthy to be done. 'Oh. OK then. Whatever.'

'No.'

The firmness of Luke's tone startled Ally and she looked up. 'No what?'

'No, I can visit the night shelter another time. The day after tomorrow will be fine. What do you say?'

Ally stood on tiptoe and just managed to kiss him over the massive mountain of her stomach. 'It's a date.'

There was an autumnal snap in the early-morning air as Miranda's car drew up outside Zee's house. He was already waiting on the doorstep, waving goodbye to Emma as she waved back at him from the neighbour's car that was taking her to school.

God bless him, thought Miranda, still surprised by her failure to despise such a pathetic creature. Just look at those trousers: any

234

shorter and they'd be pedal-pushers. And his hair looks like Emma cut it with the bread knife.

'Ready?' she enquired.

Zee stood up straight, took a very deep breath, and then deflated again as he let it out. 'Not really,' he confessed. 'But hey, let's get it over with.'

'That's the spirit.'

'At least I feel better knowing you're with me,' Zee said shyly as they drove out of Cheltenham.

'Hm. Well don't expect me to bail you out if she turns nasty. You can fight your own domestic brawls, chummy.'

It was getting on for lunchtime when they reached Northampton. Zee's stomach was making horrible noises, but not because of hunger. 'I'm scared,' he announced as they turned into the road whose name was scribbled on the back of the road map.

'Tough. It's too late to go back now.'

'Do you think Kate's there, waiting to do something unspeakable to me?'

'That's right, look on the bright side.' Miranda slid out of the car and slammed the door. 'Mind you, I did say we ought to bring a cricket bat just in case.'

Miranda's black humour only made Zee feel worse. By the time they were standing on the doorstep of number 13 (what an omen, thought Zee), his face had turned as white and clammy as a haddock fillet.

The bell sounded deep inside the ordinary-looking fifties' semi. And then footsteps sounded softly on the carpeted hallway floor. The chain rattled on the inside of the door; then it swung open.

'Hello,' said the middle-aged woman in the brown cardigan. 'I'm Ellen Morton, Kate's mother. Come in, I've been expecting you.'

Zee and Miranda sat side by side on a brown plush sofa in Mrs Morton's tidy sitting room. An assortment of china dogs gambolled across the mantelpiece, there were Jack Vettriano prints on the walls, and on a small table beside the bay window stood five or six framed photographs of her daughter. It was all very cosy and ordinary.

Zee perched uneasily on the edge of the sofa, his hands shaking so much that his cup of tea rattled on its saucer. 'You wanted to talk?'

'About Kate, yes.' Mrs Morton sat down in an armchair by the fireplace. Her voice sounded more tired than angry. 'And the ... baby.'

Zee's teacup rattled even more loudly. Miranda gave his shoulder a reassuring squeeze. 'I can assure you that none of this is Zee's fault,' she said, before he had the time to say something silly or incriminating. 'He's done nothing wrong.'

'No,' agreed Mrs Morton, much to Zee's astonishment. 'He hasn't. From what I can gather, Mr Goldman, you've been the perfect gentleman throughout.'

'But I thought ... ' babbled Zee. 'I mean, well, when Kate phoned me from the hospital she was quite ... forthright.'

'She accused him of causing the miscarriage by harassing her,' explained Miranda. 'Now, we're very sorry that your daughter's in hospital, but saying that kind of thing is frankly cruel and unfair.'

'I agree,' replied Ellen Morton. 'Especially as there was no baby in the first place.'

The silence that followed these few words was intense, mediated only by the distant sound of a clock chiming the half-hour.

'What did you say?' asked Zee.

Ellen Morton gazed at the scuffed toes of her lace-up shoes. 'Kate has a few problems,' she said slowly. 'She is in hospital ... but she's on the psychiatric ward.' She swallowed hard. 'It isn't the first time she's done this kind of thing.'

Zee and Miranda stared at each other, heads teeming with whys and hows; neither knowing quite where to begin.

Miranda chose her words carefully. 'What kind of thing would that be ... exactly?'

'A few years ago, when Chloe was just a toddler, Kate and her husband decided to have another baby. Kate was five months pregnant when they were involved in a car crash, and she lost the baby. Her husband was ... ' She paused. 'Killed.' Mrs Morton looked up. 'I take it she didn't tell you any of this?'

'I knew she'd lost her husband but she never mentioned the baby.' Zee said sadly. There was an awkward pause.

'Please, go on,' said Miranda.

'Kate was badly injured in the crash too, and afterwards she was told she couldn't have any more children. Since then ... well, she just doesn't seem to be able to come to terms with it. Somewhere

236

at the back of her mind, she seems to have this idea that if she meets the right man, everything will be all right and she'll get pregnant.'

Miranda was beginning to understand. 'And that's how she felt when she met Zee?'

Kate's mother shrugged her shoulders. 'I assume so. That's what happened the other two times.'

'So . . . she meets a man, convinces herself she's going to get pregnant, even believes she is pregnant? It's all one big fantasy?'

Mrs Morton nodded. 'And when she can't sustain it any longer, she runs away, convinces herself she's miscarried and blames it on the man. I'm sorry Mr Goldman,' she went on. 'I really am. I would have warned you if I could, but Kate doesn't tell me very much these days. It's taken me this long to track you down.'

She looked at Miranda, and then back at Zee. 'I'm glad to see you've found yourself a nice new girlfriend,' she said. 'Someone to help you to forget all this.'

Zee reddened. 'Actually, Miranda's not—'

'No,' smiled Miranda, 'I'm not Zee's girlfriend; just a friend who happens to be a girl.'

'Well, you never know. I've an eye for these things, and you do make a lovely couple.'

Afterwards, as Zee and Miranda got back into the car, Mrs Morton stood on her doorstep and watched them go, a solitary figure in brown, hugging herself for comfort.

'I guess I ought to be relieved,' remarked Zee as they drove out of Northampton. 'But all I feel is sad. Especially for poor Chloe.'

'Kate's in the best place,' pointed out Miranda. 'Maybe this time they'll be able to help her – you know, really get through to her. And I'm sure Chloe's being well looked-after by her grandma.'

They drove on in silence for several miles until Zee broke in with: 'So . . . erm, we make a lovely couple then?'

Miranda laughed and gunned the accelerator pedal. 'Don't push your luck, sunshine; I'm a respectable married woman!'

'Oh no, there's the doorbell and I'm not ready yet!' Ally fussed around, on her knees in front of her temperamental gas oven.

Luke had warned Ally that Psyche was ferociously well organised, so she wasn't over surprised when the doorbell rang at seven thirty on the nail. But that wasn't much consolation when you were

237

still up to your armpits in half-cooked vegetables and the tofu roast was refusing to look anything like Nigel Slater had sworn it would. That's the last time I rely on you, mate, she thought, casting the recipe book to one side and cranking the gas up to eight.

'I'll go, darling,' said Luke, ramming the roast back into the oven and helping his enormous wife back to her feet. 'Are you all right?'

'Fine. Just a bit tired.' She threw off her apron and tried to smooth the creases out of her tunic top. 'What did you say Psyche's other half is called?'

'Dunno. I'm not sure she's ever said.'

Ally rolled her eyes. 'Men! A woman would've found that out within the first five minutes.' She rubbed an ache in the small of her back. 'God, I'll be glad to sit down.'

'It's my fault,' agonised Luke, 'lumbering you with a dinner to cook when the midwife told you to slow down.'

'Darling, all she said was that I had a little bit of protein in my wee. Nothing to worry about, she promised.'

'Your ankles have been swelling up, too. And you've been getting headaches.'

'Stop fussing darling, looking like the Michelin Man is all part of being pregnant.'

The doorbell sounded a second time, but Luke was more interested in Ally.

'I still think you ought to drop the show, you know.'

'I can't!'

'Yes you can, you know full well they've got a Plan B, so they can manage perfectly well without you.'

Ally hesitated. What Luke said was true, after all. Even the ever-buoyant Doreen Grey-Burroughs had to admit that pregnant performers meant potential problems; and she'd cleverly got Ally to record her musical numbers so that if the worst came to the worst and she gave birth in the wings, somebody else could go on and mime. That wasn't the spirit of show business though, was it? And it meant a lot to Ally to prove that being pregnant didn't have to mean sitting around being helpless.

'I'll think about it,' replied Ally, which Luke knew meant that she wouldn't. 'Now answer that door, before whoever it is freezes to death!'

Luke's rangy frame covered the distance between the kitchen

238

and the front door in a couple of seconds.

'Oh, there you are,' chirped Psyche as he opened up. 'I thought you'd flushed yourself down the loo or something. Bottle of vino for you and some flowers for Mrs B,' she added, thrusting it into his hands. She sniffed the air. 'Mm, something smells ... interesting.'

Luke stepped aside to let Psyche through and she skipped past him into the hall, followed rather more hesitantly by a tall, attractive brunette in her thirties. 'Hi. You must be Luke.' She stuck out a hand and smiled quite shyly. 'I'm Rebecca, but everybody calls me Reb. Psyche's told me a lot about you.'

'Oops, silly me!' Psyche spun round. 'You two haven't met before, have you? Reb, this is Luke. Luke, this is Reb. She's my partner.'

Ally's tofu roast sat in the middle of the dining room table like a burnt offering at an Aztec sacrifice. It's a good job Mum and Dad had a prior engagement at the Bowls Club thought Ally. All her mum's suspicions about vegetarian food would have been instantly confirmed.

'I think it went a bit wrong somewhere,' she lamented as her dinner guests viewed it in all its charred glory. 'I'm really sorry – I'm not very good at vegetarian.'

'No problem, I love crispy things,' piped up Psyche, instantly banishing any residual animosity from Ally's heart. She even sawed off a corner and crunched at it. 'Mm, nice. It's sort of – caramelised.'

'No, I think the word you're looking for is carbonised,' Luke corrected her with a chuckle. 'It'd make a damn fine replacement for that cracked paving stone on the patio though,' he added.

'It's very characterful. Maybe you could give it a fancy name and sell it to the Tate Modern,' suggested Chas, entering into the spirit of things.

'It's all very well laughing about it,' pointed out Ally when all avenues of hilarity had been explored, 'but what exactly are we going to eat tonight? With three vegetarians, somehow I don't think that steak and kidney pudding in the fridge is really an option.'

'I know,' declared Reb. 'Let's get a takeaway! Everybody give me your orders, and I'll drive over and collect them.'

And so it was that little more than half an hour later, they were all sitting in Ally and Luke's lounge, eating Indian food out of metal trays. It wasn't haute cuisine, but it was friendly and informal, and Ally decided she liked it.

'This is fun,' declared Chas, echoing her thoughts. 'Takes me back to my student days. A few cans of lager and some baked beans, and you had yourselves a party.'

'Who needs baked beans?' Luke chewed on an onion bhajia. 'You know Ally, I bet Miranda's never done anything like this in her life.'

'Who's Miranda?' asked Reb.

'Ally's sister. Lives in a big house, eats in fancy restaurants – you know the sort. When she organises a party it's one of those great big charity balls where people go to get their photographs taken being generous.' Luke took a swig of beer. 'Not my idea of a party. Not my idea of charity either, come to that.'

'Luke!' hissed Ally.

But he continued. 'I mean, it's not as if it costs her much personally to set up parties and lunches and stuff, is it? And she's so well off that it's peanuts to her anyway. So she gets to have a nice time and looks good doing it. Put her on the night-time soup round in the High Street, and I bet she'd see things a whole lot differently.'

Thankfully, the embarrassed silence only lasted a few seconds, and then somebody cracked a joke and the evening was back on track again.

Some time later, as Luke was on his way to the kitchen for another bottle of wine, Chas intercepted him in the hall. 'Can I have a quick word?'

'Sure. What about?'

'Your wife's sister.'

'Miranda?' Luke's brow furrowed. 'Why? Oh I get it, you're going to tell me off for having a go at her, aren't you? But she kind of deserves it, you know.'

'You think so? Listen to this.' Chas related his recent visit to the bishop. 'Now, I'm not even supposed to know this, so it stands to reason I'm not supposed to tell you, but I'm going to anyway. The bishop told me that Miranda Hesketh has made some really big donations to his pastoral fund over the last few years.'

'Miranda!' Luke was utterly flabbergasted.

'And to ChelShel too. A whole host of local charities that he

240

knows about, so Lord knows how many others there are that he's unaware of. And before you tell me she only does it to look good, apparently all her donations are meant to be anonymous.

'Whatever else you think of your sister-in-law, Luke, she's no publicity-seeker. Everybody deserves a chance to prove their worth. Maybe one day you should sit down with her and have a chat. Maybe you'll find out other things about her that you never knew.

'You might even end up liking her. Stranger things have happened.'

After everyone had gone home, the kids had been checked on and Ally had retired to bed with her aching back and legs, Luke poured himself one last drink and sat down in his favourite armchair.

It had been a good evening, but a strange one too, spiked with unexpected revelations. How had he not guessed that Psyche's partner was a woman? Inwardly he laughed at himself, invaded by a feeling not of disappointment but relief. Now he knew that she was a lesbian, he could stop being neurotic. He could allow himself to like her because he found her funny and sweet and intelligent and committed; and stop asking himself if there were any subconscious sexual undertones to their relationship – even though he was quite sure there weren't. He was certain that Ally would be relieved too, for the very same reason.

But the feelings that teemed inside him were not all positive, for he also felt stupid, uncertain, ashamed. Lately he had made so many mistakes; including big ones that had threatened his marriage to the only woman he had ever truly loved. He ought to have learned a bit from them, but of course he hadn't. And now he knew he'd been wrong all over again; this time about Miranda.

How could you know someone for so many years and yet not really know them at all? What else did he not know about her? And was it too late for him to find out who she really was?

Maybe Chas was right, and he might end up liking her. But more importantly, was there a chance that Miranda might one day end up liking him?

The day after the least formal dinner party Ally had ever hosted, she woke up feeling stiff, sore, bloated and with a headache that

241

might have been called a massive hangover if she hadn't kept to orange juice all night. What's more, her legs were really swollen. Serves me right for standing around in the kitchen for hours, she thought. And all for nothing. Next time I invite people for dinner when I'm seven months pregnant, I'll just know in advance to order in takeaways and leave it at that.

Next time? She laughed at her own joke. Next time was simply not going to happen.

She took a look at herself in the bathroom mirror as she brushed her hair, and decided that advanced pregnancy was definitely not a good look. Whatever idiot had said that pregnant women looked radiant was clearly either an international supermodel like Miranda, or in urgent need of an eyesight test. With this puffy face, she thought to herself, I'm a dead ringer for a Cabbage Patch Doll.

At least the head teacher at Pussy Willows had agreed to let her take maternity leave earlier than planned, so once the kids had been safely deposited at school, she could veg out on the sofa and watch daytime TV. Rather, that's what she'd expected – until the phone rang.

Heaving her bulk to the other end of the sofa, she answered it. 'Hello?'

'Ally, is that you? It's me.'

Something inside her turned a somersault and it had nothing to do with the baby moving around. 'Gavin?'

'I'm, er, sorry I haven't been in touch.'

I'm not, thought Ally. But she knew she'd been stupidly optimistic, imagining that she could erase him from her life just by not thinking about him. Whether she liked it or not, the guy was still her brother-in-law. 'I thought we'd agreed that it was best to keep our distance,' she reminded him, 'after what nearly happened.'

'Don't you sometimes find yourself wishing it had happened? Wondering what it would have been like? Knowing we had something special – a real connection?'

'Actually, no,' replied Ally with perfect honesty. 'I just thank my lucky stars that it didn't happen. And so should you,' she added, though she felt less than comfortable taking the moral high ground. 'You've got a beautiful wife, a thriving business, and you're going to become a dad in a few weeks' time. Did you really

242

want to mess all of that up with some ... some drunken fumble?'

Gavin sighed. 'Miranda and I have been having a few problems, Ally.'

'We all have problems. It's no excuse for going out and making a whole lot more. Look Gavin, things will be fine once the baby arrives.'

'Will they?' he pondered gloomily. 'Right now it feels like everyone wants to destroy me. Did I tell you about Liam? My ex-gardener? The one I sacked because he wasn't doing his job properly?'

'What about him?'

'I knew he wasn't happy about losing his job, but I had no idea how deep it went. The police have just arrested him for poisoning your friend's dog and making all those threats against me.'

'Oh,' said Ally, momentarily shocked. 'But that's good, isn't it? Now they've caught him, there won't be any more trouble.'

Gavin laughed humourlessly. 'You think so? Well guess what, there already is. You know the big lake at Nether Grantley? Some local eco-bastard has managed to "discover" a colony of great crested newts living in it.'

'Great crested newts? Aren't they a protected species?'

'Exactly. Now, I'm sure they weren't there before and I'm equally sure they were planted. There's a conspiracy among the locals, you see. I just can't prove it. And the fact is, while those bloody amphibians are in residence, I don't have a hope in hell of getting my plans approved for the equestrian centre. So I'm stuck with a piece of land I can't do anything with.'

'Maybe it's not that bad,' ventured Ally. 'Circumstances could change in the future. Perhaps you could turn it into a nature trail or something, and get parties of schoolkids in, make some money that way. Or one of those treetop walks that are getting so popular? And at least you have the baby to look forward to.'

'Yes, yes, I suppose so,' replied Gavin moodily. His tone took on an insistent edge. 'Are you sure you don't know the sex?'

Ally was in a spot. She and her sister did of course, but she could hardly let on that Miranda hadn't told her own husband; so she sidestepped the issue. 'I didn't ask, remember. Miranda was adamant she didn't want to know before the birth.'

Something between a groan and a grunt escaped from Gavin's lips. 'For God's sake ... '

Thoughts ran through Ally's mind. Should she or shouldn't she? She didn't want to cause problems for Miranda, but on the other hand, this baby affected her life, too. 'Gavin,' she began, 'if there's some reason why you really don't want the baby to be a girl, you can tell me.'

'What reason?' demanded Gavin.

'You know, any reason.'

'What's Miranda been saying?'

'She just happened to mention that you had a sister and she died very young. And I wondered ... '

'It's none of your damn business,' snapped Gavin.

But all that did was rub Ally up the wrong way. 'Excuse me, but I think it is my business! In case you've forgotten, I'm carrying this baby. I'm its biological mother. Miranda said you'd told her it wasn't a hereditary disease. Is that the truth? If there are health considerations, I ought to have known about them before I ever decided to go along with this surrogacy arrangement.'

'Well there aren't,' replied Gavin curtly. 'I told Miranda the truth. It was just one of those things. Nothing that could be passed on or anything like that. So you can stop fretting now, can't you? Jesus, Ally. You find a woman you think is different from all the others, somebody who understands; but in the end it turns out she's just like all the others.'

'That would be me, I suppose?'

'What do you think?'

And with those parting words, Gavin slammed the phone down on Ally.

Quite coincidentally, Miranda called in on Ally later that afternoon, bearing gifts: a huge platter of fresh tropical fruits ('because all those cream cakes are going straight to our bums'), and some hyper-expensive massage oil that supposedly prevented stretch-marks. Since, at almost eight months gone, Ally's stomach already resembled a map of the British motorway network, she held out little hope for the massage oil; but she was more than happy to snack on fresh mangoes and pineapple – it seemed churlish to admit that she'd rather have had a giant chocolate éclair.

'I had Gavin on the phone,' she told Miranda as they ate in front of the telly. 'He asked me about the baby's sex, and I didn't know what to say.'

244

Miranda tried to lick the lychee juice from her own chin. 'So what *did* you say?' she asked worriedly.

'I think I got out of saying anything much, just that when we had the scan we didn't bother asking. And I sort of picked a small fight with him for not telling me about his sister. I'm sorry,' she added, 'I probably wouldn't even have picked the phone up if I'd realised it was Gavin.'

Miranda flopped back on the sofa, wiping her sticky fingers on a tissue. 'I have to tell him, don't I?'

'I think you do, yes.'

'It's just that I'm really scared, Ally.'

'I can't imagine you being scared,' said Ally with a laugh and a shake of the head.

'Well this time I am. I've made my decision; I'm going to tell him about the baby being a girl – I have to – but what if it just adds to all the problems we've been having lately?'

'You don't know that it will,' pointed out Ally, though in her heart she shared her sister's apprehensiveness.

Miranda reached out and took both her hands. 'Do you really think so? Do you really think things will be better between us when the baby arrives?'

With all her heart, Ally wanted to say yes. But try as she might, the words just wouldn't come.

# Chapter Twenty-Four

Miranda found Gavin in the home-office where he masterminded all his deals, emailing on his Blackberry and simultaneously having a telephone conversation with his assistant. He never seems to do just one thing at a time, mused Miranda; it's always two or three. Even if you talk to him you get the feeling that half of his mind is somewhere else, planning some great business coup.

As it was, she had to wait a good five minutes before Gavin finished his phone call and deigned to notice she was there.

'Hello darling.' He reached forward and planted a small kiss on her cheek. 'What can I do for you?'

'I have something to tell you,' said Miranda, her throat horribly dry and constricted. It had taken her the best part of the day and several vodkas to get her this far. 'About the baby.'

'Mm?' he murmured, as he jabbed something into his laptop.

'The baby, Gavin.' Miranda took a long, deep breath. 'It's a girl. I accidentally found out.'

This time, she knew she had Gavin's full attention. His eyes locked with hers. 'A girl? Are you sure?'

She nodded, holding her breath; certain that any moment now he would say 'That's not what I wanted at all, you stupid woman – go and get me a boy,' or something along those lines.

To her surprise, after a few seconds his tense expression relaxed into a smile. 'Well, well. A girl, eh? I had a feeling it might be.'

Completely disorientated by this unexpected reaction, Miranda just stared at him. 'Y-you're not ... upset?'

Gavin chuckled amiably. 'Why on earth would I be upset? It doesn't matter darling; it really doesn't matter at all. And I mean that.'

\*

246

If Miranda had had the power to read minds, she might have understood why Gavin wasn't upset about the news. Alternatively, she could have put an ear to the door of his office about five minutes later, and listened to his next telephone conversation. But being the trusting wife that she was, she went off back to the design studios, leaving Gavin to his wheeling and dealing.

Once he was certain he was alone, he opened his briefcase and took out his private mobile phone – the one he'd used to call Ally. Then he dialled up someone he hadn't seen in six years.

'Tash? It's Gavin. Yes, yes, I know; but I've been thinking over what we talked about over lunch with my solicitor, and after the results of the DNA test . . . well, I have no doubts at all now. I'm one hundred per cent convinced that little Cosmo is my son.

'The question is, where do we go from here? And do you still have feelings for me? Because I certainly do for you.'

'Honestly Zee,' Miranda scolded playfully, 'I've never seen such a heap of old junk in my life.'

Zee puffed out his chest and acted wounded. 'That's not a very nice thing to say about your new business partner!'

Miranda swiped him about the ears with a rolled-up Led Zeppelin poster circa 1971, showering him with dead flies and ancient fluff. 'Business partner? You should be so lucky! All I'm doing is helping you clear out this disgusting old lock-up – and I'm beginning to wonder why I bothered. I mean, what in the world is this?'

She held up something that looked like a filthy cardboard box on the end of a piece of string.

'Hey, careful with that – it's an antique!' Zee retrieved it from Miranda's sceptical grasp and gave it a quick polish, leaving dust all over the sleeve of his jumper. 'That's an authentic World War Two gas mask case, I'll have you know.'

'Zee, it's got squatters,' pointed out Miranda, opening the lid for him to see the thriving earwigs' nest inside. 'Who on earth would want to buy it like that?'

'Somebody,' insisted Zee, a little defensively. He was finding it half-amusing, half-difficult, watching his beloved accumulation of potential treasures reduced to the status of junk by someone with a more critical eye and a sharper tongue; even if that someone was a person he was starting to be rather fond of. Mind you, if he

247

hadn't been fond of Miranda, by now he would probably have run her through with the genuine Zulu assegai propped against the back wall, amid a forest of dismembered antique chair legs.

'Oh come on,' urged Miranda. 'If you're planning to make a go of the antiques business you'll have to be more ruthless. What possible use are thirty-two chair legs with no seats or backs? Or an old harmonium that doesn't even work?'

'But . . . I like them,' said Zee, his puppy-dog eyes pleading for clemency. But Miranda was already chucking the chair legs into a skip; and he knew she was right. 'Can I at least keep Mickey Mouse?'

Miranda surveyed the sorry object. 'Zee, he's got no ears.'

'He's my lucky mascot.'

She gave him a look of hopeless indulgence, and replaced the aurally challenged Mickey Mouse inside a cracked Victorian chamber-pot. 'Is there anything good in here?'

Zee gazed at the scuffed toes of his shoes. 'I don't think so,' he admitted. 'I should probably just tip the whole lock-up into one great big skip and start all over again.'

'You know,' mused Miranda as they sat down for a cup of tea amid the clutter, 'you're not the only one who could do with starting again. Though . . . I suppose that's hardly surprising really. You know, becoming a parent and all that. It really makes you rethink your life.'

Zee nodded. 'The minute you hold that tiny bundle in your arms, you know that life is never going to be the same. Nothing can ever be as important as your child. And you know you'll spend the rest of your life trying to be good enough to be that child's parent.' He smiled wistfully. 'Of course, you never are.'

Miranda swung her feet back and forth, drumming her heels on an old tea chest. 'I really feel I need a new direction,' she declared. 'I guess that's why I'm enjoying this so much: it's different. But I can't talk to Gavin about it.'

'Why?' puzzled Zee.

'Because I can't talk to him about anything. Everybody thinks we must be so close at the moment, with the new baby coming and everything, but the truth is, most of the time he hardly says a word to me. He's so cold and distant.'

Zee offered her a comforting biscuit. 'Do you . . . suspect something?'

248

'I don't know. It could be just his business worries ... Still, somehow I've just got this feeling there's more to it than that.' She laughed. 'If this was Los Angeles in the 1940s, I'd get myself a private eye. But frankly I wouldn't know where to start round here.'

'Well, I don't know any private investigators,' admitted Zee, scratching his head with his teaspoon. 'But ... er ... would I do?'

'Pardon?'

'I've always been quite good at finding things out. And nobody ever notices me – I'm one of life's invisible people. It can be an advantage sometimes.'

'Zee, you're mad,' declared Miranda.

'It's taken you this long to notice?'

'I guess it might just work ... you know, a few discreet enquiries ... '

They were still chatting about Zee being the world's most unlikely private investigator when something caught Miranda's eye. 'Those paintbrushes, over there.' She pointed. 'The ones jammed behind that crate.'

'What about them?'

'Can you grab them for me? I want to have a look at what they're standing in.'

What they were standing in was the filthiest, most paint-spattered old jug Miranda had ever seen. But something about the shape of it rang a bell in the darkest recesses of her memory, and as she scratched gently at the old emulsion it flaked away, revealing a flash of metallic reds and blues. A big smile spread over her face.

She handed the jug to him. 'I want you to put that down somewhere very, very carefully.'

'Why? What is it?'

'You know that treasure you've been looking for?' Zee nodded. 'I think this might just be it.'

While Miranda took away the jug to get it properly cleaned, Zee and Ally were in Ally's car, heading for the local school hall. Tonight was the final dress rehearsal for *The Sound of Music*.

Ally peered through the passenger window at the darkening streets of Cheltenham. 'Did I tell you Gavin phoned?'

Zee's foot twitched involuntarily on the accelerator and the car

249

bounded forward. 'No,' he replied suspiciously. 'What did he want?'

'What do you think?' Ally turned back to look at Zee. 'Don't worry, I told him to go to hell.'

'I should bloody well think so too. That bloke is seriously bad news. I wish I could tell Miranda just what he's really like,' Zee added. 'But you're my best mate and I don't want to drop you in it. I need to think of a roundabout way of doing it ... '

Ally could just imagine the scene if Zee decided to spill the beans to Miranda right now: "Oh by the way, your husband's been trying to seduce your sister for months, and she's only just told him to bog off. Just thought you might like to know." Oddly, she felt quite calm, almost detached even about that situation. She'd been incredibly dim, even a little bit underhand; if she was going to be made to look bad, well, maybe it was no more than she deserved.

'Tell Miranda what you think she should know,' Ally said. 'Don't worry about me.'

'That's the trouble, Ally; I do. All the time.'

The car bumped over some of Cheltenham's premier potholes, and Ally winced.

'Are you all right?' asked Zee.

'To be honest I don't feel so good,' Ally confessed, 'and I don't think it's just stage-fright. I've got the most God-awful headache.'

Zee took a close look at her. 'I'm worried about you,' he said. 'You don't look well at all. Your eyes are all puffy and your face is all red.'

'I think my fingers are a little bit swollen too,' agreed Ally, trying to wiggle them without much success.

'A little bit? Ally love, they look like sausages!' He thought for a moment, then pulled in to the kerb and switched off the engine.

'What's the matter?' asked Ally.

'I can't rant and drive at the same time,' he explained. 'Now look, I know you've got the most gorgeous singing voice between here and La Scala—'

Ally burst out laughing. 'Hardly!'

'But I think Luke was right: you should have told madam chairman where to stick her mother abbess. A whole week of Climbing Every Mountain, and you'll be fit for the knacker's yard.'

'Well thank you very much!' Ally wasn't sure whether to be amused or indignant. 'I don't think I'm quite that bad yet.' Deep down, however, she wasn't so sure. 'Anyhow, it's far too late to have second thoughts.'

'You shouldn't let Doreen push you into things,' scolded Zee.

Ally hooted with laughter. 'Says the man she once persuaded to perform in the nude!'

'That was art!' protested Zee, red to the roots of his hair. 'Biblical, even! You can't play Adam with your trousers on. And she did give me a decent-sized fig-leaf. Anyway,' he went on, 'stop changing the subject. Doreen's got her precious CD of you singing all the musical numbers, and an understudy who knows the lines. So what are you waiting for? Go for it: tell her you're not well and you're not doing it.'

'Pull out? Oh, I don't know ... '

'All right, tell her the doctor's ordered you not to do it. That'll shut her up.'

'She'd probably give me a lie-detector test. And you know what a bad liar I am.'

Zee offered up a small prayer for patience. 'Do you want to give birth in the middle of the show?'

'Of course I don't! But that's not going to hap—'

Zee cut her short. 'Tell her, Ally.' He shot her an uncharacteristically stern look. 'Or I will.'

Back at home, Luke kissed the kids goodnight for the fourth time, confiscated Kyle's PlayStation Portable from underneath his duvet, and switched off the upstairs lights.

Suddenly the house seemed very dark, very silent and very empty. Something was missing, and Luke was well aware what – or rather who – that something was.

In the old days, the days before he'd foolishly decided that Miranda's surrogacy plan was a really great idea, he'd grumbled about Ally's drama-club nights, but in all honesty he'd hardly noticed when she wasn't home. He'd been out most evenings anyway, and when he was in he was generally too tired to do much more than doze in front of the TV and worry about tomorrow's quota of homeless people. But now, each time Ally went out it felt as if she'd taken a little of the house's soul with her; and a little of his along with it.

251

He wasn't the only one who sensed the loss, either. As he pushed aside Josie's discarded toys and sat down on the sofa, Nameless plodded silently across the carpet towards him, jumped up and curled himself up next to Luke. Luke rubbed his head absent-mindedly and was rewarded by a soft, liquid-sounding purr.

'It doesn't feel right without her here, does it mate?' The cat nuzzled his hand, as though in agreement. 'Do you think she knows how much we love her?'

No more than a couple of miles away, just across town, Ally would be getting made up and costumed for her final dress rehearsal. He'd wished her luck before she left, though they both knew he wished she wasn't doing the show at all. What he hadn't explained to her – and he really wished he had – was that he was beginning to understand her motivation; why she felt this burning need to drive herself so hard when there was no logical or practical reason for it. Being somebody's mother might be the most important job in the world; but sometimes, he had realised, Ally needed to prove both to the world and herself that she could do something else too, and do it well. Similarly Luke had come to understand that he needed to be more than just a bloke whose entire life had gradually been reduced to one holier-than-thou social crusade.

I'm proud of you Ally, he said silently. I only wish I'd told you so earlier.

Still, never mind. There'd be plenty of time to tell her when she got back.

'A London show without London prices!' proclaimed the posters outside the school hall where St Jude's Community Players were about to present their version of *The Sound of Music*. Doreen Grey-Burroughs did not believe in selling the Players – or herself – short. As far as she was concerned, tomorrow night's audience was in for a treat. And since she had managed to wangle the use of the hall at the local public school, they would even have comfortable seats to sit on. What more could anyone ask for?

Inside the hall, there were nuns and novices everywhere in various stages of undress. Some wore jeans underneath their habits. The von Trapp children, all sourced from the same

252

enormous local family, were swearing loudly at each other, while a pretty but almost inaudible Maria was being wired up to a radio-mike. A couple of German soldiers were sitting on the edge of the stage, legs dangling, stuffing themselves with Maltesers, while Baron von Trapp was doing the rounds of the cast, asking everybody if his wig was on straight. In short, everything was going according to plan – or as nearly as it ever did.

Doreen tapped her feet and checked her watch again. A whole three minutes late. This was simply unacceptable, most unprofessional.

She relaxed a little as her mother abbess finally walked or, more accurately, waddled in, accompanied by Zee. 'Sorry we're late.'

'Where on earth have you been? It's supposed to be overture and beginners in twenty minutes, and we haven't even started on your make-up!'

Ally opened her mouth to apologise, but to her surprise Zee pre-empted her. 'Ally's not very well,' he announced. 'I don't think she should do the show.'

The colour drained from Doreen's ruddy face. 'Not do the show? But this is the final dress rehearsal! Alison dear, if you don't go on tonight, how on earth will you cope tomorrow?'

'She won't,' was Zee's simple reply. 'Like I said, I don't think she should do the show. At all. And her doctor agrees,' he added as Madam Chairman's mouth opened to object.

'This is a disaster.' Doreen took a step back and flopped dramatically onto a chair. 'How am I expected to stage a full-scale musical without my mother abbess?'

'That's what understudies are for,' Zee pointed out. 'Deirdre can go on instead of Ally. And you've got the back-up CD.'

'Haven't you heard? Deirdre's appendix burst last night! There *is* no understudy.'

'I think I'd better do this, Zee,' said Ally, steeling herself against his critical gaze. 'I can't leave them in the lurch. I'm sure I'll be OK.' She rubbed at her aching temples. 'Fine.'

'That's the spirit!' Doreen's eyes lit up. 'Once you get up on that stage, the adrenalin will take over. You'll be marvellous, Alison, just you wait and see.' She paused, peered more closely at Ally and repeated, 'Alison? Are you OK?'

But Ally didn't reply.

*

253

As Ally walked into the hall, the bright lights and noise had hit her like a brick wall. Her head was throbbing and the skin around her eyes was so swollen that she could hardly see; and she felt like the fattest, heaviest thing in the universe – a sort of black hole on legs. The last thing she felt like was climbing mountains; even imaginary ones.

But a promise was a promise, and when Doreen revealed that Deirdre was out of commission, Ally knew there was nothing for it but to don the abbess's habit and get on with it.

The only problem was that she really was feeling very peculiar. Her vision was blurring, and sounds seemed to fade in and out for no particular reason. She could feel her heart thumping like someone pounding the inside of her ribcage with a mallet. And that headache ... it was without a doubt the worst one she'd ever had in her life. Why did she have to get a migraine attack tonight, of all nights?

All at once, a wave of dizziness invaded her and she stumbled. She heard first Doreen's voice, then Zee's, asking if she was all right; but they sounded as though they were coming from the far end of a very long tunnel. She tried to answer, only all the words were mixed up inside her head, and her limbs felt leaden and useless.

Then, quite suddenly, a circle of darkness appeared at the periphery of her vision, growing thicker, thicker, thicker until there was no light left save a tiny dot of brightness at the centre.

At last that, too, disappeared.

'Oh my God, what's wrong with her?' wailed Maria. 'What's happening?'

'It's some kind of fit,' said one of the older nuns. 'Look, she's twitching all over.'

'Yes, but what do we *do*? Apart from wait for the ambulance?'

Zee was on his knees by Ally's unconscious body as it was shaken by spasm after spasm.

He stroked Ally's sweat-dampened hair back from her forehead. 'They'd better get a bloody move on,' he said quietly. 'Because I don't know the first thing about illnesses, but even I can tell this is serious.'

He reached into his pocket, took out his mobile and began making a series of calls that started with Luke. The least thing he could do for Ally was to make sure that there were people she loved around her when she woke up.

A shiver of dread ran down his spine. If she woke up.

# Chapter Twenty-Five

'But what is it?' gasped Luke. 'What's wrong with her?'

'I don't know, the paramedics weren't very forthcoming,' admitted Zee. 'Anyway, she's in the ambulance on her way to the General. I thought you'd want to know.'

He then had the same conversation with Miranda, Maureen and Clive. Finally he thought about Gavin. Miranda would no doubt phone him . . . but then again, he could be hard to reach and Miranda was in a complete state; maybe he ought to try too? He'd have preferred not to, but when all was said and done Gavin was the father of Ally's baby, so Zee reluctantly decided he had a right to know.

He phoned directory enquiries to get the number of Gavin's company but of course it was after hours, and the security guard had no idea where he was. After much wrangling, he was finally put through to Gavin's PA, Karen, who was working late, and managed to persuade her to phone the news through to Gavin's mobile. Zee breathed a sigh of relief. At least he wouldn't have to talk to the guy.

'Right, I'm going,' he announced, putting on his coat and grabbing his car keys.

'Going? Going where?' demanded Doreen Grey-Burroughs.

'To the General of course. To be with Ally.'

'You can't do anything for her there,' objected Doreen. 'Besides, you can't go. We have a show to put on, remember?'

Zee stared at her in disgust. 'You mean you're going to go ahead with the dress rehearsal?'

'Of course.'

Zee felt a surge of anger. 'Don't you care about what's happening to Ally?'

256

'We can't allow one person's misfortune to stop the whole show,' Doreen insisted. 'We open tomorrow night, and think of all the people who've bought tickets. Besides,' she added, 'I'm sure Ally would want to show to go on.'

'You've got no mother abbess,' Zee pointed out. 'Or an understudy.'

Doreen drew herself up to her full five feet one. 'If need be, I shall play the part myself. Now, go and put your costume on, Zee. We're running late already, and it's curtain up in ten minutes.'

Zee could hardly believe his ears. 'Doreen, I'm playing third German soldier, not King flipping Lear. I've only got two lines, and one of those is "Ja". So I think you can manage very well without me.'

'But what about your part? You can't just leave us in the lurch!'

Zee slung his German uniform at Doreen. 'Why don't you play that one yourself as well? Face it Doreen, you're made for the part.'

With that he marched out of the hall and drove as fast as he could to the Cotswold General, praying he hadn't left it too late.

In a smart country-house hotel somewhere in the West Country, wintry sunlight oozed through quaint casement windows, casting golden accents on pale, naked flesh.

There were two figures in the four-poster bed: an attractive, blonde woman of perhaps twenty-eight, and a man with the kind of darkly handsome looks, hard physique and piercing eyes that make women moan with desire and men groan with jealousy.

He rolled over, pulling her on top of him. The sheet slid down her body, revealing small, round breasts and generously curving hips. 'You are gorgeous,' he murmured, teasing a nipple between finger and thumb. 'God, Tash. Do you realise how much I still care for you, after all these years?'

She sat astride him, running her fingers lightly over his naked body. 'You're not so bad yourself, Gavin. I can't think why we didn't make a go of it back then.'

'Didn't you think . . . when you got pregnant . . . didn't you think about calling me?'

'I wanted to do everything on my own. Besides,' she added with a smile, 'I was still mad at you.'

He sighed and rolled over again, this time pinning her beneath

257

him. 'I must have been crazy. You have no idea how appalling my life is at the moment.'

Tash gave a sceptical-sounding laugh. 'Come on Gavin, you're married to an ex-supermodel for Christ's sake.'

'You think that's everything?' He hrrumphed. 'Well it isn't. If it's not Miranda going on at me day and night about her stupid business, it's eco-terrorists and their sodding newts.'

'Their what?'

'Great crested newts,' he said, enunciating the words with extreme venom. 'The bastards planted them in my lake, I swear they did. Probably in league with that fucker of a gardener who tried to poison my dogs and set the whole village against me. And what does Miranda say? She thinks it's all my fault, says I'm up to "dodgy dealings". I'm telling you, Tash, I need a woman who understands me.'

'A woman like . . . me?'

'How did you guess?'

'I'm married too, remember. And then there's Cosmo to think of.'

Cosmo. The boy. *His* boy. My son, he thought, and his heart began to race with joyful anticipation. 'Don't worry about Cosmo,' he assured Tash, 'you know I'll love him one hundred per cent, or you would never have contacted me.'

'I'm sorry he wasn't more . . . forthcoming when you met him the other day,' Tash apologised. 'But he's only six, and the only dad he's ever known is Steve, my husband. Guess we'll just have to give it time.'

Gavin was agreeing when his 'special' mobile rang and he delved with a groan into the jacket he had slung over a bedside chair, and checked the incoming number. 'Oh, nothing important. Just Miranda; she can wait.'

'Sure you wouldn't rather be with her?' enquired Tash with a half-smile.

'Hardly.'

He threw his mobile onto the bedside locker, only for it to ring again, a few minutes later. 'Not again!' He glanced at the incoming number. 'Oh, it's only Karen.'

'Another of your girlfriends?' enquired Tash.

Gavin struggled to keep a straight face. 'Er . . . I don't think so! She's got ankles like a rhino and a hairy neck. Cracking typist though. Karen's my PA.' Firmly, Gavin switched the phone off. 'Well, whatever she's got to say, it can wait until later.'

'What if it's important?'

He laughed. 'How could it be as important as this? Now, come here and let me show you how much I've missed you.'

Luke went through every possible scenario he could imagine as he forced his old car through the traffic, desperately longing to stick his head out of the window and scream: 'Let me through, you bastards! Can't you see this is a matter of life and death? Don't you realise my wife could be dying?'

But of course they didn't. And Luke himself knew precious little; Zee had gabbled something about Ally having a fit, and then the paramedics being really worried about her blood pressure; but none of that meant much to a man who habitually flicked past the health pages in magazines because they made him feel so queasy. Now, he just felt confused and terrified. And profoundly grateful to Maureen for offering to drive over and babysit the kids at five minutes' notice.

After an interminable drive, Luke finally reached the Cotswold General. The bloke on the desk in A&E explained that Ally wasn't there and that he'd come to the wrong place; and he redirected Luke to the Mildred McNulty Maternity Wing, where all the obstetrics emergencies were apparently taken.

Obstetrics emergencies ... Luke didn't like the sound of that one bit. Then again, he didn't like any of this, not one iota. All he wanted was for time to go back a few short hours; then he could persuade Ally not to go out and, just maybe, this might not happen.

He plodded through the endless hospital corridors with his eye on the signs and his mind teeming with horrible imaginings. At long last he turned a corner that looked like all the others, and saw Miranda and Zee sitting side by side. Zee was motionless, staring into space; but Miranda was rocking back and forth on her chair, and as he came nearer Luke saw that she was weeping silently.

A lump rose in Luke's throat. He wanted to cry too, but it didn't seem right. Not manly. He didn't bother with the usual 'hellos', just stammered out the one question that mattered: 'Is there any news?'

Zee looked up at him with haunted eyes. It wasn't difficult for

259

Luke to understand why he was going through hell too. A few short years ago, this was where his wife had been taken from him. Luke and Ally had been here that night, which suddenly seemed like yesterday.

'The doctor says it's pre-eclampsia,' Zee said. 'That's why Ally had the fit. Her blood pressure is really high . . . oh, and he thinks the placenta's failing.'

'Oh Jesus,' whispered Luke. It was the nearest he'd got to praying since he was a small boy in school assembly. Cold sweat had collected around his hairline, and now it was beginning to trickle down his face. He wasn't even aware of it. 'What's going to happen to her?'

'They've taken her down to theatre for an emergency Caesarean,' said Zee. 'Apparently they have to get the baby out as fast as possible. They said they'll let us know as soon as there's any news. I'm sorry, mate, but it's a bit . . . well . . . touch and go.'

Luke sank onto the empty chair beside Miranda. 'She's going to die, isn't she? Ally's going to die.'

'They won't let her,' insisted Zee, a hint of steel entering his voice. 'This time it's not going to happen.'

All this time, Miranda had been completely silent, just rocking back and forth with the tears forming a wet veil over her pale cheeks. Even in his agony, Luke couldn't help noticing that although her red-rimmed eyes were framed with dripping mascara, she was still beautiful. Miranda Hesketh was quite possibly the only woman in the world who could look beautiful with a snotty nose.

'It's my fault,' said Miranda suddenly.

'What is?' wondered Luke.

'All of this. Ally.' Miranda wiped the back of her sleeve across her face, smearing her make-up even more.

'Don't be silly, how could it be?' demanded Zee.

Miranda glanced at Luke, then her gaze dropped to the floor. 'If I hadn't gone on at her that night about wanting a baby – practically blackmailed her – she'd never have got pregnant. And she'd be well now, not . . . ' she took a long, halting breath in an attempt to control her jerky sobs, 'not dying.'

The last vestiges of self-control crumbled, and she curled up into a sobbing ball of misery, her cries echoing along the empty

260

corridor. 'Now I'm going to lose my baby, and I'm going to lose my sister as well. And it's all my fault, Luke. It's all my fault.'

Luke wanted to tell her that she was wrong, that it wasn't so; but he couldn't. All he could do was put an arm about her shoulders, and try to make her understand that if this was anybody's fault, it was his.

The world was a fuzzy place, full of distant voices, and faces that loomed up close and then suddenly zoomed away, out of range and out of focus. Somebody was speaking, but she couldn't work out what they were saying. And then the tiredness washed over her again, and she drifted back into the darkness.

When Ally opened her eyes again, everything was much sharper: the lights, the voices, the faces – and the pain.

She winced as she tried to sit up and then memory flooded back into her head, but she couldn't quite work out what had happened to her. The hall . . . a really bad headache . . . feeling really strange . . . and then –

Nothing.

Lying there on her back, propped up on crisp white pillows, she took a deep breath and forced herself to focus. This is a hospital, she decided. A private room. My belly hurts. Have I had an operation? She gasped with panic. The baby! Her hand slid down towards her belly, but she already knew that it was gone. They'd taken the baby away.

The pain of realisation hurt far more than any physical pain from the operation wound. The baby was no longer a part of her. It was no longer 'her' baby. She didn't even know if the little girl was alive . . .

Moments later the door opened and a midwife looked in. 'Ah, you're awake, Mrs Bennett. Some visitors for you.'

I don't want visitors, she thought. I want to lie here and be alone and miserable. But I also want to know. And when she saw Luke and her sister's faces, she knew she had to try not to fall apart, for their sake.

'You're all right!' Miranda's jubilation spilled over into a powerful embrace that half-suffocated Ally. 'Oh sis, I was so afraid.'

'Careful Miranda,' cautioned Luke. 'You'll hurt her.' He sat down beside the bed and took his wife's hand. 'Everything's all right darling. Everything.'

Ally licked her parched lips. 'My—' she corrected herself, 'the baby ... where's the baby? I was only eight months gone ... '

Miranda's face was a picture of pure joy. 'She's going to be fine, Ally. She's a little bit small so they've taken her away to warm her up, but she's just great. Oh Ally, she's so beautiful. Wait till you see her! And the nurses are being wonderful, aren't they, Luke? They've dealt with surrogate births before and they know exactly what to do. They've even put "Hesketh" on her name tag! Oh Ally, thank you, thank you ... I can't believe I'm a mum at last!'

Ally forced a smile, but inside she was awash with fear. How on earth was she going to look at this tiny child, take her in her arms, and not betray the desperate, aching need to be her mother? She'd sworn to herself and to everyone else that this wasn't going to happen, and now look at her: not happy for her sister but full of jealous anguish.

Miranda's baby. How many hundreds of times have I spoken those words? she wondered. This is Miranda's baby, not mine, and that's how it was always meant to be.

So why was she finding it so difficult to accept? And how long would it take for this feeling to go away – if it ever did?

'Look,' whispered Miranda, clutching Luke's sleeve. 'Look, she's kicking her little legs. They're so tiny ... '

'I don't think I've ever seen anything so small and perfect in all my life,' whispered Luke as he and Miranda stood at the window of the special care baby unit, gazing at little Baby Hesketh in her incubator. He knew she couldn't hear him through the glass, yet she seemed so fragile, her skin so transparent and delicate that the slightest sound might hurt her.

'Do you think she'll be all right?' worried Miranda. 'She's quite small, even for eight months.'

'The sister said she's going to be fine,' Luke reminded her. 'Her lungs are starting to work really well now she's had the injections. I expect they'll keep her in for a week or two, to be on the safe side, but all she needs now is a little TLC and a chance to grow.' He smiled at his sister-in-law, experiencing a rapport with her he'd never dreamed for a moment he could feel. A lot of things inside him had changed – and were still changing. 'And plenty of love, and I know that won't be a problem with you.'

He didn't mention Gavin. Neither of them did. Maybe Miranda was still clinging to the desperate hope that some catastrophe had prevented him even phoning her, but Luke suspected that reality was now too much a part of his sister-in-law's life for any fantasy to survive for long. He was quite sure, surer than he'd ever been, that the image of Gavin as a caring father was just that.

Miranda pressed her fingertips to the glass. 'Oh Luke – look, she's making tiny little fists. She looks so stern and . . . and . . . '

'Determined?'

'Yes, that's it; determined. She looks just as if she wants to take on the whole world!'

'Perhaps she is. She's a little fighter, after all,' said Luke, and he offered up a prayer of gratitude for his wife's survival. 'Just like her mother.'

Their eyes met and he realised what he had said. 'Sorry, I meant—'

'It's OK, Luke, I know what you meant.' Miranda's eyes travelled back to the tiny figure in the incubator: not grey any more, but a healthy, defiant pink. 'Ally *is* her mother. But I'm going to do my very, very best to be her mum.'

Luke nodded, and laid a supportive hand on her shoulder. No further words were necessary.

# Chapter Twenty-Six

It was the following day, and Ally was feeling very strange. Much better, certainly, but definitely strange.

Propped up in bed in the private room Miranda had insisted upon paying for, she gazed at the flower-filled vases that surrounded her, and struggled to reconcile what had happened to her with the way she felt. Her breasts were heavy with milk. She kept fingering the Caesarean wound that ran across her bikini line and which sent stabs of pain through her whenever she forgot and moved too suddenly. How could she have carried a child for all those months, got ill with it, given birth to it, and yet have no baby at the end of it all? It felt almost like a still-birth must feel; a bereavement.

But of course there was a baby. Just not her baby.

So far she'd avoided seeing the little girl, made excuses about being too tired and sore to be wheeled down to the special care baby unit, about wanting Miranda to have plenty of time with her new, instant family. But for how much longer? I can't be tired and sore for the rest of my life, she told herself. Sooner or later I have to face up to what I've done.

Just before lunchtime, Miranda came visiting. Ally had never seen anybody look so happy. She didn't just walk into the room; she floated on air.

'Hiya Ally!' Miranda beamed rays of sisterly love at Ally, totally transformed from the selfish little madam who'd driven her younger sister mad for most of their childhood. 'How's the best sister in the world?' She planted a kiss on Ally's cheek and bounced onto the bed. Ally winced. 'Oops, sorry. Still a bit sore, huh?'

Ally couldn't help smiling at her sister's guileless view of child-birth. Whichever way you did it, it hurt; but how could Miranda appreciate that, when all she'd ever seen were yummy mummies and supermodels, who apparently went into private clinics for elective Caesareans and emerged two days later, looking fabulous and two stones lighter?

'Just a bit,' she admitted. 'You know what they say – only when I laugh.'

Miranda grinned. 'Better not tell what Zee told me then.'

'What about him? What's he been up to now?'

'I'm tempted to let him tell you himself, but the story's too good. You know he walked out on *The Sound of Music* so he could come here with you?'

Ally nodded. 'Very noble, and very unnecessary. Bless him.'

'Well, what he didn't tell you is that because they were one German soldier short the whole cast had to be shuffled round, and Doreen Grey-Burroughs ended up playing the mother abbess herself.'

'Just as well they made my habit a big one then,' mused Ally, conjuring up a mental picture of the mountainous Doreen.

'Zee showed me some photos, and believe me, she looked like an elephant in purdah. But that's not the best bit. Halfway through "Climb Every Mountain" the sound system crashed, and she had to actually *sing* the rest of the song.'

'Ooh, nasty. Did I ever tell you she's tone-deaf?'

'The whole of Cheltenham knows now. Zee's bringing the local review in to show you. Oh, I forgot.' Miranda thrust yet another bouquet into Ally's hands. 'Just a little something.'

'You don't have to keep bringing me things, honestly you don't,' protested Ally.

'I know, but I like doing it. It's kind of difficult for me,' confessed Miranda. 'After all, how do you say thank you for the most amazing present anyone could ever give?'

Ally felt a pang of something that was not quite sadness and not quite joy, and closed her eyes just for a second, until it went away.

'Are you OK?' asked Miranda. 'Shall I get the nurse?'

Ally forced a big smile. 'Don't be silly, I'm fine. Just you wait until you have an operation and get stitches right across your middle, young madam.'

265

There was a short pause. Ally knew the question was coming, but she still felt her stomach turn over when Miranda spoke it. 'I've blagged a wheelchair. Shall I push you down to the unit and you can take a look at little Gracie?'

Ally swallowed as a pang of jealousy twisted her heartstrings. 'Grace? Is that what you've decided to call her?'

'That's right. Because she's my little princess. Grace Alison actually,' she added with a smile.

'That's nice,' said Ally brightly. 'That's really kind of you. "Grace Alison Hesketh", it sounds good.'

Miranda gave her a dark look. 'We'll have to see about the Hesketh bit,' she replied. 'Right now, my darling husband has one hell of a lot of explaining to do.'

For just the briefest of moments, a crazy thought captured Ally's mind. If baby Grace no longer had a natural father to look after her, maybe she could keep the baby herself? After all, she was her natural mother: its closest blood relative in the whole world. Wouldn't she be better off with me and Luke? she asked herself.

And then she looked at her sister's shining eyes, and shame overwhelmed her. How could she even begin to think such a thing? It was a stupid, stupid fantasy and the truth was obvious for all to see. Grace needed to be with her mum.

Miranda.

'Now.' Miranda stood up and patted her clothes back to their usual immaculate state. 'Hop out of bed and into the chair, and I'll introduce you to the newest member of the family.'

After only the briefest hesitation, Ally threw back the bed covers. 'I'd really like that,' she declared. 'Let's do it right now.'


A few hours later, Luke arrived with Kyle and Josie.

'Hello Mum, we've been to see the baby,' announced Kyle, submitting to his mother's embrace. 'It was all pink and ugly, just like a piglet.'

Josie was incensed. 'It was not! It was cute. And it's not an it, it's a she and it's got a name.'

'Yeah – Piglet,' insisted Kyle.

'Not!'

'Piglet, Piglet, Piglet.'

'Well you look like a . . . a big fat ugly . . . fat thing!' declared Josie, as her limited vocabulary failed her.

'Calm down kids,' ordered Luke, in the voice he used when he really, really meant it. 'Right now. Your mum's had a big operation and she hurts a lot, and she certainly doesn't want to hear you arguing.'

'I only said—' began Kyle. But his father gave him a look of instant death, and he promptly shut up and started exploring Ally's locker for uneaten chocolates.

Josie clambered up onto the bed and cuddled up to her mother. 'Are you two being good for Daddy?' demanded Ally.

Josie nodded. 'We helped Daddy get Nameless down when he went up the chimney, didn't we Daddy?'

'What?' Ally looked at Luke.

He put a hand over his face. 'I forgot to put the fireguard back after the chimney sweep came, and then next door's bull-terrier got in when I left the back door open . . . I think you can imagine the rest.'

Ally shook her head and tried not to look too amused. 'Are you really this hopeless when I'm not around to organise you all?'

'Oh yes,' replied Luke. It sounded heartfelt.

'When are you coming home, Mum?' asked Kyle. 'Dad's cooking sucks.'

'Soon,' Ally promised.

'Today?' Josie enquired hopefully.

'No, not today. But soon.'

'Will you bring the baby home too?'

Ally felt that old twist of the knife in the heart all over again. 'No sweetheart,' she said, stroking her daughter's soft brown hair. 'I explained, don't you remember? I was only looking after the baby for Auntie Miranda until it was born. She'll be taking the baby home with her in a week or so, as soon as little Grace is well enough.'

'Oh yes,' said Josie, sounding disappointed. 'Now I remember.'

'Well I'm glad,' declared Kyle. 'Who wants another little sister? I wouldn't have minded if it was a boy though,' he added after a moment's reflection.

You and Gavin too, thought Ally. She wondered where the hell the prodigal father had got to, while half hoping he never turned up again.

267

A little later, the kids went off with Auntie Miranda for burgers and fizzy drinks in the nearby fast-food joint, leaving Ally and Luke with the first substantial time they had alone together since the emergency began.

Luke closed the door behind him, drew up a chair and sat down beside the bed. He took Ally's hand between his and a look of concern crossed his face.

'You're all hot and clammy.'

'It's OK,' she soothed him. 'I haven't got a fever or anything, it's just hot in here. You know it's always hot in hospitals.' She stroked the hair back from his forehead, spotting a few grey hairs in among the brown that she hadn't noticed before. 'You worry so much,' she said with a smile. 'You could worry for the whole world.'

He squeezed her hand tenderly. 'I've been thinking that maybe I should stop worrying about the whole world, and start just worrying about you instead.'

Ally chuckled. 'Then who's going to worry about the world?'

Luke let out a long sigh. 'I dunno. Somebody else. Let's face it, darling, while I'm off trying to change things and failing miserably, I'm neglecting you and the kids and ... well ... courting disaster.'

'Don't you think you're being rather hard on yourself?'

'The fact is,' replied Luke, 'I keep comparing myself to Gavin and I don't come off that well.'

'Oh Luke!' scoffed Ally. 'You're nothing like Gavin! You'd never disappear when you were about to become a father.'

'No? Well maybe I wouldn't on purpose, but look at all the times I've not been there for you. Look at all the times I've been out dispensing soup and good intentions to the poor of the parish, while you've been sitting at home nursing the kids through mumps or just feeling lonely and bored.'

'I've not always been around either,' she pointed out.

'Ally, one night a week at the drama club is hardly in the same class – and I've even begrudged you that!'

'What about ... that business with me and Gavin?'

Luke shook his head dismissively. 'You wouldn't have given him the time of day if I hadn't treated you like some ... some added extra in my life.' He thought for a moment, then laughed.

'Does that sound ridiculously pompous?'

'Only a little bit,' Ally assured him. 'And anyway, it's true.'

Just for the merest moment she had a tiny flicker of doubt; after all, she *had* always felt that powerful attraction to Gavin – until now. But no. That had proved to be far less than it had seemed, or felt: just a schoolgirl crush on forbidden fruit. If nothing else, she thought, it had taught her that she could never love anybody the way she loved Luke.

He leaned his forehead against her hand, then drew his face slowly upward until her fingers brushed his lips. 'I want things to be different, Ally. I've been scared out of my wits, I've been selfish and stupid, pompous as hell, and I don't want to be away from you any more.' He looked up at her, and she saw that he was genuinely afraid. 'Is that OK with you?'

Ally laughed through the tears that were welling up in her eyes. 'Of course it is, of course it is!'

They sat there in companionable silence for a few minutes, Luke's head resting on Ally's hand. 'I don't know whether to give you an Oscar or a medal for bravery,' he said, sitting up and looking at her.

Ally was bemused. 'I don't understand.'

'I know, Ally.'

'Know what?'

'I saw it in your eyes the first time Miranda told you how well *her* baby was doing. It hurts you every time she chatters away about all the plans she's got for Grace, all the things she's going to do for her. This is tearing you apart, Ally. You're hiding it so well and all the time your heart's breaking.'

The tears were prickling again beneath Ally's eyelids. 'It's not so bad as all that,' she said. 'I mean, you can't really bond with a baby when you don't see it until days after it was born, can you? Luke?'

It was obvious from the look on his face that he wasn't fooled. 'Don't give me that, Ally. You loved that baby all the time you were carrying her, and you bonded with her the moment you set eyes on her. I'm willing to bet you'd love to run off with Grace and never bring her back. And yet you still manage to be happy for Miranda's sake.'

Ally shrugged. 'In the end you do what you think is right, don't you? You of all people must understand that.'

269

Luke nodded. 'But sometimes it's hard working out what that is. I thought it was saving the world, but it looks like I took a wrong turn somewhere.'

'Oh I don't know. Psyche's right: you've saved a few bits of it along the way. And you've done some pretty brave things too. I'm not saying I've always agreed with them, but you've never been afraid to have the courage of your convictions.'

'Well I think you're the bravest person I've ever met.' He put up a cautionary finger as she opened her mouth. 'And don't you dare interrupt when I'm telling you how much I love you, or how proud I am that you're my wife.'

They were still kissing several minutes later when Zee stuck his head round the door, thought better of it and was about to sneak away when Ally called him back. 'Zee? Where are you going?'

'Er . . . lousy timing. You look like you two would rather be left alone.'

Ally and Luke laughed, in an unfettered way they hadn't shared for months. 'Don't be a dickhead, Zee, come in and grab a chair. I'm sure you've got some great news to tell Ally about the show.'

'And I want to see those pictures,' Ally reminded him.

'Actually,' said Zee, coming in and sitting down, 'I've got some other news. Did I mention that Miranda asked me to do a little . . . digging about Gavin?'

'Some *what*?' exclaimed Ally.

'Ah – obviously I didn't. Well believe it or not Zee Goldman, dealer in worthless junk and part-time private eye, has actually managed to dig something up. The trouble is, I don't know whether I should tell Miranda or not.'

While Zee was relating his exploits, Miranda was sitting in the hospital cafeteria after dropping Kyle and Josie off at their grandparents'. It was a chance to be by herself for a little while; to sip coffee out of a polystyrene cup and let her new situation sink in.

I'm a mother, she told herself over and over again as she tried to keep a lid on the great fizzing cauldron of excitement. I've got a daughter. Mum and Dad are grandparents again. Can I really believe this? Can I allow myself to believe that it's finally happened?

270

And what the fuck has happened to—

'I thought I might find you here,' said a voice behind her. A voice that jolted through Miranda's heart like an electric shock.

She spun round, deluging herself and the floor with NHS coffee. 'Gavin! Where the hell have you been?'

He stood there, hands in pockets, looking as handsome and as unruffled as ever; not even having the grace to look ashamed. 'I think we need to have a little talk,' he said.

'Too fucking right we do,' replied Miranda.

'Hang on mate, you've lost me,' said Luke, laying a hand on Zee's shoulder to stop him as he rattled on. 'Who's this "Hairy Pete" guy again?'

Zee rolled his eyes. 'I told you! He's the cousin of the friend of the gardener Gavin sacked. The one who's been charged with threatening him and Miranda, and poisoning poor Molly.'

'Oh ... him. The one you met in the Poacher's Arms?'

'Exactly. The smelly one with the ferret. And he's the one who told me how he and his mates were offered all this money to sneak onto the Nether Grantley estate and dig up any sign that there had ever been any sheep's tongue orchids growing there.'

'Offered?' Ally drew herself up the bed, pulling a face as her stitches tugged at the wound. 'Who by?'

'Ah, well that's the interesting bit. According to Hairy Pete, it was that environmental scientist bloke from the Ministry, who came up from London to do the environmental impact survey.'

'But why would he want to get rid of the orchids?' asked Luke.

Ally answered before Zee had a chance. 'He wouldn't. But Gavin would.'

Luke scratched his head. 'You're sure this bloke wasn't just making it all up after you'd bought him too many pints of rough cider?'

'I didn't have to buy him anything. Gavin Hesketh's not a very popular bloke around those parts, or so it seems.'

'So it could all just be a grudge,' pointed out Ally.

'Maybe. But I don't think so. And he and his mates told me all kinds of other things – rumours about Gavin's finances. About him having fingers in a lot of pies, and not all of them kosher. At the very least you've got to admit that Gavin doesn't come out of it looking too good.'

271

'Not a great start for a man who's just become a father for the first time,' commented Luke. 'First he disappears into the ether, and now you're telling us he's probably a crook as well.'

He looked at Ally, perhaps half expecting her to come up with some kind of defence. But her face betrayed no sign of emotion.

Inside, a single thought took possession of her mind: how much better it would be for everyone if Gavin never came back.

Zee looked at them both expectantly. 'So?'

'So what?' they answered, almost simultaneously.

'Do I tell Miranda about all this, or not? I mean, I know she said she wanted to know if there was anything dodgy about Gavin, but maybe she doesn't really want to know – if you know what I mean?'

'Zee love,' sighed Ally, 'if you go on worrying like this, one of these days your head is going to explode. Now, if I know my sister, the one thing she really wants to know is the truth. And if you really believe that's what this is, I think you should go and tell it to her.

'Now.'

Miranda's face was white, cold and stony-eyed; her voice a steady, venomous hiss. 'What do you mean, you don't want to see your daughter?'

Gavin leaned forward across the Formica-topped table with the vase of plastic carnations, almost took his wife's hand, and then thought better of it. 'It just seems like it's for the best,' he explained. 'You know, under the circumstances.'

Miranda's jaw muscles clenched like ropes of twisted steel. 'The circumstances being, I take it, that you've met up with this woman and her brat, and bingo! suddenly you don't need me or Grace any more, because the brat just happens to be a boy.'

She glared icily at him, her chest rising and falling with emotions that were simply too strong to be expressed. The few other customers in the café had given up any pretence of reading their papers or having conversations, and were all savouring the live show. As for the woman behind the counter, she was so engrossed that she'd poured a pint of milk into the teapot before she realised what she was doing.

'Miranda darling—' began Gavin, who obviously hadn't learned much from the conversation so far.

272

'I am not your darling,' she spat back at him, leaving little dots of spittle on his face and his crisp shirt-front. 'This whore of yours is your darling now – apparently – and if you want to convince yourself that her bastard son is yours, who am I to interfere with Love's Young Dream?'

'There's been a DNA test of course,' said Gavin calmly. 'Cosmo is definitely my son.'

Miranda just restrained herself from smashing the flower vase over his smug head. 'And Grace is very definitely your daughter! What the hell is it with you, Gavin? What's all this macho crap about?' Ruthlessly she fought back the ghost of a tear. She wasn't going to let him see her crying over him. He wasn't worth it. 'How can you reject your own flesh and blood, just because she's a girl?'

For the first time, Gavin actually looked uncomfortable. He ran a finger around his shirt collar, as though it had suddenly become just a fraction too constricting. 'I'm not rejecting her,' he insisted. 'I'm perfectly willing to support her financially.'

'You know that's not what I mean.'

She tried to fix him with a cold stare, but he glanced aside. 'And you know ... about my problems. My sister ... '

'Don't give me all that shit about your sister; that's just a pathetic excuse. It's pretty obvious, Gavin. You're an old-fashioned woman-hater. Oh, and by the way,' she added, 'for the record, I know you tried to seduce Ally, and I also know that she blew you out. She told me so herself. Good for her.'

Gavin just gaped at her, open-mouthed and speechless.

'Now, where was I? Oh yes. You spent your childhood resenting your sister because your mother was always spending time caring for her instead of you – that's what the psychiatrist said, isn't it? And you resent your mother because she killed herself? Very sad and very Freudian, I'm sure. But you know something, Gavin? I don't give a shit if you're a basket case. I don't even give a toss if you move in with a trollop and a kid you haven't bothered to track down once in the last seven years. In fact I don't care about anything except *my* daughter.' She savoured the wounded look in his eyes. 'Yes Gavin, *mine*. And all I need from you now is your signature on this document, the parental order, so that I get to keep Grace – and you will sign, Gavin. Believe me you will.

273

'And when you've done that, as far as I'm concerned the faster you go to Hell, the better off the rest of us will be.'

# Chapter Twenty-Seven

While Ally was healing and Luke was making a thousand resolutions, Miranda had an awful lot of learning to do.

Every day for the next week she came to the hospital and spent hours with Grace, trying to pick up the fine art of being a mother. Grace was out of the incubator now, and about to move off the special care baby unit; everyone was saying how soon she'd be ready to go home. It was a prospect that both thrilled and terrified Miranda.

It didn't matter how many parenting classes she'd attended with Ally, how many Internet forums she'd joined, or how many nappies she'd changed on other people's babies: Grace was a tiny little fragile newborn, who was going to depend on her for everything – including life itself. This was a child she didn't get to hand back at the end of the experiment. Oh, Ally might be there to consult while she was still recovering in hospital, and the nurses and midwives were full of friendly advice. But there was no avoiding the subtext of what they all said: get the hang of this now, because very shortly you'll be taking your new baby home, and then you'll be completely on your own.

Just how completely, not all of them realised. Even some of her supposedly 'close' friends didn't know yet abut the break-up. Miranda hadn't made a big song and dance about Gavin's betrayal, and that puzzled even her. Normally she'd have flounced into full diva mode, made an exhibition of herself, got herself photographed throwing champagne cocktails over her errant husband and his floozie in some fashionable nightclub. But that kind of thing just didn't seem worth the candle any more. It felt juvenile and frankly not her style. Not now that she was somebody's mother.

If Gavin wanted to bugger off and leave her and his daughter, that suited Miranda just fine, just as long as he completed the legal formalities that made Grace officially her daughter. What didn't suit her was that he should get everything his own way and come out of it smelling of roses; particularly since it was becoming increasingly obvious that Gavin's shady dealings were in danger of rebounding on her. She hung on every word Zee told her, storing each tiny piece of information in her memory for future reference. If revenge was a dish best served cold, Miranda vowed to ensure that hers was frostier than the Arctic tundra.

A couple of weeks after Grace's birth, Miranda found herself at the ChelShel office after hours, with Zee, Luke and that slightly odd receptionist girl who called herself Psycho but looked like a skater chick and spoke more like a stockbroker's daughter.

'Where's Chas?' enquired Zee, looking around as if he expected the priest to materialise from behind a filing cabinet.

'We had a little chat,' explained Luke, handing out mugs of coffee, 'and he decided if we were going to be getting up to anything illegal, it might be better if he wasn't here.'

Miranda's elegantly pencilled eyebrows arched in surprise. 'Illegal? You're intriguing me already.'

They drew up chairs in varying stages of decrepitude, and gathered around Luke's desk. 'You know you asked me to find out everything I could about Gavin?' Zee reminded Miranda.

'Of course I do, Zee, I'm not senile,' she replied drily.

'Well you've had everything I could get. I'm convinced he's been up to all kinds of things he shouldn't, I just don't have the skill or the brains to get at the really interesting stuff. But fortunately,' he went on, 'Luke knows somebody who does.'

'Not me exactly,' admitted Luke. 'It's Psyche – or rather, one of our clients she's been working with. Billy. He was Jake's best mate at the housing project and had a job and a council flat until he got convicted for computer hacking—'

'Hacking!' Miranda's eyes sparkled. 'Now I'm beginning to understand.'

'Then he lost his job and his flat, and ended up in the next room to Jake. Psyche knows him quite well, don't you?'

Psyche twiddled a strand of hair about her finger. 'Let's say we share an interest in, um, the security aspects of computer technology.'

276

'In other words,' translated Zee, 'she's a hacker too.'

'Just not a very good one,' laughed Psyche. 'But Billy – wow, slip him a few quid and he can find out anything you want to know. And I mean anything.'

Miranda put her mug of black coffee down carefully on the corner of the desk. 'Let me get this straight: we pay this Billy chap, and he dishes up the dirt on Gavin?'

'If there's any dirt to dish,' Psyche reminded her.

It was Miranda's turn to laugh. 'Nobody keeps his financial affairs locked away from his wife like Gavin did, unless they've got something they'd rather she didn't know. Besides,' she added, the smile fading, 'I was stupid enough to invest some of my money in his projects. I need to know if I'll ever see any of it again.'

'How much money do you think this guy Billy will want?' asked Zee.

'I already asked him, and he swears he won't take a penny,' replied Psyche. 'He was Jake's best friend, remember. OK, maybe it wasn't Gavin who bought up the housing project and threw him back onto the street, but it was somebody *like* Gavin. And it's no secret now that it's Miranda who's been keeping ChelShel going for God knows how long.

'Let's just say he's happy to do it just for the job satisfaction. For his friend's sake.'

Ally was learning too. Learning how to let go.

Physically she was feeling much better now. A day or two more and she'd be back home again with Luke and the kids. Just the *two* kids. Come on, you've only had an operation, she kept telling herself – like having your appendix out or something. Miranda had a baby and you had an operation; that's the best way to think of it.

It was a ridiculous way to deceive her brain, although to a degree at least it worked. When she was away from Miranda and Grace, Ally genuinely almost believed that the baby was her niece; yet when she set eyes on Grace, or saw her in her new mother's arms, the ache of loss still caught her by surprise every time, taking her breath away.

But things were getting better, and so was Ally.

One evening, when the hospital was settling down into the long, grey slide to bedtime, Ally put on her robe and slippers and

277

gingerly shuffled along the corridor to the lift. The nursery was only on the floor below. She'd just sneak one tiny peep and then go back to bed.

A friendly face smiled at her as she hobbled towards the nurses' station. 'Good evening . . . Mrs Bennett, isn't it? Popped in to see the little one?'

Ally nodded. 'Just for a minute, if that's OK. It's not too late in the evening is it?'

'No, it should be fine. As a matter of fact her mo—,' the nurse corrected herself in mid-word, 'Mrs Hesketh is with her at the moment. Shall I tell her you're here?'

That selfsame jealous pang returned to knife Ally in the heart; only this time, it wasn't quite so horrible, not quite so viciously sharp. 'No, don't disturb them. I'll just watch through the window.'

Unseen by Miranda, Ally stood at the window that gave onto a little indoor car park of babies in cots. There, over the other side, sat Miranda, with baby Grace in her arms. A faint sound, tremulous but sweet, penetrated the thickness of the glass. At first, Ally couldn't quite make it out; then suddenly she recognised it: Miranda was singing 'Let Me Call You Sweetheart' – the same old song their grandmother had sung to them both when they were little and couldn't sleep.

Tears came to Ally's eyes and she had to look away. But this time they were tears of joy.

As she made her way back to the ward, the picture of Miranda and Grace stayed in her mind, but it didn't torment her, the way it had done before. Transforming herself from mother into proud auntie was going to be one of the hardest thing she'd ever do in her life; but finally she was beginning to get there.

In the tiny gaps between her visits to the hospital, Miranda struggled to keep the rest of her life on track. In all honesty, she wasn't that interested. Fortunately the design business more or less ran itself since she'd appointed a competent manager, a couple of months previously. Even then, she'd felt a waning of her inner drive to succeed at all costs; or at least to succeed as a businesswoman. Succeeding as a mother was quite another story. In fact it was the only thing she really cared about now.

After she'd spent an invigorating morning slicing up some of the

278

designer shirts Gavin had forgotten to clear out of the wardrobe when he left, Miranda took the 4x4 across to Cheltenham to see Zee. Over the past weeks she had gravitated more and more to him; she still wasn't quite sure why. It was more than just the fact that he was kind and sweet and funny in a geeky way. Maybe it was because he never treated her as anybody out of the ordinary. That was quite a novelty to Miranda, who'd been the golden girl ever since she won her first beautiful baby competition at the age of six months. Even Emma seemed far from overawed by the presence of a former supermodel in the house.

'I like your jumper,' remarked Zee's daughter as Miranda took off her coat, revealing a rather spectacular cashmere number that had cost a bomb in Milan.

'Thank you,' beamed Miranda.

'They've got some just like it in Primark,' Emma chirped on amiably. 'Only theirs are a bit nicer.'

'Everything ready for the little one?' enquired Zee as Emma skipped off upstairs and he brewed up one of his pots of industrial-strength tea.

'As ready as they'll ever be,' replied Miranda, making no attempt to disguise her nervousness. 'The nursery's all set up; all it needs now is, well, the baby.'

'Have you managed to find a nanny yet?'

Miranda shook her head. 'Actually Zee, I sort of think I might not bother.'

'Really?' Zee's expression fell somewhere between stunned, worried and impressed. 'Do you think you can, um . . . ?'

'Cope?' Miranda spread her hands wide. 'God knows. But I thought I might try, before I start calling in the Seventh Cavalry. I mean, I know Ally's much better at this mothering thing—'

'Hey, that's not necessarily true,' cut in Zee; and Miranda instantly loved him for it, even though she knew perfectly well that he was just being kind.

'But I just won't feel like a proper mum if I don't give it a go. Besides, my chum Priscilla's a real sweetie, and she said she'd come and stay for a couple of weeks. Isn't that kind of her?' She giggled. 'Is that cheating?'

'Oh, I think we might let you off,' replied Zee. 'Mind you, as I recall, Mum said that when I was born my grandma moved in for six months and they couldn't get rid of her.'

279

Miranda pulled a face. 'Six months? Oh my God, that'd better not happen. I mean, Priscilla and I get on OK but ... six months! Oh, by the way,' she added, 'did I tell you? Mum's staying at Ally's for a week to help Luke with the kids and take care of Ally now she's home.'

'Hm, interesting,' commented Zee. 'You don't suppose your mother's actually starting to see Ally in a different light?'

'Lord knows, it's about time. Between you and me, I think she's feeling guilty. Mind you, so am I,' admitted Miranda. 'I was really vile to her when we were little, you know. And Mum and Dad always gave me the best stuff. And I've kind of been lording it over her since I got successful, haven't I?' She looked down and picked at a loose thread in her jeans. 'Now Ally's giving me the best thing anybody ever could. She really ought to hate me.'

'I don't think Ally holds it against you, I really don't,' advised Zee. 'Any of it. And she certainly doesn't hate you.'

'Well, I still think I have some making up to do.' Miranda was silent for a moment, then sat up and smiled. 'Here I am prattling on, and I haven't even told you the reason why I'm here!'

Zee put on a downcast face. 'You mean you're not just here to admire my stunning good looks and excellent taste in house décor?'

'Kind of,' replied Miranda, and laughed at Zee's look of surprise. 'Well, the taste bit anyway. Remember that jug we found in your lock-up – the one with all the crusty old paintbrushes in it?'

'How could I forget? It left a great big ring of white gloss all over the top of that imitation Sheraton table.'

'Ah well, bugger the table,' declared Miranda. 'Just look at this!'

She reached into her shoulder bag and, with a flourish, produced something that looked about as unlike a jug full of paintbrushes as anything could. Well, unless it was a spaceship or a frozen chicken, which it patently wasn't.

It was a jug; but there wasn't a speck of paint on it. It was finely shaped and almost translucent beneath the shimmer of multi-coloured metallic glazes. It was the kind of jug you might love or hate; but it certainly wasn't the kind of jug you could ignore.

'I, er, got it cleaned up a bit,' she said.

'Hell's bells,' whistled Zee. 'It must've taken forever. I hope you think it was worth it.'

This time Miranda didn't just laugh; she guffawed. When she had wiped her eyes, she answered: 'Just about, dear. This little thing here could fetch as much as ten or fifteen at auction. More, if there's a specialist collector there.'

'What – ten or fifteen pounds?' enquired Zee in all innocence.

'Thousands, you twerp,' replied Miranda. 'Congratulations Zee, I think you've found your treasure.'

'So do I,' agreed Zee. But funnily enough he wasn't looking at the jug.

It was all arranged, and under the circumstances Gavin was feeling pretty pleased with himself.

He did still harbour some pangs of conscience about leaving Miranda in the lurch with the baby, but when everything was said and done he'd signed her precious papers, and a baby was all that Miranda had ever wanted; and if she wouldn't take his cash, what else was he supposed to do? Not crawl back, that was for sure. Not now that Tash had invited him to move in with her and Cosmo; until things were settled and they bought a place of their own, obviously.

Cosmo. A warm tingle of excitement coursed through his veins. Cosmo, his son.

OK, so at the moment Cosmo wasn't exactly elated about Gavin replacing his recently dumped stepfather, but that was only to be understood. Time and a spot of good fathering would put that right. Gavin smiled to himself as he imagined all the cool father–son things they would do together. Manly, fun stuff, with not a pink pony in sight.

He was about to leave the hotel room where he was staying when his mobile rang and Tash's number flashed up.

'Tash, sweetheart. Everything's sorted out, and I'll be bringing my stuff over tomorrow afternoon. By tomorrow night, we'll really be together.'

There was a brief but uncomfortable silence.

'Tash?' he repeated, wondering if he'd lost the signal.

Then her voice came on the line. 'Actually, Gavin, I'd rather you didn't move in tomorrow after all.'

'Oh. When then? You name the date and I'll make the arrangements.'

'Er – not at all.'

'What?' He stared at the handset as though it was playing tricks on him. 'What did you just say?'

'I said, I don't want you to move in. I'm really sorry Gavin, but it was all so rushed and I was upset over breaking up with Steve, and I guess I was kind of on the rebound. Anyhow, Steve and I have been talking and I think if we really try we can make it work.'

All colour drained from Gavin's face. 'You . . . and Steve? But . . . you said you wished he was dead!'

Tash at least had the good grace to sound embarrassed. 'I know, but the thing is, when your life's upside down and you've convinced yourself you're in love, you'll say anything. Do anything, come to that. Won't you?'

Gavin didn't answer, because he couldn't deny that she was right. About him as well as about herself.

'And, well, the other thing is . . . Cosmo. I thought he was just being a bit shy and missing Steve, but the fact is, Gavin, he just basically hates your guts.'

'Hates me? But I'm his father!' Gavin sank onto the end of the bed.

'No, Gavin, Steve's his father – at least as far as Cosmo's concerned. And I love that boy to bits, you know that. I'm hardly going to move in with some guy he hates, just because he once shagged me a couple of times, am I?'

There was no arguing with the vicious logic of Tash's argument. The ruthless, relentless, unstoppable Gavin who always got exactly what he wanted seemed to evaporate with every additional word she spoke. By the time she rang off, he was little better than a puddle on the floor.

'Oh fuck.' He flung the mobile at the wall, hitting the minibar and leaving a dent in the door. Still, he could pay for it. That was about all he could do.

He sat there for quite a long time, watching the sky darken as afternoon melted into evening. It was a weird and embarrassing feeling, being alone, and not at all to his taste.

Maybe he'd sleep on it and things would look better in the morning. And then maybe, just maybe, he might make a phone call to Miranda.

# Chapter Twenty-Eight

It was only late October, but already you could feel winter in the air, like gathering snow. To Ally it felt like a tingle on her skin, an unspoken excitement she remembered from way back, when she was a small child and winter meant Christmas.

Back home from the hospital, she submitted to Maureen's mother-hen clucking and lay on the sofa for hours on end while her mum disinfected the doorknobs, harried the cat and polished the children, and Clive sang loudly as he waltzed the vacuum cleaner around the house.

They were like different parents since Ally had become Miranda's surrogate. It was as if the realisation that Miranda wasn't perfect, that there were things she couldn't do but Ally could, had blown their cosy prejudices out of the water; and now they were trying to make up for three decades of unfounded favouritism. It was almost too much of a change for Ally to cope with. Being fussed over was hard to adjust to after years of being habitually ignored.

As usual the kids were already talking about nothing but what they wanted for Christmas, and doubtless they wouldn't pipe down until the shops closed on Christmas Eve. At least it was a distraction. Ally had dreaded this time: the inevitable, massive down after the birth, when Miranda got the baby and she got the blues. But curiously it wasn't like that at all. Instead of mourning what she couldn't have, she found herself genuinely excited for her sister, and even slightly relieved not to be facing nappies, two-hourly feeds and permanent exhaustion. I've done all that, she thought to herself. Twice, in fact – and never again. I've got two nice kids and a husband who loves me. I must have been insane to give Gavin Hesketh a second look.

No more maternal angst for me. This time I'm going to sit back and enjoy just being Auntie Ally.

Later that morning, while Ally was drinking coffee with Zee and planning a visit to a big winter antiques market, two men in leather jackets and jeans were knocking on the door of a hotel room in Swindon.

'All right, hang on, I'm coming,' complained a voice from within.

It took an age for the door to open, revealing a man whose handsome looks were somewhat marred by bloodshot eyes and a five-day growth of beard. When he opened his mouth to speak, a gust of alcoholic breath filled the corridor. 'What do you want?' he demanded, running a hand through his uncombed hair. It might be almost lunchtime, but it was pretty obvious he'd only just rolled out of bed.

. 'Are you Mr Gavin Dexter Hesketh, of Sunnybank House, Grantley?' enquired the taller of the two men.

'Yes ... no. I used to be.' Gavin cleared his throat. 'I moved out a few weeks ago. I'm living here now – just temporarily,' he emphasised. 'Until I, er, sort things out with my wife. Who are you, anyway?'

The second man flashed a warrant card. 'Swindon CID, sir. And the sergeant here is from the South-West Fraud Unit. Would you mind coming down the station with us? We'd like to ask you a few questions.'

When Luke arrived home from work, around teatime, he found Ally and Miranda having a big girly pow-wow on the sofa.

A smile came into Ally's eyes. 'Hello darling! You're early again.'

'Told you I was turning over a new leaf.' Luke bent down and planted a lingering kiss on his wife's lips. 'Are you complaining?'

'Hardly. Can the office manage without you though?'

Luke sat down on the arm of the sofa, next to Ally. 'It'll have to. Work may mean a lot to me, but you mean more. Besides, Psyche's like the human tornado: she can do three people's jobs in half the time. Oh.' He paused. 'Did I tell you about Chas?'

'Is there something wrong?'

Luke shook his head. 'No. But he's off to South America in the New Year, and Psyche's taking over his job. It looks like I'm going to be a bit more deskbound, so I might actually be home at a reasonable time most nights, which is what I really wanted.'

Miranda was clearly amused by this. 'South America? What's he done – a bank job?'

'I think it's been hard for him here, ever since his little niece was killed,' replied Luke. 'So he asked his bishop if he could have a change of scene – and, well, it looks like he got it. He's going out to help a charity that rescues street children. Ally and I are even going to sponsor one, aren't we darling?'

Ally nodded and looked at Luke, waiting for him to admit that this was a challenge he would have liked to take on himself; but he didn't. He must have read her mind, because out of the blue he said: 'Once upon a time I might have wanted to go too; but not any more. All my priorities are here now – aren't they, Piglet?'

'Hey, who are you calling Piglet?' she laughed, poking him in the stomach. 'Fat boy!'

'Charming!' Luke tickled her in the ribs and they play-fought on the sofa, with much giggling.

'Dear God, you're like a pair of teenagers! Much more of that carry-on,' declared Miranda, 'and people will start thinking you've fallen in love all over again.'

'That wouldn't be such a bad thing, would it?' ventured Ally.

Miranda winked. 'Don't mind me, these days I'm just an old cynic where love is concerned.'

'Hardly surprising in the circumstances,' sympathised Ally.

'Have you heard from Gavin?' asked Luke, voicing Ally's thoughts.

'Sort of,' replied Miranda with a dry laugh. 'Would you believe I got a call from his solicitor in the middle of the night, asking me if I'd stand bail for him?'

Ally's jaw dropped. 'Bail! So he's actually been charged then?'

'Yes – well, after all that stuff Psyche's friend dug up the police didn't have much choice – all those dodgy offshore accounts he didn't want anyone to know about, and the tax evasion didn't help, not to mention stealing my money – but I'm sure he'll wriggle out of it. Gavin's one of those Teflon-coated people who always do,' mused Miranda with a sigh. 'Anyhow, I told his solicitor I couldn't afford to stand bail for him, not since he sank half my money in his dodgy deals. And cleared out all our joint savings . . .'

'Maybe it'll do him good to spend a night or two in the cells,' ventured Luke.

'Unless the warder's a woman and he wraps her round his little finger.' Miranda chuckled. 'Told you I was a cynic. Anyhow, enough about him. Go on Ally, tell Luke my big news.'

'What big news?' asked Luke.

'Grace is coming home from the hospital tomorrow!' A warm tide of emotion washed over Ally. She didn't have to pretend to be happy; she genuinely was. 'Isn't that wonderful?'

'*And* . . . ' prompted Miranda.

'Oh yes,' said Ally. 'And Miranda's moving house. To Cheltenham!'

Ally was amazed by the way she felt about all of this. Not so many months ago, the prospect of her sister moving to a house just down the road would have filled her with absolute horror. Now, she positively liked the idea. Maybe it's hormonal, she wondered. Perhaps it'll wear off and I'll end up hating the sight of her. But somehow I don't think so.

'Money's not going to be quite so plentiful now,' explained Miranda. 'Not since Gavin made some of the worst business deals in history: with my capital. We're going to be fine though,' she added, seeing the look of concern on her brother-in-law's face. 'The business is doing well and I still have some savings. Anyhow, the main reason for moving is that I wanted to be closer to you. How the hell am I going to survive as a first-time mother without Grace's number one auntie around to mop up my mistakes?'

'You'll be fine,' Luke assured her.

Ally and Miranda looked at each other and smiled. 'No, *we'll* be fine.'


A couple of days before Christmas, Psyche paid a visit, bearing gifts of Fair Trade chocolate and something that might have been a poncho, crafted by a native women's collective in Cuzco, plus a small cuddly alpaca for Ally to pass on to little Grace.

Psyche was full of excitement. 'I can't believe it Ally – the developer backed down and the whole thing's been called off!'

Ally put up a hand to slow her down. 'Hang on, you've lost me. What's been called off?'

'You know, the developer who bought Winston House – the housing project on the Bluebell Estate – and closed it down. He had a change of heart after that massive demo we staged outside his offices in Gloucester, and now he's even given the project managers some money to help them open up again!'

'Wow,' said Ally. 'That kind of thing doesn't happen very often.'

'You're telling me!' Psyche's cheeks were pink with exhilaration. 'You know, I'm a complete atheist but suddenly I'm in danger of believing in the magic of Christmas. Mind you,' she admitted in conspiratorial tones, 'my mate the hacker found out one or two interesting things about the guy, while he was looking for stuff on Gavin. I guess that *might* have helped a little . . . '

'You *blackmailed* the developer?' Ally knew she ought to be scandalised but couldn't help being impressed. 'You never did! What if he'd reported you to the police?'

Psyche shrugged. 'It's not about individuals, is it? It's about what's right.'

Luke shook his head and smiled. 'You know something, kid? You really are a psycho. In fact you remind me of me – fifteen years ago.'

'But now you're a middle-aged couch potato with a wife, two kids and a mortgage?' suggested Psyche.

'Something like that,' agreed Luke. He turned towards Ally. 'And d'you know what? I think I'm learning to love it.'

An hour or two later, after the fifth pot of tea and a second portion of Maureen's special chocolate cake, Luke, Ally and Psyche were still chattering away in the front room. In fact they were so deep in conversation that they didn't even hear the front doorbell ring.

Moments later Miranda appeared, cradling a tiny bundle in her arms. 'We were on our way back from having our vaccinations at the clinic, and Grace wanted to say Happy Christmas,' she announced. 'The nurses are so pleased with her, aren't they sweetie?' she beamed. 'She's right up to her proper weight already!'

Even Psyche melted at the sight of the baby, snub-nosed and blonde with blue eyes that Ally had convinced herself were like Clive's, not Gavin's. It was easier that way. 'Oh look – she's soooo cute!' gasped Psyche.

287

'Want to hold her for a while, so I can take my coat off?' enquired Miranda.

'Heck, no!' Psyche took a step backwards in consternation. 'I'm hopeless with babies; I'd probably drop her.'

Ally held out her arms. 'I'll take her.' The little bundle nestled just perfectly into the crook of her arm. 'How's Auntie Ally's little girl today then?'

'Auntie Ally's little girl has just had a clean bill of health from the clinic,' replied Miranda proudly. 'And she's putting on weight like a prize wrestler.'

'Oh, that's a point.' Psyche's hand flew to her lips as she remembered something. 'I meant to ask you something. About babies, that is.'

'Such as?' enquired Ally, expecting a question about nappies or weaning or some such run-of-the-mill topic.

'Surrogacy,' said Psyche brightly.

'Oh,' said Ally.

'You see, I've got this pair of gay friends – Simon and Xander – and they've been together for absolutely ages, only they're desperate for a family, and it's just about impossible to find a baby to adopt. So they're thinking of looking for someone to be a surrogate mum.'

Psyche smiled appealingly at Ally. 'I don't suppose you'd be interested, by any chance? You've had experience of it, and you'd be doing such a wonderful thing for Simon and Xander. You know, giving them the chance to experience what it's truly like being a parent.'

Before Ally had a chance to say, 'Over my dead body,' Kyle's young and plaintive voice came floating down the stairs and through the door into the lounge.

'Mum,' it wailed.

'Yes Kyle?' Ally called back.

'Mum, I can't find my pants.'

# Epilogue

**Eighteen months later: the garden of number 22, Brookfield Road ...**

It was a beautiful June evening, and the swifts were swooping low over the Bennetts' back garden.

As a horticultural achievement it still wouldn't win any prizes, but over the past year Luke had been spending a lot more time at home with the family. He'd finally managed to tame the jungle, lay some decent turf for the kids to play on and even persuaded Zee and Psyche to help him install some trendy decking. Ally still couldn't quite believe the transformation in him, but she thanked her lucky stars for it every day.

As she lazed on a lounger in the evening sunshine, with Nameless slumbering blissfully across her legs, a light breeze carried across appetising smoke from the barbecue, together with the sounds of children's laughter as Kyle, Josie and Emma threw a Frisbee around at the bottom of the garden.

Zee, clad in a striped apron and chef's hat, plus the new trousers he had had to buy when Miranda threw all his other pairs out, shouted something about cheeseburgers and there was a minor stampede towards the barbecue. Ally couldn't be bothered. She was far too comfortable where she was, relaxing and working out a vague plan in her head for tomorrow's music session at Pussy Willows.

Just for a second, through sleepy, half-closed eyes, she almost imagined that the tall, slim figure in the distance by the apple tree wasn't a member of the ChelShel board, but someone quite different: Gavin.

289

Not that it could be, of course. Up to a point, Miranda had been right about him wriggling out of trouble. At least he had avoided a custodial prison sentence. But twelve months, suspended, plus a six-figure fine and plenty of damning press were enough to dent anybody's reputation; and as soon as he was free of probation, Gavin had headed abroad. The last they'd heard of him, yet another 'love of his life' was pregnant. Ally wondered how long Gavin would persist; it seemed as if he was engaged in an eternal search for a woman who could produce a son who wouldn't hate the sight of him.

And in the meantime, the odd Coutts cheque made its haphazard way into Miranda's letter box. Not that she ever spent any of the money, just stashed it all away in a high-interest account for when Grace was older. She was managing quite nicely in her modest detached, running her business and bringing up her daughter. Ally had never seen her happier.

Mind you, that might have something to do with the fact that Zee and Emma had been living with her for the last year. At first it had been just a business partnership, buying and selling antiques and bric-à-brac, but within months they'd become an item. Ally had dreamed it might happen, but had been too afraid to match-make: too convinced that she would break the spell and ruin everything. Now she looked at the two of them exchanging ketchup-smeared kisses, and somehow the whole world felt right.

Luke strolled across and sat down on the grass beside her. 'Burger?' He handed her a plate, and she sat up with a yawn.

'Mm, don't mind if I do.'

'Penny for 'em.'

Ally laughed. 'I was just thinking how funny it is, the way things work out. It doesn't matter what you do, they never come out the way you think they will. Look at Zee and Miranda – they never had the time of day for each other, and they're so great together.'

'Ah, but what about us?' enquired Luke with a twinkle in his eye and mustard on his chin. 'Are we great together?'

'Would I be here if we weren't?' countered Ally with a smile.

Side by side they gazed into the middle distance, where Kyle was playing a highly competitive game of Frisbee with a smaller, ginger-haired boy called Owen. 'They seem to be getting on OK so far,' hazarded Luke. 'I mean, Kyle hasn't killed him yet or anything.'

290

'You never know,' agreed Ally. 'This fostering business might just work out.'

How strange, thought Ally, that after all the trauma of giving away baby Grace, she and Luke had suddenly decided that they wanted to do something that involved giving away children all the time. Taking them in, caring for them, learning to love them; and then losing them. Every time. Maybe it was the very experience with Grace that had put the idea into Ally's mind, made her realise that she had developed the strength and the skills to do a job that few people could bear to do.

It had meant building an extension, of course. But out of the blue, Maureen and Clive had offered to help, and with Ally's extra teaching hours and the little bit extra Luke was making at ChelShel, it had proved affordable.

Ally watched the two boys chasing each other around, laughing fit to burst; and felt in her heart that they'd made the right decision. Maybe they'd found another way of bringing more love into the world.

As they sat there, munching and sharing their burgers with the cat, Miranda and Zee came across, with little Grace toddling confidently between them, her blonde curls bobbing like a golden halo around her head. At the sight of her aunt, a huge smile lit up her face.

'Al-ly! Al-ly cud-dle!'

Ally swept her up in her arms and buried her face in her niece's soft hair, breathing in the delicate, fragile scent of babyhood. 'How's our darling girl then? How's our little Gracie?'

She's so beautiful, thought Ally as the little girl wriggled and giggled in her arms. And the strange thing was that Grace even looked like Miranda, not Ally. It was as if nature knew that she was destined to be Miranda's child.

Well, it had taken a little time but Ally was cool with that. She knew that her decision to be Miranda's surrogate had been the right one. And now, she told herself firmly, I'm going to try to be the best auntie in the world ever. Maybe even the best foster-mum. But as for surrogacy . . .

Just don't ever ask me to go through *that* again.

**Be My Baby**
Zoë Barnes

Lorna had given up her career as a midwife to have her own baby. Happily married to Ed, she had looked forward to telling him that Leo would soon have a baby brother or a sister to play with. But fate had stepped in and left her widowed with a young son and another baby on the way.

Eighteen months later, Lorna misses Ed as much as ever, but knows she must get out and make a new life for herself and her children. When her mum and dad suddenly find themselves desperate for somewhere to live, what could be more natural than for them to come and live with Lorna? It'll be a great opportunity for her to go back to her job, while they get to know their grandchildren.

But that's before the mishaps, the arguments over childcare, or the rows that break out when Lorna announces that she's met a hunky doctor and is ready to start dating again.

**Praise for Zoë Barnes:**

'bloody good read' *New Woman*
'Top ten book…feel-good escapism' *Heat*
'Zoë Barnes writes wonderfully escapist novels, firmly based in reality' *Express*

## Wedding Belles
Zoë Barnes

Nothing is going to go wrong with Belle Craine's dream wedding to Kieran. Her mum won't let it. Unfortunately, nobody's told an Australian girl called Mona Starr, who turns up on the Craines' doorstep without warning and announces that she's Belle's long-lost half-sister. It's bad enough, but Belle also has to face the fact that her fiancé, Kieran, is spending an awful lot of time with ex-model Mona – a fact which her teenage sister, Jax, delights in pointing out.

Is Belle being paranoid, or has she got a fight on her hands if she wants to keep her man? And more to the point: is he worth fighting for?

# A SELECTION OF NOVELS AVAILABLE FROM PIATKUS BOOKS

| 978 0 7499 3788 1 | Wedding Belles | Zoë Barnes | £6.99 |
| 978 0 7499 3677 8 | Be My Baby | Zoë Barnes | £6.99 |
| 978 0 7499 3468 2 | Split Ends | Zoë Barnes | £6.99 |
| 978 0 7499 3734 8 | The Adultery Diet | Eva Cassady | £6.99 |
| 978 0 7499 3774 4 | Sweet Nothings | Sheila Norton | £6.99 |
| 978 0 74993 735 5 | Love Potions | Christina Jones | £6.99 |